A Handful of Ashes

Born and brought up in Parkstone in Dorset, Janet Woods now lives in Perth, Western Australia, although she returns to her English roots on a regular basis to visit family and friends.

A Handful of Ashes

Janet Woods

POCKET
BOOKS
LONDON · SYDNEY · NEW YORK · TORONTO

First published in Great Britain by Simon & Schuster, 2004
This edition first published by Pocket Books, 2004
An imprint of Simon & Schuster UK
A CBS COMPANY

1 3 5 7 9 10 8 6 4 2

Simon & Schuster UK Ltd
1st Floor
222 Gray's Inn Road
London WC1X 8HB

www.simonandschuster.co.uk

Simon & Schuster Australia
Sydney

A CIP catalogue record for this book is available from
the British Library

ISBN 9781849833530

Typeset by SX Composing DTP, Rayleigh, Essex
Printed and bound in Great Britain by
Cox & Wyman Ltd, Reading, Berkshire

Dedicated with my thanks
to fellow writers, and friends,
Wendy Evans and Karen Saayman.

*

The author is happy to receive feedback from readers
via her website
http://members.iinet.net.au/~woods
or by post
PO Box 2099
Kardinya 6163
Western Australia

1

It was the middle of the morning, late in the July of 1841. The Dorset countryside was a tapestry of colour. The meadowlands, dotted with blue cornflowers, flaming red poppies and golden buttercups, were displayed at their prettiest. A light breeze set the leaves dancing on the fingers of the boughs spreading overhead.

With Francis Matheson at the reins and a handsome chestnut trotting between the shafts, the overhang made a welcome shade for the occupants of the two-seater phaeton as it bowled through the tunnel of soft jade light, for the weather had turned warm in May and had remained that way.

Between the two adults, three-year-old Bryn, his honey-brown curls ruffled by the breeze, pressed hard against Siana Matheson's side and squealed with delight. 'Gee-up, Papa.'

Francis inclined his head to smile at him, at the same time exchanging a rueful smile with his wife. 'That boy has more energy than the five girls put together.'

Siana kissed Bryn's head, squashing the tremor of guilt she felt at the pride Francis displayed in him. But what her husband didn't know couldn't hurt him – it couldn't hurt anyone. Only one other person knew the secret of Bryn's parentage, and he'd never tell.

Francis slowed the carriage to a halt when he spotted a pair of red deer up ahead, grazing at the side of the road. Siana took advantage of the interlude to place a kiss at the side of his mouth. That mouth stretched into the smile she loved so much as he turned her way, the grey depths of his eyes seething with his awareness of her.

Their relationship had been passionate since his return from Van Diemen's Land, an island off the coast of Australia, the year before. The event of his arrival had been greeted with much joy, for Siana had been informed of her husband's death by drowning and, although she hadn't been able to totally believe it then, her hopes had been beginning to fade.

His hand slid to the nape of her neck, holding her, so he could kiss her more thoroughly. Somewhere near, a speckled song thrush trilled a song.

'Me too,' Bryn demanded, his lips and eyes screwed into a ferocious-looking pucker as he tried to push them apart.

Glancing down at him, Francis laughed. 'I heard your mamma call you her baby cuckoo the other day. Now I know why.'

But Francis didn't know why, Siana thought, her heart leaping in alarm. She must guard her tongue from now on. Gathering the child up, she smothered his face with kisses, making him giggle and diverting her mind from the vague feeling that somehow her happiness was threatened.

2

Bryn suddenly spotted the deer and yelled out, 'Horsies!' The startled animals sprang off to the safety of the trees before Siana could blink.

'You'll see plenty of those if we buy the house we're going to look at. And they're not horses, they're deer.'

'Horsies,' Bryn insisted and made a clicking noise with his tongue. 'Gee-up, Papa.'

Francis set the rig in motion again, slower now, for they'd soon be on the outskirts of Wareham. Rivervale House, the property they were about to inspect, had once been a rectory. It had been replaced by one of more manorial proportions when a legacy had increased the size of the rector's fortune.

The property had been suggested to them by Marcus Ibsen, the new owner of Cheverton Manor. 'I considered Rivervale when I first decided to come here, though it was occupied by the rector at the time,' he'd told them. 'The house has a great deal of charm, and I was taken with it.'

'Is there a reason why didn't you buy it?'

'I needed a property with land attached. Besides, I believe the house has been waiting for the right person to claim it,' he'd said and, although Francis had grinned at such a fanciful notion, Siana had known exactly what Marcus meant.

As they turned through wrought-iron gates into a wide carriageway, which curved gently upwards between lilac bushes interspersed with copper beech and silver birch trees, Francis said to her, 'Are you sure you won't mind leaving the house at Poole? I know you're fond of it.'

The Poole property they currently lived in had been a

gift to Siana from her first husband. 'I'll enjoy living in the country again, especially in a place that is ours. The Poole house will attract a good rent, but if the need arises we can sell it. I already have a buyer waiting.'

His face expressed his surprise as he turned towards her. 'Who?'

'Josh,' she said with a grin.

'Your brother?' Francis chuckled. 'Hasn't he acquired enough property in his short life?'

'He wants it to live in.'

'What about the house he always planned to build over Branksome way?'

'He's got plans for that when it's built. He's decided to turn it into a residential hotel. He says there are plenty of wealthy families looking for places to leave their unwanted relatives. Besides, he'd rather live in Poole. He's used to the place and likes to be in the thick of things.'

Francis slowly shook his head. 'Trust Josh to come up with something like that.' He whistled to himself as they rounded a curve and the house came into view. 'If we decide to buy this house, you might *have* to sell the one at Poole to him.'

Unexpectedly, her heart gave a little wrench at the thought, though it was quickly forgotten at the sight before her.

The early Georgian House was build of red brick. It stood in a spacious garden which, although slightly unkempt, was a riot of colour as bergamot, delphiniums, poppies, daisies and flowers of every hue jostled for position in the flowerbeds.

Francis picked a bloom as he stooped to retrieve the house key from its hiding place under a boot scraper, securing the flower amongst the ribbons on her bonnet.

A flight of steps led up to the porticoed front door, over which a high arched window of stained glass reached up to the second level. Ranged either side were two large, square windows. Two more were set each side of the door, with smaller ones at garden level. White and yellow roses rambled over trellises affixed to the wall.

Siana had fallen in love with the house at first sight. She loved the inside even more, with its handsome staircase and panelled rooms. The stained-glass window, decorated with a border of red roses, depicted a woman with flowing hair holding aloft a garland of lilies. Her other hand was cupped protectively around a small boy's head as she cuddled him against her thigh.

The child reminded her of Ashley, the son from her first marriage. The heir to Cheverton Estate and the last of the Forbes family, he had succumbed to scarlet fever nearly three years previously.

Anguish stabbed so strongly at her; she wanted to sob with the unfairness of it. Instead, she stood in the quiet hall, with the light from the window streaming in on her, cherishing the precious living memory of her firstborn. It escaped from her too soon, slipping away like his short life had, leaving her in pain. Closing her eyes, she absorbed the peace of the house into her heart and felt herself grow strong again.

'What were you thinking of?' Francis asked.

'Ashley.' She managed a smile. 'Can we afford this house? I would very much like to live here.'

'That remains to be seen. I have the money from the sale of my house and the legacy my brother Will left me. I intend to keep the Van Diemen's Land property and the logging business for the time being, as it brings in a good income.'

'And I have my allowance from the Forbes investments. There was not much left from the sale of the estate once the debts were settled. Perhaps I could sell those diamonds Edward bought me. I rarely wear them.'

He laughed at that. 'We are not so impoverished that we need to sell your jewellery. Neither do I want to touch your allowance, or oblige you to sell your house.'

She took his hands in hers, making them one. 'We agreed to pool our resources and live in something that was ours alone. This house is convenient for your medical practice.'

'I want to provide for you and my children myself.'

'But three of the girls are not yours. Daisy is my sister, Goldie is a foundling I decided to keep, and Susannah is being fostered only until her mother is in a position to have her back.' She deliberately pushed Bryn to the back of her mind.

'You cared for Maryse and Pansy when I was away.'

Exactly how well she'd cared for Maryse, he'd never know. 'That's different. They're grown up and we're more like sisters. I don't know what I would have done without their company.'

'Which makes me feel old.' He grinned. 'Are you going to argue with me all day, woman?'

'It's you who is arguing with me.' She brushed a kiss against his cheek. 'I feel this house belongs to us, even though we haven't seen it properly yet.' She looked around them. 'Where's Bryn scuttled off to?'

Francis pulled her against him and gazed into her eyes. 'Stop fussing. He's all right, I can hear him chattering to himself.' He ran a finger down her nose and gave a teasing grin. 'Thank you for giving me my son, Siana. You told me you were expecting a daughter in your letter. What happened to the Welsh sight you inherited?'

His words brought to mind a thought of her great-aunt, Wynn Lewis. The Welsh woman had gazed at her with undisguised bitterness on the occasion of Siana's necessary visit to Wales. Her nerve ends prickled at the sudden thought of her, for Siana was sensitive in ways that many others didn't understand.

She wondered if the lie could be detected in her eyes when she answered; 'It must have deserted me.'

'All the same, I'm sorry I wasn't here for Bryn's birth.'

Siana wasn't sorry. The future would have been very different for Bryn if Francis hadn't been absent at the time. Guiltily, she murmured, 'It wasn't your fault you were detained in Van Diemen's Land. One day, I'll give you another son.'

Hugging her tight again, he whispered, 'There was a time I thought I'd never see any of you again. I'm thankful for all of my children.' He released her when a door slammed shut and a frantic banging noise came from behind the panels, and offered her a wryly amused grin. 'For most of the time, anyway. It sounds as though Bryn has shut himself in. I'd better fetch him before he kicks up a fuss.'

7

Bryn emerged from behind a door, indignant, red-faced and on the verge of tears. He was covered in dust. Siana brushed the grime off him when he rushed into her arms to be comforted. Giving him a cuddle she handed him over to Francis to carry. The child fell asleep on his shoulder while they were inspecting the house.

'At least Bryn will be rested when we visit Marcus,' Francis said. 'I'll be interested to find out how he's getting on with the village.'

Siana loved every inch of Rivervale House, which had a fine view over the wetlands of the Frome river valley and the misty hills beyond. The landscape was dotted with sheep, their eyes framed by curled horns.

Her eyes alight with the pleasure she felt, Siana turned to him, her enthusiasm all too apparent. 'This is exactly what we need. Please can we buy it?'

Francis sounded doubtful. 'I shall have to think about it.'

A couple of miles away, Marcus Ibsen was looking over plans for the new village of Cheverton Chase.

The work had already started. The village would be situated a mile from the present workers' accommodations and the best of the old cottages would be repaired and retained. They would house the itinerant workers, who were hired every year to help bring in the harvest.

'Cob cottages need a good bonnet and boots,' the builder had told him. 'If the walls get too boggy they'll become straw and mud again, and if they're allowed to

8

dry out, they'll crack. A good coat of lime will keep them sound. I allus burn my own limestone for mortar, so it be constant in quality.'

The cottages were to be semi-detached, two storeys high and thatched with longstraw, which had been specially cut from the previous year's corn harvest. The cottages would share an oven, have two rooms up and down, and flag-stone floors rather than packed dirt. Extra space would be provided under the roof.

Marcus wanted to have a model village. Built on a gradual slope, the twenty cottages would have a generous allotment apiece for growing vegetables, a sty for a pig, and a privy for each family. A water pump was to be situated at the top end of the village, well away from the privies so the water couldn't become contaminated by seepage and cause diseases such as dysentery or typhoid.

Building the village had proved to be a costly exercise. Marcus had tried to take that into account when bidding for Cheverton Estate, but without much success. A grin lifted his finely boned face and his coal-dark eyes sparkled with amusement. Siana Matheson had seen right through his ruse.

Leaving the plans, he strolled over to the window, gazing over his rustic domain with pride in his eyes. Marcus was content, but slightly bored with life, even though he'd acquired a fine library with the manor. It was about time he found a wife and bred some children from her, he thought. But was the girl he had in mind ready to partner him in such a responsibility?

When the Matheson carriage came up the

carriageway his heart gave a leap. But the exquisite, dark-haired woman with the pine-green eyes on whom his glance fell, was not Maryse. It was her stepmother, Siana, and Maryse's father, Dr Francis Matheson. His spirits lifted at the sight of Siana. He admired the woman greatly for her beauty and compassion, but mostly because they were kindred spirits.

He greeted his visitors himself, his long legs carrying him down the staircase and out through the door before the carriage came to a halt. Risking a frown from Francis, he kissed Siana's cheek as he helped her down, his hands supporting her elbows. Her taffeta skirt was of the palest lilac and rustled over her many petticoats as he set her down on dainty slippers. A faint scent of bergamot lingered about her. He spotted a sprig of heliotrope in her bonnet, a darker purple amongst the lilac ribbons.

He turned to greet her husband, a smile on his face. 'I'm pleased to see you, Francis. How is my godson?'

'Quiet at the moment, he's just woken up.'

Marcus took the boy from his father's arms and kissed his cheek, which was round and flushed from sleep. Before he handed Bryn to his mother, his glance clung to Siana's over the child's head for a poignant moment.

Both of them recalled a hill in Wales, where they'd buried the body of her stillborn daughter, and remembered a moment when he'd placed this ill-gotten boy against her breast. Bryn had tasted of her milk and claimed her as his own. She'd been helpless against the attraction of that suckling mouth, as Marcus had known she'd be, for the mothering instinct was strong in her.

Leaving the horse and carriage with the groom they strolled together into the dim, quiet space of Cheverton Manor hall.

'It's a fine day, we'll take tea on the terrace,' Marcus said to a hovering servant. He turned, smiling widely as he ushered them through to the back of the house. 'Bryn will be able to stretch his legs there without getting into too much mischief, while you tell me how you liked Rivervale House.'

'I adored it.' Gazing at her husband, Siana's smile had a melting quality to it, but her eyes were slightly anxious. 'Francis hasn't decided yet, have you Francis?'

Francis Matheson, a sensible, professional man of middle years, grinned like a youth under the onslaught of her smile. 'I've decided to find some way of buying it for us,' he said, a pronouncement which earned him a hug. 'If need be, I can raise a loan from the bank.'

Marcus said, 'It's been on the market for some time. I've heard that the owner is desperate to make a sale and will seriously consider any offer.'

Francis nodded at him. 'My thanks. I shall bear that in mind.'

Marcus envied the closeness of this pair. They balanced one another. The doctor kept the pagan in Siana under control. He'd made himself aware of that aspect of her behaviour on occasion, no doubt, as any man with red blood in his veins would.

Under Siana's silk and satin was an earth mother who loved to run barefoot on the wet grass of the hills, and would defend her own with tooth and claw. She was tender-hearted, passionate and loving, courageous when needed. But there was a streak of ruthlessness in her, mostly in the loyalty shown to those she loved. If her back was against the wall, he thought she might kill in defence of them.

As for Francis, a sensible, impatient and sometimes arrogant man, he was, nevertheless, a good healer. Francis was Siana's refuge when she was hurt, but he didn't smother her. It was as if the measure of independence she enjoyed in the marriage was tied to the end of a velvet rope. And that rope was strong, for it had kept them connected across a wide expanse of restless ocean – time keeping them apart, faith and the love they held for the other bringing them back together again.

Unease trickled up his spine as he looked at Bryn. But would that love prove strong enough if Francis found out she'd deceived him over Bryn?

He could sense Siana watching him. It was disconcerting when she knew what he was thinking. Uncanny, as if the fates had conspired to bring them together. When he thought of Maryse Matheson, he knew why.

'Francis,' he said when they'd settled themselves and were waiting for the refreshment to arrive. 'There's something of the utmost importance I wish to discuss with you.'

Siana rose unhurriedly to her feet, trying to hide her jubilant grin. 'I'll go and rescue Bryn. The last time he smelled the flowers, a wasp stung the end of his nose.'

The two men watched her go, beginning to laugh when Bryn caught sight of her and took off at a run. Tossing her bonnet and shoes aside, Siana lifted her skirts and pelted after him, dodging around the flower-beds with agile grace. When the pair finally collided they fell into a giggling heap together.'

'You're lucky to have her,' Marcus observed.

Francis's grey eyes were firmly fixed on his wife and his voice was tender. 'Yes, I know. What was it you wanted to talk to me about?'

'Miss Matheson.'

'My daughter?' Francis turned towards him with a frown. 'What of her?'

'Don't take me for a fool, Francis. You must be aware my regard for her goes beyond friendship. I would like your permission to pay court to her.'

'And if I don't give it?'

'There's no reason why you shouldn't, for I'm of good character and a suitable match for her. However, bear this in mind: if you reject me, you might condemn your daughter to a life of spinsterhood.'

'It's true that Maryse has refused all offers so far, but what makes you think she'll accept you?'

'Miss Matheson is a sensitive soul. Instinctively, she knows and trusts me. I more than admire her, Francis. I fell in love with her the first moment we met. She knows that, for I told her so.'

Marcus smiled when there was a quick intake of breath from Francis. 'I needed to plant a seed in her mind, for a romantic notion in a young girl's heart can only blossom and grow. If nothing else, she can admire me for my constancy. As it is, of late, I fear she might be pressured into a marriage without love. So I'm speaking out now in the hope that my petition can be considered.'

'Aye, her aunt is most persistent, I must admit. Maryse has not allowed her head to be turned, though. I sense there might be a reason behind that, because she has changed so much in my absence. Her aunt thought her behaviour to be erratic and totally out of character while I was away.' His eyes became almost mercurial bright as he turned his way. 'How was she in Wales?'

The hairs prickled along Marcus's arms. Francis sensed something had occurred, but knew not what. 'I had nothing to compare Miss Matheson's behaviour with, but your daughter struck me as being quiet and well behaved.' He gave a faint smile. 'She seemed to enjoy learning the domestic chores of the house, helping your wife in the garden and drawing the scenery around her. She told me she enjoyed the peace and quiet of Wales, despite its rusticity. You understand, of course, that I was living in the barn, not the house. I saw very little of them, except at mealtimes. But we have already talked of this.'

'Of course. But you didn't tell me before of your declaration to my daughter.'

'It wasn't a declaration as such, more the establishment of my future intention. Such understandings are kept private between the couple concerned, for I doubt if Miss Matheson has informed you of it either.'

'No, she has not. And neither has Siana.'

'It could be that she simply dismissed it. But if Miss Matheson has confided in your wife, it would be reasonable to expect her to honour the secret between them, especially where a female confidence was concerned. Women are not as strong as men. They need the

14

support of each other where matters of the heart are concerned.'

An astute glance came his way again. 'You profess to understand a devil of a lot about women. Known many, have you?'

Marcus tried not to grin. 'I was brought up by my uncle and aunt in the company of six female cousins.'

'Ah, I see,' Francis said, looking a trifle shamefaced. When the doctor nodded to himself, Marcus knew he had him almost convinced.

'I promise to treat Miss Matheson with the greatest of respect, and not declare myself until I consider the match agreeable to her. I have no wish to be made to look the fool if she accepts in haste then changes her mind. Believe me when I say that my greatest desire is to secure your daughter's happiness.'

'In that case, you have my permission to court her,' Francis said gruffly. The two men shook hands on it just as the refreshment arrived.

Bryn, his nose casting at the air like a hungry dog when he saw the servants arrive with the tea trays, suddenly remembered his manners. Taking his mother's hand he led her back to the terrace.

Before he snuffed the bedside candle that night, Francis propped himself up on one elbow and gazed down at Siana in suspicion. 'Did you know Marcus was going to ask for Maryse's hand?'

'Sooner or later. He has always loved her.'

'Why didn't you tell me?'

'I thought it was obvious from the way he looks at her,

15

and the way he always asks after her. Why do you think he visits us so often?'

'I thought it was you he admired.'

His disgruntled voice made her chuckle. 'Would you mind very much if he did?'

'Would you?'

'Certainly not. I like Marcus a lot.' She grinned and idly ran her fingers through his hair. 'Of course, that's not to say I wouldn't mind if another woman admired you. I would most likely poke her eyes out and squish them under my feet.'

He chuckled at that and, snuffing out the candle, drew her into his arms.

2

Josh Skinner was wearing his black evening suit over an embroidered waistcoat of pearl grey. He never knew what to do with his top hat, especially on a windy day, but it added a bit of dash so he decided to carry it along with his cane and gloves, rather than wear it. He didn't think he could fit his head into it now, anyway. His manservant had tonged his fair hair into side curls for the evening.

'You're enough to make a cat laugh,' his sister, Siana, would probably say to him when she saw his new hairstyle and discovered he'd hired a personal servant. Bentley doubled as a butler as well, though he was a bit slow, at times. Still, he couldn't expect too much of such an elderly codger as Bentley.

A right dandy Josh had become of late. It hadn't taken him long to appreciate the feel of good cloth against his skin, or note the extra dash a tailor could add to the cut of a garment. And although Siana didn't know it, he'd been taking dancing lessons from a married couple who ran an academy in their parlour. He was receiving invitations to more and more parties with fancy folk, and needed to learn all the social skills he could. Tonight, he was determined to sweep Miss Pansy Matheson off her feet in a waltz, and without making a fool of himself.

Clodhopper boots and dead men's coats and trousers brought from market stalls were a thing of the past. He was *Joshua Skinner Esquire* which, according to Bentley, meant he was a man of substance.

Picking up the stiff, embossed invitation he cracked a wide grin as he read: *Mrs Francis Matheson requests the pleasure of the company of Joshua Skinner Esquire on the occasion of her husband's forty-second birthday*. Siana and Francis were also celebrating the purchase of Rivervale House, the first home the pair had set up together as a family.

The occasion was also an opportunity to celebrate Francis's return from the dead, for his brother-in-law had been reported drowned almost three years ago, when the ship he'd been travelling on to Van Diemen's Land was wrecked in a storm. His subsequent trials had been a test of endurance for Francis, and for Siana's abiding love for her husband.

'Requests the pleasure,' he repeated softly. 'Be damned if that blue-blooded doctor my sister married hasn't made a lady of her without even trying.'

It was odd how well he and Siana had adapted to their changed circumstances over the previous eight years. They wore their adopted status like a second skin. More so Siana, who'd needed the trappings to survive in the society she'd married into. When they were alone together she relaxed a little, but it wasn't often her peasant blood put in an appearance now – unless her temper got the better of her.

'I have to be careful for Daisy's sake,' she'd told him. 'I promised our mother I'd care for her, and I want her to grow up to be socially acceptable. I didn't enjoy being poor, and I try not to let my background show in case I embarrass Francis.'

Daisy couldn't recall a life other than the one Siana had provided for them all by marrying well. Their younger sister had never known hunger, cold or cruelty since then, and at the age of nine was a confident, pretty child – if a little self-centred.

'Don't wait up for me,' he said to the elderly gentleman's gentleman who had faithfully served his last master for forty years. Taking pity on the dignified old fellow, who'd been tossed onto the labour market after his master's death, Josh had hired him for himself. But being waited on hand and foot by someone old enough to be his grandfather made him feel a little guilty. 'You have a little nip of my good brandy and take yourself off to bed early, Mr Bentley.'

'Yes, sir.' Mr Bentley didn't even flicker an eyelid as he held out Josh's cloak. 'You'd better take this, sir, it might get cold later.'

'Thank you.' Taking the cloak from the servant's arm, Josh strode out to the horse and phaeton. As he climbed into the rig and picked up the reins, he reckoned life couldn't get better than living near the top of the hill.

Below him spread the harbour of Poole, reflecting the lights of the town. There was money to be made if you knew how to go about it, and wealth brought with it respect. Not the respect good breeding brought, the sort Francis Matheson commanded. But all the same, it was good to be called sir by shop assistants, or Mr Skinner by bank managers.

Joshua Skinner Esquire. He grinned with the pleasure of it, wishing his ma and pa had lived to see it. He wasn't the richest businessman in town by any means, but then, it wasn't so long ago he was digging up cockles, with a bit of smuggling going on on the side. Now, he and his partner owned a fair portion of the property in town, and were thinking of expanding those interests. Although he was only twenty, Josh knew he'd never forget his former poverty.

He glanced at the house he'd just bought from Siana, and smiled. A canny one, his sister. She'd made him pay a fair price for it, too.

One of these days he'd marry, and he'd make sure his family never wanted for anything. There was a girl he liked and got on well with, but . . .? He shook his head as he reached the end of the carriageway. No, Pansy Matheson was too far above him, and it was no good hankering after a girl he couldn't have.

Nineteen years old, Pansy Matheson was torn between the choice of pale blue watered taffeta, or a pink silk gown with puffed sleeves and a bodice decorated in artificial roses.

Standing in front of the mirror in her stiffened petticoats, corselette and drawers, she held first one against her, then the other. 'Help me decide, Maryse?'

Maryse, the elder of the sisters by a year, folded her

hands into a skirt of dark blue silk and slanted her head to one side. 'You haven't worn the taffeta yet. It will look pretty with your hair curled and those silk flowers in your hair.'

'It also makes a nice sound when I walk, like shuffling my feet through autumn leaves.' Pansy caught a reflection of her sister's grey eyes in the mirror. There was something sad about them. 'I suppose the uncles are all coming.'

'The whole Matheson family is coming. You and I are the only females not spoken for. We're going to be worn out from dancing with everyone.'

'I'm sure the other women will help out. Is the admiral bringing his intended?'

Maryse smiled. 'He is, but if she's as old as he is, she won't do much dancing.'

'Well, cousin Roger might bring his fiancée. I bet Aunt Prudence is cock-a-hoop over him winning the hand of the wealthiest heiress in the district. I met her once. Her name is Lalage Lewisham. She's terribly languid in manner, speaks as though she's out of breath and smells of violets, like a funeral cortege. Imagine how ridiculous it will sound when she marries the viscount and we have to call her Lady Lalage. I'm sure I shall burst into song. When I pointed this out to Aunt Prudence, she made a long face and snorted, "Stop being facetious, Pansy Matheson."'

Pansy's imitation of the Countess of Kylchester made Maryse giggle, something her sister didn't often do now. 'Cousin Alder is pestering me to become engaged to him now Roger has settled his suit. He says he's waited long enough, and demands that I give him an answer tonight.'

'Alder has made his intentions towards you quite clear right from the beginning. He deserves to have an answer, Pansy.'

Pulling the skirt over her head, Pansy's muffled response came from within its depths. 'I like him enormously, of course, Alder is such good fun. But Maryse, I don't love him and my instincts keep warning me he's not right for me. Besides which, the thought of a lifetime of Aunt Prudence nagging me over every little thing is quite intolerable.'

'Then you must tell Alder so.'

Emerging from the gown with her hair all over the place, Pansy pulled a face. 'I have. He is quite persistent. He just laughs, then informs me that he has ways to make me learn to love him.'

Maryse gave a small shiver.

'He says I should have grown used to his mother, by now. Aunt Prudence is on his side, of course. Well, she would be with him being the absolute favourite of her sons. She's spoiled him terribly, so he's used to having his own way. I don't suppose you'd be interested in marrying him in my stead, would you?'

'You know very well I've vowed never to wed. Besides, I've been in Aunt Prudence's bad books for several years, so having me for a daughter-in-law would simply not please her as much as having you.'

'Then perhaps I'll make a vow not to wed until after you are settled, since it's traditional for the eldest daughter to wed first. If I wed Alder it will set the seal on your spinsterhood. Dearest Maryse, I want so much for you to come to realize that your notions about remaining unwed are foolish, since it's possible you may fall in love.'

'You have no reason to imagine such an event,' Maryse said.

'Then we shall grow old together, a couple of spinsters with tabby cats rubbing against our ankles, all vinegar and spit. We can sit by the window with our embroidery, playing games of "do you remember when", and gossip spitefully about the passers-by.'

'That's a perfectly horrible suggestion. I'm sure I'll be able to find better things to do.'

'But what if you *do* fall in love?'

Maryse closed her eyes for a moment, and Pansy could have sworn she saw a glint of tears when she opened them. 'That will never happen.' Rising, she moved towards her sister, abruptly changing the subject. 'Turn around while I do up the buttons on your bodice. Do you want your hair curled? If so, I'll go and heat the curling irons. Rosie is busy.'

Maryse's shining brown hair was parted in the middle and drawn back into a satin bow at the nape of her neck. It was an elegant style, but too severe for Pansy's taste. It seemed as if Maryse didn't want to appear attractive, which was almost impossible, since her sister had a finely drawn delicacy to her face that would always be striking, whatever the hairstyle.

Although she and Maryse were alike, Pansy knew she was the more robust and animated of the two. She attracted labels such as jolly, lively and hoydenish, while

Maryse was regarded as sensitive, artistic, and of late, oddly eccentric.

It was unfair of Aunt Prudence to say things like that about her sister, but it had come about because Maryse had continually thwarted the countess in the quest to marry her off. Maryse had now refused to endure the ordeal of another season in London, so they would never hear the last of how ungrateful and stubborn she had become.

Pansy brought her hand up to cover her sister's. 'What has happened to make you determined not to wed?'

'Nothing has happened.'

Maryse closed her eyes in anguish, wishing she didn't have to lie to her sister as she remembered the horrifying events on the night of the harvest supper a few years previously. Everything that had coloured her life since, had happened then – the two men, their hands groping her flesh, the smell of scrumpy cider on their breath, the tearing of her innocence as they brutally violated her, one after the other, leaving her bloodied and loathing herself. They had stolen all that was dear to her, then tossed her aside as if she was worth nothing.

She lived in dread that she might be confronted by those men again, and the other three, the ones who had walked away and left her to her cruel fate, that they'd look at her with the knowledge of what had been taken from her, see what they'd soiled. She'd die rather than have that happen, and she couldn't take such a secret into a marriage. Maryse only just stopped herself from shuddering. To dwell too long on the subject made her hate herself even more.

'I'll go and fetch the curling irons,' she said when the last pearly button was secured. Turning on the heels of her blue satin slippers, she hurried towards the door, feeling as if she needed to be sick.

Siana wore a black silk corsclette and a froth of petticoats as she walked into the dressing room separating her bedchamber from her husband's.

Francis was still in his robe. She slid her arms around him and hugged him lovingly, marvelling that the man she adored had come back to her after a two-year absence. But he was not quite the same Francis who'd gone away, for under her palms she felt the ridged scars on his back. The scars were the result of a brutal flogging when he'd been mistaken for a prisoner who'd escaped from the Port Arthur Prison in Van Diemen's Land. Now and again, he suffered from melancholy and withdrew from them all, going into his study to be by himself for a while.

'It's nothing serious,' her husband's partner, Dr Noah Baines had told her. 'Just provide a loving home for him and give him time to adjust.'

She traced gently along one of the scars with her fingers she felt his skin tense. The flogging was something Francis didn't talk about. 'I can't imagine how awful this was for you. Can't you bring yourself to tell me about it?'

'One day, perhaps.'

'I love you so much,' she whispered against his ear.

When he cupped her face in his palms and kissed her, her response was immediate. 'Make love to me.'

'Our guests will be arriving soon.'

'Then it means you might be late for your own party. Don't you like me, Doctor Matheson?'

The warm smile he gave her robbed her of breath. 'When you're flaunting yourself in your petticoats like a strumpet I can't resist you, as well you know,' he grumbled, and subsiding onto a chair he pulled her onto his lap so she straddled him.

She laughed and nipped the end of his nose. 'We've never made love in such a position as this, but it does make me feel like a strumpet.' Already, he had responded to the suggestion in no uncertain manner, and she teased, 'If you'd prefer to, you can ignore my flaunts.'

'I don't prefer and I couldn't.' He kissed the rise of her breasts before loosening them from their bondage. His tongue sought the nubs, sliding across and around them, bringing them moist and swelling to bursting point, like a couple of ripe hazelnuts.

'I didn't realize your tongue was so very long,' she murmured with a sigh of pleasure. 'What else can you do with it?'

He laughed at that. 'Unfortunately I haven't got time to show you. That demonstration was purely in the interests of anatomy.'

Undoing the fastenings on his robe she chuckled when she saw what his attention had done to him. 'Your anatomy is definitely interested.'

Pushing his hands under her petticoats, he slid his

palms under her buttocks and lifted her onto him, easing himself gently into the moist velvety depths of her.

Her breath caught in her throat, then left it in a long, soft, ecstatic murmur. Nothing could ever spoil such happiness.

'I do love you, my Francis. I always will.'

'Siana looks delicious tonight, like a piece of raspberry tart waiting to be devoured.'

'Judging by the smug look spread on his face, and the smile on hers, our brother has already had a bite of her tonight.' Raoul Matheson took two glasses of red wine from a serving maid and handed one to Augustus. 'Have you ever seen a gown as monstrously ugly as Prudence is wearing? She resembles a striped toadstool.'

'The countess never did have any fashion sense. I admit the colour is unbecoming when matched to her complexion, and she's a little bit on the skinny side for my taste. Still, Ryder has his delightful little *amore* tucked away.'

Raoul chuckled. 'Yes, I've met her. A simple soul. Ryder doesn't keep her for her mind, though. Where's your intended bride, by the way? I'm dying to meet the companion you've chosen for your retirement.'

'Constance has gone upstairs with Pansy, who has promised to read a story to the two girls.'

'It's a long way up to the nursery. Pansy will be obliged to help Constance downstairs again, no doubt.'

Augustus Matheson's eyes filled with laughter as he gazed at his brother. 'They're coming back down now. What d'you make of my bride?'

Raoul was temporarily struck dumb. In her early thirties, Constance was an attractive woman with a warm smile and a trim figure. Her bright blue eyes came to rest on Gus, whose wink brought a wide smile to her face.

Raoul nudged him in the ribs. 'Shame on you, Gus. Even when set next to our sweet Pansy, Constance looks young enough to be your daughter. How did you manage it?'

'It's the naval uniform; women can't resist it,' Augustus drawled, his eyes assessing as he watched the pair come towards them. 'I'm certainly looking forward to parting her ringlets.'

On the other side of the drawing room, Josh sipped his drink and watched Pansy talking to her uncles. He smiled when she laughed. He couldn't help it, for she looked so merry.

Followed by the admiral and his fiancé, Raoul Matheson escorted Pansy onto the dance floor. He gazed around him at the spectators. 'We need two more couples to make up a square for the Quadrille?'

Immediately, they were joined by Maryse, who was partnered by the Earl of Kylchester. Then Francis stepped forward, pulling behind him a reluctant Siana, who was frantically protesting. 'I don't think I can remember the steps, Francis.'

'I'm sure you will when you hear the music,' he said, and he signalled to Prudence, who was taking her turn at the piano.

They all bowed to each other, then to their corners,

then they went into the *chaine anglaise*.

Josh grinned and nodded his head in time to the music, trying to remember the sequence of the figure '*Balancé*,' he whispered to himself, and four bars later, '*Change partners.*'

One of Pansy's cousins came to stand beside him. 'Talking to yourself, Skinner?'

'I'm trying to remember the sets.' Josh held out his hand. 'It's Alder, isn't it?'

Alder ignored both his hand and his question. 'Fancy yourself as a dancer, do you?'

Josh's gaze sharpened. Alder, grey-eyed like all the Matheson family, seemed to be the worse for drink. He certainly had a mean look in his eye. Josh, who never invited trouble into his life unless it was inescapable, thought it might be judicious to humour him. 'Not at all, I'm just learning.'

'What does a farm labourer want with dancing lessons?'

'I'm a businessman not a farm labourer.'

'Odd, but I can still smell the bull shit on you.'

'Be careful I don't rub your nose in it, then,' Josh said pleasantly, and exchanged a smile with Pansy when she caught his eye.

'Don't forget you're partnering me in the waltz, Josh,' she called out just before she was whisked off down the line.

'Lay one finger on my cousin and I'll have you, Skinner,' Alder warned, then walked unsteadily back to where his elder brother stood watching the dancing. Roger had a beautiful but rather vapid-looking woman attached to his arm. The two men spoke together, then looked his way and laughed.

Josh ignored them and fetched Pansy a glass of lemonade to quench her thirst. When the dance ended she took it gratefully from him. 'Thank you, Josh. What was Alder saying? Was he being mean?'

Josh didn't want to say anything to make her any more anxious than she already sounded. 'Why should he be mean?'

'I've just turned his marriage proposal down.'

'It isn't the first time, is it? He should be used to it.'

'The trouble is, to Alder the marriage is a foregone conclusion, so he doesn't believe me. And this time he sounded different, sort of hectoring, as if Aunt Prudence had told him to put his foot down.'

Usually full of spirit, Pansy sounded so forlorn that Josh felt sorry for her. It must be hard to be a young woman who was under pressure to wed. 'Perhaps you should talk to your father about it, let him sort it out.'

Her fine grey eyes came up to probe the depths of his. 'My papa wants me to marry well, so is in favour of a marriage between Alder and myself.'

'Nevertheless, he's fair-minded. He wouldn't want you to be unhappy, would he?'

'Of course not.' Before Josh's eyes, Pansy relaxed and offered him a merry smile. 'You always make matters sound so simple.'

'Matters usually are, Miss Pansy. It's folks who are complicated.' He grinned. 'I'm not much good at paying pretty compliments, but damn me if you don't look as pretty as a dappled pony in that gown.'

'Joshua Skinner, are you flirting with me?'

'That depends if you like being compared to a dappled pony or not. Most girls wouldn't.'

The spontaneous giggle she gave faded as her glance darted past him. 'Quickly, my father has taken over the piano and he promised he'd play the waltz for me before supper.'

Noticing Alder heading towards them, Josh swept her onto the floor and began to twirl her around in time to the music.

'You're good at dancing the waltz,' she said a few moments later, laughing and breathless.

'I learned it especially, so I could dance it with you.'

'Truly?'

His eyes caught hers for a moment and he grinned with the happiness he felt flowing inside him, though it made his cheeks grow warm. 'Truly.'

From the corner of his eye, Josh saw Alder return to the company of his brother, a churlish expression on his face.

The waltz stopped and the Roger de Coverley was called, which signalled the end of Josh's dancing. He was elbowed aside by Alder as the women and men made lines opposite each other.

When Alder turned to glare at him as he bowed to Pansy, Josh backed away, the skin along his spine prickling. He could smell trouble coming his way.

Siana could also sense trouble, but it wasn't in the immediate vicinity. It appeared as a fleeting uneasiness when she snatched a moment before supper to check on the children.

Daisy and Goldie were still awake. How pretty they both looked with their golden hair captured into linen caps, their blue eyes still shining with excitement, for Miss Edgar, their governess, had allowed them onto the upper landing to watch the dancing.

She leaned over to kiss her sister Daisy goodnight. 'Sweet dreams, my darling.'

Daisy's arms came up around her neck in a hug. 'I'm going to dream that I'm grown up so I can wear a pretty gown, marry a rich man and and stay up for the dancing.'

Siana stifled her smile and turned to her foster child, Goldie, whose darker, spun-gold hair escaped in wisps from under her cap. 'What about you?'

Goldie thought for a moment, then smiled. 'I'm going to look after the sick people, like Papa does.'

Daisy informed her, 'Only boys can be doctors. Girls don't like seeing blood. They faint.'

'I'm going to be a printer, then, like my brother. The last time I visited him he said I could help him in his shop when I grow up.'

'I'm sure you'll be wonderful at whatever you do.' Siana gave Goldie a hug and went through to the nursery, where Susannah and Bryn were fast asleep.

How dainty Susannah was and how like her mother she looked. Siana smiled as she smoothed the girl's foxy hair back from her forehead. Her good friend, Elizabeth Hawkins, wouldn't recognize her daughter when next they met, for Elizabeth had been found guilty of a crime she hadn't committed and transported to Australia for four years.

Siana turned to Bryn, uncovered and lying completely relaxed on his back with his arms and legs flopped out. She pulled the cover over him then stooped to kiss him, her heart filled with love. 'Goodnight, my little cuckoo.'

Unease hit her strongly then, a feeling that brought coldness with it and goosebumps racing over the surface of her skin. It was as if the world had shifted, reminding her that happiness could be fleeting. Bryn wasn't her child, none of them were. The two children she'd carried in her womb had already perished; her son taken by scarlet fever and her daughter, Elen, snatched away before she had lived, in childbirth.

She thought again of her great-aunt, Wynn Lewis, wondering if the woman knew of what had taken place. She hoped not, for Wynn Lewis had always been surrounded by darkness.

Siana had no time to brood over it, however, for Francis came up behind her to slip his arms around her waist. 'I'm always amazed that there's nothing of you in Bryn's face.'

'The Matheson look in him is very strong.'

'Aye.' He gazed down at Bryn, a fond smile playing around his mouth. 'There's no mistaking where he sprang from.'

'You do love him, don't you, Francis?'

'Of course I do. He's my son.'

'I do so want to give you another son.'

'I'm content with Bryn.' Turning her in his arms he

33

tipped up her chin and gently kissed her before leading her out of the nursery. 'I love his mother, too, and nothing will ever change that.'

Once again, Siana felt uneasy. How easy it was to create a lie. But living with the deception when it involved somebody as fine and as honest as Francis was another thing altogether.

They went down the stairs to be met at the bottom by Marcus Ibsen, who bore her hand to his lips and kissed it. Dark-haired and tall, his eyes a ferment of liquid darkness, she experienced a sense of excitement at the raw power emanating from him.

'I'm sorry I'm late. Unfortunately, I was detained in town. Mrs Matheson, you look exquisite, like a wild poppy blowing in the wind.'

There was a moment when his words conjured up a sensation of a breeze drifting like cool silk over her skin and the sensual smell of midsummer wildflowers. She gained control of her imagination, and had the sense to avoid his teasing grin. Flirting with danger was part of Marcus's make-up and hers, but Francis would not appreciate a public display of it, she knew.

Lightly, she said, 'Maryse overheard Raoul compare me to a raspberry tart, and Augustus said I looked like a glass of burgundy.'

'Obviously, the Matheson men are lacking in soul.'

Francis laughed. 'I'm afraid we're concerned with the tangible aspects of life rather than the ethereal. We're just going in to supper, Marcus. Will you join us?'

'Most certainly, and I'll look forward to the entertainment afterwards.' His glance went past them, to where Maryse stood talking to one of her uncles and his wife. Beckwith was a magistrate and the more serious of the brothers, the father of two young sons and husband to a wife who fussed. Siana watched the woman brush a piece of lint from her husband's shoulder, shake out her skirts and straighten the wrinkles in the fingers of her gloves, all in the same few seconds.

As if Maryse knew she was being observed, she turned her gaze to where they stood, her head slanted to one side. Her blue silk skirt gleamed along its folds as her body assumed an elegant pose. The serene smile she wore faltered when her glance met that of Marcus. A delicate tracery of pink tinted her skin.

Marcus slowly edged out a ragged breath.

Recovering her composure, Maryse excused herself and came towards them. 'Mr Ibsen, you've missed the dancing.'

'Something I regret now I see how well you look, Miss Matheson, even though I'm an indifferent dancer. It would be my pleasure if you'd allow me to escort you in to supper.'

'Thank you, Mr Ibsen.' Maryse took the arm he offered.

'I thought we were friends,' he said as they strolled away

'We are.'

'Then why don't you call me Marcus?'

'Why don't you call me Maryse?' she countered.

Marcus chuckled. 'Because I'm trying to make a good impression on your father.'

'Why? Oh . . . I see!' An impatient note came into her

voice. 'You know I've determined not to wed, so please don't waste your time.'

'Being in your company is never a waste of time, even when you're being a shrew.'

Maryse opened her mouth to speak, then shut it again and gave a soft laugh. 'I'm not going to allow myself to fall into that trap, Marcus, for you'll wrap me up in conversation like a spider in a web and before I know it my mind will be changed for me.'

He slid Maryse a melting little smile, and said tenderly. 'I'll keep that in mind. You remind me of the first bluebell of summer in the wild woods.'

Laughing, Siana glanced at Francis. 'I do so love a man with a romantic soul and a honeyed tongue.'

'Bluebells! Poppies!' Francis snorted under his breath. 'What next . . . cowslips? God, save me from my daughters' suitors.'

3

Bright though it was, the light from the moon didn't save Josh from disaster. Nearing the gates of Cheverton Manor, the rope stretched across the road between the two trees was invisible to him until he was upon it.

It caught his horse at chest height and brought it down. One of the shafts of the rig splintered along its length. The whole lot tilted sideways and catapulted over. There was a loud snap.

Thrown out of the rig, Josh rolled sideways into a ditch at the side of the road. His horse, held fast on its back, began to squeal and thrash its legs. Dazed, Josh crawled out of the ditch on his hands and knees. He had to set it free.

He stepped gingerly amongst the wreckage of the rig, thankful he hadn't been going any faster. His gelding didn't appear to be badly damaged by the way its legs were moving but the beast's eyes were rolling and blood-flecked foam gathered around his mouth.

'Hush, boy, you've had a fright. I'll soon have you out of here.' Loosening the straps of the rig, Josh took the reins in his hand and tried to help the gelding to regain his feet. Squealing and blowing, the animal made it to his knees before rolling on his side again. Tremors ran along his flanks and an odour of fear rose from him. The gelding's breath came in harsh bursts and blood bubbled from a wound in his heaving chest.

Josh swore. 'Cowardly bastards!' he yelled, punching at the air. 'What did the poor horse do to deserve being maimed in such a manner?'

Untying the rope from the tree, Josh hurled it into the ditch. He'd just straightened up when an arm came around his neck from behind and Alder appeared in front of him. Josh managed to throw a punch and something crunched when it landed. Alder grunted and drove a fist into his midriff with some force, driving the wind from him. The neck hold released, he began to double over when a punch to the chin snapped him upright again, propelling him backwards. He landed heavily on his outstretched arm, which immediately snapped under his weight.

'Christ!' The pain of it made him shriek and he curled into a ball. A kick to the head from his assailants brought darkness crowding in, but it wasn't hard enough to dull the excruciating pain of a second kick to his crotch from behind.

As he began to retch, a voice said against his ear, 'Let that be a lesson to you, Skinner.'

There was the sound of horses galloping away. Above the thump of his own heartbeat and the rush of blood in his ears, Josh heard the laboured breathing of his horse and its whickers of distress. His own injuries kept him lying there for a full half-hour as he alternately passed out from the pain, or woke up to vomit.

Eventually, he heard hoof beats approach and managed to pull himself into a sitting position to shout out a warning to the rider of wreckage on the road. The rider slowed, then came to a halt. It was Marcus.

'Josh! Good God, what's happened?'

'A rope across the road brought me down. I've been set upon and my arm is broken. Take a look at my gelding first, would you, Marcus? He's suffering.'

A few seconds later Marcus came to squat upon his haunches next to him. 'Part of the shaft has snapped off and has been driven into his chest. His lung is pierced. I have a pistol in my saddle bag. With your permission I'll put the poor fellow out of his misery. It will be kinder than allowing him to linger.'

Miserably, Josh nodded. A few minutes later a shot rang out.

'Can you mount my horse?'

Josh managed a wry smile. 'I doubt if I can even stand up. My balls got a good kicking, as well as my head. I don't know which is worse.'

'Then I'll go and rouse my household and come back with a cart. It's nearly dawn. They can clear the debris, send for the knacker and fetch the doctor.'

'Make it Noah Baines, would you? I don't want my sister Siana alarmed, and I don't want Francis involved at this time.'

'I understand.' A cloak was tucked over Josh's body. 'Try to relax, I won't be long.'

Once they were back at the house, Josh found himself

39

tended to by Marcus. Soon, he was lying on a soft bed, wrapped in a nightshirt. Marcus made a face when he splinted his arm. 'The bone will have to be manipulated if it's to set properly, but at least it hasn't broken through the skin.' Dark eyes came up to his. 'The procedure will be painful.'

Josh nodded.

'Care to tell me which of the Mathesons did this? Though it wouldn't take much to guess it was Roger and Alder. Both were the worse for drink and behaving loutishly. You can bring charges against them, you know.'

'They're Francis's family, and it would be uncomfortable for both him and my sister, should I decide to do that. They won't get away with it, though. A pity about my horse, the poor beast didn't deserved what he got – that he didn't.'

Noah Baines was announced. His examination was thorough. 'Luckily you have a thick skull, for the concussion is slight, and I can fix the arm.' He shook his head when he examined Josh's groin. Face straight, he announced, 'The balls will have to come off though.'

Josh's eyes widened in alarm. 'Not bleddy likely, Doc. I've got long-term plans for them.'

When Marcus whooped with laughter, Noah cracked a grin. 'Right, Mr Skinner, let's get that bone pulled into place. It's going to hurt like hell but I'll give you some laudanum to dull the pain. As for your manly bits, it's a temporary disablement. Bathe them in cold water four times a day until the swelling subsides, and don't attempt to exercise them until the bruising has gone, whatever the temptation.'

Noah handed over a dose of laudanum, watching while it was swallowed. Then he began to lay out padded splints and strapping. Josh's ears took on a pleasant buzz and he felt so relaxed he had a job keeping his eyes open and kept grinning.

Baines smiled to himself, then turned to Marcus. 'You made a good job of the splint. I'll need assistance with this arm. Are you up to it?'

Marcus nodded. 'I know what's expected, I studied anatomy and basic surgery techniques for a while.'

'Ah, that accounts for it. Ready when you are then, Marcus.'

The next minute Marcus had Josh held firmly below the elbow, and Noah Baines was pulling on his wrist. A searing pain shot through him.

Before he had time to shriek, Josh passed out.

At Rivervale House, Francis was attempting to straighten Alder's bloody nose.

'Damned fool to fall off your mount,' Ryder said without compassion. 'What were you doing out riding at that time, when we have the journey home to make? Don't you know there are itinerant workers abroad who would cut your throat for a shilling from your pocket? Most of them are Chartists, out to unsettle the labourer force with their demands.'

Francis glanced up from what he was doing, saying with some satisfaction and a smile, 'Not hereabouts, Ryder. Marcus Ibsen has improved both conditions and wages at Cheverton, and the Chartist cause has run out of momentum. You met Marcus earlier.'

'Ah yes, that fellow with an eye to Maryse. He might be a good choice for her. She's a nervous filly and he looks the type who would stand for none of a woman's nonsense.'

Francis was not about to get into a discussion with Ryder about his beloved daughter, especially when Maryse was being compared to horseflesh. He manipulated Alder's bloodied nose less gently than he should have in retaliation for the remark, heard him suck in an agonized breath. 'I'm afraid there's nothing I can do about this, Alder. The swelling and pain will subside in a few days, and your nose will settle into its new shape.'

'It looks like it was caused by a punch to me,' Ryder grumbled. 'Are you sure you haven't been set upon? If so, we can lay charges and have the fellow transported.'

'With all those boxing medals from Cambridge to his credit, would Alder have come off second best?' Roger scoffed.

'We haven't seen the other fellow.'

Alder exchanged a glance with his brother. 'There is no other fellow.'

Ryder's eyes narrowed.

Later that afternoon, a servant from Cheverton Manor delivered an account to Rivervale House, addressed to Alder Matheson. It was intercepted by Ryder, who hadn't believed a word his sons had told him.

The earl discovered Alder in a secluded part of the

garden, arguing with Pansy. He stopped to listen for a while.

'I'll dance with whoever I wish, Alder. You're my cousin, not my father.'

'But Josh Skinner is a low peasant.'

'You are acting lower.'

'When we're married I'll bring you to heel, by God, I will!'

'I'm not marrying you, Alder. What are you doing . . . let go of me, at once.'

There was the sound of a slap and Alder swore. 'Damn you! Mind my nose.'

'Damn your ugly nose, then! I hope it drops off and the crows eat it.'

Though Ryder grinned at her retort, he thought it was time he made his presence known.

Pansy had an outraged look on her face, tears in her eyes and angry patches of colour in her cheeks. She seemed relieved to see him.

Rubbing his face, Alder took a step back.

'From what I overheard, you owe Pansy an apology, Alder.'

'Sorry,' he muttered.

Pansy glared at him. 'You're becoming a bully and a bore, Alder.'

Ryder laid a calming hand on her arm. 'Enough, Pansy. We'll sort this out later. Alder, an account has arrived from Joshua Skinner requesting reparation for a horse and rig, plus the services of a doctor. Would you mind telling me how this has come about? And no deceit, this time.'

Alder's face mottled red as he flicked a glance at Pansy. 'It's a private matter between Skinner and myself.'

Ryder was insistent. 'What happened last night, or do I have to ask Mr Skinner?'

'The fellow was leering at Pansy all evening, and he had the cheek to waltz with her. I warned him off earlier, but he didn't listen.'

'Joshua Skinner was a guest in your uncle's house. You had no right to warn him. Pansy is sensible. If his behaviour had been improper towards your cousin she would have informed her father, who would have dealt with it, no doubt.'

'Damn it, Pa, Pansy is my future wife. I don't want some low type handling her on the dance floor.'

The earl gazed from one to the other. 'Am I to understand that Pansy has accepted your suit?'

Spirited little filly that she was, Pansy sent his son a glare. 'I certainly have not! On the strength of what has happened now, it's doubtful I ever will.'

'Ah, don't get so miffed, Pansy, I know you don't mean it, since the fellow means nothing to you.' Alder turned towards him and shrugged. 'Mamma said Maryse is having an unsettling influence on Pansy. I think she's right.'

'Pshaw!' Pansy snorted, sounding so exactly like his wife, Prudence, that the earl nearly chuckled when she demanded to know of his son, 'What did you do to poor Josh?'

'Tied a rope across the road so *poor Josh* would come a cropper – and he did. It serves the upstart right, too.'

44

Her face became ashen. For a moment Ryder thought she might go into a faint, then she sucked in a breath and whispered, 'How could you do such a terrible thing, Alder? Is Josh injured?'

'He was breathing when I left him, which was more than he deserved. He did break my nose, after all.'

This was worse than Ryder had imagined. 'You caused a fatal injury to a man's horse, destroyed his rig and left him lying unconscious on a public highway? That was the act of a coward.'

His son's face adopted a sullen expression. 'I was drunk, Pa. I'll pay the fellow off and that will be the end of it.'

'It might only be the beginning of it. Being the son of an earl carries certain responsibilities along with the privileges. Not only could you be charged and hauled up before a magistrate for what you've done, you could also drag the family name through the mud.'

'No lawyer would take his case against me.'

'It appears Skinner doesn't intend to press charges if remuneration is forthcoming. Fetch Roger, would you? Attend me in your uncle's study and we'll discuss a suitable settlement.'

'Pa . . .'

'*Now, Alder!* I will not tolerate dishonourable behaviour, such as has happened here. I'm ashamed of you.'

After he'd gone, the earl turned to his niece and offered her his arm. 'I cannot apologize enough, Pansy. Don't think too badly of Alder, for he's allowed his regard for you to blind his good sense. So far, he's shown

45

remarkable patience in his pursuit of you, but no young man of mettle likes to be kept waiting for such a long time. I realize that Skinner is of little consequence to a girl of your breeding. If you were to accept Alder before we leave for home I'd be the happiest man alive, for you know how fond of you we all are. It would settle him down to be sure of your affection. Your father would be pleased with the match too.'

'You've discussed it with my father?'

'Of course. He's eager to see his daughters settled into advantageous marriages.'

Pansy muttered something non-committal as they strolled back to the house.

'Alder will apologize, of course.' Ryder kissed her gently on the forehead. 'Perhaps you'd find your father and ask him to join me. He was going into the library the last time I saw him.'

Her father looked up from a book and smiled when Pansy joined him. 'Why so glum, my precious?'

'There's been some trouble. The earl wants you to join him in your study.'

Laying the book down on a table Francis came to where she stood. 'Does the trouble concern you?'

'Only indirectly. Alder took exception to Josh Skinner dancing with me last night, and set about him.'

'Oh, so that's where the broken nose came from.' Placing a finger under her chin, he lifted it so she met his eyes. 'Since my two daughters are of exceptional beauty, it was bound to happen. But Alder being jealous of Josh is simply preposterous. You'd have more sense than to encourage a youth so socially beneath you.'

'You married Siana, and they are brother and sister,' she pointed out.

He frowned. 'As my wife, Siana is accepted. Besides, she was married before and had adapted to a different life than the one she was used to.'

'Josh was badly hurt.'

His eyes sharpened. 'How badly? Has he been examined?'

'A rope was stretched across the road, his horse was killed and they left Josh unconscious on the road. Dr Baines was called out to attend him. He could have died.'

'They?'

'Roger was in on it, too, I think.'

'It's worse than I thought, then. I'll go to see Ryder at once.' He kissed her on the nose. 'Try not to worry, Pansy. We'll sort this out so Josh is well compensated and Alder and Roger keep their good name intact. Money always talks sense to Josh.'

'Not only to Josh, it seems, except he's worked for his and deserves it.'

The coldness in her voice brought a frown to her father's face. 'You'd better explain that censorious remark, Pansy.'

'Alder was the ringleader, he always is. He needs a good flogging. Any recompense should come from his allowance and he should apologize publicly to Josh.'

'Should he now? Your opinion on this matter is of little consequence, since Alder is too old to be flogged and his punishment is for his father to decide. I doubt if that will include a public grovelling by the son of a peer to entertain Miss Pansy Matheson.'

Nearly gasping at the rebuke, she took a step back, prepared to do battle on Josh's behalf. 'Then you're going to condone Alder's behaviour?'

'I certainly don't intend to condone your lack of courtesy towards me. Am I to suppose you harbour tender feelings towards Josh Skinner?'

She slanted her head to one side, feeling tears prickle in her eyes. 'Of course not, he's merely a friend. But what if I did?'

'You're being silly and argumentative. Please remove yourself to your room. I'll be in my study later if you wish to offer me an apology.' He strode off, his back as stiff as a broomstick.

'You're perfectly horrible when you're with your brothers,' she whispered after he'd gone, which wasn't quite true, for she had overstepped the mark and should have accepted the reprimand. Now she was angry with him. Bursting into a storm of weeping, she fled into the garden instead.

Alder found her there a while later, her temper repaired, her eyes quite dry but still red from weeping. 'Go away. I feel horrid and ugly.'

'You look wonderful to me.' Alder handed her a red rose. 'I'm sorry if I upset you, Pansy. I'm a brute.'

'I know,' she sniffed, and because she'd grown up with him and couldn't totally dislike him, she asked, 'Did you get into much trouble?'

'I deserved it. I've taken all the blame which lets

48

Roger off the hook and I'm going to see Skinner now, to apologize. Come with me.'

Her eyes widened. 'Alder Matheson, do you intend to make a fool of yourself by apologizing to him in front of me? My papa said you wouldn't be expected to abase yourself in such a way.'

He grinned at her. 'I'll grovel on my belly if it will make you feel better and allow you to like me again. I thought I might offer him my new horse as a replacement. I really didn't mean to go as far as I did.'

'Really, Alder, that's wonderful.' She threw her arms about him in a hug, surprised and pleased by his generosity.

His fingers stroked through her hair. 'We've known each other since childhood, Pansy. I hate it when you're furious with me.'

'I'm not furious, now.'

'Your father said you thought I should be flogged.'

She shrugged and sat up, smiling at him. 'So I did, and if you were a man I would have flogged you myself. But you can be quite sweet when you try.'

He slid from the seat and onto one knee, taking her hand in his. 'I know I don't look very pretty at the moment, but Pansy, my darling, honour me by saying you'll wed me. I'll be sweet all the time, then. I love you quite desperately.'

From the other side of the hedge came the muffled sound of her father's voice, followed by that of the earl. Then came the loud, aggrieved voice of her aunt Prudence. 'Girls in my day did as they were told. They had no opinions.'

'Ah,' said the earl, 'I imagine they were storing them up for their old age.'

Stifling a giggle, Pansy whispered, 'Get up, you fool. Our parents are here.'

His eyes full of laughter, Alder begged, 'Say you will, or I'll shout it to the skies. *Pansy Matheson!*

She placed a hand over his mouth and hissed, 'Stop it this minute, Alder.'

Taking her hand in his he kissed her palm, then his arm came up around her waist and she was drawn onto his knee so he could steal a kiss from her mouth. Her face heated, for she hadn't expected to like it. Placing her hands against her cheeks she said in a flustered voice afterwards, 'I'm mortified.'

'Marry me, Pansy. I won't let you go until you give me an answer.'

The voices came closer. Oh God! It would be too embarrassing for them to find her like this. 'All right, Alder, I will . . . but not until I'm of age. Now, let me up.'

She scrambled back onto the seat just in time, for the earl popped his head around the corner the next moment. 'I thought I heard voices. What are you doing on your knees, Alder?'

He sprang upright and drawled, 'Actually, Pa, I was proposing marriage to Miss Pansy Matheson. Although you've arrived at an inconvenient time you shall be the first to know. Pansy has just done me the honour of accepting.'

Prudence gave a loud scream and Pansy found herself enveloped in a crushing hug while Ryder beamed a smile at her. 'There, I knew you'd come round. We shall have a grand dinner party at the hall to celebrate, and the nuptials will take place in London. Next July will be a convenient time, for the London season is just about over but the guests will still be in their London residences.' Prudence began to prattle on happily about who to invite and who not to invite.

Pulling herself from her aunt's arms, Pansy replenished herself with a breath before going to hug her father and whispering, 'I'm sorry I was so horrid to you, Papa. I love you, I can't bear it when we're at odds.'

'I think we were all a little rattled by what has happened. Let's go and tell Siana the good news. She'll be so happy for you.'

'Does she know about Josh yet?'

'You are the only female of the house privy to that information. Josh doesn't want Siana to be alarmed for the time being. Yes, Siana will be told eventually. I thought I might tell her tomorrow, when the earl and his family have departed and Alder has had time to put things right between himself and her brother. I do so enjoy the company of my family and would prefer relations to remain harmonious between us. Josh understands that.'

Harmonious! Was that what this demonstration in the gentlemanly art of brutality and justification had been? She managed to bury the exclamation of annoyance she felt as they strolled with their arms about each other's waists, back to the house. 'Can you stop Aunt Prudence from doing things her way? I'm not going to wed until two years have passed, and I want a small wedding with just family, not masses of people who I don't really know.'

'Aunt Prudence has always wanted a daughter, and kindly assumed the role of mentor after your own mother died. Indulge her if you wish to please me. A wedding lasts only for one day, marriage for a lifetime.'

A coldness crept over Pansy then, and it was nothing to do with the fact that her father had decided not to pander to her wishes in this.

The feeling of coldness intensified when she visited Josh with Alder. Laying on the bed a bunch of flowers she'd picked she gazed upon his bruised and blackened face with concern. The beating had been more brutal than she'd expected. 'Dearest Josh, Alder has come to apologize for what he's done. Please forgive him.'

Alder cleared his throat and said gruffly, 'I've brought my horse over for you, Skinner. I daresay the nag is worth a lot more than the one you lost, so I hope you'll accept it in the spirit it's offered. You'll be recompensed for the rig and any expenses, of course.' He held out his hand. 'No bad feelings, I hope. All's fair in love and war, eh?'

After a moment's hesitation, Josh took his hand. 'Is it? I must remember that.'

Alder's laughter was forced. 'By the way, Pansy has done me the honour. We're to become engaged.'

Josh paled as he gazed at her for a painful moment. 'Are you happy, Miss Pansy?'

'Of course she is. We'll leave you now, Skinner, the visit seems to have tired you out.'

Ignoring Alder, Pansy leaned over the bed and kissed Josh on the cheek, murmuring, 'Get well soon. I'll visit you again in a day or so, with Siana and Daisy.'

Alder took a propriatorial grip of her upper arm and brought her upright. 'Come on, Pansy my love, our business here is over now. The fellow needs his rest.'

When they were halfway home, Pansy realized not one word of apology had left Alder's lips.

The next day Siana and Maryse were in the stillroom when Francis came back from visiting Josh at Cheverton Manor. The air was strongly flower-scented. Flattened open before them on the table was a book titled *Domestic Cookery*.

'What are the pair of you up to in here?'

Siana turned, a frown of concentration on her face. 'We're attempting to make some pot-pourri. Later, we're going to make pomanders to place in the cupboards, for it repels the moths. Maryse is better at it than I am.'

'That's because I had some tuition from Aunt Prudence.'

Sagely, Francis commented, 'Prudence has many skills to pass onto others, it seems.'

Siana laughed when she caught the amusement in his eyes. 'You've distracted me. I've forgotten how many cups of rose petals I've measured into the pot.'

'Nine,' Maryse told her. 'There's about fifteen cupsful to a peck. Isn't it about time we put some more jasmine in?'

'We used that in the last layer. It's the turn of the lavender next, then a handful of laurel leaves.'

'Can you put that witchery aside for a moment? I need to talk to you. It's about Josh.'

Her gaze intensified on his face. 'He's hurt, isn't he?'

'Not badly. How did you know?'

Siana's fey sense had let her down this time. The undercurrents of uneasiness she'd felt of late were nothing to do with Josh. They seemed to be related to something much bigger. But then, the sight rarely came to her outside of the quiet times, and the house had been anything but quiet of late. 'I didn't, but you had your doctor face on when you you went out, and came straight back to me when you arrived home. What has happened?'

'He had an . . . *accident*. His arm is broken and he sustained some bruising. He'll be recuperating at Cheverton for a few days.'

She began to untie her apron. 'Why didn't you tell me of this sooner? I could have gone with you.'

'Josh didn't want you to be unduly alarmed. I wanted to see how bad his injuries were for myself before I told you. My brothers concurred with my decision.'

'Your brothers?' There was a certain evasiveness about his answer she didn't like. She envied the sense of camaraderie the Matheson brothers possessed and noted the deference afforded to Ryder in his position as earl. There was a definite pecking order amongst them. Francis was the youngest, therefore the least important. He accepted that. She didn't, especially when information of such importance was kept from her.

'How did the accident occur?'

His glance flickered away from hers for a moment, then came back. His sigh had a slightly irritated sound to it, so she wished she hadn't asked. 'Alder deliberately caused the accident. He had too much to drink and took offence when Josh danced with Pansy.'

Maryse gasped.

Even though her insides churned with the anger she felt, Siana gazed calmly at Francis, waiting for the rest of it. It wasn't forthcoming.

He shrugged. 'The argument has been resolved, an apology made, compensation offered and accepted. It was a family matter.'

'Josh is a member of *my* family.'

'I'm well aware of that, but you must allow me to act on your behalf in such disputes, and as I see fit. A needlessly unpleasant atmosphere might have developed and caused dissent amongst our guests had the matter been handled differently.'

Siana felt like stamping her foot. 'When did all this happen?'

'The day before yesterday.'

'I see. So my brother was criminally attacked and badly damaged by a member of your family and the matter is to be hushed up. What would have happened if it had been the other way round, Francis?'

Siana, resenting that his brothers took precedence over herself in matters such as this, dropped her apron to the bench, pushed past him and out of the door without another word.

Her path took her the hill behind the house. Reaching the top, she kicked off her shoes and threw herself on her stomach in the long grass to gaze down on the River Frome, a sheet of silver water shining amongst the meadowlands.

From here she could see only the chimney stacks of the house amongst the trees. There was a hint of autumn in the air, a slight curl and amber tint to the leaves. More gold than green, the grass had assumed a dry whisper, the prickly husks of the chestnuts were dropping to the ground and splitting open and acorns were pale brown beads in their cups.

Yet the sun warmed her back and calmed her as she pressed her ear against the earth to feel the beat of its ancient wisdom. Presently, she heard footsteps. A shadow came between her and the sky as Francis seated himself beside her.

'I'm sorry. I should have told you sooner. I was brought up to believe that gentlemanly compromise was preferable in such matters.'

She rolled over onto her back and smiled, inclined to be forgiving now he'd come after her. 'I should have understood that consulting me would have diminished you in the eyes of your brothers. How tedious you all are when you're together, as if it's a game you play.'

'I've never thought of it that way. It's just something I've grown up with.'

She thought of her own childhood then, of the poverty and the ill-treatment by her stepfather and of the promise she'd made to her dying mother to care for Daisy and Josh. She'd kept that promise, for she'd married above her. It was easy to love a man who treated a woman tenderly, and she'd found love with both her husbands, especially Francis, who had captured her heart completely. She reached up to trace the curve of his mouth.

Francis thought he'd never seen anything so lovely as this woman of his. He loosened her hair and spread it to gleam darkly amongst the grasses, then took her hands in his and inhaled the heady fragrance of pot-pourri on her palms.

She watched him from the wild darkness below the surface of her eyes, the pagan in her parting her luscious mouth in a faint smile, so his love for her spread through his veins in a river of heat. She brought him alive with her passion for life and loving, with the compassion that flowed from her to embrace every living thing.

He bent to kiss the soft, pale flesh of her breasts, felt himself surge against her thigh.

She laughed against his ear, the sound husky and teasing. 'Whatever has come over you, my stuffy blue blood?'

He grinned down at her and growled, 'You've bewitched me.'

Her peal of laughter was spontaneous. 'I wouldn't do anything so unnatural.'

'Then why do I have this sudden desire to spread you out on the grass and make love to you?'

'It's the herd instinct. You're king of your own castle again, and you need to reclaim what's yours for reassurance.'

'That's an uncomfortable thought and you're too clever by half. Perhaps it's just because I love you.'

'Or because I love you.' She guided his hands to the fastenings of her bodice and, while he was fumbling there, her mouth found his and she kissed him long and hard.

She was perfection, and he would never allow anything to come between them.

Francis didn't notice the shadow of a cloud passing over the sun, just felt his wife give a tiny little shudder.

4

It was the end of October. The Cheverton harvest had been a good one, generating a healthy profit. Marcus was well satisfied, his only regret was Maryse had not attended the harvest supper with her family the previous month.

'My daughter is indisposed and she sends her apologies,' Francis had told him.

When they had a moment alone together, Siana had informed him exactly why the girl he loved was indisposed.

'Maryse could not bring herself to revisit the place where she was brutally assaulted. Her emotions are very fragile and you should have known she wouldn't attend.'

Marcus didn't blame Maryse one little bit. He'd resolved right there and then to remove the barn and the copse. He'd have a garden designed and laid out in its place, especially for Maryse's pleasure.

Gazing at himself in the mirror, he grinned widely. He looked like a man with courting on his mind in his new full-skirted coat with fur collar and matching cuffs, and his side-braided trousers. He was off to Wareham, where he intended to collect the garden design from the landscape artist.

Siana had told him that Maryse and her sister would be attending an exhibition and sale of local crafts in the town hall. He intended to invite them to the tea rooms if he ran into them, which was more than probable, because he intended to keep an eye out for them.

He declined refreshment with the landscape artist, and placed the plans in a satchel in his saddle bag. Scarcely twenty minutes later he cantered across the bridge over the Frome and past Lady St Mary's Church. Forced to slow down as the road grew busier, he threaded his horse through the foot traffic, dismounting at the road junction outside the town hall.

Leaving his mount to be minded by one of the lads eager to earn a few pennies, Marcus strode across to the Red Lion Hotel and, taking up a window seat, refreshed himself with a glass of ale while he observed the comings and goings at the town hall.

He saw the rig arriving. What a stroke of luck! Josh Skinner was at the reins. Marcus hadn't seen Josh since he'd spent time recuperating at Cheverton Manor after being set upon. He was of a mind to teach the young man personal defence skills, something Marcus had learned, along with the art of meditation, from an oriental gentleman he'd formerly been acquainted with. He was pleased to see Josh had fully recovered, for the attack upon him had been unwarranted, and also savage.

Pansy, dressed in pink, laughed as Josh helped her down. A shame she had committed herself to her lout of a cousin, Marcus thought. The man was a bully and would seek to crush her spirit.

Maryse followed. She wore a dark blue mantle over her gown for warmth. A matching bonnet of demure proportions framed her face and was tied to one side with a bow.

His heart began to sing like a bird as he drank in the sight of her delicate face. Soon she'd be his to cherish. The inevitability of it grew inside him, for he knew they were meant for each other. He'd known it as soon as he'd set eyes on her, and so had she. All he had to do was convince her, and the defensive shell she'd built around herself would begin to crumble.

He waited a while, giving them time to make their purchases from the goods on display. Finally, abandoning his vantage point he strolled across to the hall, deciding it would be better to make the meeting seem accidental, so as not to embarrass her.

Goods of many designs were on display, from tapestries, beaded lamps, jewellery, bird displays mounted under glass domes, to exquisitely dressed dolls and painted fans. He saw Maryse examine a fringed shawl of light grey silk. It was decorated with intricately embroidered blue butterflies in random flight.

Josh stood behind them, his arms full of parcels, a long-suffering look on his face.

'How lovely it is,' Marcus heard Maryse say to Pansy.

'You should buy it. It would suit many of your gowns.'

Wistfully, Maryse shook her head. 'I haven't got enough money left, and I need some new gloves.'

Pansy opened her reticule to peer into its depths. 'I

have a small amount. If you offer them less, they might take it. Your gloves can wait and so can my new bonnet.'

Maryse shook her head. 'Aunt Prudence said that bonnet was a disgrace.'

Pansy laughed. 'She regards everything I do and wear as a disgrace. I don't know why she was always so keen on me marrying Alder, when she disapproves of me so.'

'That's just her way. How could she disapprove when you're so bright, happy and lovable. It's impossible to be melancholy when you're around. I'm going to miss you so much when you're wed.'

'I've told them I won't wed Alder until you're settled.'

'Which means she'll redouble her efforts to find me a husband. Really, Pansy, how could you make me responsible for your happiness?'

Pansy looked a little crestfallen by the rebuke. 'I want you to be happy, too, Maryse.'

'How can I be when you've made me feel guilty for the decision I made? You are doing exactly the same to me as was done to you, trying to push me into something I don't want.'

Pansy grinned. 'But I wasn't in love. You are, for I can see it in your eyes every time you look at—'

'Stop it, at once, Pansy Matheson.' Obviously flustered, Maryse blushed as she turned to walk away.

Marcus's eyes narrowed. As soon as they moved out of sight he hurried forward and purchased the shawl, placing the parcel in the saddle bag he was carrying over his arm. He'd hardly closed the flap when the party returned.

Maryse's blush returned when she saw him. It charmed him. 'Marcus, what are you doing here?'

'I was in Wareham on business, and was attracted by the crowd. There are some pretty goods on sale.'

'Yes. Her glance went to the table and she couldn't quite hide the flare of dismay in her eyes. 'There was a shawl I rather liked, but it's gone. I was going to ask them to keep it for me.'

'Oh, that's a shame.' He greeted Josh and Pansy, saying casually, 'I was just going to the tea rooms for some refreshment before I return home. Will you join me?'

'In a little while. Miss Pansy has offered to help me choose dolls for Daisy, Goldie and Susannah,' Josh replied. 'Escort Miss Matheson, and take some of these parcels, if you would. I just haven't got long enough arms to hang everything on.'

'I have some plans for the Cheverton gardens I'd value your opinion on, later.'

It was Maryse's opinion Marcus valued, and while they waited in the tea rooms he watched the changing expressions on her face with genuine pleasure as she studied the plans.

Once, she looked up and gazed straight into his eyes. The raw pain in them staggered him. 'If you have the copse removed, surely the ground will become even more boggy there.'

'The bog will be turned into a lake, which, in turn, will drain into the stream.' His hand hovered over the plan and he stabbed a finger at it from time to time as he explained, 'There will be a bridge there. At this side of it, a weir with a sluice gate, because the lake might need

63

draining from time to time. Some of the existing trees will be retained for protection against the wind, and to provide shelter for the birds. Here, where the barn is, an artificial hill will support a pavilion, and an avenue of elms planted. The project will be called Maryse's garden.'

'Why would you want to call it after me?'

'You know why. The lake we'll call *Gwin Dwr*.'

She gave a sudden gasp, biting her bottom lip as she was reminded of the cruel assault she'd been subjected to – of the consequence, the secret child she'd given birth to in Wales. She had never spoken of it to him, but she did now.

'So, you believe the presence of the lake will wash away my shame, as it was purported to do in the cave of the wine water in Wales?'

The *Gwin Dwr* had been real, a cave where Welsh virgins had supposedly been thrown after being violated by the English soldiers. Legend said that only the pure of mind could safely bathe there, and if the souls of the virgins found them wanting, they would drown. If they survived their sins were washed away. Maryse had bathed in the waters, emerging alive and imagining she was cleansed. But she was older now, and Marcus knew she'd believed because she'd wanted to at the time. Her words confirmed it.

'Do you really believe that happened, Marcus?'

His hand slid over hers. 'Maryse, you have done nothing to shame yourself.'

Her eyes came up to his again. 'You must be blind if you truly think such a thing.'

'I know it must be true, for the virgins of the cave of the *Gwin Dwr* found you without sin and cast you from their midst. Like them, I believe you were sinned against. Can you not forget the past and admit you love me just a little?'

Unexpectedly, she said, 'I do love you, more than you'll ever know. You are noble and kind, and you deserve someone much better.'

A description far from the truth. Maryse had seen only what he'd wanted to show her, for she was too fragile to learn of the darkness in him. 'There is nobody better for me. Wed me, Maryse. No one else will cherish you as much, or love you so well.'

He held his breath as she evaded his eyes, her expression telling him she was considering the idea. Finally, she looked again at him, the grey of her eyes shining with unshed tears and uncertain in their resolve. 'If you can love me without censure, the least I can do is have faith in you. But I'm scared, Marcus, for I don't know if I can bring myself to be a proper wife to you.'

With his heart soaring, for he was confident he could overcome the damage which had been done to her, he said, 'It would be my pleasure to instruct you in the gentle ways of loving, for I would want some children from the marriage. You know I'd never deliberately hurt you.'

She sucked in a sob of a breath, then nodded. 'I know. So yes, I will become your wife.'

Marcus felt like a young lad with his first love as he took her trembling hand in his. He vowed he'd never allow anyone to hurt this girl again. He'd kill them first! 'When shall it be?'

She gave a faint smile at his eagerness, rewarding him with an answer that took his breath away. 'Before Christmas, with no fuss and with only my immediate family present.'

At the end of the following month the pair were wed in the Cheverton church.

It was a cold, grey day, with the smell of rain in the air as the Matheson family set out. The fields were a dark crumble of ploughed earth and mud, the hedges a twist and gnarl of grey sticks, browning leaves and orange berries.

Inhaling the damp, mossy smell of early winter, of leaves crushed underfoot, and experiencing the chill as the wind breathed into the warm space between her collar and bonnet, Siana smiled. The weather invoked memories of her childhood, reminding her how lucky she was to have enough to eat and a sturdy roof over her head.

Smoke drifted from the chimneys of the cottages in the new village Marcus had built. Already the neat, bright thatch was beginning to weather, eventually to meld with the landscape. It provided a warm home for wintering mice. Here and there, on the solid cob walls around windows and porches, ivy or climbing roses were beginning to take hold, gardens were green with rows of winter vegetables. Chicken, geese and hogs sent out a cacophony of sound, familiar to those who lived there.

Apart from themselves, only Josh and his friend, the misshapen and mute Sam Saynuthin, would witness the vows. Marcus had paid for a barrel of ale to be tapped at the local inn for the estate workers to celebrate.

Maryse would become mistress of Cheverton Estate, as Siana had been in her brief first marriage. She would be able to support her husband in ways Siana still found difficult. Maryse could socialize with ease, arrange dinner parties, and knew the order of preference without having to consult with another. Her manners were innate. She would not be made the recipient of condescension, however well meant it was.

But Siana was ever aware of and, grateful for the love and support offered to her by Francis. If she lost that she would find the strength to go on for the sake of the children, but she knew the essence of something inside her would shrivel up and die.

She and Francis had been wed in this very church by the same man. When she slid her hand into her his, he turned towards her and smiled, remembering the vows they had exchanged together, perhaps, as she was.

Maryse, elegantly gowned in blue silk, wore the shawl Marcus had bought her for warmth. The pearls at her throat had once belonged to her mother. She was calm, speaking her vows in a clear voice.

Afterwards, when they exchanged hugs, Siana became aware of the tension her stepdaughter was trying to hide. She guessed the reason behind it. 'Be happy, my dearest Maryse. If ever you need me, you know where you can find me.'

There were tears in Maryse's eyes as she whispered, 'Thank you for being so good to me always.'

Beyond Maryse, something shifted in a shadows, causing Siana to experience a moment of such dread that she nearly cried out with the shock of it. Feeling faint she clutched at her husband for support. Not noticing anything amiss, Francis said quietly to her as he handed his family into the carriage, 'I already miss her.'

'Maryse will not be living far away, Papa,' Daisy reminded him. 'She said she'll invite us all to tea when she's settled in properly. I can remember living at Cheverton Manor. There were ghosts in the attic. Do you think they're still there?'

Goldie's blue eyes widened in remembrance and she shifted closer to Siana. 'They used to rattle the door trying to get out. I saw one standing by the window in the attic once. She was wearing a green gown.'

Siana laughed, but uneasily. 'That was a portrait of a woman who used to live there.'

'What happened to her?'

'She became very sad because her daughter died. She went to heaven to be with her.'

Siana wasn't about to tell them that the woman in the portrait had been deranged and had been kept a prisoner at the manor for many years, that her own fey sense had been heightened there and the presence of the woman had seemed to haunt her – especially when she'd been with child. She shivered, wondering if the portrait had been disposed of.

Her sister snuggled up against her side. 'I'm glad you didn't go to heaven when Ashley died.'

A sudden stab of anguish ripped through Siana as Daisy reminded her of her precious son, her little squire, who'd been so handsome and robust. His life had been withdrawn from his body after a prolonged period of suffering, despite the fight she'd put up. She tried to stifle a tiny, involuntary sob as the blood drained from her face. Francis took her hand and held it, offering the only comfort he could.

She drew on his love and the depth of strength she knew she had inside her. 'I was lucky. I still had you and Goldie to love. And now we have Susannah and Bryn too.' Though Susannah would soon be claimed by her mother, and Goldie was going for a prolonged visit to her brother in London in the spring.

Maryse found it hard to adjust to marriage. Her wedding night had proved to her that her fears were correct. Marcus had been wonderfully gentle with her but, although she tried to relax and respond to his advances, at the last moment she became so rigid with fright she'd had to grit her teeth to stop herself from screaming. Afterwards, she felt dirtied and sick at heart.

'My love,' he'd said, making a valiant effort to hide his disappointment, 'we will grow used to each other in time.'

Because she loved Marcus and wanted to please him, Maryse put up with his attentions. Although she grew used to it she knew she'd never find pleasure in the marital act. Sometimes, she was physically sick afterwards. Eventually, Marcus must have realized it, for he began to make fewer demands on her and the disgusting act became less prolonged.

He spent a night away from her just before Christmas, returning slightly pensive. 'I had someone to see in Cornwall,' was all he would say, and would be drawn no more on it.

Had Maryse known that her husband had killed two men on her behalf, she would have been horrified.

Christmas came and went, celebrated in pleasant company at her father's house. It snowed heavily that year, making the journey to Kylchester Hall impossible. Spring swiftly followed, new plants pushed through the earth to embrace the sky.

'The daffodils are out,' Marcus said to her one day and led her to the window. Blazoned across the lawn in bobbing gold flowers were the words, 'I love you, Maryse.' She broke down, sobbing her heart out in his arms.

Maryse's courses ceased. She knew what it meant and was beset by melancholy. She hid it under a mantle of calm, because everyone else was delighted. The only pleasure for her was that Marcus ceased to press his attentions on her.

Her baby was due to be born in August. Pale and listless from constant sickness, she sat by the window to while away the days by working at her embroidery or stitching a garment for Marcus's child – for she couldn't think of the expected infant as hers – and watching the new garden taking shape.

'It's beginning to look pretty,' Maryse murmured to herself, seeing the lake fill with water as the stream was diverted. Soon, it became hard to remember at all the spot where she'd been assaulted, for it had disappeared under the water. 'The lake we'll call *Gwin Dwr*,' Marcus had said.

He'd been humouring her. This lake could never be the legendary *Gwin Dwr*. But she was grateful the scene of the crime was no longer there to mock her.

Dear Marcus. He was so patient with her, even knowing she couldn't love him as well as she wished.

By June, her garden was completed. Water lilies began to spread across the surface of the lake and reeds and irises thickened into clumps along the banks. Two ducks and a drake moved in. On the other side and up the hill a sweet little pavilion had been erected.

Her heart suddenly lightened. Marcus had worked so hard and she had been so ungrateful. She went down to join him. He smiled as he straightened up to lean on his hoe, his face smeared with perspiration and dirt.

'What are you planting?'

'A bed of roses for you. Next year we should have a good display. Come next month there will be baby ducks on the pond, for I've found a nest hidden amongst the reeds.' His eyes went proudly to her bulging stomach. 'It will be a good harvest all round, this year.'

'Will you take me across the bridge to the pavilion? I want to see it.'

'You're feeling better, aren't you?'

'A little. I didn't feel so ill today.'

'Good, I've been worried about you.' He offered her his arm and led her down to the bridge. 'The mud is beginning to settle on the bottom of the lake now. See

71

how pretty it is with the water tumbling over the weir. It was well worth doing.'

The hill to the pavilion was steep for someone in her advanced condition, and she was gasping for breath when she reached the top. Inside, were two chairs and a small table. The door opened outwards to give a view over the lake and the avenue of elm saplings. Maryse sank gratefully into one of the chairs, panting slightly. The climb had been taxing.

'Sit and rest for a while, my love. I'll go and fetch some lemonade so you can refresh yourself. Now you're here, I've got a surprise for you.' He strode off down the hill again, crackling with energy. She could see part of the house past the trees, the weathered Portland stone softened by rambling ivy. Marcus stopped for a moment to speak to a servant, who went scurrying off into the house. Then he disappeared into the stables.

It was pleasant to sit in the open air with the birds singing all around her. Presently, Maryse grew drowsy. Inside her, she felt the movement of her infant, a sly push against her ribs. She wished she could love it, for her disinterest seemed unnatural to her. But this was something Marcus had wanted, not her. She hoped it was a boy so he would have his heir.

Something wet pushed against her hand. Startled, she opened her eyes. A little white dog was gazing up at her, its tail wagging. It had a black spot on its back. Her mouth dried and her tongue clove to the roof of her mouth. It looked like her sister's dog, Spot, lost all those years ago when he'd been a pup.

Then a man suddenly came into view and called the

dog to heel. Whipping his cap from his head, he mumbled, 'Beggin' your pardon, ma'am. 'Tis a long time since I've been in these parts and the Cheverton barn used to be here.'

Heart pounding with the horror she felt, she gazed at him, managing to choke out, 'The barn has been moved to beyond the trees.'

'Thank you kindly, ma'am.' He moved off, the dog at his heel.

Weakness flooded through her. Thank God he hadn't recognized her! She felt safer when she saw Marcus striding up the slope. He carried a box with a cloth over the top. Bringing up the rear was one of the footmen with a tray of refreshments, and he was trying to keep up without spilling anything. A grin on his face, Marcus placed the box on the ground in front of her. 'For you, my love.'

Scrabbling sounds came from the box. 'What is it?'

At his urging she pulled the cloth from the top. It was a pair of peacocks. The male of the pair gave a harsh squawk which echoed over the grounds and, after taking stock of his surroundings, he sprang from the box and urged his drab mate to do the same. Spreading his tail feathers and regaining his dignity, he ushered her towards the lake.

'They're beautiful.' She fought to control her quivering voice. 'They'll have to be taken to the barn each night, otherwise the foxes will kill them.' Still trembling, her glance went to the man and his dog, nearly out of sight now.

Marcus relieved the servant of the tray, placing it on

the table before dismissing him. Almost casually, he asked her. 'Who was the man you were talking to?'

'Someone looking for the barn.'

'Ah yes, Phineas Grundy is hiring itinerants this week. Did the man bother you?'

'Why do you ask?'

He seated himself opposite her, his eyes as sharp as those of a hawk. 'Because I saw your reaction when he approached. He's left you pale and trembling, my love.' He sighed and stared at her hands, which were busy shredding her handkerchief. She dropped it to the floor.

'Do I have to ask him why he left you looking so terrified?'

'No!' she almost shouted, then she began to cry.

He drew her into his arms. 'Was he one of them?'

'No. But he was one of the men with them. That dog belonged to my sister. It was just a pup, but he took it with him when he left, even though the others told him to kill it.'

His face darkened. 'The man knew what was about to happen and made no attempt to put a stop to it?'

'I don't think he recognized me. What if he remembers . . . what if the others come?' She gazed up at him, her face haunted by misery and fear.

Two of them will never come, Marcus thought. No wonder Maryse tried to isolate herself all these years by secluding herself in her room. He couldn't bear it that she felt so vulnerable. As his heart burnt for her, his eyes and heart hardened. How on earth would she have managed without Siana's strength to draw on? 'I'll deal with the problem.'

'How?'

She didn't need to know how. 'Trust me to do what's best for you, Maryse.' He poured her a lemonade. 'Drink this, my love. Let's get some colour back into your cheeks before we go back to the house. As soon as you're settled in bed I'll be going out for a short time.'

'You didn't say you had a meeting.'

Marcus avoided her eyes, for he'd resorted to taking his ease now and again with a widow woman in Dorchester, and felt guilty about it.

'This is just a quick visit to see Reverend White. I'll be back in time to kiss you goodnight.'

The night was misty as Patrick Pethan settled himself into one of the cottages in the old Cheverton village. He'd been issued with a blanket, candles and rations, the cost of which would be deducted from his wages.

Patrick had hardly recognized Cheverton. He'd decided to come here after parting with his former companions in London. The pair had become increasingly violent over the previous four years. They'd drunk heavily and the rooms they'd rented together, within spitting distance of Covent Garden, attracted the most dubious of characters. The activity they'd boasted about had sickened Patrick.

After committing several robberies with Henry Ruddle, Silas had got the wind up and had signed on as crew on a merchant ship. A week later, Henry had killed a young girl in a drunken rage, and had thrown her body into the gutter.

'She was a slut,' Henry had told him when Patrick had

75

protested. 'Nobody will miss her. If you don't like it, you and the bloody dog can piss off.'

It had been Patrick who'd reported the murder to the constables, receiving a reward in the process. Henry had been transported for life, but his former companions had threatened Patrick and he'd been forced to leave London in a hurry.

Patrick had saved a bit of money over the years and the reward had added to his next egg considerably. Now, he hoped to get a permanent job on the estate and find another ratter as good as Spot. He had a craving to settle down with a wife of his own, and he had always liked the countryside here.

When Spot whined and gazed towards the door, he smiled. 'There'll be plenty of rats around these parts for you. And the country girls are as fat as butter, with bellies as round and as quivering as a greased hog. They keep their comforters hidden under little beards, so they stays warm and moist. A man can slide right into her. There be nothing like a warm and willing woman, Spot.'

Spot gave a little yap.

'That one we saw today was a bit on the slender side. Suits somebody, though, for she's got one settled in the pod. Scared to death when she set her eyes on us, as if she'd seen a ghost, or something. I knows her face, but I can't bring the where or how of it to mind.'

Spot barked and leaped at the door latch.

'Want to cock your leg up, do you? Now don't you go down any rabbit holes. Remember, you're not used to the country, even though you was born here.' Patrick opened the door and watched the dog run off up the lane into the mist, yapping something fierce. There followed a couple of squeals, which abruptly stopped.

Odd, Patrick thought, shaking his head when his whistle brought no response. Spot must've gone down a rabbit hole. Somewhere in the mist a horse whinnied. It was getting dark. Patrick went indoors to light the oil lamp and prepare his supper of bread, cheese, and a slab of raw onion.

A scrabbling at the door brought his head turning, and he went to let the dog in. His smile faded when he saw the man. This was no rough labourer. 'Who might you be, then?'

The man's smile didn't reach his glittering eyes. 'My name is Marcus Ibsen. I own Cheverton Estate.'

Taken aback, Patrick retreated a step and said respectfully, 'How can I be of service, sir?'

'The lady you spoke to this afternoon in the garden pavilion is my wife.'

Puzzled, Patrick stared at him. 'I meant her no disrespect, sir. I didn't mean to startle the lady, or to trespass. The last time I was in these parts there was a copse and a barn where the garden and lake are. I lost my bearings.'

'Ah, yes, the copse. Do you remember two men. They were called Henry Ruddle and Silas Barton. They assaulted and raped a young girl there.'

The blood ebbed from Patrick's face as he remembered why the woman's face was familiar. She had been little more than a maid, then. He recalled the girl pleading with Henry and Silas as he walked away. Suddenly he felt sick. 'I had nothing to do with that, sir. Honest.'

His employer gave a weary sigh. 'Ah, so you remember what happened to my wife. I want to know where I can find the other two. I intend to bring them to account.'

'Silas Barton went to sea on the *Mary O'Connor*. Henry Ruddle has lately been transported to New South Wales for the term of his natural life. It was me who reported his crime, sir. He killed a girl.'

'He killed part of a girl here to, and left the other part of her suffering. Can you write, Mr Pethan? I need a witness statement.'

'Yes, sir.' Handed a piece of paper and a pencil, Patrick scribbled down the information his employer required, making sure his own innocence was accounted for. Marcus read the document and gazed at him. 'This pleading you mentioned. Didn't it occur to you that it was your duty to prevent the assault on her going ahead?'

'I was drunk, sir. We all were. Henry and Silas would've killed me if I'd interfered. Their blood was up, see. I pleaded with them to leave her alone, though.'

'Thank you so much, Mr Pethan. My wife was very young at the time and she suffered a great deal from that assault. I intend to redress that by making the perpetrators pay for their crime.'

Beginning to sweat a little under the man's steady gaze, Patrick hung his head. 'I'm sorry, sir.'

'We have a problem. My wife wouldn't want this vicious assault on her to become common knowledge.'

'No, sir. I won't say a word to anyone. As I wrote in my statement, I had no part in the attack.'

'Ah, but you're wrong, Mr Pethan. You did. The assault was a cowardly act against a young girl who was helpless to prevent it. Just as cowardly, you left her to her plight. It was a great pity you didn't attempt to stop them, really it was, then this wouldn't be necessary.'

As the man took a step towards him, Patrick became aware of an aura of danger surrounding him. Suddenly filled with fear, his head jerked up. When he tried to push past, the man's arm looped almost casually around his neck. There was a swift tightening, then sharp pain as his neck was twisted.

Patrick barely heard the crack.

Laying the body on the bed, Marcus gazed down at it with an indifferent smile. It had all been so easy. Gently, he tipped over the oil lamp. When the flame took hold he dropped the witness statement into the flames, watching while the damning document curled and blackened.

'Tried, found guilty and punished,' he said dispassionately as he strolled from the cottage and closed the door behind him.

He should dispose of the dog as well, but he didn't have the heart. Stopping to retrieve it from the bushes, he released the handkerchief tied around its snout. It gave a little yelp and cowered against his body, a bundle of quivering flesh.

Marcus was wondering what to do with it when he saw the lights of Croxley Farm. He remembered the Ponsonby family had several children. There was a rich aroma of mutton stew coming from the house.

Dismounting, Marcus crept up to the front door and left the dog in the porch. He'd hardly returned to his horse when the dog set up a series of whines and yelps.

''Tis a poor little stray,' he heard one of the children say.

'Let's 'ave a look at 'im, then, our Timmy. He be a ratter by the looks of him. Happen he could catch that big black un that takes off with the hens' eggs.'

A round shadow appeared in the doorway. 'Can thee smell smoke, our Rudd?'

'Of course I can smell smoke. I've just put a log on the fire, 'aven't I? Bring the dog in. We can't leave the poor little creature out in the cold to starve. Likely, he'll enjoy a bowl of your mutton stew, Abbie.'

When the door closed, Marcus mounted his horse and rode unhurriedly away, ignoring the faint red glow where the old village stood.

5

It had been many years since anyone had left the isolated Welsh village. The last to have done so had been Megan Lewis who'd lain with the preacher, Gruffydd Evans, and had got herself with child. Although the village women had shorn the hair from Megan's head and thrown dirt at her for her sins, Megan had kept her chin held high as she'd walked out of sight.

'Twenty-seven years ago,' Wynn muttered. She remembered it well, for Megan Lewis had been her niece, the preacher man, her own intended. Both were dead now, and good riddance to them.

More recent was the visit to Wales by the bastard girl born from the coupling. The bastard was as beautiful as her mother had been, with the same green eyes and her hair as dark and as glossy as the coal wrested from the heart of Wales. It had been a shock seeing the girl at *Bryn Dwr*. So like her mother, she was, for her chin had been tilted with the same proud spirit. She'd been named Siana, after her great-grandmother.

Despite the circumstances, Wynn had admired the spirit of the Lewis bastard. She'd spied on her for the remainder of the time she'd stayed at the house her father had left her. It hadn't taken long to figure out why she was in Wales. There was another girl with her, hardly out of childhood. Both had swollen stomachs, but only one had a wedding band on her finger. And only one infant had left the place with them. The man with them had stayed at *Bryn Dwr* before, and had been supportive of them both.

The girl with Siana had braved the dangers of the *Gwin Dwr* to wash away her sins. Such suffering had been in her face, and an abundance of sympathy and love Siana Matheson had shown her, too. Siana had taken the girl's sin upon her own back, showing her more compassion than had been shown to her mother by the village women. Wynn remembered the man watching over both of them, telling the younger girl of his love for her.

'Siana's compassion will bring her no favours,' Grandmother Lewis had said when Wynn had told her what she'd observed. 'The Welsh-born child is a catalyst for tragedy.'

The village was nestled in the foothills of the Black Mountains, fed from a spring which disappeared underground before it reached there. Its flow was captured by an iron-handled pump situated in the middle of the village square. The pump was a meeting place for the village women, and a hive of gossip.

Wynn could almost hear the talk that would be left behind her, if she found the courage to do what she was thinking of doing.

'*Gone?*' they would say. '*Poor old Wynn Lewis, her as sour as onions because she never had a man?*'

'Gone. Who, that dried-up old lizard?'

'Her tongue is as sharp and nasty as the stinger on a wasp. How will she live, for nobody will employ her?'

Who indeed, Wynn thought, feeling sorry for herself, for she had no skills.

The village community generally lived on the produce they grew. The men planted vegetables in the surrounding allotments or, with their dogs, tended to the sheep which roamed the hills growing fat on the lush grasses. The fleece was spun into yarn. Some was woven and fashioned into garments, the rest sold to the wool merchant in Monmouth. The animals which didn't end up in the pot were driven into market. Life had a certain rhythm to it, born out of routine and centred on survival. They made a living, but not a profit.

At one end of the village was a small chapel which was filled to overflowing on Sundays. Mostly they were God-fearing people, and respected the law, which was applied with a slathering of Methodist fire and brimstone.

Wynn had spent much time on her knees in the chapel over the years, praying for something to happen so she could escape.

Now something had happened. Grandmother Lewis had died.

She gazed around the cottage she'd once shared with the old woman. Now she was gone, Wynn had to leave the cottage which had always been her home. She had to make room for her young nephew, who was about to be wed.

At sixteen years of age, Gwynneth, the bride, was to

all intents and purposes a woman. Already, the girl had ingratiated herself into the good graces of her future parents-in-law. Having made her arrangements with the elders of the family, today, not an hour after the service to save Grandmother Lewis's pagan soul, Gwynneth had taken it upon herself to visit her future home, to decide which pieces to keep.

Wynn protested, 'My mother left certain pieces to her English great-granddaughter, the rest is left to me.'

Gwynneth shrugged. 'It's greedy, you are, Aunt Lewis. It's not as if you'll be taking it to your brother's house, for there's no room there for it.' Her eyes gleaming, the girl fingered a piece of the fine lace. 'And how will the Lewis bastard know she's been left anything? Is it taking it to your great-niece yourself, you'll be doing? Not that it would be a bad thing, mind you. The Lewis family doesn't know what to do with a dried-up old spinster woman, especially one whose disposition is as mean as a witch. Mind you, you don't frighten me, poor sad old thing that you are. It would save us the trouble if you left altogether, see.'

So that was the way the wind blew. It might not be a bad thing at that. After Gwynneth had departed, Wynn locked the door and sat on the bed to think about her position. Normally, she would never have dreamed of opposing her brother. But when he'd mapped out a life of servitude for her it had been a shock. She deserved more respect after a lifetime of looking after Grandmother Lewis. She hadn't found the courage to say so, though.

'You'll help my wife in the house for your daily bread

and sleep in the room off the kitchen,' he'd told her after the burial. It meant a life of hardship ahead for her, for she'd grown too bitter to appreciate anyone else's company but her own. She didn't get on with her sister-in-law.

Now, on her last night in the quiet little cottage where she thought she'd end her days, Wynn's mind was in a turmoil. She should have set her pride aside and left the village long ago. But someone had needed to look after Grandmother Lewis. Wynn had been left her mother's savings, the money earned from selling her lace work, telling stories, or predicting the future for those who would pay her.

And the old woman had said just before she died, as peaceful as a lamb in her rocking chair before the fire, 'Don't let the past sour the rest of your life, *cariad*. Gruffydd Evans is dead, and glad of it, I am, for the man was a black-hearted scoundrel. Release your angry thoughts so they no longer lie ugly upon your face, my Wynn. You have a journey to make, but beware. Seek not to reveal the past, for it will destroy you.'

Although she'd never believed in her mother's pagan sight, Wynn had experienced a flicker of excitement at being told there was the possibility of something beyond the Welsh borders for her. She wasn't afraid of hard work. Perhaps she could find a job in England in one of those grand houses, be paid for her efforts. Perhaps her great-niece would be kinder to her than her brother's family. She would take her the old woman's legacy, there was no harm in that, mind. But as for Gruffydd Evans, the preacher man, she would never forgive him and she hoped he rotted in hell, for the man had broken her heart.

Her mind made up, Wynn collected together the things Grandmother Lewis had wanted her namesake to have. There was precious little. Her finest hand-made, lace pieces, a love spoon given to the old lady by her husband so many years ago, the wood now worn smooth by constant handling. There was a lock of dark hair fashioned into a brooch.

Then there was the book of poetry written by someone called Hywell Llewellyn. It was written in the old language, so the girl wouldn't be able to understand it. Still, it was a pretty piece. Illustrated in gold leaf, the colours seemed as bright as the day they were laid onto the page. Wynn wrapped it carefully in a cloth.

To her bundle she added her Sunday dress, made of thick blue cotton, and a warm jacket. The dress was plain, like her. A yard of vinegar, her sister-in-law had called her. Well, she would not stay where she was not welcome.

Her cache of coins went into the toe of one of her spare boots, a hairbrush and a clean bonnet into the other. Tying the boots around her neck, she pulled her shawl over the top then donned her mother's black hat.

Two boiled eggs, a piece of cheese and an apple were wrapped in a clean cloth and tucked into the pocket of her apron with a chunk of bread. Her bible went under the bib, for she went nowhere without the good book to guide her.

Wynn took the quilt from her bed. Rolling it tightly, she fashioned a harness from rags and slipped it over her arms to carry on her back. There now. She was weighed down like a beast of burden and could carry no more.

Seated on a chair by the window, Wynn waited until the sun was a warm golden light shining through the glass. She waited longer, until the shadows of the cottages were laid low along the ground. Lighting a candle, she drew the curtains across as she usually did.

Only when the purple dusk sank into blackness did Wynn pick up her bundle and her mother's walking stick. She slipped from the cottage and trudged silently and surely through the darkness, the air a humid kiss against her cheek. She'd walked these hills since childhood. Even in the mists that rolled stealthily down from the Black Mountains to shroud the green valleys, she knew her way, though others may be lost.

When she reached the top of the hill she looked back, down over the village. She could see the light from candles through the chinks in the curtains, smell the smoke rising from cottage chimneys. She suffered a moment of remorse at leaving what was so familiar to her.

They would not miss her until morning. By that time she'd be long gone. Her limbs began to tremble. It would be easy to return now, before they discovered her flight. When they did, there would be no turning back, for the doors would be closed against her.

But there was a sense of freedom in her now and an inner voice seemed to urge: *It's just as easy to go forward. The English border isn't far, you can see it from the top of the next hill.*

A sudden gust of wind lifted the black hat from her

head and sent it bowling back towards the village. An omen? She laughed out loud, dismissing the thought, for the sense of destiny was strong in her now. 'Going back to where you belong, are you? It's just as well, for the English would laugh at you, funny old Welsh thing that you are.'

Above her, the stars burnt holes in a sky of darkness, giving her a glimpse of something mysterious and infinite beyond. It was a moment of beauty within the vastness of the silence and for once, Wynn felt at peace as she said, 'God, strike the devil from my shoulder and guide my footsteps.' When the moon rose over the next hill to light her path, her spirits lifted and her stride lengthened.

Reverend Richard White was about to eat some bread and cheese for his breakfast, when the woman presented herself at his kitchen door.

'I'll be speaking to the woman of the house?' she said, fixing eyes as dark and as shiny as autumn berries on him.

'I have no wife. I'm Reverend Richard White, rector of the church over yonder. I live here alone.'

'I've been walking for several days, sir. Can you spare me a drink of water and perhaps allow me a little bread?'

Richard hesitated. The women was handsome in a gaunt, worn sort of way, with brown hair streaked through with grey and twisted into a bun at the nape of her neck. She looked harmless, but tired and dusty.

It was his Christian duty to offer her sustenance, but his housekeeper had recently retired to her brother's house with the rheumatics. So far, Richard had been unable to hire another woman, for it was harvest time and all the available workers had been taken on by Cheverton Estate.

'I can pay for the bread, mind,' she said sharply.

He stood aside, smiling a little at her lilting Welsh accent as he gazed at her over his glasses. 'That's not necessary. But the food you see on the table is all I have at the moment. My housekeeper has recently retired after looking after me for many years, and I find myself unprepared for domestic matters. The bread is three days old, but I'd be happy to share it with you.'

The woman dumped the bundle she was carrying onto the floor and gazed critically around her, her sinewy hands planted on her hips. 'It's a new house-keeper you'll be needing then, is it?'

The reverend shrugged. He did, but wondered if it would be wise to hire this stranger. But the kitchen stove had gone out, and although someone came in to dust occasionally the house had taken on a neglected air. 'Are you looking for work?'

'The Lord must have guided my feet to this very spot. I'm not too proud to earn my bread cleaning up after others. Neither am I too old to manage the vegetable garden, even though the good Lord has seen fit to fill yours full of weeds. I can read and write and do sums, too, so can keep household accounts. I'm used to economizing, too, mind you, for I've had to all my life, though I'll want to be paid a proper wage.' She gazed wistfully around her. This house would suit me just fine because the Lord dwells within its walls.' That said, she folded her hands into her sleeves and stood there, gazing at him.

'Have you references, Mrs . . . um?'

'No, sir, I do not, for I've spent most of my life looking after my mother, who has recently died. But I'm honest and God-fearing, and would be willing to work for a week to see if we suit each other. Would chicken be to your liking for dinner?'

Her sudden change of direction confused him. 'Chicken . . . I um . . . I'm not sure if we have one?'

In a way that reminded him forcibly of his childhood governess, she replied, 'There are several fussing around in the vegetable garden, and a scrawny bunch they are, too. Have the eggs been collected lately?'

'I couldn't right say, Miss . . . um?'

'Then I'll find some coal, light the stove and collect some, and I'll fry that stale old bread on a skillet if you have some drippings in the larder, to go with the eggs. After we've eaten I'll go through the larder and make a list of what's needed. Will that be all right with you, Reverend?'

'Perfectly, Widow . . . um?' Richard said faintly, hoping the Lord had sent this woman to him, not the devil. For despite her travel tiredness, she was crackling with energy.

'Wynn Lewis, lately of Wales,' she threw firmly over her shoulder as she headed out of the door. 'Indeed to goodness, what made you think I was a widow? I've never been married, nor am I likely to be, now. I'm here to seek out some kin of mine.'

Lewis? Richard shook his head when she stomped off.

Now, where had he heard that name before? It was a while before he remembered. That had been Siana's maiden name when she'd lived and worked at the rectory before her first marriage. He'd taught the girl to read. Unease filled him then. There had been enough trouble in Siana Matheson's life. He would watch and wait, discover what the Welsh woman wanted with her.

Later that night, Wynn knelt by the side of her narrow bed and thanked the Lord for his goodness.

'Thank you for sending me to this door. The reverend is an honest man, indeed, Lord, though in sore need of being looked after. Didn't he take me in on trust and give me the food meant for his own stomach? And if you could take some of the whip from my tongue when I talk to him, I'd be much obliged, for I like the peace of this place and feel the destiny Grandmother Lewis spoke of pulling at me.'

When an unexpected chill ran through her, Wynn shivered. 'Mind you, not that I believed her, for she was misguided in her wicked, pagan ways. Since I am a true believer, no doubt a more fitting destiny awaits me.' About to open her eyes, she added. 'God bless your servant, Reverend Richard White.'

A faint breeze came through the open window, bringing goosebumps rippling along her arms. Rising, Wynn snuffed the candle and climbed into the bed, where she pulled the blue and white quilt over her body and sighed with pleasure at the comfort of a mattress under her body, the pillow for her head and a purpose in her life.

Somewhere, an owl hooted. Wynn smiled before she drifted into sleep. She was not to know her presence was to be the catalyst for disaster.

Maryse had expanded to a greater size than she'd expected and couldn't get comfortable.

Now, three weeks after the cottage fire, she woke in the early hours of the morning, feeling extremely uncomfortable. Moreover, the bed was soaked through.

For a moment she lay there in the dim glow of the guttering night light, watching the shadows leap and dance on the wall behind it and listening to the silent, dark spaces of the house.

This was a house with a secretive atmosphere. She'd always liked, and felt comforted living here. Something creaked above her, a mouse scratched in the wall. Her spaniels, curled cozily on their cushions, whimpered and sighed in their sleep.

An ache started in her back, gathering in strength as it broadened to clutch at her distended stomach. It ebbed away, receding like the tide and leaving her face covered in perspiration.

It had started – the long, painful process of labour to bring Marcus's infant into the world. She should be ringing the little bell on her bedside table so her maid could alert Marcus. She didn't. It was too early and she wanted to be alone with her thoughts. Besides, he had come home late from his meeting and his breath had smelled a little of brandy when he'd said goodnight. He needed his sleep.

The little gold carriage clock on the mantelpiece

chimed two o'clock. She rose from the bed, her nightgown clinging and sodden against her legs. Another pain and more water gushed in a warm stream, leaving a series of little puddles across the floor as she went to gaze out of the window.

Moonlight laid a haunting luminosity across the landscape. She couldn't remember ever having been up at this time before and revelled in the solitariness of it. The lake gleamed like polished pewter in the moonlight. The lawn was covered in dew, which would rise in the dawn as mist. She would probably be a mother then, for she'd heard that second children birthed in a faster time.

Somewhere, a door began to rattle. Odd, when there was no wind. She suddenly remembered the time when she'd become a mother before – in Wales. Her infant had died. She didn't even know whether the child had been a boy or a girl. Even with Siana by her side, she'd denied the child's birth. She hadn't cried out and hadn't cared. It was unnatural for a mother not to care about her child, she thought, not to want to see it, or love it.

But Siana wasn't with her now, and her stepmother wouldn't be so understanding with regard to this child, who'd been conceived and born in wedlock. She must learn to lie, to pretend she loved it when it arrived.

Maryse pushed restlessly at her stomach. How big and how ugly it was. She didn't want this infant. It would remind her of the other one, the one she tried to deny. Giving a small cry of distress she rode out the next pain, which was stronger, like a fire burning at her insides. When it was over, she angrily dashed the tears from her eyes. She would be strong and bear this child in silence, too. Then when the birthing was over, nobody would know how weak and shameful she was.

The spaniels were awake now, sniffing around her legs, whining, their tails stirring the air for attention. 'Go back to bed,' she ordered, and off they went, their eyes gleaming as they watched her move towards the table.

That rattling attic door would soon wake everyone in the house. Lighting a candle from the night light, she made her way through the corridors and up the staircases, stopping every now and then to ride out the pains, which came more often now, so it was hard not to cry out.

The attic door vibrated under her hand as she pushed it open. Moonlight streamed through the window onto a portrait on an easel opposite of a woman in a green gown. Dripping molten wax on the table beside the portrait, Maryse stuck the candle to it. She gazed at the portrait again. Breathtakingly beautiful with her dark hair and pale green eyes, the woman reminded Maryse of Siana. Though Siana had eyes as dark as pine and had a warmer look to her. Both of the women had been wife to Edward Forbes, whose family had once owned this estate. Both of them had lost the child they'd borne him.

The door creaked shut behind her, the latch clicked. She hardly heard it as she sank to her knees with the strength of the next pain. The mouth of the woman had a cruel twist to it, her eyes glittered in the candlelight.

Maryse felt as if she was being split in half by the pressure on her pelvis. Something slipped from inside her. It made a mewing sound and brought no relief. A few moments later the pressure inside her became unbearable and the pain went on and on. The woman in the portrait stared down at her, smiling. Then Maryse's foot caught against the easel and it began to topple. The candle flickered in a draught and extinguished. The smell of hot wax filled the air as the portrait fell upon her, heavy and suffocating, the frame trapping her across the chest.

Although she tried to push against it, she couldn't quite shift it.

The pain of labour went on and on unceasingly. Maryse, hardly able to breath for the crushing weight upon her chest, took shallow breaths and began to moan. Then as her son relentlessly began to push his way into the world, she gave a prolonged and agonized scream.

Downstairs, the spaniels came alert and began to bark frenziedly.

His heart pounding, Marcus sat up in bed. The dawn was a crack of pale yellow across the window. His instinct for danger was screaming. Pulling on some trousers and a shirt, he flung his dressing robe over the top and headed through to Maryse's room. The bed, bloodstained, empty and rumpled, told its own story.

He headed into the corridor outside, the spaniels yapping at his heels, and was about to dash downstairs when he saw a blob of candle wax on the stair leading into the upper reaches. He moved on up, here and there coming across a small stain, then more wax.

The attic door was closed, but unbolted. The dogs

flung themselves against it, scrabbling at the wood. Two scared-looking maids in their robes and nightcaps appeared, woken by the scream. He reached for the doorknob and, finding the door held fast, had to thump his shoulder against it to open it.

He saw his infant before he saw Maryse. The heavy frame had just missed her, but the tiny girl seemed to be dead. She'd obviously been too small to survive. Pulling the frame from his wife's body he gazed anxiously at her. She was deadly pale, barely breathing. Blood ran from her and, as Marcus went to lift her, he saw the second child between her thighs.

Pinching the boy's ear, he was rewarded with an indignant squawk.

'Go and rouse the servants, and take those noisy damn dogs with you. Send a woman to me with all haste with some sheets to wrap my wife and the child in,' he shouted at the maid who'd followed him up. 'Tell the groom to fetch Noah Baines without delay. Have my wife's bed made ready, then come back with something to wrap the dead infant in.

He covered the pair with his robe, and was about to moved his poor, unfortunate daughter when she made a tiny, mewing sound. His heart melted. She sounded as though she was begging him to rescue her. Wrapping her in his shirt he held her against his heart, waiting with some impatience for the maid to return.

As he stroked the soft, pale skin of his wife's face, he wondered what she'd been doing up here. That damned portrait! He'd laughed when Siana had told him to get rid of it. He should have listened, burnt it along with the others. At the time, it had seemed a shame to spoil the exquisite beauty of Siana's predecessor.

Now he gazed at it with hate in his eyes, thinking irrationally that the bitch had nearly killed his wife and daughter.

The woman gazed calmly back at him.

'I'll burn you,' he whispered, 'just as I did the other one.'

Beside him, his wife made a noise, a low, gurgling chuckle. The hairs on the back of his neck stood on end. It hadn't sounded like Maryse.

6

'I'm not going to visit Uncle Ryder and Aunt Prudence this summer,' Pansy told her family at breakfast.

Speared through a morsel of bacon, Siana's fork hovered midway between her plate and Bryn's mouth, already open to receive the titbit, which was a reward for eating his oatmeal without complaint. The fork wandered temptingly back and forth, just out of his reach, his eyes following it like a dog's begging for a snack. 'What about your wedding? Won't your aunt Prudence need you there to help?'

'Since she's inclined to argue over every little detail, I daresay she can manage quite well without me.'

Francis tucked the napkin back under Bryn's chin and guided Siana's hand until the boy was able to close his mouth around the morsel. 'Don't forget to chew it properly,' he advised, and joined in the conversation. 'Have you no desire to see him?'

Pansy gazed calmly at her father. 'No doubt I shall see him every day when we're wed. Maryse needs me now.'

When Francis sighed, Siana wondered why her

husband couldn't sense the reluctance in his daughter to marry Alder.

'You could be just the tonic Maryse needs, I suppose. But your sister is married with her own household now. Wouldn't it be better to wait for an invitation?'

'Marcus has almost begged me to come. He's at his wits' end, for Maryse is suffering from the glooms. She just sits in her room, takes no interest in anything and mopes all day. I can't think why. Her babies are so adorable I could munch their little fingers off. Marcus said she shows little interest in them. What's wrong with her, Papa?'

'Noah Baines takes care of Maryse. But since you're showing concern, you should know that it's a common occurrence for women to become a little melancholy after giving birth. Maryse will recover in time and will become her own dear self again.'

'But Maryse hasn't even shown any interest in naming the twins.'

'Then I'm sure you'll be of great help to her in making suggestions. Perhaps you could suggest that she names the girl after your mother.' Francis rose and kissed his daughter on the forehead. 'Make sure you don't over-stay your welcome. Your sister is a wife and mother now. She has responsibilities and pandering to her won't help her realize them. Make sure you're accompanied.'

'Don't worry, Francis,' Siana interjected. 'I'm going to visit Maryse, too. Josh has some business with Marcus and will drive us over and bring me back.'

He turned towards her, an enquiry in his eyes. 'Josh seems to visit Marcus a lot of late.'

'They've become firm friends. Marcus has taken an interest in him. He's been teaching Josh the oriental art of personal defence. Apparently, you can learn to defend yourself without damage to your attacker. It's a little like wrestling, Josh said, and he might set up his own school when he's learned enough.'

Francis rolled his eyes. 'Trust Josh to turn his knowledge into profit.'

Pansy grinned widely at them. 'Josh said he has plans to buy a real school when the present owner retires next year. He said I can be the headmistress, if I want. I should very much like to do something like that.'

'You'll be married next year. I doubt very much if Alder would agree to you indulging in such an occupation.'

'Alder?' Pansy frowned. 'He will not be allowed to dictate to me in any way, shape or form.'

'My dear, Pansy, there are certain expectations within a marriage. One of them is that a wife's duty is to defer to her husband's wishes.'

'Please do not remind me of such a distasteful notion, Papa. I'm not wed yet and, since I came of age nearly a month ago, I shall exercise my right to think for myself until I am.'

'As if you ever did anything else. You've always been the more independently minded of my daughters,' he said with a sigh, taking his watch from its pocket to gaze at it. 'Now, I must make all haste, for it's my turn to visit the infirmary. I'll check and see if any letters have arrived for us when I'm in Poole.'

'We haven't heard from Goldie for a month or so. I'm so worried, Francis.' Siana murmured

'No doubt she's having a fine time. Her brother has wed since her last visit and she'll have a new stepmother and stepsister to spoil her.'

Daisy, pretty in a pink, flower-patterned dress, and with her blond tresses in ringlets, said. 'I miss Goldie when she's gone, even though we argue. I hope she doesn't decide to like her new stepsister better than me. I'll hate it if she goes to live with them for ever. She can't love them more than she loves us, since we took her in and saved her from death.' Daisy conveniently over-looked the fact she had nothing to do with the rescue. 'Until her brother appeared, she was quite happy with us.'

'If she leaves us it won't be until she's much older. She'll be welcome to stay here, but she must decide for herself where she'd prefer to live then.' Francis's glance swept around at them all, his smile taking on a new tenderness when it alighted on Bryn. Along with Susannah, Bryn was on his best behaviour. It was the one day of the week that the two younger children were allowed to join the family for breakfast without their governess, Miss Edgar, in attendance. 'When Pansy weds, there will only be Daisy, Goldie and Bryn left in the house,' he said.

'You've forgotten Susannah,' Siana told him.

'Since Elizabeth Hawkins's sentence is just about due to expire and she's now married to Jed, no doubt she'll want to reclaim her daughter as soon as possible. I'm expecting a letter to that effect, any day.'

Siana's heart gave a little jolt of dismay as she gazed at the dainty little Susannah. The child seemed unaware that she wasn't a permanent part of their family, even though Siana often spoke of Elizabeth to her. She'd be sorry to lose the child.

As if he'd read her mind, Francis gently squeezed her hand. 'You've always known she'd leave us one day.'

'It doesn't make it any easier, Francis.'

Daisy used the moment to push her own agenda. 'Well, I'm not going to leave you, ever.'

'Nor am I,' said Susannah.

But Daisy wasn't about to relinquish the floor. 'I'm eleven, and too old for the nursery now. Please may Goldie and I share the room Maryse used to have?'

'Then Bryn will be lonely.'

'He has Susannah for now, and you could get another baby to keep him company,' Daisy suggested artlessly.

Siana exchanged a wry glance with Francis. There was nothing she wanted more than to conceive his child and suckle it at her breast. But her husband's glance was still on Bryn, stealthily reaching for the honeypot with his spoon. Francis's eyes were full of affection and pride in the boy. Uneasiness settled in her stomach like a lump of cold gruel.

'You've had enough,' Francis said quietly. When Bryn turned and offered him an angelic smile, he chuckled. 'That smile only fools your mother and your nursery maid.' He nodded to the servant, who wiped the boy's sticky hands and face with a wet flannel. His smile disappearing, Bryn began to wriggle and protest at such cruel treatment.

'Stop being naughty. You'll give Miss Edgar a head-ache, and she won't let you play with the animals in the Noah's ark on Sunday,' Susannah informed him primly.

Siana exchanged a grin with Francis as they edged out into the hallway, for he rarely escaped in the morning without them all trying to delay him with one thing or another.

'I hope Goldie's brother doesn't bring her back from London with a sore throat again,' she said. 'And it took months to remove the printer's ink from her fingers and clothes. I sent a letter to Sebastian Groves, reminding him to make her wear the aprons I packed. Did you remember to give it to him?'

Pansy had followed them out. 'Be thankful Goldie arrived home with nothing worse. London is a dis-gusting place. The roads are so full of horse dung you're compelled to lift your skirts to cross a road, and sweeps are employed to clear a path for you. Sometimes the air is so foul you can hardly breathe, and a thick yellow fog rises from the River Thames. It's so vile and choking that everyone walks around with handkerchiefs clutched to their faces, in case they catch lung sickness from it.'

Francis gazed at her, a slight frown upon his face. 'I thought you enjoyed going to London with Aunt Prudence.'

'Actually, it was easier to give in to her than oppose her. To be fair, I did enjoy it at first. The parties and dressing up were so exciting and new. But I was still a child then. Now it's worn off and I find it such a bore. But Alder loves London and wants to live there. We're having a big argument about it. He calls me a country bumpkin.'

'My dear, you will have to learn to compromise.'

'Why should it be me who does the compromising? Alder is so stubborn, and he wants his way all the time. Well, he shan't get it with me. I'd much rather stay here with people I love.'

All this was said indignantly. Pansy will never marry Alder, Siana suddenly thought, and her heart lightened.

Pansy gave her father a kiss before dashing up the stairs, two at a time. She turned at the top. 'Goodbye, dear Papa. Don't work too hard today.'

'Give my grandchildren a kiss from me. Tell Maryse I expect them to have a name by the time I get home.'

'Don't worry. I shall suggest so many names she will choose one, if just to shut me up,' floated down at them.

Francis gave her a wry smile. 'I doubt if Prudence will ever make a lady out of her. And now, my dear, I must be off. I might be late home tonight.'

'I know.' Siana gave him a prolonged hug to help him on his way, then gave voice to the niggling little worry lingering in her head. 'Do you think all is well with Goldie? She usually sends us a letter every week when she visits her brother.'

'Of course it is. Sebastian would have written otherwise.' A kiss landed on the end of her nose. 'Stop worrying, Siana. Sebastian Groves is a responsible young man. He's aware that Goldie has lived a different life than the one he can offer, and it will take time for them both to adjust. I've made enquiries, however, and am assured that he's decent, honest and trustworthy. If

I didn't think so, I wouldn't have allowed Goldie to visit him in the first place. Now, I must go. I have patients waiting.'

Her worry now eased, she sent him off with a kiss. 'Take care.'

Had they but known it, things were far from well for Goldie in Sebastian Groves's household.

She'd been handed over to her brother by Francis and introduced to his wife, a handsome woman some six years older than Sebastian. Betty had a daughter from a previous marriage whose name was Alice.

The friendliness had fled from the woman's smile as soon as Francis had departed.

The accommodation over the print shop, previously adequate for Goldie and Sebastian, was now too small. Alice had claimed the spare bedroom as her own. Similar in age and size, Alice lacked Goldie's fair, rose-tinted complexion, her shining hair and her clear blue eyes. Alice looked grey. Her hair was lank, her skin dull and her eyes small, muddy and artful.

'Don't think I'm giving my bed up for you,' she said sullenly at dinner that first night. 'You'll have to sleep on the floor.'

'Goldie can share the bed with you,' Sebastian told his stepdaughter, sounding none too pleased with her manners. 'She'll be standing in for Betty in the print shop during the day, so your ma can have a bit of a rest.'

'You promised I could work there,' Alice cried out immediately.

'And so you can, but not yet. You're not as good with

your letters as Goldie. While she's here you can help your ma with the housework.'

Goldie helped her brother quite happily. Her skills were mostly used at the composite bench, reversing the characters as she arranged the metal type in the compositing sticks, then the sticks and illustration blocks into the iron chase, her fingers flying nimbly over the compartments to pick out letters and punctuation. Time passed quickly, for it was work that made her concentrate. It wasn't long before it became second nature to her to read print back to front.

She'd stand and watch her work reproduced by the letterpress in a variety of types. There were business cards, theatre posters and sometimes wanted posters, with pictures of criminals so fearsome, their faces made her shiver. She was careful to stand back when the heavy platten was lowered onto the tympan, in case she was careless and her fingers were caught between the two and crushed.

The print shop was situated in a narrow street. They worked in a back room, the shop front the other side of a curtained doorway. The shop itself was a small space with a counter, samples of work and a variety of personal card styles in a glass cabinet attached to the wall.

'A pity she isn't a lad,' Zeke, the journeyman who came in on a daily basis told her brother. 'You could take her on as an apprentice, then.'

Sebastian winked at her. 'Perhaps I'll take her on anyway. We could always cut yer hair off and call you Alfred, after the prince. You'd have to live here, though.

But I daresay you'd rather be with your own brother than living in that big draughty house in Dorset and having to mind your manners all the time. We could give you your own bedroom under the shop counter.'

When she gazed in uncertainty at him, he laughed. 'Don't worry, love, I won't make you do nuthin' you don't want to do.'

Goldie couldn't help thinking about it, though. She'd been happy when she'd learned she had a blood relative after years of knowing she was unrelated to the Matheson family. Yet she loved them with all her heart, and Siana, the woman she thought of as her mamma, in particular. Siana often told her of the incredible story of how she'd been found.

'I discovered you in the burnt-out shell of a cottage, starving and frightened and snuggled against the body of your dead mother. Your hair danced like flames on the wind and I knew the spirit of your mother had drawn me to you. She wanted you to be loved before her spirit could rest. And fancy, it was the very cottage I grew up in,' Siana had told her, making Goldie feel very special. 'Life sometimes brings trials for us to face and we must face them with courage, as you did then, even though you were so very young. It strengthens us and helps us to trust the people we love.'

But her mamma was like that. Siana made each one of them feel special. Sometimes she sensed things others didn't, and although that was odd, she made it seem so natural. Goldie often wished she was the same.

Goldie had grown to like her brother, Sebastian, who was easy-going and happy, and who sometimes reminded her of Josh Skinner with his cheery ways. However, she felt no special attachment to him. When the time arrived for her to choose, she knew she would not stay in London with him. Used to country life and her family in Dorset, she would miss them all too much, especially Daisy, who was more of a sister to her than Sebastian was a brother. She considered London to be smelly, noisy and confusing. It was such an easy place in which to get lost, with its back alleys, twists and turns.

When she went upstairs that first night, it was to find that Betty and Alice had been through her trunk. The girl was parading in the gown and shoes she kept for best.

'Why have you been through my things?' Goldie said, outraged by the invasion of her privacy. She was dismayed when she saw that Alice was wearing the silver bangle Daisy had given to her for a Christmas present. 'And that's my bracelet. It has my name etched inside.'

'What if it is?' Betty snapped. 'Alice was putting your stuff away in the cupboard, you ungrateful miss. She was just trying the dress on, wasn't you, Alice dear?'

Alice gave a sly smile. 'Course I was. You don't mind, do you? I ain't never had anythin' pretty to wear, like this. This bracelet's fit for a toff to wear. Them people you live with . . . got plenty of money have they?'

'I don't know. My sister, Daisy, gave me that bracelet for Christmas.'

Hands on hips, Alice swayed forward. 'Sister, is it? Well, there's a thing. That being the case, I'm your niece, so wotcher goin' to buy me for Christmas, then, Auntie?'

'I won't be here for Christmas.'

'Then I'll keep the bracelet, shall I? It's share and share alike around here and your sister can afford to buy you another.'

'But what will I tell her?'

'That it was snitched off yer arm by some dip in bad old London town. It'll only be the truth.'

'Shut yer trap,' Betty snarled, jerking her head towards the door. 'D'you want him to hear?'

Alice poked Goldie in the chest with her finger. 'This country bumpkin doesn't know what a dip is, and if she says anythin' I'll thump her from here to next Monday, then back again. I might even set me uncle onto her. He'd give her what for.'

Alice smiled falsely at Sebastian when he came in just then, saying swiftly, 'Look what Goldie gave me, Pa.'

'And a right princess you look in it, too,' Sebastian said with a smile. 'That's real generous of you, Goldie. You're a good girl. I'm glad you two are getting along.'

Alice's eyes narrowed warningly on her. Finding it impossible to protest now, and not wanting any trouble during her visit, Goldie pressed her lips tightly together.

Alice smirked.

Over the next few weeks, most of Goldie's things gradually disappeared. When she dared to question it, Betty gave her a stinging slap across the face. 'I had to sell them to pay for your keep, didn't I? And don't you tell that brother of yours, else it'll be the worse for you.'

With tears in her eyes and nursing her sore face, she whimpered, 'I'll tell my father when he comes for me.'

Betty shrugged. 'Tell him, then. He can keep you as

far as I'm concerned. Her hands came over her stomach. 'We won't have room for you anyway. I've got a brat in the oven, though with a bit of luck it'll not be there much longer.'

Two days later Betty went out, returning pale and tired-looking. She went to her bed, leaving a grumbling Alice to do the housework.

Later that night, when Alice and Goldie were in the living room, there was an argument between husband and wife in their bedroom.

'What do you mean, you got rid of it?' Sebastian yelled. 'That was my infant, as well as yours.'

'Well, I didn't want it. Now it's gone. It wasn't your brat, anyway.'

'If I'd known I never would've wed you. You took me in with your weeping widow act. I wouldn't be surprised if you was a street slut with all the tricks you brought with you.'

'What if I was a slut? My tricks kept you happy, didn't they, and they cost you nuthin'?'

'Except a roof over your heads and food in your stomachs.'

'Well you *did* wed me. I'm your wife, and you'll have to put up with me.'

'Will I, by God? You tricked me into marriage as as far as I'm concerned. You can go back and keep house for your damned brother.'

'I'm staying right here. I'm your wife and it's your duty to look after me. I'm not having that sister of yours put before me and Alice, either. From now on, she can sleep under the shop counter.'

'Don't you tell me what to do in my own house. Goldie is worth ten of you and Alice. At least she earns her keep.'

The sound of a slap was followed by an obscenity from Sebastian. 'You're a scheming witch, and you and your nasty little daughter can pack your things and get out – right now.'

Betty began to scream and hurl abuse at him. There came the sound of a meaty blow followed by a crash – then silence.

Looking scared, Alice picked up the heavy poker.

'What are you going to do with that?'

'I'm going to see what's going on. I might need it to defend myself with. Coming?'

'No.'

'Coward,' Alice taunted.

Petrified, Goldie sat there, listening to the floorboards creak as Alice crept away. A few moments late she heard Betty sob, followed by Alice's voice. 'He's bleedin'. What the hell have you done?'

'Crowned him with the chamber pot.'

'Is he done for?'

'I reckon he is. There's blood on the floor.'

'What about the girl?'

'She heard everything.'

'Then we'll have to stop her going to the police. Give me that poker. We'll give her a couple of good thumps and throw her in the river.'

'Gawd, Ma, you're not going to do fer her as well, are you? She's connected to those posh folk. They'll come lookin' for her before too long.'

'They can't hang me twice, and it's either her or me.'

'We'll chuck her out, then. If she sets up a hue and cry, we'll tell the peelers she did it and ran away. She won't last long on the streets by herself. If the police find her and she rats on us, we'll just say she's lying. By that time we'll have found someone to witness for us and they'll probably transport her. If she keeps quiet they'll take her to the workhouse, and no harm done.'

'What about her folks?'

'We'll send a letter from her every month, saying she's all right, telling them she's decided to stay in London a bit longer.'

'They'll know it's not her writing.'

'You can print it, and I'll sign it by hand. I've been practising her signature. You never know when things like that might come in handy.'

'You're as artful as a cage of monkeys, you are,' Betty said, admiration in her voice. 'I'll do it now, you go and watch the girl.'

Goldie edged herself into a corner behind a chair, where she tried to make herself very small as she shook and shivered with fright while Alice stood over her, the poker clutched in her hand and a smirk on her face. Betty returned, thumping heavily up the stairs.

Goldie, wondering if she should make a run for it and try and find her way back to Dorset, where she'd be safe, tried to scramble away.

But she ran out of courage when Alice's hand clamped down over her wrist, strong and wiry. 'No you don't, else I'll thump you. Now, come outta there.'

'I won't tell, I promise,' Goldie yelled as Alice began

to drag her out. 'I want my mamma and papa.'

'Well there's a pity, 'cause mamma and papa ain't here. Instead, me and my ma are goin' to take you on a tour of the city, yer ladyship.'

'Not in them clothes, someone'll have them off her,' Betty said sharply. 'It might as well be us, for they'll fetch us in a bob or two.'

Ten minutes later, Goldie found herself dressed in a ragged skirt and bodice. Alice threw her a dirty shawl. 'Put that around your head, girl. Hang on tight to it if you want to keep it. Best to keep that hair of yours covered, too, else someone'll take a cut-throat to it.'

'It's nice and long. We should cut it off and sell it to the wig-maker,' Betty suggested.

'We need something to attract the attention of the police. What better than that flaming, carroty hair of hers?'

Betty laughed when Goldie put her hands over her hair. 'If someone sees it, they'll likely take her scalp as well.'

'That's her hard luck. I reckon she won't be out there long before she gets caught by the police, for we'll leave her nice and handy to them.'

Tears trickled down Goldie's cheeks as they bustled her out of the door. Betty and her daughter dragged her along dark alleys that turned this way and that. Although she tried to keep track of the twists and turns it became impossible, and soon she was lost. To complete her confusion they blindfolded her and took her on another long twisting route.

There was a screeching sound as a gate opened on

rusty hinges. 'Sit there for a minute,' Alice said, pushing her down onto a hard and cold surface. 'We're just going to check on something.'

Betty and Alice went to an inn, from which Betty had once plied her trade.

'How's married life then, Betts?' the landlord shouted out. 'Has yer husband thrown you out on yer arse, yet?'

'It beats lying on me back in the dirt, though its not quite so lucrative. No, my old man is working late and we've been over to visit me bruvver. We was on our way home and got thirsty. Pass me a pot of ale and a watered-down one for my girl, here.'

The landlord leaned over the bar and pinched one of Alice's nipples. 'Let me know if she needs a job. I've got a client who would pay a pretty penny for a young 'un like 'er.'

'Sod off,' Alice snarled and the man laughed.

'She's got spirit, too.'

'Leave her be, will ya? She's not gettin' into that game.'

'I hear tell you've got another one staying with you.'

'My sister-in-law. A sullen little cow, she is. She doesn't get on with her brother and is vicious towards Alice. My girl is covered in bruises where the little shrew kicks and pinches her. She needs a good crack around the ear, if you asks me. We left her with Seb. He says he's going to sort her out, tell her what's what. Otherwise, she can bugger off back to that fancy family who took her in. Fancy or not, they didn't teach her no manners, for she thinks she's a cut above the likes of us.'

Betty quaffed her ale in several gulps and smacked her lips. 'Well, must be off. My Sebastian will be waiting for his jollies.'

They went noisily up the street, determined to be noticed by waving to a couple of their neighbours, the fishmonger who rented the premises next door, and the woman from the bookshop on the corner, who was married to a Jewish gentleman.

The print shop premises were in darkness.

'I thought you left the lamp burning,' Betty whispered, suddenly nervous.

'It must've blown out.' Groping their way through the shop they lit a candle from the kitchen range and crept upstairs to the bedroom.

'Blind me if the bugger ain't gone!' Alice said.

They searched the rest of the house, with no result. Perplexed, they stared at each other.

'It's no good making a fuss now. He'll probably turn up in the morning with nothing more than a headache. If he does, we'll tell him the girl ran off. Fetch us the scrubbing brush and pail, Alice. I'll clean the blood off the floor.'

Goldie had sat there for several minutes, her heart thudding in her chest, her breath coming in little whimpering sounds. It was a while before she realized that they'd left her there. Pulling off the blindfold she gazed around her. She was seated on some stone steps, a door at her back. Before her was an iron fence. Beyond, the street was almost empty, except for the sound of a couple of men in the distance, who were singing a raucous ditty.

They staggered under a pool of light spilling from the gaslight on the corner. She averted her eyes as the pair stopped to relieve themselves. As they came nearer she edged into the corner, covering her head and shoulders with the shawl. The men passed her by without seeing her, weaving drunkenly from side to side.

She stayed huddled in the corner like that, undetected. The night sounds terrified her. There was the sound of drunks passing by, their voices raised in song or mouthing obscenities, the loud laughter of fallen women, the sudden, explosive yowls of cats and the squeaks of rodents.

She seemed to be in a garden, and bit back a sob. She would stay here until morning, then try and find her way back to Dorset. Her papa would know how to help her, her mamma would cuddle her until she felt safe again, and Daisy would listen wide-eyed to the story of her adventure. Gradually, Goldie's quivering nerves relaxed and she fell asleep, only to be jerked awake when a hand descended heavily on her shoulder.

The scream she gave would have woken the dead, if the flesh attached to the bones in little crypt behind her hadn't corrupted several years previously.

Not more than a mile away, Sebastian Groves staggered towards the infirmary, blood dripping from the wound in his head.

He didn't quite make it. Dogged by a pack of young felons who found him easy prey, he was dragged into an alleyway and brought down.

His pockets yielded nothing, his only riches being the

clothes on his back. The youths graduated from thieving to murder by taking it out on his body.

Sebastian was identified by his hair. The next morning Betty Groves was informed of his demise, and became a respectable, grieving widow.

7

Siana was in the garden weeding the border when Francis arrived home. Straightening up, she ran towards him, trying not to look too worried. 'Was there anything at the postal office from Goldie?'

Francis had a smile a mile wide when he fished the letter from his waistcoat pocket. She grinned at him. 'You're just as relieved as I to have received a letter from her.'

'Aye, I shouldn't be at all surprised, for I'm very fond of the girl.'

'What does she say?'

'I haven't read it yet.'

She slit the envelope open with her thumbnail. 'Oh, the letter is printed.'

'And badly spelt,' Francis observed, reading it over her shoulder.

'I suppose printing is harder than writing. Goldie told me the letters were set back to front in printing, which seems odd to me, for how does it turn out the right way round?'

Francis chuckled. 'No doubt she'll explain if you ask her.'

'Oh, you.' When she turned to frown at him he kissed the end of her nose. 'She said we mustn't worry if she doesn't write very often because she's helping in the print shop.' Siana gazed at her husband, beset by a moment of unease. 'There's something odd about this letter.'

'What do you find odd about it?'

'I don't know. The wording. It doesn't sound like Goldie's voice.'

He laughed. 'You worried because you didn't receive a letter, now you're worried because you have. It probably doesn't sound like her because it's printed, so appears to be much more formal. Goldie is ten years old now, and a very capable girl. She must be given the time to get to know her brother so she can make her mind up as to what her future will be.'

'All the same, I can't bear the thought of losing any of them, Francis. Will she be working long hours, do you think? I wouldn't want her brother to take advantage of her, and she doesn't mention coming home.'

'His wife seemed a nice enough woman. She has a daughter about the same age. I'll be going to London in a couple of weeks. Why don't you come with me? We can check on her.'

'Promise.'

She laughed when he gave an exaggerated sigh, lifting her face to his so she could be kissed.

'Don't forget we're going to the christening of your grandchildren on Sunday.'

'You mean Maryse has finally decided on names?'

'Marcus and Pansy have. The girl is to be Jane Louise, as you suggested.'

'Aye, I did, didn't I?'

She linked her arm in his when his face took on a slightly pensive expression and said softly, 'It's fitting that she's been named in remembrance of your first wife.'

'Jane would have liked that. What about the boy?'

'Alexander Marcus, after his Ibsen grandfather.'

Francis nodded. 'A good name.'

'Now, before you relax, there's some doctoring you need to do.'

His eyes slanted greyly towards her. 'I've already kissed you.'

'I thought it was I who kissed you.'

So he kissed her again, taking a little bite of her bottom lip which promised much for later, when they were alone together and unlikely to be disturbed.

'It's Bryn,' she said, afterwards. He tumbled down the steps, scraped his hand and cut his lip. I've put ointment on it, but he's been limping all day. He told me it was because I'm not a proper doctor.

Bryn wasn't limping when they gazed around the nursery door. Kneeling, he was lining his wooden soldiers up in rows. When he finished he pulled himself upright, took several steps backwards, then ran and kicked them all over the nursery.

His nursery maid came through from the other room. 'That's naughty, Bryn. Help me pick them up again. You were supposed to be in bed. Susannah is already asleep.'

Bryn put his hands on his hips and stuck his bottom lip out. 'Won't. I'm not going to bed. Not ever.'

'You most certainly are,' Francis said.

'Papa!' A smile spread across Bryn's face and he flew across the room, expecting to be picked up. Francis gazed down at him. 'Say sorry to your nursery maid for being rude to her, then help her pick up the toys.'

Bryn's hands went to his hips again. He thought better of it when he saw the glint in Francis's eyes, brought them down to his sides and hung his head. 'I fell down and hurt myself. I want you to make it better.'

'So your mother told me. Go and pick the toys up, then we'll talk about it.'

Bryn went off with a sigh, nursing an exaggerated limp. 'Sorry,' he said reluctantly to the maid as he helped her collect the scattered toys, then hugged her. 'Sorry, sorry, sorry.'

Siana tried not to laugh as she gazed at Francis. 'I think he just wanted your attention.'

'It's nice to have someone like him, who desires my attention.' He took the boy on his lap when he'd finished his task, gazing at the scratches on his hand and his cut lip. Those will be better in day or two. How bad is your leg?'

Bryn pulled on his wounded expression. 'It's broken, Papa.'

Francis didn't so much as twitch a lip. 'We'll have to mend it then. I'll rub some arnica on it, and you can go to bed and rest it until morning. It will be better then.'

Bryn hugged Francis tightly as Siana handed over the salve, and said, 'Where did you go today, Papa. I was looking for you everywhere.'

'To work. I had sick patients to see.'

'I want to come with you.'

'You can't. You have to stay here and learn your letters, then, when you're older, you can become a doctor too.'

'I want to be a soldier and march up and down.'

'Tomorrow, when your leg is mended, then.' Laughing, Francis gave him a final hug before handing him to the nursery maid.

As they went downstairs Francis kept glancing at her. She grinned at him. 'Is my face dirty?'

'I was wondering where Bryn's nose came from. It's nothing like mine, or yours. In fact, I can't see anything of you in him. You'd think there would be something in him. An earlobe or a dimple, perhaps.'

Siana's heart gave a sudden, sickening thud. 'He's very much a Matheson.'

Francis shook his head. There's a lot of Matheson in him, but there's something entirely different too. He must be a throw-back to one of the ancestors, though I grew up with their portraits hanging on the wall, and can't recall anyone like him.'

'You're not the only one with ancestors. His looks might have come from my Welsh forebears. Apart from my father and mother, I have no idea what any of them looked like.'

'If they produced you, they must have been exquisite. Let's go and visit Daisy in her new quarters.'

'Daisy is feeling very grown-up about moving out of the nursery.'

But they arrived to find Daisy's clothes strewn about all over the place. Seated at the dressing table, Daisy was gazing despondently into the mirror. Francis frowned as he glanced around him. 'There's a cupboard and drawers for your clothing.'

'Usually, Goldie helps me put things away.'

'Goldie isn't here, so you'll have to manage for yourself.'

There was an unexpected moment of envy. 'I expect Goldie's having a lovely time in London, going to social events, while I'm stuck in the country, being bored.'

'I doubt it,' Siana told her, losing her initial thrust of anger when she remembered Daisy couldn't recall their former poverty. She'd been only a baby when their mother died. 'Goldie's brother isn't well off. He runs a small printing business and Goldie helps him in the shop.'

Daisy seemed to cheer up at the thought. 'Good, that sounds even more boring, and she won't want to stay there. I was hoping Pansy would take me to Kylchester with her for the summer, but she's gone to Cheverton to look after Maryse, instead. Have we been invited to Kylchester for Christmas? I'm so dying to see it.'

Francis gave a small sigh. 'I'd prefer to celebrate Christmas here, with my own family and friends around me, this year. We'll have the twins to celebrate.'

'When I get older I want Aunt Prudence to give me and Goldie a season in London, like Maryse and Pansy had. Then we can marry wealthy husbands, and Goldie won't have to work in the print shop.'

Daisy didn't realize that the countess considered her as lower class. The chances of her being taken to London for a season were remote. Siana exchanged a wry glance with Francis, who lifted his eyebrow and left her to answer.

'Daisy, my dear, as you know, you and Goldie are not part of the Matheson family by birth, as Maryse and Pansy are. There will be no season in London. You will have to learn a useful profession to earn your keep. That's why it's important for you to learn as much as you can from Miss Edgar, for you may wish to become a governess, like her.' Her fingers grazed gently across the back of her husband's hand. 'Besides, marrying for love is better than marrying for wealth.'

'Then I'll fall in love with Thomas Matheson and marry him. He's nice as well as wealthy. He's the same age as me, and gave me a shilling the last time he was here. He's going to be a pirate and look for treasure. I daresay I'll go with him.'

That settled, Daisy gazed at the clothes on the bed, and sighed. 'Will you tell Rosie to come and help me hang everything up?'

'No, Daisy,' Siana said as gently as possible. 'You thought you were grown-up enough to move out of the nursery. Now you have to accept the responsibility of looking after your own things.' She gazed at the little china clock on the mantelpiece. 'If you leave your clothes thrown all over the place they'll be creased the next time you wear them and you'll appear untidy for the christening at the weekend. I expect them to be tidied away before you come down for dinner, which will be in half an hour. Understood?'

'Yes, Siana,' Daisy said, making a face. She began to pick up her clothes as Siana had known she would, because Daisy always liked to look her best and be admired. 'I wish I had my own maid,' she wailed as they walked away.

It was a cold, gusty day late in November. The Matheson family had come from Hampshire for the christening of Jane and Alexander Ibsen in the Cheverton Church.

Pansy was a godparent, as was Josh Skinner. Proud to be chosen, Josh grinned from ear to ear as he looked down on his dark-haired, dark-eyed little goddaughter.

Wynn Lewis stood at the back of the church. She was observing her great-nephew and her two great-nieces, while remaining unobserved herself. Siana was the image of her mother with her dark hair and green Welsh eyes. There was none of the preacher man, Gruffydd Evans, in her, which gave Wynn a huge amount of satisfaction.

Siana was holding a boy on her lap. It would be the child born in Wales by the look of him. But he bore such a resemblance to the younger woman, there was no mistaking who his mother was. And she was standing up with the man who'd been in Wales with them. He was no longer in the robe of the penitent, but looking as proud, dark and handsome as the devil himself.

So, it was not as she'd always believed. The pair were

married. It was Siana who'd lost her child in Wales. And none to replace it by the look of things, though a fine upstanding man she had. A physician and surgeon by profession, Reverend White had told her. A smile softened her lips when the pair gazed at each other for a lingering moment. Now there's a match, she thought. But Siana had best mind herself, for her man has a look of no nonsense about him.

Siana appeared quite at home with the company she was in, though a haughtier company Wynn had never seen. The older man was an earl, no less. Just fancy, the bastard girl was rubbing shoulders with an earl. Grandmother Lewis would have laughed at that.

'Not that he's much to look at, mind,' she whispered, in case the old woman could hear her. 'And his lady looking like a chicken with that scrawny neck and great beak of hers.'

Daisy and Joshua, children from Megan's marriage, didn't resemble their sister, much.

'They have a different father to Siana, see,' she muttered. 'The young man is a bit like my brother, though he's fairer in colouring and lacks his dour expression. The younger girl is bonny, but she'll lose her pretty looks later in life, for her face is not fine-boned and dainty like that of her sister. Skinner, the reverend said the two younger ones are named. The men will be around the girl like bees to the honeypot in a few years. They should marry her off early, else she'll be trouble later, mind you.'

And so Wynn carried on, talking softly to herself. She passed comment on the English gentlemen with their funny way of talking and their fancy ways. She watched the kin she'd never known, different to her, but feeling part of them nevertheless. And she smiled upon the reverend, a gentle and learned man, who listened to her opinion and prayed privately with her. It was her pleasure to serve him and to worship him from afar. She didn't dare to hope for more, though he consulted her over his sermons, helped her in the garden and took her to market on Thursdays.

Wynn twitched with nerves. Today Reverend White had promised to introduce her to her great-nephew, Joshua Skinner. The church had nearly emptied when the reverend beckoned her forward. The tall young man beside him turned to gaze at her, curious, but without awareness.

'Joshua, I've asked you to stay behind so I can introduce you to your great-aunt, Miss Wynn Lewis. Miss Lewis is employed as my housekeeper.'

Wynn nearly bobbed a curtsy, but Josh took her hand in a firm grip, preventing her. Close up, Joshua Skinner's eyes were blue and astute, which made her feel uncomfortable. No fool, this one, despite his affable nature.

'There's no love lost between my sister and myself with the Welsh kin. So why are you here, Miss Lewis?' he said straight away.

'I have something for your sister. A legacy from her great-grandmother Lewis.'

'So, it's Siana Matheson you wish to see. I don't know whether she'll see you.'

Wynn blinked back a tear. 'Will the pair of you be

turning me aside when I've travelled all this way? Is that what you'll be after doing to your own kin?'

'Isn't that what happened to my own mother?' he said bleakly. 'I believe she was cast from her village, and not one of you cared whether she lived or died.'

'It wasn't my doing. I was also sinned against, for the preacher man, Gruffydd Evans, had promised himself in marriage to me. I chose to believe the lies rather than the truth your mother presented when it was seen she was with child. My heart was full of revenge and I had no pity in me,' she admitted. 'But if a sinner finds it in her heart to repent, surely to goodness those sinned against can forgive what is past and gone.'

He laughed and gently mocked her. 'Indeed to goodness, Aunt Wynn, you have a glib tongue. I think you could talk the moss off of a stone if you put your mind to it. My ma has been dead and gone since I was a young lad of twelve years. But the song in your voice brings back memories of her, as if she were standing in front of me. Her voice was full of love, though, where yours is not. She was a good mother, for all our poverty. For that, I'll acknowledge you. My sister, no doubt, will make her own mind up. Here she comes now.'

With Siana was the mother of the two newly christened babes. She was hand in hand with the Welsh-born boy, and smiling down at him. Behind her came the dark-eyed man, with the beak-nosed countess, whose eyes darted this way and that in case she missed something.

Siana gave her brother a smile. 'There you are, Josh. Prudence has left her reticule on the seat, have you seen it?' When he turned and stepped to one side, the smile suddenly fled from her lips. 'What are you doing here, Wynn Lewis?'

Goodness, such agitation the girl had in her face. 'Your great-grandmother has died. She asked me to bring some bits and peices she wanted you to have.'

The day was fast turning into a nightmare, Siana thought as Richard White smiled at her, oblivious to the undercurrents in the air. 'I've employed Miss Lewis as my housekeeper, and she expressed a desire to meet you.'

'I hope your God forgives you for what you've done this day, Richard,' Siana breathed, sensing darkness and danger crowding in on her.

Maryse was poised with her hand against her heart, her face ashen.

Sensing there was something amiss, something she should know about, the countess said, 'Since Miss Lewis is part of Siana's family, perhaps you'd like to bring her along to the christening feast, Reverend?'

'No!' Maryse said sharply. 'I won't have her.'

'Mamma,' Bryn said, cuddling himself against Siana's skirt. She picked him up, snuggling him almost defensively against her as she stared at the woman.

Wynn Lewis shrugged. 'Your boy, then, is he? He looks so much like the lady here, I thought it was the infant she gave birth to at *Bryn Dwr*. It was her infant who was buried up on the hill, then? Stillborn, was it?'

'Shut your mouth,' Siana hissed. 'It's none of your business. Go back to Wales, you're not welcome here.'

Francis slanted her a puzzled frown. 'Siana?'

Maryse gave a low moan and sank into a pew.

Marcus chose that time to stride into the church. 'What are you all—? He gazed at the small, frozen tableau, then crossed to Wynn. His face was as still as stone, yet the devil's fire burnt in the depths of his eyes. The Welsh woman shivered when he spat out, 'What spite have you been spouting, you witch?'

'I didn't know,' she whispered. 'I didn't know.'

'Get out, before I kill you,' Marcus said, his voice a whiplash. He turned towards Maryse, bringing her into his arms so she was sobbing against his shoulder. 'It's all right, my love. I'll never let anybody hurt you.'

She lifted her head then, gazing at him through tragic, tear-sodden eyes. 'Tell me the truth, Marcus. Is Bryn my son?'

Marcus's glance came over Maryse's head to join with Siana's. There was no profit in lying now, but neither of them could get the words out, so they remained mute, staring at each other.

'I'll have your answer on this, and I'll have it now, Siana,' Francis said sharply.

'Yes,' she whispered. 'Bryn is Maryse's son.'

'Hah!' Prudence said triumphantly. 'I knew something funny was going on with that girl, but nobody would listen. Got herself into trouble, did she? That's what happens when you bring the lower class into the family, Francis. Their morals are inferior and it's bound to rub off.'

'Perhaps you're right,' he said, his face stricken.

Siana flinched, for his words had inflicted a damaging wound.

The countess became shrill. 'I did try to tell you. And who fathered the child, that's what I'd like to know?'

'No doubt you would,' Marcus cut in, 'but it's really none of your business, my lady. I'd be obliged if you'd join your husband and ask him to send everyone on their way. Your insensitive remarks are only adding to my wife's distress.'

'And so they should do, for she's brought shame down upon the Matheson name. When I've finished with her she won't be able to show her head in decent society again.' Prudence stomped off in an affronted fashion, her eyes glittering.

'Ryder will stop her,' Francis said almost inconsequentially, sinking onto the nearest pew.

Siana knew the earl wouldn't be able to prevent the gossip spreading through the family. She also knew that Maryse would find it impossible to face their censure.

Francis gazed at Bryn, who'd joined him and was trying to climb on his knee. Harshly, he said. 'Who fathered him? Is anyone going to tell me?'

'I want up, Papa,' Bryn said, holding out his arms to him.

Francis ignored him. 'Siana?'

Placing her hands over her ears Maryse shook her head from side to side. 'Don't tell him. *Please* don't tell him, Siana. I can't bear it.'

'He will have to know, my dearest. I'm so sorry.' She turned to her husband, the sense of doom inside her almost deadening. But not here, Francis. We will go where it's quiet and I'll tell you everything. Just know that my actions were motivated by the best of intentions.' The glance he offered her was bleak. 'Don't look at me like that, my Francis. I can't bear it.'

Picking up the fact that all was not well between the two most adored people in his life, Bryn began to grizzle and cling to his knee. Francis set the boy away from him and rose to his feet. '*You* can't bear it? It's I who have been deceived. Take the child to the carriage, Siana. You are right. This must be sorted this out at home. I will insist on knowing everything. Marcus, bring Maryse.'

'Maryse has done nothing wrong, Francis, as you will learn,' Marcus replied. 'I'm taking her home so she can rest. Tomorrow, we'll talk, but only if she feels she is able.'

Francis looked set to explode. 'You're overriding me, her father?'

'I think I have that right as her husband. You've allowed your pride and, dare I say it, your temper, to override your good sense. Once the facts are set in front of you, you'll see that what was done was for the best.

'If you think that Maryse having an infant out of wedlock, concealing the fact from me, her father, then having that infant foisted upon me as my son, is for the best, you must be insane. My daughter has brought shame down upon my head.'

'If you were not her father, I'd kill you for saying that.'

The two men stared hard at each other, father and husband both seething with passion.

Bryn began to scream, went to Maryse and laid his head in her lap in a bid for sympathy. A shudder went through her and, with loathing on her face, Maryse pushed him roughly to the floor. 'Get away from me!'

Picking up the bewildered boy, Siana cuddled him against her and left the church, stopping for a moment to speak to an ashen-faced Pansy, who stood at the door clinging to the jamb for support. 'I beg you not to hate your sister, Pansy. It wasn't her fault. She was attacked and violated and she'll need your support, for I doubt if she'll ever accept mine, now.'

The girl seemed to gather strength to her. 'I could never hate my sister, whatever she did. Poor, poor Maryse. Aunt Prudence was telling everybody, gloating about it before uncle Ryder silenced her. It was awful. Alder was laughing about it, said he hoped I wasn't promiscuous like my sister. I shall never marry him now. Never.'

'I'm so sorry, my dear.'

'Don't be. I'm glad. I hate them all. They're shallow and mean. All they care about is position and money.'

'Don't be too hard on them. Pansy. This has come as a shock to them and they're coping the best way they can at the moment. Once they're made aware of the facts they'll be more forgiving.'

Josh came to where they stood, sliding his hand under her elbow. 'I'll settle you in the rig. Will you be all right? I'm taking the twins and their nurses back to the manor. I could take Daisy off your hands for a while, if you like.'

'Thanks, Josh. I'll tell Miss Edgar to pack her a trunk. Daisy needs a firm hand so I'll send Miss Edgar too. As for the rest, this has to be between Francis and myself. Look after Pansy for me now. She wants to be with Maryse.' She gave her stepdaughter a hug. 'I love you, my sweet girl. Stay strong. Whatever happens, try not to take sides, for the only innocents in this whole affair are Bryn and Maryse. If the issue is not handled with compassion and love they'll become victims for a second time.'

'You'll cope with it, Siana.'

But how she was going to cope with it was beyond her now. All she could do was tell Francis the truth and hope he'd understand. But already he'd erected a barrier between them. She could feel it, like an impenetrable wall.

The christening party was scattered by a sudden downpour of rain. Tears in his eyes and looking as though his heart was breaking for her, Marcus lifted his softly weeping wife into his arms and carried her out into a rain-soaked day. She hid her face from the light, burying it against his shoulder.

Siana waited a long time, sitting in the rig and sheltering herself and the children as best she could. She was glad Susannah wasn't with them, for the girl's throat was slightly sore, and the long wait in the rain might have worsened it. Bryn, his usual exuberance deserting him, fell asleep between herself and Daisy. Her sister knew something was wrong, but she said nothing as the horse fretted between the shafts.

Finally, Francis strode from the church, his face looking as if it had been carved from granite. He ignored them all. Picking up the reins, he set the rig in motion. Soon, the passing countryside was a blur.

'Slow down,' she cautioned.

He ignored her. The rig began to sway and mud

sprayed up over them. The horse's breathing became laboured and Daisy began to cry as they were tossed about.

Siana struck him on the arm. 'Stop it, Francis. You're frightening Daisy.'

Her hand was flicked off, but he heeded her warning, gradually easing off the reckless speed. They turned into the carriageway of their home at a more sedate pace. Throwing the reins to the stable hand he jumped down and strode into the house, leaving them to fend for themselves. She'd never seen him so out of control, and she wondered what the outcome of today's events would be.

As they entered the house, the door to his study slammed shut ominously.

Reverend White was shocked to the core by the events that had taken place. His attempts to counsel Francis had brought him an ear-blistering reply – a blunt warning to keep his nose out of Matheson affairs. Falling to his knees, Richard began to pray long and hard.

Back at the rectory, Wynn Lewis's mind was in turmoil. What had she set in motion today with that careless remark? It was as if the devil himself had sent her amongst the sinners to wreak havoc.

But who were the sinners? She had seen the girl called Maryse go into the cave of the *Gwin Dwr* and emerge, free of sin. The legendary virgins whose blood stained the water red, had let her go. Wynn had watched her emerge triumphant, her soul and body cleansed, her husband waiting for her. Only he hadn't been her husband then. And neither was he the father of that boy.

Hugging her hands against her body, Wynn rocked backwards and forwards, hating herself. What sort of God could set something so awful in motion? Why had she been appointed the devil's advocate in this, when all she'd ever wanted was to love and be loved?

Would the *Gwin Dwr* judge her and find her free of sin? As soon as the thought lodged in her head, the idea grew so strongly she began to believe that the sight her mother had possessed had now embraced her too. She was so certain of what she must do, as if a voice inside her head was giving her direction.

Going into the reverend's study, she drew a piece of paper towards her and began to write. When she'd finished, she set the letter on top of the small legacy Grandmother Lewis had left for Siana.

All she owned in the world was her blue and white quilt, an item she'd stitched with such hope in her heart so long ago. It had been intended for the marriage bed she'd never reached. She folded it, adding it to the pile. If she came back she would make another, stitching it with love as she sat by the reverend's fire in this house where she'd found herself, and discovered a different life. Now the chance of happiness had eluded her again, and by her own actions.

Stoking up the fire so the house would be warm when the reverend returned, she left quietly, closing the door behind her.

She didn't bother looking back as she set off along the road. She had no need, for she knew every stick and stone of the place, and if she came back it would be waiting for her.

If she didn't come back . . .? She shrugged. She was a woman who'd never experienced the love of either a man or a child. Nobody would miss her.

Wynn had enough money in her purse to pick up a stage coach when she got to Dorchester. With each passing mile the sense of doom inside her increased.

When she reached Wales, she had nothing of value left, except a pair of stout boots, a warm cloak and a stick to lean on. That was all she needed.

'My soul comes before you naked,' she said to God.

But it was the pagan gods of her mother who stirred in her blood and answered. The Black Mountains were shrouded in mist, but they seemed to call to her as she climbed the foothills, to the sanctuary of the house called *Bryn Dwr*.

There will be a reckoning.

8

Siana spent a nerve-racked night, searching her conscience as she tossed and turned. She finally fell asleep at dawn, waking towards noon. As she struggled out of sleep she saw Francis sitting in the chair by the window, his face in profile. He looked haggard, as if he'd been awake all night.

Of Rosie, her maid, there was no sign. 'Francis?'

He turned to gaze at her, his eyes devoid of expression. 'Tell me what happened. Now, when you've just woken from sleep and have no time to concoct a story.'

Hurt thrust through her. 'Remember the harvest supper the night before you left for Van Diemen's Land, when Maryse hurt her ankle?'

'What of it?'

'Maryse had been raped by two of the itinerant workers.'

The silence was broken only by the harshness of his breathing as he tried to keep the horror she saw in his eyes under control. 'And you let me depart without telling me? What type of woman are you, Siana?'

'One who requests a fair hearing from her husband before he passes judgement.'

He sighed and inclined his head.

'I didn't know until a few months later, when I learned she was with child . . . indeed, that we were both with child. Maryse was so upset and ashamed by what had occurred that she'd gone up onto the cliff top to try and kill herself.'

Anguish filled his eyes.

'She nearly succeeded. My father had died and left me his home up on the Welsh hills. So I took her there, I didn't know what else to do. I was going to farm the child out. Maryse never knew she'd given birth to a son. She didn't want to know so I thought it would be best if I told her the infant was dead.'

'What happened to the child you were carrying?'

'Our daughter, Elen? She was stillborn. I lost her as I was taking Bryn to the farm where he was to be left. We buried her on the hill, Marcus and I.' She closed her eyes for a few seconds, remembering the sweet, pale face of her daughter, so peaceful in death. 'We said words over her.' Her voice faltered as she murmured the words she'd spoken then: 'May the womb of the earth goddess nurture my daughter, Elen.'

'Marcus answered, "And may the daffodils and lilies reflect her purity every spring." Then, knowing how much I'd wanted our child, he placed Bryn against my breast to suckle. I had no choice, then, but to love Bryn, for we fulfilled the need in each other.'

'I've heard enough of this pagan rubbish. You said Marcus Ibsen touched your breast?'

'Not in a disrespectful way. He knew what was in my heart and acted on his instincts. Bryn looked so much like you, it was easy to love him and make him my son. Mine and yours, as if it had been I who'd carried him in my womb and brought him into the world.'

'He's not your son, Siana. He's the result of a base crime. A bastard of uncertain parentage, a child who is the lowest of the low.'

Siana winced at such a cruel description. 'Children aren't just blood ties. They're bonded to the heart of their parents by love, as you bonded to Bryn.'

He shrugged her words aside. 'I thought Bryn was my son, born of my seed. What kind of woman would dupe her own husband in such a manner?'

'Didn't you make him yours? When I got back from Wales it was to the news that you'd been lost at sea. Then I lost my son, Ashley, to scarlet fever. Bryn kept me sane, for part of you lived in him. I did it with the best of intentions, believing Maryse would never discover the truth.' She rang the bell for Rosie. 'I must get dressed. I want to find out how Maryse has fared. She'll need all the support she can get now, though I don't know if she'll ever forgive me.'

'Rosie has gone. I questioned her and have dismissed her for her part in the affair.'

'She only obeyed my instructions, and her loyalty is to be commended rather than scorned.' Her eyes came up to the implacable grey of his. 'And will you dismiss me also, Francis?'

'I've not yet decided.'

Her heart filled with dread as she remembered Bryn.

The house was unnaturally quiet. Throwing back the covers she scrambled from the bed and, pulling her robe around her, raced along the corridor and up the stairs to the nursery. Susannah was on the nursery maid's lap. The woman gazed in alarm at her when she shouted, 'Where's my son?'

'In the other room, ma'am, with Jessie.'

The tension drained from her. Thank God Francis hadn't taken it into his head to send Bryn away. Rattled by the thought, she returned to her room and spat at him, 'If you do anything to hurt Bryn I shall hate you for ever.'

'Be that as it may. I haven't decided yet what Bryn's future is to be.'

She glared at him, incensed by his coldness. 'I don't understand you. Why should he be punished for something that's not his fault?'

'He'll be punished anyway. Do you think my family will tolerate such a child in their midst? You made a fool out of me, Siana.'

'Damn your family! You've made a fool out of yourself for listening to them instead of to your heart,' she shouted, and burst into tears.

He gripped her by the upper arms, shaking her until she quieted, then thrust her on to the bed. 'Compose yourself and get dressed. I'll be in the study when you think you can discuss the problem rationally.'

Discuss it rationally? She'd never be able to discuss it rationally. Bryn was her son, a child she loved unconditionally. Picking up her hairbrush she hurled it at the mirror, giving vent to her feelings as the glass shattered into silver daggers. *'Damn you! damn you! damn you!'*

Daisy had left on her visit to Josh. Aware that something was going on, her demands to know fell on deaf ears. One of the nursery maids had said to her, 'It's something which doesn't concern you, Miss Curiosity.'

Miss Edgar kept her counsel. She was happy to return to the house in Poole, though, and soon settled back into her old routine. She just wished that Goldie was with them too, instead of in London. She wondered, was the girl being fed and looked after properly?

Goldie had been taken to a workhouse, where she'd been examined for infections by a doctor.

'She says her name is Goldie Matheson and she lives in Dorset,' Mrs Tweddle, the gaunt-faced woman in charge, told him. 'She said her father is a physician and is the brother of the Earl of Kylchester.'

'Did she, did she indeed?' The doctor cackled with laughter. 'Well, she certainly has a sense of humour, considering the rags she arrived in. If your uncle is an earl, girlie, how did you end up in St Martin's cemetery, eh? Answer me that.'

Goldie couldn't tell him of the crime Betty and Alice had committed, in case she was charged with the murder of Sebastian herself and hanged by the neck until she was dead. So she kept quiet.

'Hmmm, there's no answer for that, is there girl? Hang out your tongue. Say ah.'

'Ah.'

'How old are you?'

'Ten, sir.'

'Good.' He turned to Mrs Tweddle. 'She doesn't appear to be suffering from malnutrition, and neither does she have any sore or parasite infestations.' His hand rested on her bare thigh. 'Good straight bones, too. Physician's daughter, indeed. He must be a poor sort of doctor to keep you in such rags. And what's he doing in Dorset while you're in London, all alone?'

'She's probably a maid of all work who's run away from her mistress.'

'Most likely. Ten is a bit young to be working as a maid of all work, though.' He gently rubbed Goldie's nipple between his finger and thumb. 'She seems older in development. Put her down as twelve.' His hand cupped one of her buttocks, rested there, making her feel odd and awkward. 'Do you know any letters, girl?'

She moved away, picked up the coarse grey dress they'd given her, holding it against her. 'Yes, sir. May I get dressed now?'

He gazed at her for a moment. 'Good . . . good. Mrs Tweddle will test you. If you can read, you can assist the schoolmaster for the time being. Go and fetch a slate, Mrs Tweddle.'

She scrambled into the dress when the woman left, jumping when he pinched her. 'You're a pretty little thing. Do you know what the age of consent is?'

'No, sir.'

He chuckled. 'That's good then, for, no doubt, I can help you better your lot by finding you a post somewhere. I know someone who'd like a nice little thing like you working for them. In the entertainment business, she is.' He drew her closer, so she was standing between his thighs. 'I must tell Mrs Tweddle not to cut that hair off. I will be an asset in the job I have in mind for you. I have a thruppenny piece in my pocket, would you like it?'

Goldie thought about that. Thruppence might buy her a coach fare to Dorset, so she nodded.

'Come, sit on my lap, then. I'll guide your hand into my pocket so we can find it.'

After a few moment, she said, 'There's no thruppenny piece, only a hole in your pocket.'

'It must have fallen through.' Just as she was about to withdraw her hand he took her by the elbow and pushed her fingers through the hole. He grunted when her hand encountered something soft and warm. That's the little puppy I keep in my pocket. He's a sweet little thing who enjoys a stroke. I'll find your thruppence afterwards.'

When he heard Mrs Tweddle coming along the corridor he hurriedly withdrew her hand and pushed her away from him. 'Some other time, eh.' Taking a handkerchief from his pocket, he mopped his sweating brow. 'Ah, Mrs Tweddle, that was quick.'

She gazed from one to the other, her eyes sharp. 'Yes, I like to make sure the new ones are properly supervised. A clean bill of health then, is it? Well, I don't need to detain you any longer, sir. No doubt you have plenty to do.'

The doctor rose to his feet. 'I certainly do, Mrs Tweddle. Leave the girl's hair alone, would you? It would be a shame to cut it off.'

'Workhouse regulations, sir.' Besides, it would fetch Mrs Tweddle a few shillings from the wig-maker.

'Since when did we obey rules?' He pinched the woman's cheek. 'We must get together with a bottle of brandy one of these days, just like we used to. You haven't lost your looks, my dear.'

Mrs Tweddle simpered a smile at him.

'May I have the thruppence, sir?' Goldie said as he began to leave.

'Thruppence? Dear me. If I gave you thruppence that would make me poor and you rich. Thruppence indeed. He went off shaking his head.'

'Did I see your hand in his pocket just as I came in?' Mrs Tweddle asked her.

'He had a puppy he wanted me to stroke.'

'A puppy. Is that what he calls it? And he promised you thruppence to stroke it?' Mrs Tweddle's mouth settled into a straight line when Goldie nodded. 'A dirty old sod, that's what he is. Keep away from him if you can, dearie. Holler real loud if he corners you again. I'll cut his bleeding puppy's tail off for 'im one of these days, that I will.'

Wide-eyed, Goldie gazed at her.

'You do know what I'm talking about, don't you, dearie?'

'Yes, ma'am,' she whispered, thinking it a shame that the puppy would have its tail cut off.

'Good, then I'll know who to blame if it happens again. Now, let's see what you can do, 'cause you've got to work for your food around here, little enough though that is. You look to be a smart young lady, and you speaks real nice. Perhaps the board of guardians will find a suitable post for you if I draw you to their attention.'

Later, Goldie found herself lying on a hard metal bed with a straw mattress under her that smelled of stale urine. Two other girls were squeezed in the other end, with the beds either side of her similarly occupied. Goldie cried a little for her brother, Sebastian, and more still for her family in Dorset, who she thought she might never see again.

She prayed to God they were all well, and imagined them eating together at the table. She wondered if Daisy had managed to talk her sister into letting them have Maryse's old room to share. Daisy could talk people into anything if she tried. She wished she was there with them now. 'Please God, look after me. Help me find the courage to run away and make my way home to the people I love,' she whispered. 'If you can't do that, please send them to find me.'

'Run away and you'll have to run fast,' one of her bed mates commented.

The other one laughed. 'You'd better stay on the right side of Mrs Tweddle or she'll make your life a misery and you'll never get out of here.'

Life turned out to be a misery in the workhouse, even when seemingly on the right side of Mrs Tweddle. It soon became apparent that there was not enough food to go round. Breakfast consisted of pails of thin gruel. There was pea or cabbage soup for the main meal, with small pieces of mutton floating in it. A slice of coarse barley bread was issued to soak up the grease floating on the top.

Goldie was assigned to the schoolroom, a long, cold, grey room packed with two hundred or more grey-clad children. The only light came from skylights in the roof, which were nailed shut, so no air circulated. They leaked when it rained. Goldie handed out slates, corrected sums and spent long hours on her knees, scrubbing the floors or benches.

Even though she learned to eat every scrap set before her, she began to lose weight and was soon as thin and grey as the rest of the children. Her hair was a dimmed flame, held captive in a dirty braid tied with rag at the bottom.

Although Goldie didn't realize it, her hair would eventually gain her freedom.

Maryse had been weeping for two days. She had once thought she might learn to be a better wife to Marcus. He was so patient and kind, so eager to serve her every need.

Now this! Heartsick, she couldn't stop crying. She would never forgive Siana for betraying her, for stealing the bastard child to bring up as her own. She'd never speak to her again. Oh, why hadn't her stepmother allowed her to die in the first place, when she'd realized she was carrying the bastard child and had attempted to throw herself off the cliff? Why had she been forced to stay alive to be confronted by the result of her shame? Now she was reliving the violence of that act against her, over and over again in her mind.

She felt so soiled. Turning restlessly in her bed she spared a thought for her husband and children. She was an unnatural mother who felt nothing for her children. Neither of them looked like her. They were the children of Marcus, made in his image, for both had coal-dark eyes and dark caps of hair. Marcus spent more time in the nursery gazing at them with adoration in his eyes, than he did on the estate.

'They're perfect,' he'd say, and she'd nod, smile and agree. They didn't feel like her children, though, and she didn't care if she never saw them again.

Not only was she an unnatural mother, she was a bad wife to Marcus. He loved her so much that she constantly felt guilty because she couldn't live up to his expectations. She hated to see disappointment flare in his eyes when he saw the untouched meal, or failed to respond to the effort he made to please her, like when he'd placed the little vase with a spray of holly on her bedside table.

She gazed at the red berries clustered along the twig like globules of oozing blood, at the dark leaves with their sharp spikes. How gloriously cruel a plant it was.

A knock came at the door. It was Pansy bearing a tray in her hands. 'I've brought you some broth.'

'Why don't you go home, Pansy? Papa will need you.'

'You need me more. He has Siana.'

'Siana,' she said bitterly. 'He'll never forgive her for her deceit.'

'She did what she thought was best.'

'Best for her.' Giving a sob, Maryse turned her head away. 'He'll never forgive me either, for he is too proud. I'll never be able to look anybody in the eyes again, for

I'll see nothing but pity, shame or loathing in their eyes. I wish I was dead.'

Alarm came into her sister's eyes. 'You're not going to do anything silly, are you?'

'Of course not. You have always been more courageous than I.' What was silly about putting an end to her own suffering? Then she would no longer be a burden to those she loved. Calm crept over her. 'Set the tray down, my darling Pansy. I'll eat your broth, if only to take the worry from your eyes.'

'She seems a bit better,' Pansy reported later to Marcus. 'She ate the broth.'

A relieved smile touched her brother-in-law's exhausted face. 'Good. I'll go up and say goodnight to her later. Don't worry if I go out tonight. There's something I must do in Poole, and I might not be home until early in the morning.'

'Are you going to see Josh?' she said, her eyes lighting up.

Managing a grin for her, he teased, 'I do believe you like Joshua Skinner a lot more than you should, Miss Matheson.'

Pansy blushed a little, then confessed, 'I have always liked him, but that seems to have grown into something more. Only I didn't realize it until that awful time at the christening. Josh was so calm and supportive to everyone, when all the others became still and awkward and sniggered about my sister.' Her expression contorted into a scowl. 'I hate the Mathesons. If my father disowns Maryse I may very well never speak to him or his family again.'

'You mustn't estrange yourself from your father, Pansy. Would you like me to give Josh a nudge in your direction?'

The laugh she gave was assured. 'Certainly not. I've already indicated to him that I now have no intention of marrying Alder. I have yet to write to Alder informing him of the fact. When I have, and I consider the time is right, I intend to ask Josh outright if he'd care to pay court to me.'

Marcus laughed for the first time in two days. 'He'll be mad if he doesn't. You're a perfect gem, Pansy Matheson.'

Having learned from the late Patrick Pethan that one of the perpetrators of the crime against Maryse was now employed as a seaman on the collier *Mary O'Connor*, and having heard from Josh that the ship was due in harbour to unload a cargo of coal, Marcus slipped from the house just before dark and headed for Poole.

He left his horse tied to a tree and went in on foot, moving fast.

The ship was tied up against the wharf and riding low in the water, for her cargo was still intact, awaiting unloading in the cold eye of morning.

It took Marcus a little while to single her out from the tangle of masts swaying and creaking in the heavy fog, and he had to edge up close to make out the dirty lettering on her bow.

The ship was quiet, the deck inhabited by a single watchkeeper, who was shrouded in an oilskin. Slumped on a coiled rope, a rum bottle cuddled against his chest, the seaman snored loudly enough to wake the dead.

Shaking him into befuddled wakefulness, Marcus said, 'I'm looking for Silas Barton.'

'Who're you?'

'His saviour.'

'That bastard needs one if you asks me,' the old man said, his eyes beginning to fog with sleep again. 'He'll be at the Jolly Hornpipe, I reckon. He's got a slut he sees there when we're in port. Round the back in the lean-to. You can't miss Silas. He has a mermaid tattooed on one hand and King Neptune on the other. He's a bad bugger, though. He keeps a knife up his left sleeve and another in his boot.'

'Thanks,' Marcus grunted and, placing a couple of coins in the man's pocket, he allowed him to sink gently back into oblivion. As he made his way back along the quay a door spilled open and light spilled across the cobbles. He drew back into the shadows as two men staggered out.

Access to the back of the Jolly Hornpipe was made via an alleyway. He heard Barton before he saw the faint light coming through chinks in the door of the lean-to. He was grunting as he thrust into the whore.

''Ere I didn't say you could do that, that,' the whore protested, her voice muffled as if her face was shoved into a pillow. 'It ain't natural and it hurts.'

'Shut your mouth else I'll shut it for you.' The grunting continued, faster and faster and the woman began to squeal and protest.

Marcus imagine Maryse, sweet and clean at the age of seventeen, looking forward to a happy future, suddenly being subjected to such brutality. His mind sent him a picture of Maryse begging for mercy, and that mercy being denied her as she was violated by this man. Throwing open the door he dragged Silas out by his collar, then pulling him backwards across his knee, he broke the vertebrae in his neck. The man twitched in his death throes and a strong stench gusted from him. Wrinkling his nostrils, Marcus let his body fall.

The girl edged past him and began to run, screaming at the top of her voice, 'Help! Murder!'

Men seem to appear from everywhere, shots were fired.

'Shit!' he grunted. Dodging through the back alleys he headed for his horse at a run, with what seemed to be an army of men in uniforms after him.'

He heard a horse come up alongside of him. 'Grab my arm,' Josh hurled at him. Swung up behind Josh, he and the younger man soon gained ground and Marcus was finally reunited with his horse.

Leaping into the saddle, he gazed at his rescuer. 'What were you doing there?'

'I saw your horse and decided to keep an eye out for you. Just as well, for you'd have been caught in five minutes. The way you were running, anyone would think you'd committed a crime instead of being with me all evening. They'd have hung you on the spot. The revenue men are out in force tonight. Come on, let's head around the back and come into town from the other direction.'

'Are you mad?'

'Sometimes, but it seems I ain't the only one. Trust

me, Marcus. They won't suspect anyone coming from the opposite direction.' Setting his horse in motion, Marcus had no recourse but to follow.

They were stopped by a couple of revenue men as they came back along the quay.

'Rein in. Oh, it's you, Mr Skinner,' one of them said.

'Mr Weaver. How are you this fine night?'

'Fine, it isn't, for a man has recently been murdered. His neck was broken.'

Josh's next breath was a cautious quiver. 'No business of the customs, surely, Mr Weaver. Do we know the victim?'

'A seaman called Silas Barton.' Henry Weaver's smile was all friendliness. 'And as you know, the revenue men stick their noses into all sorts of business, Mr Skinner.'

Marcus had been told about Josh's run-in with Weaver in the past, how the man had given Josh a strong warning about his smuggling. It had set him back on the straight and narrow. Josh chuckled now. 'And a mighty fine job they do of it, too. Have you met my companion, Mr Marcus Ibsen, the owner of Cheverton Estate? He's just about to head for the manor before this fog gets any thicker.'

'It will probably thin out beyond Upton.'

'I'm counting on it, otherwise I'll have to escort him all the way to the manor. Don't shoot me when I come back through, will you, Mr Weaver?'

'I'll try not to.' Weaver extended his hand. 'I'm pleased to have met you, Mr Ibsen.'

Marcus took it in a firm shake. 'And you, Mr Weaver.

Do you have a description of the felon in case we run into him?'

'He'll probably be large and strong, for Barton's neck was broken without a sign of a struggle, and he was no sparrow. His female companion said it happened so quickly she didn't see the attacker's face.'

'That was unfortunate. Well, we'll be getting on, then. Goodnight to you.'

'Take care. Do you have a weapon to hand?'

'I have a pistol in my saddle bag.'

'Don't hesitate to use it if you have to. Robbery wasn't a motive for the killing, for the man's purse was left intact. It was probably a grudge killing.'

'That's a relief,' Josh said with a laugh. 'Marcus has just won a packet from me at cards, and I'd like him to live long enough so I can win it back from him.'

'Thanks for the favour,' Marcus said, clapping Josh on the shoulder when they parted. 'I won't forget this.'

'Think nothing of it.'

Friends like Josh were hard to come by, Marcus thought as he rode away.

Maryse was wide awake. Her husband had hesitated outside her room, then quietly entered. She'd closed her eyes when he'd crept across the floor to lovingly kiss her cheek, wishing she could respond to him.

She wondered where he'd been. Did Marcus have a mistress? Not that she minded. It would be unfair if she did, for she had no desire to keep him satisfied in that way.

Marcus was a good man. Without a doubt, she loved

him. But someone so fine deserved someone better than herself. She couldn't bear to see the worry on his face over her. Siana would have made him a better wife, Siana who she'd once loved, but now hated for her deception. Eventually her father would forgive Siana for her part in this, for she'd always been able to get round him. Then Maryse would have to spend the rest of her life knowing Bryn was her own child – hers and one of the devils who had hurt her. A sob came to her throat. *Hating hurt . . . how it hurt!* But she didn't know how to stop.

Maryse could think of only one way to take her revenge – one her father would never forgive Siana for. Her action would split asunder the family Siana had drawn around her.

Later, she heard her children crying to be fed, their thin, complaining voices coming from a distance. Poor little wretches. They had a mother who didn't love them and who wouldn't sustain them, so Marcus had hired a wet nurse for them. But he had enough love inside him for both of them. She was glad they looked like him, for then they wouldn't remind him of her.

When all was quiet she rose and dressed herself. Boots in hand, she made her way downstairs, the spaniels following at her heels. Quietly letting herself out, she stood for a moment, shivering in the cold, moist air, her courage almost deserting her.

The dogs sniffed around, then pushed at her hand and whined. Maryse thrust them back inside the door. She listened to them scratching on the other side for a moment, then heard their feet pattering away.

The water in the garden Marcus had designed for her glinted as it rushed over the little weir. Silly that he'd thought to erase the act from her memory in such a way. It didn't matter now. Nothing mattered except to carry out the act that would stop her hating herself and everyone else.

She picked up speed, following the line of trees. An hour later she could smell the sea. The sky had lost its blackness and was a surly grey between the lighter clouds. The horizon was a thin streak of silver where the moon still shed some light.

Another half an hour and the salt smell was strong in her nostrils, the tide an ebb and flow of noise against her eardrums.

The hill sloped downwards towards the cliff. She stood on the very edge, her mind teetering dangerously between exhilaration and dread, her cloak billowing around her. She stared down into the darkness, where the water surged and churned over the rocks.

She thought she heard Marcus call her name from a distance and there was a faint sound of her dogs yapping.

The sea called to her, its voice louder, more insistent. *Come to my embrace, I will end all the pain inside you.'*

Holding out her arms she fell forward into the void. For a moment her cloak filled with wind and she flew like a bird. Then it folded up over her head and she plummeted.

The pain lasted for only an instant.

9

Siana woke with a sense of real dread, which didn't leave her even when she felt a familiar wave of sickness engulf her.

Could she be with child? Her monthly course was overdue for the second time. She ran her fingers over the flatness of her stomach, allowing herself to savour a small quiver of excitement. Sometimes, her husband had surprised her with his unconventional behaviour and his passion, so it was a wonder that an infant had not been conceived sooner.

Dressing quickly, she pulled her hair into a loose braid and hurried downstairs. Now was not the time to tell Francis, when he was so worried about Maryse.

The day was overcast and gloomy. There was a sense of doom, of waiting. When was the last time she'd felt the strangeness so strongly in her? It had been the day her first husband had lost his life. She'd felt like this then, as if there was an overwhelming darkness living inside her. There was nothing she could do about what it would bring about, she knew that now. The earth had its own ways, and although she may have the instincts to be aware of them, the mere knowledge was a privilege bestowed on her. She'd learned not to try and work against it, for there was always a reckoning.

She went upstairs to the nursery. Bryn and Susannah were playing happily together under the eye of the nursery maid. She gave them both a hug, saying to the maid, 'Have you seen my husband?'

'He went out early, Mrs Matheson. Noah Baines came for him. Dr Matheson looked to be proper mazed too, all pale and shaking, like he was suffering from the ague.'

Siana's sense of doom deepened, but all she could do was wait.

She was glad when Reverend White was announced. He looked sad and lonely as he placed a string-tied bundle on the desk. 'Your aunt has returned to Wales. She left these things for you, and a letter. I'll miss her, for although she was a servant, she was beginning to be a good companion.'

'I'm sorry,' she murmured.

'Also, I thought I'd tell you that I've employed your former maid. At least you will know where Rosie is, should you be in the position to retain her again. She was very distressed when she came to me.'

'Thank you, Richard, that's kind of you. Francis dismissed her without reference, even though she'd been acting on my orders. I was worried about her. She's such a good-hearted woman, and a hard worker. Give her my love and tell her I'm managing.'

Siana ordered refreshment and, while they waited for it to arrive, she read the letter from Wynn Lewis.

Dear Mrs Matheson,

When I left Wales to seek you out, my intention was to right the wrongs of the past. Instead, my interference has worsened matters. Please accept the legacy from your great-grandmother. I should like you to have the quilt too, for it is the only possession I have. Perhaps you will see some beauty in the design, and bear in mind that the stitcher was the bitter old woman who came into your life with the means, but not the will, to destroy.

My only hope for redemption is if the Gwin Dwr cleanses the stain from my soul. I beg your forgiveness too.

Your great-aunt,

Wynn Lewis

Fear lodged heavily in Siana's throat. The *Gwin Dwr*? The sacred pool would not redeem this woman, she knew it without a doubt. But she had no sympathy to spare for Wynn Lewis, for the woman had caused too much damage to those Siana loved.

'The book she left you is the poetry of Hywell Llewellyn, Richard White said. 'I feel very privileged to have seen it. It's very old and is hand illuminated. It's probably worth a great deal of money.'

'Then I'll look after it carefully.' Siana lifted the brooch from the lace work and gazed at the lock of dark hair, which had been woven into an intricate design. Feeling sick at heart, she slowly shook her head as she turned the brooch in her fingers, unconsciously copying the movement her great-grandmother's fingers had made before her.

'This is my mother's hair. She was taken advantage of

by my father, the man we both knew as the preacher, Gruffydd Evans. He was a man who couldn't control his urges. The village women cut my mother's hair from her head before sending her from their midst to fend for herself.' Her palm closed around the precious memento and she gazed at him, her eyes full of tears. 'Why must your God make women suffer so, when the sin is not theirs?'

Richard White spread his hands in defeat. 'I have no answer for you, Siana. You've had a sad time of it over the years, my dear.'

It was going to get sadder. She knew it. 'Pray for my relative's soul, for I haven't the charity inside me to do so myself,' she said, as he stood to leave. 'She will need it, I think.'

When Francis returned, Siana had never seen him look so haggard. Pansy was with him, her eyes puffy and red from crying.'

Siana gazed an appeal to him as he came into the house. 'Francis?'

He pushed past her without a word, making his way up the stairs looking like an old man. Her heart filled with dread, Siana turned to Pansy. 'Is it Maryse?'

'She's taken her own life.'

Maryse, dead! Her beautiful, sensitive stepdaughter, so full of life and grace, gone from them.'

'How?' she whispered. But she didn't need to ask, for the how and place had been revealed to her in the past, and she'd risked all to snatch the girl back back from the brink.

But it wouldn't do to remember too much. There was a purpose to everything, and Maryse had left behind two beautiful children. Nobody could help the dead, they could only comfort the living. In front of her was a wonderful girl who'd always walked in her sister's shadow. Pansy's grief and bewilderment surrounded Siana. She drew a pair of cold, shaking hands into her own and felt them tremble as the girl said in a tragic voice, 'She threw herself off the cliff on to the rocks below. Oh, Siana, Maryse was so badly damaged and the waves were pink-frothed with her blood. Marcus was beside himself. He climbed down the cliff into the water and held her in his arms so she wouldn't float away with the tide, while I ran to get help.

'Luckily, Josh came to Cheverton on his way to Dorchester. He's so strong and calm; he's helping Marcus. Why did she do such an awful thing? I hate her for making me suffer like this. I hate her!' Pansy burst into another flood of weeping.

Folding the girl in her arms, Siana wept with her. 'You don't hate her, my dearest. Maryse suffered so much. She felt betrayed by me and didn't know where to turn in her distress. Sometimes, it takes more courage than someone possesses to live with the consequence of what one has gone through. But although it might have seemed like the easiest way for her to solve her problem, it took a greater degree of courage to do what she did.'

Siana held Pansy at arm's length. 'Being women, there's one more thing you and I can do for her. We can prepare her for the undertaker, so when they come to lay her in her coffin, her body will have remained private except to the women closest to her. Do you have the strength to help me perform such a task? It will be the last act of love we can offer her.'

Pansy nodded. 'I can do no less.'

'Good, then I'll fetch my cape. We'll go before the horse and rig is stabled.'

'What about papa?'

'I'll tell him before we go. Wait outside for me.'

But the study door was locked. 'Francis,' she said softly against the panel. 'Pansy and I are going to the manor, for there are tasks we must do.'

She received no answer.

'I'm sorry,' she whispered, biting back on a sob because she could sense and understand the torture he was going through. She listened for a few moments and, getting no reply, joined Pansy outside, taking the reins herself as they made their way through the damp, miserable morning to Cheverton Manor.

Maryse's spaniels came running out to greet them, their ears flapping as they yelped with the excitement of seeing her. Marcus followed, giving Siana a hug. His clothes were still damp and, although he was composed, he looked haggard and the skin surrounding his eyes were puffy, as if he'd been weeping. She held him close for a long time, absorbing some of his distress and wishing there was some way she could comfort him.

'I'm glad you came,' he said.

'Are you coping, Marcus?'

'I feel numb, but perhaps that's for the best. No doubt we'll find time for guilt and recriminations after the conventions have been observed, when someone is looking to place the blame for this tragedy.'

It didn't take much to realize who that someone might be, but she wasn't about to enter into such a conversation in front of Pansy. 'With your permission, we are here to prepare Maryse for burial.'

He nodded. 'I thought you'd want to do that last act for her. Josh has gone to inform the undertaker and will be back as soon as possible. Is there anything I can do to help?'

'It will be better if you leave it to us now. Send a female servant up with water and soap. A sensible, older one would be best. We'll call you when you're finished.'

Tears came to his eyes. 'Be gentle with my sweet Maryse. She's suffered enough for one day.'

'And so have you, Marcus. You're still wet. You'll catch a chill if you're not careful. Here is your servant. Go with him and change into dry clothes.'

'Does it matter?'

Just then, a small distant cry reached their ears. 'There are others who love and need their father, are there not? It's your responsibility to stay healthy,' Siana admonished.

The smile he gave was a painful wrench of his lips. 'My love left me a legacy, and you will keep me obligated despite my pain.'

'As you did me.' The future of Bryn, the child who had precipitated this tragedy, was suddenly obscure. So was her own happiness. But it was best not to think of that now. There were tasks to be performed and arrangements to be made. 'You'll need to see Reverend

White to arrange the service, so must send a servant to inform him of what has taken place.'

Something distressing occurred to her. 'I'm not sure what the procedure is in cases such as this.'

'Don't worry, Siana, Maryse will not be shamed again. Noah Baines has certified her death as accidental. She'll be buried in hallowed ground next to her mother.' He nodded to his servant. 'Mrs Matheson will require the services of an older female and I will need some hot water and a dry suit of clothes.'

Later in the morning, Siana and Pansy joined hands and looked down on the lifeless body of Maryse. They'd used wax to carry out the tasks necessary to keep her body sweet before burial. Afterwards, they'd gently washed and dried her bruised and broken corpse, then rubbed sweet-smelling lavender oil into her skin.

The injuries she'd sustained were shocking. Fortunately, her face had remained uninjured. So they bound her limbs and body tightly in strips of linen, then dressed her in a grey silk gown which covered her up to her chin. Her stockinged feet were placed in kid slippers, her hands in silk gloves.

Around her shoulders they placed the gift of love Marcus had given her, a grey silk shawl gaily decorated with embroidered butterflies. By necessity, a cap was used to cover her head and tied tightly under her chin to prevent her mouth from falling open. Her newly washed hair flowed in little gleaming rivers from under it to rest upon her shoulders and the pillow.

Her hands were crossed upon her chest, a gold crucifix on a chain arranged there. Finally, weighing down her eyelids with two coins, Siana folded a lace handkerchief and placed it across her eyes. Gently, she kissed Maryse's cold cheek. 'Goodbye, my beloved stepdaughter. May your soul find peace.'

'She looks younger and relaxed and beautiful, like she's an angel already,' Pansy whispered, biting back a sob. 'I'll go and fetch Marcus.'

'No, I'll go. You might want to snatch a few precious moments to say goodbye to your sister in private.'

When Marcus came in to gaze down upon his wife, lying there as if fast asleep, he was controlled. Siana was thankful for the strength he possessed.

'Thank you, Siana, and you, Pansy. I'd like to spend a little time alone with her now.'

'We'll wait downstairs until Josh and the undertaker arrive, and will then inform you. They'll advise you on what should be done next.' As Siana and Pansy proceeded down the staircase, Marcus gave an anguished cry, as if his heart was breaking in two.

Francis had taken Maryse's death hard. It wasn't until the day of the funeral that he spoke to Siana again. She saw or heard him come and go, sometimes with letters in his hand. Sometimes he was called out to attend a patient. When he was home he remained in his study. Siana worried about his lack of appetite when his meals were sent back to the kitchen barely touched, even though she had little appetite herself. Mostly, she worried because he didn't talk to her, not even when they passed on the stairs. But he'd stand politely aside to allow her to pass, his head averted, as though he didn't want to be contaminated by even seeing her.

Instead of being able to give way to the relief of tears, Francis kept his grief locked inside. He was wound up as tightly as the spring in the carriage clock on the mantelpiece and refused to see anybody, not even Pansy, who was obliged to turn to Siana for comfort.

On the day of the funeral they waited for him in the hall. As he came downstairs his appearance shocked Siana. He'd lost a great deal of weight, so his clothes hung on him and his eyes appeared hollow and sunken. He gazed at her from those eyes, as if he hardly knew her. 'I don't want you to attend the funeral.'

'But Francis, you need my support.'

He gave a bitter laugh. 'My family will support me adequately. I'd prefer it if you confined yourself to your room. I will send for you when I'm ready.'

'Papa,' Pansy entreated.

He ignored his daughter's plea. 'You understand me, Siana?'

'I do,' she said and, turning, walked away from him and up the wide staircase towards her room. Sick at heart, she watched them leave for the funeral from her bedroom window. Francis had reached a decision and she knew it boded ill for her.

When he returned it was without Pansy. 'My daughter has gone back to Kylchester to stay with my family,' Francis curtly told her when she enquired.

Although there were comings and goings during the next two days, Siana didn't bother to try and seek her husband out. Francis had said he'd send for her when he was ready. She would have to be content with that.

She went up into the hills, unescorted, walking for hours to try and find solace. But guilt hung heavily on her. When she went to the nursery to say goodnight to the children later that evening and discovered Bryn's bed was empty, she knew she would be content to wait no longer.

But Francis's study was empty, and though she paced the floor for half the night until she fell into an exhausted sleep in a chair, he didn't return until the next morning. She woke late and found Francis at his desk, writing a letter.

'Where's Bryn?' she shouted.

He turned, gazing at her. 'You don't need to know.'

'Don't need to know?' As if the boy was nothing to her. As if he'd never existed in their lives – had never been loved by them.

'He's our son.'

'No. He's not our son.'

She flew across the room at him, pounded her fists against his chest, shrieked. 'You *must* tell me where he is.'

Taking her by the arms he shoved her on to the chair. 'You're acting like a fishwife.'

'I hate you,' she spat at him, tears boiling from her eyes.

'That's all to the good. It will make what I'm about to say to you, much easier. You've always wanted to travel. Now you shall. The day after tomorrow you will be embarking on a long sea journey. You will take Susannah to her mother in Van Diemen's Land, which as you are aware, is an isolated island off the south coast of Australia. You will be at sea for several weeks, and will remain in Van Diemen's Land until further notice.'

'You are banishing me? But what about my children . . . who will care for them?'

'Goldie is living with her brother, Sebastian, in London, and Daisy is with your brother, Josh. I see no reason why the arrangements shouldn't continue, since the children are adequately supervised and cared for.'

He was scattering the family, depriving her of the people she loved the most. 'And Bryn?'

'Bryn is no longer your concern.'

'Francis,' she pleaded, 'don't punish Bryn for what has happened. He'll be so lost and alone amongst strangers.'

It was as if she'd never spoken. 'The ship sails from Bridport the day after tomorrow, so you have adequate time to pack. I will provide you with a letter of credit to the bank in Hobart Town, and the address of a family of Quakers who will help you buy provisions and provide a guide to the property there.'

'Will you send for me?'

Leaning his head to one side, he seemed to considered it. 'At the moment, I don't care if I never set eyes on you again.'

How wounding his words were, but he was lashing out at her from grief. 'You can't mean that, Francis.' She tried to push him into the decision she wanted to hear. 'I think I'm with child.'

He stared at her with so much disdain in his eyes that her heart quaked. 'Couldn't you have thought of a more plausible tale, Siana? I believe you to be lying, as you've lied to me in the past. You might as well know, my intention is to never father a child of yours now.'

She gasped, as if he'd slapped her. Wounded to the core she rose to her feet. 'You're behaving despicably. Am I to understand that you intend to disown any infant I may bear?'

'How could I be sure it was mine, now?'

'Then I must believe that our marriage means nothing to you. So be it. I would have it in writing, so, at least I cannot be deprived of the infant I carry, as you have deprived me of the rest of my family.'

'You're in no position to demand anything of me.'

'You're making that perfectly clear.' She made one last appeal. 'How can you be so caring with strangers and so cold to those you once professed to love? It sounds as if Prudence has been advising you. Has she convinced you that your blood is far too blue for the low peasant girl you once exchanged marriage vows with?'

He hesitated for a moment as if a struggle was going on inside him. Then his eyes hardened. 'How can I love a woman who deceived both myself and the daughter I placed in her care, especially when that deceit caused Maryse's death?'

Siana turned and walked away from him, her heart too heavy to bear any more of his censure.

She didn't see Francis before she sailed, and made no attempt to see him. Susannah, meanwhile, was puzzled by the disappearance of Bryn from her life, looking for him under the bed or in the cupboard, as if expecting him to jump out and scare her.

'We are going on a ship,' Siana told her, trying to make it sound like an exciting adventure. 'And at the end of the journey we'll find your mamma. Do you remember me telling you how much you look like her, and how much she loves you and is longing to see you again?'

Susannah nodded.

'The time has now come to take you to her.'

Only she hadn't expected it to be like this. She'd expected Elizabeth and Jed Hawkins to come home for Susannah, then settle down in the district. She hadn't expected to travel to some wild, foreign land.

They were driven to Bridport by the groom. The ship was a three-masted packet with a sturdy, workmanlike appearance. Siana shared her tiny cabin with another woman, who also had a child with her. She seemed pleasant enough, and the two girls soon made friends.

'They'll be company for one another, so they won't get bored,' the woman said, seemingly pleased she had a companion for the journey. Siana, on the other hand, would rather have been left with her own thoughts than be obliged to socialize.

'I'm Emily Scott. I'm joining my husband. He's an army officer who has just been granted a tract of land.'

'Siana Matheson. I'm delivering Susannah to her mother.'

The woman seemed to draw back. 'Oh, you're the girl's nursery maid, then?'

'No, her mother is a close friend of mine. Susannah was being cared for by my husband and myself.'

'Do you have any children of your own?'

Siana wondered where Bryn was. 'I have stepchildren.' And no more than that did she intend to tell her travelling companion. 'I'm taking Susannah up on deck to watch them cast off.'

'One of the seamen told me the ship flies over the water, so we should make good time.'

Siana thought she saw Francis, standing on the shore. So did Susannah. 'There's my papa,' she shouted out and began to frantically wave to him. 'Goodbye, Papa.'

The man turned away and headed towards a horse. Within minutes he was gone, leaving a trail of footprints in the sand.

The ship was hauled down the channel by a boat oared by several men. When the water deepened she gradually spread her sails and began to surge forward. As Siana watched the coast of her beloved homeland recede, she had never felt quite so alone.

Wynn Lewis had stayed two nights at the house of *Bryn Dwr*.

The day before she had walked to the top of the hill and looked down on her village. The house she'd once occupied looked exactly the same. Smoke rose from the village chimneys and women stopped to chat, their shawls clasped tightly around then to ward off the cold. She felt invisible, as if she didn't exist for them now.

Wynn had not lit a fire in the grate at *Bryn Dwr*. She didn't deserve to be warm.

Grandmother Lewis had visited her in her dreams the

night before. 'What are you doing, here, *cariad*?' she'd said to her.

'I'm going into the cave of the *Gwin Dwr* to cleanse the sin from my soul.'

'The *Gwin Dwr*, is it? That isn't the place for you, it's for the pure in heart as well as body. You lack the courage and the conviction.'

'I am pure, for no man has touched me. And I pray to God every day on my knees.'

'Beware, for there's no pride to take in a body that has not fulfilled its function, when the thoughts inside it are impure. The wine water has a pagan heart.'

Wynn had woken up shouting, 'You don't understand. Away with you, you silly old woman. Let me sleep in peace.'

Now she rose from her mattress and went outside. It was bitterly cold, snow drifted in the wind and powdered the mountainside.

Courage and conviction, Grandmother Lewis had said. Wynn knew she had both. She would do it now, before she had time to change her mind, and she would be cleansed.

Her bare feet made light imprints on the snow. The cave was a welcome shelter and she could see the steps leading down to a flat ledge covered in moss. There was enough light to reveal the faint red stain to the water, and she shuddered. Legend had it that the English soldiers had raped the Welsh virgins, cut their throats and thrown their bodies into the pool.

She began to understand then. The English girl had been raped. That's why they'd brought her here, to help her heal. Oh God, what had she done? This was no place for her to seek absolution.

She placed her foot in the water. After the snow it felt warm. It would be relaxing to immerse herself in it, wash the stink of the journey from her body. Then she'd make the journey back to Dorset before the snow closed over the mountain. Throw herself on the mercy of Reverend White and beg him to seek forgiveness on her behalf from his God!

She removed her clothes and gazed down at her angular body. Untouched by man though the thought of such attention had tortured her often. She was dried up, withered, like a stringy goat. No wonder Gruffydd Evans had scorned her, preferring to take her niece unto him, so long ago. It was true that Megan Lewis had tempted him. She'd always been dancing around the fields with flowers in her hair, smiling at the men. And Wynn knew that in her heart, she'd always been envious of Megan Lewis. The envy rose in her now, the bile of it almost choking her.

The water looked inviting and her body was cold and covered in goosebumps. She sat on the flat slab and slid off the ledge into the deep pool below. She went under and came up spluttering, to reach for the edge.

There, she was cleansed. Indeed to goodness, why the silly fuss about the dangers of this place? Her fingers slid from the slippery ledge as she tried to pull herself from the water. She scrabbled to get a grip, but only succeeded in pulling her clothes in after her. There was no foothold, her feet simply went under the ledge.

Unable to swim, Wynn began to thrash about as she

panicked. The cave was filled with the echoes of her screams, as if people were being slaughtered all around her. She couldn't tell whether it was her voice or those of the spirits around her. Tiring, she became aware of the chill in her body, of the fatigue creeping over her. She slid under the water, found the strength to struggle her way to the surface and take another gulp of Welsh mountain air. How sweet and clean it was.

As she began to sink again she clearly heard Grandmother Lewis's voice say, *Seek not to reveal the past, for it will destroy you.*

The water closed over her and she had no resistance to it as it crept into her nose and mouth. She swallowed it, taking in great mouthfuls until her stomach was bloated. Bubbles of air exploded from her, rushing to the surface above to spread in ever widening ripples.

Down, down, she went until the light faded and all became still.

Outside, the snow filled the imprints her feet had made.

At Rivervale House, Francis Matheson sat in the drawing room and listened to the silence.

It should have been satisfying, but it wasn't. It was empty, as though the house wasn't occupied. It took some time before he realized it wasn't the house that was empty, it was himself.

The house was full of memories – of Bryn and Susannah's squabbling, Daisy's chatter and Goldie's soft voice. It was filled with Pansy's outspokenness, Maryse's unspoken fears and his own inconsolable grief.

Something was missing from the memories, though. Love. He had swept it from his life, so he didn't have to feel anything any more. It was as if the fire in the hearth had burnt out, leaving him with a handful of ashes.

But it hadn't worked, for the broom had not swept away his pain. Grief pounded against his skull like a navvy's fist, his heart thumped painfully against his chest as the clock ticked away the hours. Would it always be like this, his grief stretching on and on into infinity?

He placed his aching head in his hands as he recalled how he'd watched the ship leave the harbour and had seen Susannah wave to him. This was not the time of year to send them to sea. What if they were shipwrecked and perished?

But the packet was new and built for passenger comfort. 'The company has just taken possession of it and their most able captain is in command,' the agent had told him. 'She's one hundred and twenty feet long, does fifteen knots under full sail and will have a regular sailing schedule as soon as the second one arrives. With a good following wind we could cut a couple of weeks from the normal sailing time.'

Tears began to track down his cheeks. He must get control of himself, but first he needed the forgetfulness of sleep.

Halfway upstairs, he gazed at the distinctive stained-glass window, at the woman with the child against her knee. Siana had said the child reminded her of her firstborn. But the woman reminded him more than anyone of Siana, who needed her children to love. She had been forced to suffer the loss of Ashley without him. In fact, she had lost both her children within a year of each other. His own child, whose existence he'd only just learned of – Elen, she'd said the girl had been named. And at the same time Siana had grieved for him too, her husband, for she'd thought he'd been lost at sea.

He thought of Bryn, of the way the boy's excitement had turned to tears at the parting. No, he didn't want to think of Bryn. Not yet! Angered by his weakness, he tore his eyes away from the window and continued upstairs.

The door to Siana's room was open, her bed sheets still tumbled. He could smell her perfume, a subtle mix of pine scents and the wildflowers of the Dorset countryside.

On her dressing table, placed on top of the shards of broken mirror, he saw a piece of folded paper. Mouth dry, he took a few steps forward and stared at it. His name was written on it in her neat, sloping handwriting.

Francis.

He remembered a time when she'd struggled to write her name, remembered the hours she'd put in to rise above her lowly birth. Even now she thirsted for knowledge and read every book she could lay her hands on.

He slowly reached out for the letter, touched the edge of the paper with his finger. His palm began to tingle, as if she'd left something of that fey, mysterious part of herself within its folds to taunt him.

Suddenly, Maryse came into his mind. Snatching his

hand away he turned and strode from the room. Pulling the door shut behind him, he turned the key in the lock.

10

It was halfway through March, the warmest time of the year in Australia. In Van Diemen's Land the sky was an infinite blue canopy overhead and birds soared high.

The spirit of Elizabeth Hawkins soared with them. She had just been given her release from a four-year sentence for setting a fire which had burnt down a shop. No longer would she be classed as a servant assigned to a master, but a respectable wife and, unexpectedly, for she was in her forties, the mother of two strapping sons in addition to her daughter, Susannah, a girl on whom she hadn't set eyes for a long period of time.

She glanced back at the verandah, laughing when her younger son gave a roar as he woke from his nap in his father's chair. Tobias was not easy-tempered on awaking. She watched him gaze around him, his face as sour as if he'd sucked on a lemon. When he caught sight of her, he stared reflectively at her just like his father did, then he grinned.

She held out her arms to him, swinging him up for a hug when he came running.

His brother, Oliver, almost three years old and the

elder by barely a year, was out with his father, perched proudly in front of Jed on the saddle. Though who was the more proud of the two was debatable. Jed had taken Oliver with him on his visit to their neighbour.

The property they occupied was owned by Francis Matheson. Francis, although under suspicion and confined to the property himself after being mistaken for an escaped convict, had made sure she was assigned as his servant, thus saving her from the worst privations of her sentence. Francis and Siana Matheson had always been good to her.

Jed had now bought an acreage and homestead in New South Wales, and they would shortly be leaving the island to travel to the mainland. Now Elizabeth had been granted her freedom, they'd move to a place where her past wasn't known. Once settled in, Jed intended to return to England to fetch Susannah. Not that Elizabeth was ashamed of her past, since she hadn't committed the crime she was convicted of. But there was no way of proving that now, and she didn't want her children to grow up thinking less of her for it.

'There will be a good future for our sons in New South Wales,' Jed had promised her. 'And we'll be less isolated.'

Elizabeth couldn't think of anything more promising than being as happy as she was now, and being married to Jed for the rest of her life. All that had gone before – her early life as mistress to a rich man, the years of mothering the bastard son she had borne him, who was now dead from his excesses – was a painful memory she would rather not recall. She was loved and cared for by a man who was worth more than his weight in gold, and she had borne two sons in the sanctity of their marriage. She was now looking forward to being reunited with the daughter of her previous marriage. What more could any woman want?

'Pa,' Tobias shouted out, pointing towards the trail cleared between Francis Matheson's property and that of their neighbour.

She gazed towards the pathway to see Jed and Oliver emerge from the trees. When Tobias began to struggle she let him down, laughing as he went running off at a trot, tumbling over and righting himself because he tried to run faster than his legs would allow, to greet his father.

Dismounting, Jed set him on the saddle with his brother and began to lead them. His honey-brown eyes met hers as he drew nearer, and he smiled. As always, she became aware of herself as a woman, though she was no longer able to primp and perfume herself, as she had in her previous life.

Here, she had dirt under her nails and calluses on her hands. Her hair was pulled untidily back into a ribbon at the nape of her neck, her face tanned and freckled from the sun. Nevertheless, her fingers went to her foxy hair, attempting to tuck the stray strands in. Her husband didn't mind her being untidy. Having worked on the land for most of his life, he was unused to a life restricted by convention.

Jed, tall, upright and grey-haired, laughed. 'Stop fussing, woman. You know the light in your hair puts the sunlight to shame.'

'Jed Hawkins. You always say that.'

'And you always blush.' He lifted their sons from the horse, picking them up by the slack of their shirts like a couple of pups, to set them gently on their feet. Taking her face between his hands, he kissed her mouth, making it his own. She'd never felt more loved in her life than when she was with Jed. 'I have some news.'

'What is it?'

'Someone was making enquiries about you in Hobart. A woman called Emily Scott.'

'Emily Scott? I can't recall her.'

'She was a passenger aboard a ship which docked a week ago, and shared a cabin with Siana Matheson and a child called Susannah.'

'Siana and Susannah?' Elizabeth's eyes widened and an unbelieving smile came and went. 'A week ago? Where are they, then? Why have they not come to us?'

'They're being cared for by a Quaker family. Apparently, Siana was taken ill aboard the ship and the child caught it from her.'

Elizabeth's hand came up to her mouth. 'Oh, God! What's wrong with them?'

'An infection of the lungs accompanied by fever, I understand.'

Elizabeth began to take off her apron. 'I must go to them.'

'No, my love. I'll go, and you'll wait here. We don't know what ails her yet. I don't want to put the boys at risk, especially since we'll be leaving here within a month. I'll leave tomorrow at first light. As soon as she's recovered I'll bring her back to you.'

It was a frustrating time for Elizabeth while Jed was away. Siana, after all these years, she thought. What on earth had possessed Francis to allow her to travel all this way by herself. But she wasn't by herself. Susannah was with her. Dear God, how she longed to see her daughter again. The girl wouldn't know her after all this time. And what of Siana, was she happy? God knew, she deserved to be after all she'd been through in her childhood.

She sat her sons down, saying to them, 'Soon you will have a sister. Her name is Susannah.'

Oliver nodded. 'Pa said.'

'Pa said,' Tobias mimicked.

Elizabeth fetched the precious drawing of her daughter, smoothing it out carefully. It had been drawn by Sam Saynuthin, the deaf mute who worked for Josh Skinner. It had been a gift from Siana, given to her before Elizabeth had left England.

'Susannah was the same age as you in this picture, Oliver, but now she's much older. She has blue eyes like me, and the same colour hair.'

The pair of them nodded solemnly. 'Pa said.'

But even Elizabeth was unprepared for the changes in her daughter, when two weeks later she was presented to her. At the age of eight, Susannah was as dainty as a porcelain doll. Elizabeth longed to take her in her arms, but the girl was clinging to Siana's side and she didn't want to frighten her.

'Do you know who I am, Susannah?'

'You're my mamma,' the girl said and gazed up at

Siana for confirmation with a trembling bottom lip.

Oliver, dragging Tobias behind him, pushed in between. 'There are some baby pigs. Wanna see? You can hold one and make it squeal.'

Gazing at Siana for permission, Susannah received a nod.

'Be careful you don't dirty that pretty dress,' Elizabeth told her. 'Good clothing has to be looked after, here.'

Susannah ignored her, saying to Oliver, 'I slept outside last night. A wild animal made a noise in the bushes. Your papa said it was a devil.'

'Were you scared?' Oliver asked.

'Of course not,' she said scornfully. 'Don't be such a baby. We have dragons in England. They blow smoke and fire from their nostrils and roar much louder. They would cook you and eat you in one bite.'

Seemingly impressed by her answer, Oliver gazed wide-eyed at her, while plump little Tobias clung fearfully to his brother's hand.

'Come on then, show me the pigs,' she said bossily.

'Where are your manners?' Elizabeth asked. 'We say please and thank you in this house.'

Susannah subjected her mother to a cool look, reminding Siana of Daisy. She tossed her head and walked out through the open door, the boys following her.

Siana smiled apologetically, as if her mothering of the child had been at fault. 'I've never seen Susannah act as badly as this. But you must remember that everything is strange to her and she's aware that I'm going to leave her here. Give her time. She'll settle down and accept her situation in a little while. I've talked to her about you, often.'

'Forgive me. I'd expected no less and you're right to remind me. You look pale, my dear.'

'The journey tired me after the infection. The land is so rugged. I'm glad Jed was with me, for there's a sadness attached to the land here, which made me feel quite melancholy.'

Elizabeth had forgotten Siana's odd perceptions. 'How is Francis, and the children?'

To Elizabeth's surprise, tears formed in Siana's eyes as she choked out. 'Something entirely dreadful has happened, Elizabeth. Maryse has taken her own life. Francis holds me to blame. He's sent me away, for he can no longer stand the sight of me.'

'Oh, my dearest.' Slipping back into her former role of mentor to the younger woman, Elizabeth took Siana in her arms and held her close. 'We will have some tea and you must tell me all about it.'

Jed shuffled his feet, dismayed that Siana was about to heap her troubles onto Elizabeth's shoulders. He hoped nostalgia for the past didn't unsettle his wife and make her hanker after returning to England.

Elizabeth gazed at him over Siana's shoulder, offering him a faint smile, though there were concerned tears in her eyes. Siana had been good to her in the past, and she wouldn't turn her back on this troubled friend, who was now in need of her counsel.

Feeling superfluous when faced with this display of shared, female emotion, Jed shifted awkwardly from one foot to the other. 'I'll go and supervise the children,' he said. 'The boys are bound to get into trouble if they're not watched.'

Over the next few days Elizabeth gradually won Susannah over. The girl relaxed and seemed to enjoy the freedom of the place, which was unregulated by household or schoolroom schedules. Elizabeth made sure she received some tutoring every day, though.

After unburdening her troubles, Siana allowed herself to be persuaded by Elizabeth that the parting would be temporary. 'Francis will come to his senses.'

'I worry about what has happened to Bryn.'

'Knowing Francis, nothing too drastic. Even if he cannot accept the boy as his son, he's Bryn's grandfather. Blood is thicker than water. In time he'll come to the conclusion that you may have deceived him, but you acted with the best of intentions. He loves you too much to let you go for good.'

Because the Hawkins family had plans to leave Van Diemen's Land to settle on their own property in New South Wales, Siana didn't tell Elizabeth about the baby she carried inside her. Luckily she no longer suffered from sickness, and her slightly bulging stomach was easily hidden.

'Come with us to New South Wales,' Elizabeth said one day. 'I don't like the thought of leaving you here alone.'

'No. I want to stay here in case Francis comes for me.' The truth was, she wanted to be alone so she didn't have to pretend she was happy when her emotions were constantly in turmoil.

As the days swiftly passed and the time of parting grew nearer, Siana made light of her problem with falsehoods. 'I'll only be here over the winter. Francis said something about joining me here in the spring. By that time he'll have recovered his senses.'

Although he suspected she was lying, Jed didn't urge Siana to take Elizabeth's advice. Having once been the steward of Cheverton Estate, which had belonged to Siana's first husband, he knew the way her mind worked. Siana Matheson made her own troubles, and didn't expect anybody but herself to sort them out. She had inner strength and was a woman with the ability to survive in the most desperate of circumstances.

'I'll go into town and make sure you're provisioned up for winter before we leave. There will be winter vegetables available, and the neighbours will come over every week to make sure you're all right. If you need help, just fire the rifle twice into the air.'

'You'll have to show me how to load it, then.'

'You'll come through this all right, lass,' Jed said to her. 'You've always been strong, for you've always had to be.'

A week later Siana was alone.

Susannah had shed a tear and hugged her tight, but no more than she'd have done for a favourite aunt, for her own mother had captivated her after the first day. Susannah was intrigued by her and Elizabeth's resemblance to one another. And it was obvious that her little brothers enchanted her. After always being among the youngest of the pack, she seemed to relish the responsibility of being the eldest.

Jed seemed to have captured her heart by just doing nothing, and she called him Pa, the same as her two brothers.

'Good luck,' Siana had said to them, doubting if she'd ever see them again.

Her friend Elizabeth had changed. She was more capable than Siana remembered, and certainly tougher. Being part of a family where she was loved and respected had given her confidence. Four years ago their paths had divided, taking them in different directions. Although they remained friends, their past rapport, which had been forged out of mutual need, no longer existed. Both of them knew it.

'Are you sure you don't want to come with us?' Elizabeth asked her on the last day.

Giving them all one last hug, Siana shook her head. 'Safe journey.'

She watched them walk out of her life with dry eyes. When they exchanged a final wave and disappeared from her sight she went back indoors, planning her schedule in her mind.

The work about the house and garden would keep her busy, she realized. It would do her good to get back to her roots and dirty her hands. In fact, she was looking forward to working in the alien soil. Although the general terrain was steeper and more rugged, and the landscape wilder than she'd ever experienced in her life, the hills reminded her vaguely of Dorset. The solidly built wooden house would keep her snug and warm when winter came, for Elizabeth had told her it was bitterly cold in the winter months.

So the weeks passed. Siana missed her husband and children but, although she felt sad and wondered about them constantly, she was aware of the child growing inside, keeping her company. She would endure the long days until she saw her family again, for she was sure they would be reunited.

She fashioned clothes for her infant, using fabrics she'd brought with her, and stitching during the day when the light didn't strain her eyes. Sometimes, she talked to the child as if she was already born. The sound of her own voice was a comfort in her loneliness, for the only visitors she had were members of the neighbouring Stowe family, who she welcomed gladly when they came to pay the occasional call.

Siana knew she'd give birth to a girl. And so it came to pass, on a cold day in June, when frost lay thickly upon the ground.

She barely had time to stoke up the fire when the pains were upon her. So swiftly and easily did the infant arrive, she didn't have time to think, let alone send for the assistance of Jean Stowe. Not that she needed her. The afterbirth came away a few seconds later, and without a tear. Tying the cord, she separated the infant from it and wrapped her daughter in a sheet. After attending to her own needs, she placed the child against her breast to suckle, and returned to her bed to rest for the remainder of the day.

The baby captivated Siana. Her head was covered in a dark velvety cap and a glimpse of her eyes showed them to be dark, too. The child bore a strong resemblance to her own mother. But there was Matheson in her too, in the shape of her hands and the tiny frown creasing her brow, which reminded Siana achingly of Francis. How delicate and perfect a being she was.

'I'll name you after your father, and also after my mother. So, my dearest little Francine Megan Matheson, all we have to do now is wait for your father to come for us. That should not be long now, for a man cannot mourn for ever, not even for a lost child.'

Over the following months she was happy being a mother to her child. She didn't stray far from her immediate surrounds except to draw water from the stream. The only threat to her peace of mind came from the wild tangle of wilderness surrounding the clearing, which seemed to Siana strangely oppressive. Siana didn't belong here, and had the feeling that if she ever ventured into the wilderness it would lay claim to her and she'd be lost for ever.

In London, meanwhile, Goldie was making an impulsive bid for freedom after finding a door to the outside swinging open. Slipping through it, she ran as quickly as she could along the streets, hiding amongst the vendors of fruit in the market.

She was looking for a coaching inn. If they agreed to take her to Poole, Josh Skinner would repay them for her fare. He used to own a coaching company and was acquainted with all the drivers. But, although she chased after each coach she saw, they soon left her behind.

The grey uniform marked her out. Twice, she evaded capture by a constable, hiding in some smelly rat-ridden refuse in an alley. By evening Goldie was ravenously hungry, but not ravenous enough to scavenge with the rats. Even the sparse workhouse food would have been a welcome sight.

Wearily, she sank into a shop doorway. It had been a hot day. The city stank of dung, rotting vegetables and the stinking, reeking mud of the river, for when the tide ebbed it left behind it an assortment of dead animals and other unsavoury rubbish.

Before long it grew dark. Curling up in the shadows, Goldie slept, oblivious to the sounds around her. Morning brought her downfall. Dragged upright by a constable she was marched back to the workhouse.

Hands on hips, Mrs Tweddle scowled ominously. 'Well, there's an ungrateful girl, then.'

Close to tears, Goldie said, 'I don't want to stay here. I want to go home.'

The breath left her body when the woman back-handed her. Goldie staggered backwards with each slap, finally hitting her head against the wall. She burst into loud sobs as she slid down the wall to the floor.

But Mrs Tweddle hadn't finished. Fetching a thin cane, she set about Goldie, whipping her across the back, shoulders and arms without mercy. Cowering away from the stinging cane, Goldie tried to shield her head from the worst of it.

'It hurts!' she shrieked. 'I won't run away again, I promise.'

'I'll make sure you don't, dearie.' Her face convulsed with fury, the woman dragged Goldie upright by her hair and threw her face-down over the back of a stuffed chair. Blow after blow landed on her legs, buttocks and back.

Goldie's stomach began to ache. She couldn't catch a breath properly and became dizzy. Froth dripped from her mouth and she lost control of her bladder. Then the room went black and she lost consciousness. Limply, she hung there, blood welling from her wounds.

Her energy spent, breathing heavily, Mrs Tweddle gazed at her victim without remorse. That would teach the ungrateful little pest to obey the rules. She dragged her through to the infirmary and gave her to one of the workhouse inmates who served as nurses to the sick.

'This one's a runaway. See to her injuries. The little madam thinks she's too good for the likes of us. When she's able to work, let me know. She can scrub the privies and floors from now on.'

'Eh, the poor little thing,' one of them said after Mrs Tweddle had departed. 'That miserable old cow has given her a right savaging. Fetch me some water, Maggie. I'll see if I can clean her up . . . some of that salve too, to stop the cuts festering. If Tweddle puts her to scrubbin' the privies, I reckon it'll kill the poor little lass.'

The words lodged in Goldie's brain as she woke. She groaned as she tried to sit up, resolving to run away again as soon as she could. She'd rather die than stay in this place longer than was necessary.

'Now don't you be scared, my luvvy. You're in the infirmary. My name's Annie Rice and this here is my friend, Maggie Coster. We'll be looking after you. But we've got to wash you and put some salve on those welts. It's going to hurt.'

Tears came to Goldie's eyes. 'I want my mamma.'

Maggie gazed with astonishment at her friend. 'Well, I never. She speaks real nice, don't she?'

Annie lowered her voice. 'And looks pretty. She still has her hair. Mrs Tweddle might take it into her head to let the doctor have his way with her. You know what he's like with the young girls. She'll end up in a house when he's finished teaching her a few tricks, the dirty old sod.' Annie turned to smile at her. 'How did you get in here, then?'

Goldie bit her lip and plucked from the air what seemed to her to be a perfectly reasonable scenario, for the death of Sebastian and the consequences to herself of exposure of the crime against her brother, were very real to her. So far, nobody had believed the truth of her background. But everyone respected what the earl said, and she knew he would vouch for her.

'I was staying with my papa's relative, the Earl of Kylchester, and I got lost. Someone stole my clothes and they left me on a tomb in a cemetery.'

'Now there's a fine tale,' Maggie said and gazed at Annie, her eyes brimming with mirth. The two women gazed at each other for a moment, then began to laugh uproariously.

Josh wished he hadn't mentioned that he intended to visit London in August, for the battle with Daisy had been raging for five minutes.

'It's not a social visit. Giles Dennings and I are going to look over some property there as an investment.'

'We could make it a social visit, though. Mr Dennings

won't mind. Please, Josh,' she begged. 'I won't get in the way, I promise. I can visit Goldie then. I'm so bored without her and I want to know when she's coming home, because even though she said she'd write, she hasn't. I'll be good, I promise.'

'You're a girl. Who's going to look after you?'

Sensing victory, Daisy gave her brother her most winsome smile. 'Miss Edgar can come too. Her sister has a boarding house in London and we could stay there. I'm sure she'd like to visit her sister.' She gave a breathless giggle. 'Besides, Miss Edgar and Mr Dennings are sweethearts.'

'The devil they are,' Josh said, his face lit up by a huge grin. 'What makes you say so?'

'He gave her a flower when he left yesterday, and Miss Edgar's face went all red. I was watching from the landing upstairs.'

Josh laughed. 'The sly old dog. I'll be damned. What else do you know?'

'That Pansy Matheson has you fair mazed,' she taunted. 'You look like a moonstruck mule when you're with her.'

The smile left his face. 'See here, Daisy Skinner. Just because you're my sister, it doesn't mean you can take liberties, unless you want to go over my knee and feel my hand across your rump. That nose of yours will fall off if you keep sticking it into other people's business.'

'How else can I find out things when grown-ups won't tell me? You're my brother and Pansy is my stepsister. I love her and I love you.' The laughter left Daisy's face. 'When is our sister coming home, Josh?'

'Don't you like staying with your brother, then?'

She crossed to where he stood, hugging him tight. 'Of course I do, Josh. But I'm lonely. Everything has gone wrong since Maryse died. Papa no longer loves us. He's sent Siana away, and Bryn as well.'

'Who told you that?'

'I heard the maids talking about it.'

'Did you now? I'll have to ask Mr Bentley to give that pair of flighty hens a flea in their ears. I'm sure Francis loves you all, but he's very sad at the moment. As for Siana, she's taken Susannah back to her mother, who lives a long away across the sea. She'll return to us before too long.' If Josh had known what Francis's intentions were, though, Siana would never have departed alone. He was relieved that Jed Hawkins and Elizabeth would be there to look after her.'

'And what about Bryn? Where is he?'

Josh hesitated, loath to tell Daisy the truth about the boy's birth. 'Sometimes people leave our lives because they have no choice. That doesn't mean we'll never see them again.' He smiled at her, then uttered the very thing that would divert his sister's mind from the subject. 'You'd better go and tell Miss Edgar to pack a trunk for London. But we're only staying a week or so. There are several places of interest we can go and see. I can take you to see Brunel's Tunnel under the river and I heard there was a monument being built in memory of Horatio Nelson, the great British admiral who died in the battle of Trafalgar. That might be finished by now.'

Daisy snorted. 'You can go and see the dead admiral if you want. I'd rather have Miss Edgar take me to the theatre to see a play and then go to visit Kew Gardens. Pansy told me it's filled with flowers.' Her eyes began to shine. 'Can we use the railway from Southampton? Mr Bentley told me that it's very noisy, and it snorts fire and cinders from its chimney like a dragon.'

'And how would Mr Bentley know that?'

'He knows someone who knows someone else who went on one, once.'

'A pity he had to tell you about it, then,' Josh said gloomily, for he'd just remembered the London and South Western Railway ran a first-class passenger service on the Southampton to London route, and the three-hour journey would cost him twenty shillings apiece.

But Daisy hadn't finished promoting his manservant. 'Mr Bentley tells lovely stories. When he was a boy he knew somebody who went up into the air in a basket hung from a bag filled with gas. Fancy that.'

'More like fanciful, is that. 'Tis him that's a bag of gas, and it wouldn't surprise me if he could fly all by himself. What's more, Mr Bentley's not paid to tell you stories. Just you let him get on with his work instead of being a bother to him.'

'Oh, you,' she said and flounced off, her pink skirts flicking up to reveal the hems of her calico drawers, below which a pair of calves disappeared into sturdy brown ankle boots.

'Little madam,' he said and choked out a laugh, trying to imagine his sister dressed in rags and digging for turnips, as he and Siana had been obliged to at her age.

*

Pansy had been furious at being packed off to stay with her aunt and uncle after Maryse's funeral. She was even more disturbed at being in London, where the season was in full swing. She felt constricted, confined and uncomfortable, and longed to be in Dorset to comfort her father.

There was something going on she didn't know about. Conversations ceased when she walked into rooms and she was beginning to feel like an outsider. Her uncle Ryder hadn't changed, but Aunt Prudence was cool towards her now, sometimes using her to fetch and carry, as she would her maid.

What was worse, Alder was squiring Justina Parsons around. Not that Pansy was jealous, for she'd quite finished with Alder. But it seemed to Pansy that her cousin was being insensitive and just using Justina Parsons to embarrass herself. And Justina didn't deserve to be used like that. Although she was a little empty-headed at times, she was a pleasant enough person nevertheless, and Pansy liked her. Matured by Maryse's death, Pansy didn't want to play Alder's foolish games.

She attended the nuptials of her uncle Augustus, who was wed to his Constance in a small ceremony conducted in the chapel of Kylchester Hall. This was followed a few weeks later by a ball and grand wedding of the earl's heir, Roger, to Lalage. Peers of the realm abounded at the latter, which was celebrated at Kylchester Hall. Her father was noticeable by his absence from both ceremonies.

A week later, Pansy requested a private meeting with the earl.

'What is it, my dear?' he asked her.

'If it pleases you, sir. I should like to return home. Siana and papa will need me.'

Her uncle drew in a deep breath, then slowly exhaled as he waved her to one of the chairs. 'My brother said he would send for you.'

'It has been several months now and there has been no word from them. We cannot mourn for Maryse for ever and I suspect something has happened that I don't know about.'

'Ah . . . I see.' His fingers tapped on the table for a moment. 'How old are you now, Pansy.'

'I'm twenty-one.'

'Then quite old enough to understand. Not only is your father mourning the loss of Maryse, he has cast her illegitimate child from his hearth. Furthermore, he has banished the peasant woman he married to Van Diemen's Land.'

A chill ran through Pansy and her eyes widened in bewilderment. How could the father she adored do such a cruel thing? 'What has he done with Bryn?'

'The boy is being farmed out with a former servant until his future is decided upon. It's most likely he'll be sent to an institution and trained to work in a useful profession, so he can support himself in the future.'

Pansy knew the reputation of the boarding schools he was referring to, most of which housed unwanted children. Many of them didn't survive their childhood. Clasping her hands to her mouth she tried to hold back the tears pricking her eyes. 'I swear, I will never forgive Papa for this.'

'My dear Pansy, the boy cannot be brought up as part of the Matheson family. Think of the shame it will bring down on us. Maryse was unwed.'

'How dare you blame Maryse when she was the victim? The shame is that the men who did this to her are still at large when the Matheson men should be hunting them down and bringing them to justice. My father has allowed his self-pity to overcome his compassion. He should remember that Bryn is an innocent, and the boy is also his grandson.'

'The boy is a bastard.'

Her eyes blazing, she lost her temper and was totally indiscreet. 'And you, my lord, are a hypocrite, since it's common knowledge you have a mistress, and have fathered illegitimate children of your own.'

Ryder Matheson stood up, bristling with affront. 'That's enough, Miss Matheson. I will not be spoken to thus, in my own home.'

'Then I will leave your home forthwith.'

'You will not. You will stay here until your father sends for you. However, I intend to write to him and inform him of the displeasure with which I now regard you. Go to your room now, please. I'll send your aunt up to you. When you marry Alder you must stop this hoydenish nonsense and behave with more dignity. In fact, it's high time the pair of you were wed, for when you are a wife, you will learn to heed the will of your husband. Perhaps we will bring the nuptials forward.'

Pansy stared at him. 'I will never marry Alder. This I have told him, time and time again.'

The earl's face was drawn into cold, haughty lines.

'Miss Matheson, I've had quite enough of this conversation. You are a disgrace to your father's name. While you are living under my roof you will accede to my wishes.'

Even though she stared at her uncle defiantly, Pansy quaked with the enormity of what she'd said. 'I will not marry your son under any circumstances. Good day, sir.' She turned and left the room, her chin held high.

11

Goldie ran away a second time, climbing on to a privy roof and dropping into a pile of rubbish in the lane behind the workhouse. But her escape bid had been observed. Intercepted at the end of the lane, she was dragged back to face the punishment of Mrs Tweddle.

After a severe beating, Mrs Tweddle hacked the hair from her head close to her scalp with a pair of sharp scissors. Then her hands were tied behind her back and she was secured to an iron ring set into the wall in a dimly lit cellar.

'You won't escape from there, my princess. You can stay until you rot, or until you decide to behave yourself,' she shouted.

Two days later Goldie was still there. The wounds from her beating had scabbed over, thirst parched her mouth and her stomach ached from hunger. A few days later her throat became sore and she began to cough. She was kept there for several more days, forced to eat the thin gruel she was offered, crouching on her hands and knees like an animal. She was freed on occasion to use the bucket in the corner. But she would not give in and say she was sorry.

One day she was untied and taken upstairs. The unaccustomed light made her blink. Her stomach ached and she felt sick, and tired. Mrs Tweddle ripped off her filthy clothes, then stood her in a bowl of cold water and scrubbed her thoroughly all over.

The woman smiled nastily at Goldie when she looked around for something to dry herself on, handing her a thin, grey towel and a clean smock to wear. 'I've found you a job, princess. But the doctor's coming to check you over, first.'

Goldie remembered the doctor's hands on her when she'd first come to this place, and shuddered. She was no longer the innocent child she'd once been, for the older girls had seen fit to educate her about the ways of men, and she lived in fear of being taken before the doctor again.

But when it happened it was a different doctor, a younger one with glasses and a perfunctory manner. Mrs Tweddle hadn't been expecting him, for she said, 'Where's the regular doctor?'

'His contract lapsed and was not renewed.' The doctor frowned when he saw Goldie's welts and bruises. 'How did the girl get in this state?'

'She ran away and was set upon.'

'My wife is looking for a maid of all work. But this girl can't be employed in her present condition. She's too thin, and has probably got intestinal parasites. She won't be strong enough to do the tasks required.'

'Please, sir, I'll work very hard,' Goldie begged,

beginning to cry. She'd do anything to escape from the workhouse. Drooping from tiredness and feeling really odd, she mumbled, 'I want my mamma.'

Mrs Tweddle spoke sharply to her. 'You don't have a mamma. You're an orphan.' She turned back to the doctor, her manner ingratiating. 'Take no notice of her, sir. The girl is queer in the head. She claims she's a member of the aristocracy. I have another girl, who might suit your wife. She's a little older and more docile. Her name is Mary Masterson.'

Goldie had a sudden fit of coughing that left her feeling weak.

The doctor gazed reflectively at her. 'How long has she had that cough?'

'Just a few days. I didn't think it bad enough to report.'

'Your job is to report all illness, for even a slight cough can result in an epidemic. And I do not believe your explanation of how she got these injuries. I'll require a truthful accounting before I leave the premises.'

'Sometimes the girls need a good caning. This one stole food,' Mrs Tweddle said resentfully. 'It wasn't much, just a slice of bread. From the goodness of my heart I didn't report her, in case she was transported for her sin. A beating seemed a less harsh penalty for the girl to pay, and it teaches them not to steal again.'

'Quite so,' the doctor agreed. 'But make the beating a little less enthusiastic next time.'

'Yes, sir,' Mrs Tweddle said humbly.

Just then Goldie was enveloped in a black haze. Her knees became weak and she buckled. The doctor caught her before she fell and laid her gently on the table. He felt her forehead for fever, then tapped his fingers against her chest. Finally, he listened to the erratic beating of her heart for a few moments. His expression was grave after he finished his examination. 'The girl's lungs are congested. She must go into the infirmary.'

'The poor dear,' Mrs Tweddle exclaimed, her voice falsely sympathetic. 'Will she survive?'

Drawing her aside the doctor whispered, 'It's early days yet, and I'll give her a tincture which might help to improve her condition, but I very much doubt it.'

Daisy was disappointed with London. It was dirty and smelly and, although Queen Victoria had a splendid palace, she couldn't see Her Majesty anywhere. The soldiers guarding the palace gates in their silly hats wouldn't speak to her, either, which wasn't polite considering she'd been using her best voice and manners.

She did like the lamp in the street outside the boarding house, though, which was lit every night by a man with a long pole. The glow shone through her window at night. At first, Daisy had thought there must be a large candle inside the lamp, but Miss Edgar's sister had smiled when she'd said that, telling her in quite a superior way not to be silly, that it was a gas lamp. But when Daisy had asked, she couldn't explain exactly what gas was.

Miss Edgar had done the smiling then, telling her sister that gas was extracted from coal.

'They can fill big bags with it, hang baskets underneath and float in the air in them. Mr Bentley's friend was there when it happened and saw it. He told me all about it,' Daisy had informed them both, enthusiastically.

'Good gracious. Your charge will have us flying to the moon in one next. My dear Sylvia, how can you bear to tutor children when they have such silly ideas in their heads?'

Miss Edgar had offered her sister a superior smile. 'Daisy is, of course, referring to the flight in the Montgolfier brothers' balloon in Paris in 1783, aren't you, dear?'

Daisy had nodded.

'Ah, yes . . . that balloon,' Dorothy had murmured.

'I think they might have used a different gas than that obtained from coal, wouldn't you, Dorothy. We must find out what it was.'

'Yes . . . yes, I suppose they would have. Is that someone at the front door, I hear?' Rising to her feet, Dorothy had hurried away, red in the face.

Miss Edgar's sister was married to a bank clerk. She was very genteel and made nice cakes. The boarding house was small and had only two rooms vacant. When Josh and Mr Dennings moved in, it was full up.

Daisy had to sleep in the same bed as Miss Edgar. The governess wore a nightgown with pretty embroidery on and a nightcap to match, from which her hair hung to her waist. She tossed and turned before she fell asleep, so the bed squeaked and woke Daisy up.

What was worse, during the day Daisy still had to do some lessons, seated at the table in the stuffy front parlour. Sometimes, Mr Dennings came in to read the newspaper.

'Oh, my pardon, ladies,' he always said, as if surprised to see them there. The curved points of his moustache would waggle dashingly as he smiled at her tutor. Miss Edgar would give a pursed-up little smile, go pink and pretend to be severe. 'Do stop coming in to disrupt Daisy's lessons, Mr Dennings.'

Then he'd wink at her and she'd turn red again. 'Not in front of the child, please. She might get the wrong idea, altogether.'

Daisy didn't mind having her lessons disrupted. She knew Miss Edgar and Mr Dennings were sweethearts and hoped that eventually they'd get married. She liked being a bridesmaid. Daisy secretly recorded her observations in a daily journal she kept, writing down everything interesting she saw, following the progress of the romance closely.

Josh and Mr Dennings went out a lot, visiting the properties available for sale and discussing them in the evening. One particular evening, Mr Dennings said to Josh, 'I thought the building we looked at today was over-tenanted. The way I see it, this city is going to keep expanding. We'd be better off buying something further out where it's cheaper.'

'But the building is right in the middle of the business district. Londoners are used to being crowded, from what I can see. That building is fully tenanted. Besides, it's only a mile from that new monument of Nelson. They wouldn't put a tribute to a hero in the area unless the value of it was set to increase. More importantly, the investment will start earning us money straight away. In a couple of years' time that building will be worth twice what we paid for it, then we can use the profit to invest in longer-term projects.'

'When can we go and visit Goldie?' Daisy got in when Josh paused for breath.

'As soon as Giles and I have finished our business here.'

'Well, please hurry up and make up your mind, Mr Dennings. Everyone says Josh is clever about buying vestments and somebody else might get the place. Besides, you promised to take me and Miss Edgar to the theatre. If you don't hurry we won't have time to go.'

'Investments, dear,' Miss Edgar corrected.

The deal was settled the next day. Afterwards, they did some sightseeing, using one of the horse-drawn omnibuses to go from place to place, most of which were hot and crowded. Josh took her to all the boring places he wanted to see first, then they visited Kew Gardens. Daisy thought the place wasn't a great deal better than the gardens of Rivervale House.

It was with great excitement that Daisy and Josh found Sebastian Groves's print shop the next day. There was a sign on the door saying it was closed. Josh, trying to peer through the window, reported he could see nothing through the grime and advertising posters. However, when he tried the door handle the door swung open. A bell held by a spring rang merrily when they advanced into the dusty interior of the shop.

A girl of about Daisy's age came hurrying through from the room at the back. 'Can't you read? The sign on the door says we're closed, don't it?'

'Doesn't it,' Daisy corrected in Miss Edgar fashion,

and the girl gave her a hard stare. Daisy stared right back.

An older man came through. 'That's enough, Alice. You shouldn't be after talking to customers like that.'

'This is my ma's shop now, Zeke Palmer. If you want to keep your job, do as you're told. Alice seated herself on a stool behind the counter and propped her head on her hands. 'Seeing as you're in, watcher want, then?'

Josh stooped to look her in the eye. 'To start with, you can watch your bleddy lip, missy, else you'll get my hand across your arse, quick smart.'

Daisy smirked when the girl flushed a dull red.

'I'm sorry, sir,' Zeke said. 'The girl didn't mean anything by it. How can I help you folks? We print leaflets, calling cards and . . .'

Poking her tongue out at Daisy, Alice whispered, 'What d'you think you're looking at, then?'

Daisy's hands went to her hips. 'A smelly pig?'

Josh gave her a stern look. 'My sister and I have come to call on Sebastian Groves.'

Alarm came into the girl's eyes. 'Ma!' she yelled.

Zeke ran a tongue over his lips. 'Sebastian passed away a few months ago. Set upon, he was. A shame, for he was a nice young man.'

'Then I want to see Goldie,' Daisy said, not taking her eyes off the girl, who was now making faces at her.

'Goldie went home with her pa.'

'No she didn't, else I would have seen her, since she's my sister.' When the girl paled Daisy turned to Josh. 'She's lying, Josh. That girl is wearing the bracelet I gave to Goldie. And that's Goldie's dress she's got on.'

'When the girl tried to hide her arm, Daisy grabbed it and held it fast. 'You dirty, thieving little rat.'

Alice's other arm shot out. Grabbing Daisy's braid in her fist she yanked hard on it.

'Eeow!' Daisy yelled, and promptly smacked one across her protagonist's ear. She then got a grip on her collar with both hands and dragged her across the counter to the floor, sending paper flying everywhere. Throwing herself on to the girl, Daisy pummelled her, both fists flying.

But Alice was used to defending herself and soon tossed Daisy off. They rolled around in the dust, their drawers on display, their skirts flying, scratching and screaming at each other like a couple of alley cats.

Josh exchanged a grin with Zeke and they both moved forward together. Between them, they plucked the struggling pair apart.

'What in hell's name is going on down here?' a voice bawled from the doorway. 'Who are you?'

'My name is Joshua Skinner. I'm looking for Goldie Matheson. Where is she?'

The woman gave him a flat stare. 'How the hell would I know? Scarpered, most like. Sly little devil, she was. She took off after her brother died. I reckon she killed him, 'cause he was found with his head stove in not far from 'ere. We haven't seen the girl since.'

'That's not what you told me, Betty Groves,' said Zeke. 'You said her pa had come for her.'

'My sister wouldn't kill anyone,' Daisy yelled at her. 'And that horrible girl is wearing her clothes and her bracelet. I'm going to find a constable and tell him.'

Hastily, the woman said, 'Er, there's no need to involve the law. I reckon the girl took fright when her brother got killed, and ran away. She said she wanted to go 'ome. We did look for her for a while, but if she stayed in the city she most likely got picked up and took to the workhouse.'

'She stole Goldie's bracelet.'

'The girl left it behind. Alice was wearing it for safe-keeping. Alice, give the girl the bracelet. As for the clothes, that dress got stained with ink and Goldie gave it to my Alice, so don't you go accusing her of stealing it, unless you can prove it.'

Daisy snatched the bracelet when it was reluctantly offered, sliding it on to her own wrist. 'Goldie wouldn't want the dress back after you've been wearing it, anyway. I expect it's got fleas in it now.'

'I hope they bite you, then.'

The two girls offered each other hard, challenging stares, while Zeke said to the woman again, only louder this time, 'You told me Goldie's pa came for her, Betty.'

She gazed at him in irritation. 'What if I did? What's it got to do with you, anyway?'

'I worked for Sebastian and his uncle before him. A right decent lad he was, till you got your clutches on him, pretending there was an infant on the way. I can't see no sign of it now.'

'There *was* a baby. I lost it.'

'Got rid of it, more like. I reckon you did young Goldie in. She was a sweet, well-mannered young lady. There was a wet patch, where you scrubbed something from the floor. I thought that suspicious because you're a slattern who wouldn't take a scrubbing brush to anything. But you left blood between the cracks. What did you do with the girl? You'd better tell us, else I'll fetch the constables myself.'

Betty began to look sick. 'I didn't harm a hair on the brat's head. I told you, she ran away. My brother will pay you a visit you won't enjoy if you spread gossip about me. Now, get out of here, the lot of you. As for you,' she said, stabbing her finger at Zeke, 'printer journeymen are fifty to the dozen in London, so don't you bother coming back.'

As soon as Josh released Daisy, as quick as a flash she sprang at the other girl and fetched her a clout that sent her reeling backwards. 'If anything awful has happened to my sister, I'll send Spring-Heeled-Jack around here to eat you.'

Alice clutched her flaming cheek and screamed abuse at her.

'Smelly fishwife.' Her hackles still raised, Daisy flounced from the shop, her hat hanging to one side and six inches of torn lace dangling from her petticoats.

Grinning at this unexpected display of aggression from Daisy, especially since she and Goldie had always been at loggerheads, Josh followed her out of the shop with Zeke trailing after.

'That's me done for,' the printer said. 'I'll never get another job at my age.'

'Yes, you will. To start with, I'll need a guide around the London workhouses. I've got to find Goldie. When we've done that I might be able to fix you up with a job. It stands to reason that you must be good with letters and numbers and stuff, since you're a printer. I'll have to consult with my partner first, but we have an office building that will need managing, if that would interest you.'

Daisy suddenly burst into tears. Miserably, she said, as she clung to her brother's waist, 'What if Goldie's dead?'

Josh took her hands in his. 'Goldie isn't dead, I know it. Don't you worry. I'll find her.'

Daisy sniffed. 'Promise?'

'When did Josh ever let you down? I'll stay in London until I *do* find her.' Handing her his handkerchief, Josh grinned cheerfully at her. 'Here, blow that snout of yours if you want to look ladylike. It's dripping on my sleeve. By crikey, you're a right little tiger cat when you're roused, aren't you? I'm thinking about putting you in a travelling side-show in the boxing tent.'

Daisy, who didn't know what a boxing tent was, and didn't really care, gazed forlornly at him. 'When's Siana coming home? I miss her. I want everything to be like it was before.'

Josh's smile faded. 'Soon, I hope, Daisy love. Soon.'

An exceptionally wet spring had been followed by a perfect summer, which had drawn from the soil a crop of magnificent abundance. When the earth had handed out her blessings she'd been particularly generous with the Cheverton Estate, Marcus thought.

Marcus was fit and tanned. He was spending long hours working as part of an itinerant team of labourers, filling the place of a team worker who'd trodden in a rabbit hole and was forced to rest his injured ankle.

His agent, the hard-working and deceptively jovial Phineas Grundy, a man Marcus had met on his travels and who he trusted implicitly, had seated the injured labourer at the whetstone. Thus he'd be gainfully employed, keeping the sickles and scythes sharpened until he recovered sufficiently to take his rightful place in the line.

One Ben Collins had been appointed overseer of the teams of itinerants. He was a large and generally genial man of local birth, with an older wife and a handful of youngsters. His son George, aged about eleven years and already solidly built, worked alongside his father, keeping a tally of the stooks and who cut what. He was quick and accurate.

The sharp-eyed lad was the nephew of Josh Skinner, who had an eye on him for a clerkship working under Giles Dennings. Besides the tally, George fetched drinks for the workers and carried armfuls of wheat to soak in the brook to keep it pliable. The soaked wheat was then woven into bands by the children, to bind the wheat sheaves with before they were placed in stooks.

At first, the labourers had been suspicious of Marcus, and awkward in their approach. Gradually they'd relaxed and accepted him, going so far as to laugh at his initial inept strokes with his labouring tools, and gently teasing him about his inadequacies.

'If you don't mind me saying so, sir, you be cutting corn not chopping down a tree. That there sickle needs to have a keener edge and thee needs to get some rhythm into your strokes.'

Enjoying himself, Marcus joined in the laughter. Gradually, he fell into the way of cutting, rotating from the spine in measured swings to build up an arm. After the first day his hands were covered in blisters and his back was so painful he could hardly stand upright.

His housekeeper, Maisie Roberts, applied salve to his palms and bound them with linen strips. 'If I can be so bold, sir, you be like the old squire in his workin' ways. He liked to get his hands dirty. He said it kept him young, and a fine upright man, he was, until the end of his days. But don't you go overdoing it. Get into it gradually.'

'Thank you, Mrs Roberts. I'll certainly take your advice.'

One of the labourers gave him a stick fashioned from a tree limb the next day. 'Best go back to your bed, sir. Thee is as bent and creaky as a tree in a gale.'

Marcus persevered, and as his back muscles strengthened he grew a fine set of calluses on his hands. However hard he tried, he couldn't quite match the speed of his workers. He earned their respect, though, and enjoyed their rough camaraderie, learning many things he normally wouldn't have been privy to, as they relaxed in his company.

One said, 'The old squire didn't mind getting a bit of shit on his boots. "Shit grows vegetables,' says he. 'We eats them, then turns it back into shit again. I make a bit of money during the process." He allus used to work in the fields alongside us when he could. He had a strong heart and could work all day once he set his mind to it.'

Another answered, 'The old squire was a farmer at

heart. He was tight-fisted, but a fine gentleman never-theless, 'cepting when his dander was up, then he thought nothing of handing out a flogging.'

Marcus thought he might have liked Squire Forbes, had he met him.

'He were a devil with the women. Shocked the gentry by getting hisself wed to a fine bit of peasant stuff afore he was called before his maker, her who be married to the doctor now. No more than eighteen years of age at the time. A man could die happy with someone like that in his bed.'

Marcus couldn't help but join in the laughter when he heard Siana discussed in this good-natured way. He wouldn't mind having her in his bed himself – he wouldn't mind it at all.

'You remember that Patrick Pethan,' one said to the other one day. 'I hear it was him died in that cottage fire last season.'

'The damned fool must have had a skinful and knocked the candle over.'

'What happened to his team?'

'Two of them split off from Henry Ruddle, reckoned he was bad news. I don't know what happened to them.'

Twitching an eyebrow, Marcus smiled to himself. He did. They were buried in Cornwall. The pair had been the first to face his justice. Officially, they'd fallen down the shaft of a silver mine and broken their necks while under the influence of strong liquor.

'I hear Silas got a girl into trouble and went to sea because her brothers were after him.'

'Silas would have been no prize, him being a light-fingered cur, and all. And Henry Ruddle got hisself transported to New South Wales for life after forcing himself on a girl then killin' her, I hears.'

Marcus's ears pricked up in case Ruddle's whereabouts or circumstances had changed.

'Best place for him too. Henry was allus bragging about the women he'd had. He reckoned he took 'em by fair means or foul. God help any woman who fell into his clutches, I say, for he was a bad bugger who was too handy with his fists.'

His eyes narrowing, Marcus experienced rage scalding his insides. Sucking in a deep breath he gradually let it out, barely squashing his fury. Henry Ruddle wouldn't escape his clutches, however far away or well-guarded he was. He would wait until he was ready, then he would find him.

They covered the fields slowly but surely, the men pitting the might of their muscle against each other. There was a deceptively unhurried pace to life. The sun was hot on his back. Marcus's body grew stronger and fitter for the toil and, even though the sweat itched and chaffed at his skin, he fell into bed each night to sleep the sleep of the exhausted, and to rise in the morning eager for another day of it.

His tragic Maryse was company to his thoughts in the wakeful hours. Without success, he tried to block from his mind the broken and bloodied, sea-soaked girl whose body had flopped limply in his arms like a bundle of wet rags. The grey of her eyes had turned purple with blood, like clouds full of storm and thunder. Her body had been empty, her soul gone to where he couldn't follow.

The thought of her kept his resolve strong, but he was thankful for those deep, dreamless nights.

Sometimes he felt guilty, because he knew Maryse hadn't wanted to marry him. He'd exerted as much pressure on her to change her mind as her relatives had. More, in fact, because he knew she was troubled and knew why and he'd manipulated that to gain his own ends. He'd thought his love for her would sustain and protect her. Maryse had trusted him and he'd failed her. The need to avenge her rose like bitter gall from time to time. His veins pounded with the fury of it.

But as surely as night follows day, Maryse was beginning to slip from him, as his body began to crave a more lusty pursuit. Marcus was a man in his prime with an appetite to match. Here in the fields he was brought closer to the baser of a man's instincts. The sight of the country wenches with their nut-brown skin and their sweat-stained bodices, their hips swaying as they walked, inflamed his libido.

He'd been celibate since Maryse died, discarding his casual liaison with the widow. Now, he badly needed a woman. He must have given out signals, for an itinerant girl of about eighteen years, one who'd previously given him the eye, found him when he was seated in the pavilion in Maryse's garden, contemplating his future without his love.

He gazed at the girl, inhaling the ripe, natural smell of her bodily musk. She was handsome rather than pretty, had clear skin, knowing eyes and a full-lipped mouth. Her voice was husky with promise, her words blatantly opportunist. 'Can I be of service to you, sir?'

216

Could she? He didn't want her body, he just needed release. He contemplated that weakness for a moment, justified it to himself. Afterwards, he would function better, especially since there would be no emotion involved.

She nodded when he stated his terms. 'Not here, though. It's in plain view of the house. I'll meet you behind the hedge in a few moments.'

When he joined her, she sank to her knees and efficiently relieved him of his burden for the price of half-a-crown.

Soon, the harvest had been successfully gathered in and the supper had been celebrated in the new barn, in the usual riotous manner. Marcus knew it was time to set his plans in motion.

One day, when rain drifted down in sheets from a miserable grey sky, he went up to the nursery to gaze adoringly at his sleeping infants. 'Goodbye, my dearest little ones. I'll be back one day and you'll be changed, but I'll carry this memory of you in my heart.'

His heart swelled with pride when he looked at Alexander, his son and heir. It melted again at the sight of his sweet little Jane Louise, so fragile and beautiful. The pair of them were too young to be aware that their mother had died, and for that he was thankful. Such love he held for these two, it was going to be a wrench leaving them, he thought, as he placed a kiss on each of their delicate, rose-tinted cheeks.

But leave them Marcus did, for his course had been set long ago and now he had more reason than ever to complete what he'd set out to do. His coachman took him first to Rivervale House. It was a sad house now, silent and forlorn without Siana and the children in residence.

He found Francis in the conservatory, staring morosely out over the sodden garden. 'I have come to make my farewell, Francis.'

Bewildered, the doctor stared at him. 'Farewell?'

'I'm leaving for New South Wales, where I have urgent business. I did tell you.'

'Yes, yes, of course. I'd forgotten.'

Marcus frowned. 'As my children's grandfather, you haven't forgotten you've promised to assume responsibility for them in my absence. My nursery staff are excellent, but if you feel the need, please don't hesitate to bring the children into your home. They are so very precious to me.'

Francis nodded as he turned back to his contemplation of the garden. 'You can trust me, Marcus.'

Casually, he said, 'I'll be visiting Mrs Matheson in Van Diemen's Land. Do you have a message you wish me to deliver to her?'

A nerve in Francis's jaw twitched. 'Tell her . . .' Marcus held his breath then expelled it in a rush when Francis said flatly, 'Tell her I hope you find her well.'

'Damn it, Francis, can't you forgive Siana after all this time?'

'I would prefer it if you attended to your own business, Marcus. I haven't forgotten your part in this.'

'Only a fool is ruled by his pride.'

'I'll make sure your children are looked after. *Bon voyage*.'

'Would you dismiss me so soon, declining me the opportunity to take refreshment with you before we part?'

With a thin smile, Francis turned to engage his glance. His eyes were hollow and haunted, filled with pain. 'Since you live but a short distance from here, I doubt if you need any refreshment. You have adequately delivered your message. I'm in no mood to be preached to.'

Marcus held out a hand to him, receiving for his trouble a handshake, impersonal and without warmth. This man knew how to keep people at arm's length. 'You're a different man without your family around you.'

Francis's query reeked of indifference. 'How so?'

'You are lonely, and diminished in your own eyes, Francis. Self-pity doesn't sit well on your shoulders. I suspect you're beginning to think the decision you made regarding your responsibilities was an ill-advised one. And it was.' He smiled slightly, wondering what he'd do if Francis punched him. 'You might as well know. I care too much for Siana to leave her isolated from those she loves. I'm going to offer her a home at the manor.'

He saw the struggle in Francis to restrain his anger, and wished the man would let go of it, for then he might begin to heal. Finally, the doctor said, 'In the past, I've noticed your regard for my wife oversteps the bounds of convention from time to time. I do not appreciate the familiarity of your *friendship*, and neither do I intend to give you permission to invite Mrs Matheson to move into your home.'

Marcus chuckled. 'I don't need your permission, for Siana is old enough to make her own decision. As for my *friendship* with her, I hope to build on that.'

Having delivered his parting shot and having had the satisfaction of watching his father-in-law's shoulders stiffen and his hands curl into fists, Marcus turned on his heel and left, hoping his words would bring the man to his senses.

12

While the ship Marcus had boarded was spreading her sails to the wind at the start of her long journey, others of his acquaintance were attending the theatre in London.

Pansy, who was attending a matinée performance at the Royal Pantheon in the Strand in the company of Aunt Prudence and Justina Parsons, wished she was anywhere but here. Despite the superior ventilation system the theatre owners prided themselves on, the place was stuffy and it smelled of stale smoke. She'd developed quite a headache.

Justina prattled incessantly, seemingly torn apart by nerves in the presence of the countess. As well she might be. Aunt Prudence was easily irritated today and snapped at the unfortunate young woman, 'Do be quiet, girl.'

Justina blushed and gazed down at her hands, embarrassed by the reprimand. Pansy felt sorry for her.

Prudence turn her censorious gaze upon Pansy, who was able to cope with it more easily, since it was something she'd grown up with. 'Alder has asked his father to purchase him a commission in the army.'

'Alder told me. He'll make a good soldier and the discipline will be good for him.'

'Discipline!' Prudence said on an ominously up-sliding note. Pansy hoped her aunt was not about to make a scene, not here in the theatre. If so, she would just get up and walk out.

'Alder would look awfully dashing in a uniform,' Justina twittered, and was immediately quelled by a look from Prudence.

'Don't be so ridiculous. How can a man look awful and dashing at the same time? I am having a conversation with my niece, kindly don't offer your opinion unless it is asked for.' Prudence turned Pansy's way again. 'It's all your doing, Pansy. Alder has quite given up hope of winning your hand in marriage.'

'After all this time I certainly hope so, Aunt.'

'I'll say this for you, you're a determined young lady, one with more backbone than your poor, doomed sister ever had. You remind me of myself at your age, though I had more sense than to turn down a good offer when I saw one.'

Pansy's lips tightened.

As the orchestra began its overture, Prudence turned again to Justina. 'I suppose you'd be willing to accept an offer from Alder. After all, he is the son of an earl.'

An excited little yelp came from Justina and she began to jiggle on her seat, like a puppy about to wet itself.

'Seeing as my ungrateful niece won't have him, I might as well tell Alder's father to advise him on an alternative match. Someone must bear his children, and your money will be compensation for him. You do admire him, I suppose?'

'Oh yes, Lady Kylchester. Most dreadfully.'

The countess grimaced.

The stage curtains were drawn aside to reveal a purple-gowned woman in a tragic pose, the back of her hand reclining limply against her forehead. 'I have lost my true love to another,' the actress said and moved her hand to her bosom as she paused to gaze dramatically at the audience.

In the dim light, Pansy allowed herself a jubilant smile.

There were a variety of acts presented, songs, monologues and scenes from plays. During one of the intervals Pansy happened to notice a familiar face in the hall below. Miss Edgar with Daisy? And wasn't that Josh with his business partner next to them? She hadn't known Josh was in London. Her heart gave a series of rather alarming thumps. How handsome he was now.

Making sure her aunt was fully absorbed by the dramatics, for apart from Marcus Ibsen Pansy had told nobody of her tender feelings towards Josh, though she'd thought of him often since they'd been apart, Pansy took a pencil from her bag and began to scribble on her programme.

When they'd been small, she and Maryse had played a game. They'd stare at the back of their father's neck and see if their steadfast gaze would make him turn around and pay attention to them.

Now she stared at Josh's profile with all the love she

felt for him churning inside her, and thought she might burst from the excitement. It was wonderful to see him, and how well he looked. This was the man she was going to marry. He just didn't know it yet.

It was Daisy who saw Pansy first. Waving, she then nudged her brother in the ribs. Blue eyes turned almost lazily her way. Recognition came into them as they gazed at each other for a moment or two. Pansy felt her cheeks heat as his mouth quirked into a smile and he blew her a kiss.

The balcony scene from *Romeo and Juliet* was followed by the death scene, which concluded the performances. The two parties met in the foyer, the countess pretending Josh didn't exist. How rude of her to cut him dead. The countess's ears were twitching with curiosity, nevertheless, and she didn't walk away.

'What are you doing in London?' Pansy asked him while they waited for the carriage to be brought round.

'Buying a bit of property, and looking for Goldie.'

'Goldie?'

'We believe she's in a workhouse, somewhere.'

Pansy paled. 'Surely my father has not abandoned her.'

'He abandoned Bryn.'

Prudence suddenly lost her air of being uninterested. 'The unfortunate boy is not abandoned. At the moment he's residing with a trusted servant until a school can be arranged for him. That is a different kettle of fish altogether. And nobody could expect anything more. The boy was passed off on dear Francis as his son by your own sister. Why should he have Maryse's shame thrust upon him, especially since it caused his daughter's death?'

Breath hissed between Josh's teeth and Miss Edgar and Mr Dennings drew Daisy away to examine a poster displayed on the wall.

'Maryse's shame didn't kill her. It was the shame attributed to her by people who professed to love her one minute and condemned her the next. Perhaps it could have been avoided had she been offered the support she needed.'

Pansy gasped at that, and so did the countess, who said, 'You are too outspoken.'

'I've learned to be of late, and if Goldie isn't found soon, I'm going to be more outspoken yet.'

'Francis would not abandon the girl, you know.'

'I know of no such thing. If he has, he's going to get a shock, because when I find her I'll be taking her straight home and giving him a piece of my mind.' He gazed apologetically at Pansy. 'Sorry, Miss Matheson, but someone has to shake some sense into him.'

'That's not your place, young man. Francis has older brothers to guide him.'

Josh snorted. 'I hope the doc turns out to have more sense than they have, then. He was as happy as a pig wallowing in muck married to our Siana, and them with a litter of kids running around the place. Now he's as miserable as sin. What sort of advice was it that made him that way?'

'Don't be vulgar,' Prudence snapped, so affronted she could hardly get the words out.

When the carriage came into view Pansy dropped her reticule. As together they bent to retrieve it, she took the opportunity to slip the programme inside Josh's jacket. 'Please let me know when you find Goldie,' she whispered.

The countess moved off, her back rigid, and accompanied by the attentive Justina, who was wide-eyed with the excitement of the encounter.

When they'd gone, Josh gazed at the note, which had been written around the margins.

Dearest Josh,
Meet me by the bandstand in Hyde Park at 3 p.m. the day after tomorrow. Aunt Prudence has a card afternoon arranged. If I beg off with a headache I should be able to leave the house unnoticed. There is something I urgently need to tell you.
Pansy Matheson

He shouldn't encourage Pansy to deceive her aunt, he really shouldn't. Josh smiled to himself, knowing he would.

Daisy had been entranced by *Romeo and Juliet*. Miss Edgar had told her beforehand that the story was about a girl and boy who fell in love, but their families hated each other so they were forbidden to marry and they both killed themselves. It was romantic and sad, and the actress was so pretty that Daisy had cried when she died, and was relieved to see her alive again when the cast bowed to the audience.

Since the Countess of Kylchester had been so horrible to Josh, Daisy decided she wasn't going to marry one of the Matheson cousins, for she didn't want to have the countess for a mother-in-law. She was going to become a famous actress instead.

It was Daisy who provided the clue to Goldie's whereabouts, finding it in the window of a wig-maker's establishment.

'That's Goldie's hair,' she whispered to Miss Edgar, whose attention had been captured by the pair of matching false ringlets that had led her into thinking much the same thing. Miss Edgar had brushed Goldie's hair enough times to know it when she saw it.

'It certainly looks like it.'

They entered the shop and the governess smiled gently at the assistant when the ringlets were brought to the counter for their inspection. 'Such a pretty colour hair. Where does it come from?'

'The workhouse round the corner, madam. We buy a lot of hair from there. That colour is rare and the hair is very fine. It will fetch a good price.'

'If it's rare there won't be a market for it,' Daisy said, her sudden logic startling Miss Edgar. 'I will pay you ten shillings for it.'

The assistant gazed at her in a rather snooty manner. 'Where would you get ten shillings from?'

Remembering she was going to be an actress, Daisy looked down her nose at the woman, saying as haughtily as she was able, 'You won't be asking questions if I fetch the constable.' She changed tack, laying her hand against her forehead like the actress in purple had done.

227

'I have lost my sister. That hair was cut from her head after she was kidnapped.'

When the assistant laughed, Daisy glared at her. 'It's not funny. She might well have been murdered. However, if we discover her alive in the workhouse, my brother will pay you a generous reward.'

'How generous?'

'Two guineas.'

'Five.'

Miss Edgar gasped as Daisy picked up the ringlets and said, 'Give this female ten shillings, Miss Edgar. That's all she will get from me.' Daisy swept from the shop with her nose regally in the air.

Dropping the contents of her purse on the counter with the hope that it would cover the negotiations that had recently taken place, Miss Edgar scurried after her errant pupil in case the assistant called for a constable herself. Or worse, an officer from the insane asylum.

It wasn't until they were out of the shop and halfway back to the boarding house that a ticket for seven shillings and sixpence was discovered on the ringlets.

Josh was informed of the find straight away and, although he was dubious, the four of them went to the grim workhouse immediately, to check the place out.

When they confronted her, Mrs Tweddle gazed at the ringlets, the colour receding from her face. 'The Matheson girl is in the infirmary. She's got sickness of the lungs and the doctor has just seen her. He said she won't last the month out.'

'You stay here with Giles,' Josh told Daisy and stared hard at the woman. 'Take us to her, at once.'

Goldie was weak, pale and dirty. Fever spots burned brightly on her cheeks.

Miss Edgar took her former charge into her arms. 'Oh, my dearest. How on earth did you get into this dreadful state?'

Goldie's eyes fluttered open for a moment and tears glittered on her lashes as she whispered. 'I want to go home.'

Choked by the anger he felt, Josh could hardly speak. 'And so you shall. Josh Skinner will take you there himself. Nothing will be too good for Miss Marigold Matheson.'

'I'll have to get clearance from the doctor before she's signed out,' Mrs Tweddle told him slyly. 'It's regulations. There will be a fee to pay, of course.'

'Damn your soddin' regulations, woman. I know what you're after, and I'm not greasing the palm of the likes of you. You sign them papers quick smart, 'cause I'm taking her now. If you get in my way I'll walk right over the bleddy top of you.' So fiercely did Josh say it, the woman did as she was told, sharpish.

They left with Goldie wrapped in the workhouse blanket.

'You'll have to pay for the blanket,' the woman protested, chasing after them.

Last in line and still playing the duchess, Daisy, who wasn't about to repeat the mistake she'd made over the ringlets, scrabbled in her pocket, turned and threw a coin at her. 'Here's thruppence, my good woman. That's all the filthy rag is worth.'

'Thruppence?' Mrs Tweddle screeched. 'Is that all?'

Her hands on her hips, Daisy dropped her grand manner and became herself, glaring ferociously at the woman. 'You made money from the wig-maker from Goldie's hair, you ghoul. Now, sod off!' She kicked the woman in the shin to reinforce her words and scurried quickly out of the way.

Unexpectedly, her governess gave her a talking-to when they were safely out of Mrs Tweddle's reach. 'Don't you ever let me hear you swear like that again, Daisy Skinner. It's vulgar.'

'My brother, Josh, does it.'

'Mr Skinner is a man. A lady does not utter obscenities and kicking people is offensive. It makes you appear common. You're being too forward by far, and unpleasant to the extreme. I can only think it's because your sister's influence has been removed. Mrs Matheson would not appreciate this display of bad behaviour from you. You remember that?'

'Yes, Miss Edgar,' Daisy said, crestfallen at being reprimanded so harshly. She sighed. 'I do wish Papa would tell Siana to come home. Doesn't he love her any more?'

The expression in Miss Edgar's eyes softened. 'Of course he does. Everything will be fine, Daisy. Just you wait and see.'

'Goldie won't die, will she?'

'She will have Dr Matheson to look after her.'

'I'm staying with her too.'

'You might not be able to, Daisy.'

'I'm staying at Rivervale House, even if papa says I can't. I'll sleep in the stable with the horses.' Her eyes began to flood with tears as she thought of what Goldie had been through. Miserably, she said, 'I'll never be mean to Goldie again, and I'm not sorry I kicked that awful woman.'

Miss Edgar gave her a kiss and took her by the hand. 'I know, my dear, I felt like kicking her too. But when you give in to such impulses it makes your behaviour as bad as theirs. However, I'll forgive you this time. Now, let's hurry, else we'll be left behind.'

Now her governess was in a good mood again, Daisy decided to ask her something which had been on her mind for a while. 'Does Mr Dennings's moustache tickle when he kisses you, Miss Edgar?'

'Daisy Skinner, you little wretch!' Her face turning bright red, Miss Edgar picked up speed and, almost jerking Daisy off her feet, hurried them forward to catch the others up.

Josh left Goldie to the private and tender ministrations of the females. The poor little wretch was half-starved, welted and bruised. Her hair had become dull, matted clumps through which the scalp could be seen in parts, where the hair had fallen out. Josh called in a doctor, who examined her and shook his head. 'Best you take her to familiar surroundings where she can feel loved and cared for until she dies.'

'I hate that doctor,' Daisy said passionately afterwards, bursting into noisy tears. 'I don't want Goldie to die.'

'It's not his fault she's sick. You stop that noise, our Daisy, lest Goldie hear you. The doctor left some medicine for her to take. If she knows people love her, she might get better in time. The best thing for you to do is to be good and help Miss Edgar look after her. That way, if she does die, you know you did your best to help her.'

'Shall I say some prayers?'

'That won't hurt her none, either.'

As Daisy knelt beside the bed, her hands piously held together in prayer, she decided she might become a holy sister. After a while, praying on her knees became boring and she ran out of holiness. Rising, she gazed down at Goldie and, remembering the bracelet she wore, she slipped it from her wrist on to Goldie's.

'I took this back from that horrible common girl in the print shop. Alice, her name was. I dragged her across the counter and knocked the spots off her. And I kicked that woman at the workhouse on the leg.'

Goldie's eyes fluttered.

'Listen, Goldie, I promise to give you my allowance for a whole month if you get better. I managed to get us a big bedroom all to ourselves at Rivervale, though you'll have to sleep in the sickroom for a while.' Daisy looked around to make sure there was nobody else listening. 'I didn't really hate you all those times I said I did. Miss Edgar said I suffer from *such* impulses. I don't know what they are, but she suffers from them as well. She wanted to kick the woman too. Imagine that.'

A soft noise came from Goldie's mouth.

Encouraged, Daisy whispered, 'There's something you should know. Mr Dennings is in love with Miss

Edgar. If they get married she might ask us to be her maids of honour.'

When Goldie's fingers fluttered against hers, tears filled Daisy's eyes. 'I do love you, Goldie. Really, I do. Try and get better quickly. There is so much I have to tell you.'

Outside the door, Miss Edgar dabbed a handkerchief to her damp eyes and thought to herself that Daisy Skinner could be an absolute angel when she set her mind to it.

Josh had tossed up between boat, rail or carriage. The trip by sea took approximately the same time as a carriage. Rail was quicker, but he'd still have to hire a carriage at the other end to take them from Southampton through to Poole.

He decided on a boat, reckoning if the weather was calm it would be more comfortable for Goldie than negotiating all the potholes in a swaying carriage. After booking a cabin for the females to use, he suddenly remembered his assignation with Pansy. How could he have forgotten when he'd been so longing to see her? Consulting his pocket watch, he decided he could make it in time, if he hurried.

The sun seemed to have deserted the sky and a chill wind had sprung up. Josh stopped long enough to buy a posy from a flower-seller, then his long legs carried him through the street and into the park. By the time he reached the bandstand, not only was he out of breath, he was perspiring. He gazed round him, seeing only a couple of nursery maids with their charges, a boy bowling a hoop along the path and an old man shuffling along with a dog on a leash.

His silver pocket watch told him it was only just past three. Surely, Pansy would have waited for a few minutes. Then he saw her hurrying across the grass towards him, clasping a silk shawl against her chest. As he went to greet her, a smile spread across her face. 'Josh, I'm so sorry I'm late. Alder delayed me.'

His eyes lapped her up like the tongue of a hungry dog lapped up food. 'I was late too. We've found Goldie. She's very ill, though, and there's some doubt if she'll survive.'

Pansy gasped. 'Is there anything I can do to help?'

'I'm going to take her home and have hired a cabin on a boat going to Poole. She'll get the best attention from your father there, for I'm sure he'll not turn her away. If – God forbid – she does die, then at least she'll have some of the people she loves around her. We'll be leaving on tonight's tide.'

'Can I come with you?'

Troubled, Josh gazed at her. 'Will your aunt allow it?'

'She'll try and stop me, so I'll leave her a note.'

'Doing this will soil your reputation, Pansy, my love.'

'I know.' Her eyes were very blue as they gazed into his. 'Am I your love, Josh?'

'Surely, you are, Miss Matheson,' he teased, and he handed her the posy he'd bought. The thought of declaring his love for Pansy Matheson was rather awe-inspiring, and he didn't know quite how to proceed.

She looked at the flowers in her hands and smiled. 'Then I'll marry you.'

Something lurched sideways in the region of his heart. 'I'm not good enough by half for you. 'Sides, I'm supposed to ask you.'

'Don't you want me, then?'

The glimmer of a smile touched his lips at such a ridiculous notion. How could he not want her? 'Your father wouldn't approve.'

'I'm of age where I don't need my father's permission. We could elope to Gretna Green.'

'We'll do no such thing, for I respect you too much,' he said sternly. 'First, I'll seek your father's approval, then I'll propose marriage to you. If you accept, we'll be married properly.' A grin stretched across his face. 'By crikey, I'd be so proud that I'd want to flaunt you in front of the congregation like a prize pony at the fair. I'm not having that old termagant aunt of yours telling people you're fast.'

'You funny, old-fashioned thing. I *am* fast.' And she flung her arms about him. 'Kiss me, Josh Skinner?'

'Try to stop me.' He took her face in his hands and kissed her sweet mouth, hoping his inexperience didn't show, happiness buzzing through him like a hive of honey bees. It was wonderful and felt so right.

'*Well, well*, Pansy,' someone drawled, sending them springing guiltily apart. 'No wonder you were in such a hurry to get rid of me. You thought you had me fooled, didn't you?'

'What are you doing here, Alder, you sneak.'

'Looking out for your welfare, you stupid little fool. Did you really think you could fob me off on to Justina Parsons?' Grabbing her by the arm, he jerked Pansy forward. 'If you want to elope to Gretna Green it will be with me. By the time we get there you'll have no choice but to accept me, I'll see to that.'

Pansy lost the colour from her face. 'You wouldn't dare. Let me go, Alder. You don't know what you're doing. You've been drinking, I can smell brandy on your breath.'

'Unhand her, you lout,' Josh said quietly.

Releasing his former fiancée, Alder took off his coat and began to roll up his sleeves. 'I'm going to give you the thrashing you deserve, Skinner. How dare you come sniffing round my cousin like a mongrel after a bitch in season. She's not for the likes of you.'

'You mind your language in front of Miss Matheson.'

Pansy grabbed her cousin's arm. 'Don't you dare hurt him, Alder.'

Flung off, she staggered backwards. When she recovered, Josh calmly handed her his coat, lest it be torn. It was tailor-made and he hadn't had it long. He smiled calmly at Alder. 'When you're ready, sir.'

Alder's fists came up and he crouched into a boxer's stance. Josh waited for him to make a move.

Alder sneered, 'Aren't you going to defend yourself, you coward?'

'I shouldn't be at all surprised.'

When Alder's fist shot out, Josh caught it, turned and jerked. Taken off balance, Alder somersaulted to sprawl on his back. Josh was still on his feet and waiting when Alder staggered up again.

His next move brought the same result. Josh rolled on to his back and threw Alder over his head. Josh was on his feet in a trice, blessing Marcus Ibsen who had taken the trouble to teach him the art of self-defence.

Losing his temper, Alder began to lash out at random, expending his energy and rarely landing a blow. Josh was able to predict and counteract every move without inflicting damage on the man, though he knew that if Alder got a hold of him he wouldn't stand a chance. Soon, Alder was out of breath and perspiring heavily.

'Had enough?' Josh asked him pleasantly.

Alder shook his head, staggered to his feet then collapsed at the knees and sank heavily onto the grass.

'I think you have.' Josh turned to Pansy. 'Miss Matheson, under the circumstances I think it would be safer if you came back to the boarding house with me. Miss Edgar and Daisy will be sufficient chaperone until I can place you in your father's care. I'll send a message to your uncle to let him know what has occurred, so he doesn't worry.'

They left Alder to his own devices. He hurled foul curses and threats after them as they walked off.

As they left the park Josh turned to see a pair of constables heading Alder's way. He grinned to himself. Alder was going to spend an uncomfortable night.

It was late in the morning. Francis was surprised to see Josh Skinner's carriage come up the carriageway.

He was even more surprised when Daisy jumped out of the vehicle, followed by Miss Edgar. His heart lurched when he saw Pansy. He'd thought she was being safely looked after by her aunt. Without thinking, he smiled at the sight of her. How well and happy she looked. If a little travel weary.

Jolted out of his melancholy by the surprising event, he headed downstairs and out of the front door. He was just in time to see Josh alight from the carriage with a still figure in his arms. His breathing seemed to stop. 'Goldie,' he whispered. 'What has happened?'

There was an accusing look from Daisy when Josh said, 'You may well ask. We found Goldie in a London workhouse. She is ill. How ill I'll leave you to discover for yourself.'

Pansy said to Josh. 'Take her inside and up to the sickroom. We'll care for her there. Miss Edgar, show Josh the way, please. Daisy, go with them and help make Goldie comfortable.' Pansy then turned to him. 'Are you coming, Papa?'

'Of course. But first, do you not have a greeting for your father after all this time?'

'I'm too heavy-hearted to indulge in social niceties. Goldie is sick unto dying. Why did you not take better care of her?'

Francis's ears began to burn as he was suddenly confronted with the unhappy consequences of the prolonged length of his grieving for Maryse. It had been so dark a time he hadn't realized he was being totally neglectful of others.

'But I had letters from her, saying she was well and wished to stay in London with her brother. And I sent money, for she said her brother was not well off and she needed new clothes.'

'Her brother has been dead for many months. Goldie

238

was robbed and thrown onto the street. His wife and her daughter are fraudsters, perhaps worse. A former employee suspects that they murdered Sebastian Groves and intended to blame it on Goldie. But we will not know the truth unless she recovers. The doctor who examined her in London thinks it unlikely, though.'

Drily, Francis said, 'The London doctor is obviously unaware of the recuperative power of clean air and country fare.' He gave her a quick hug. 'Dearest Pansy, I have no excuses for my behaviour, but the sight of you and Daisy has brought me wonderfully alive again. My heart is full to bursting.'

'And so is mine. Oh Papa, I am finally in love.'

'With Alder? I'm so pleased.'

'No, not Alder. My cousin has shown his true colours now and I find his nature to be despicable in the extreme. He was prepared to compromise me to get his own way, You should know that he was planning to abduct me, and carry me off to a hurried ceremony at Gretna Green, giving me no choice but to return to my family and friends with with my character besmirched.'

Startled, Francis gazed at her.

'Then who?'

'That, you will hear from his own lips. He will speak to you when he is ready and the opportunity arises, making his intentions known.'

She smiled and hugged him in return then, bringing such a warmth of love tumbling through him that he wanted to cry from the ache of knowing everything he'd missed over the dreadful, black months that had passed since Maryse had left them.

'First, Goldie must be attended to, for everything else must be secondary to her welfare. Shall I fetch your bag?'

'No, I shall not need it.'

A few minutes later it was with a heavy heart that he gazed down at the frail young girl he'd taken under his roof, and had now failed.

Daisy slid her hand into his. 'You'll make her better, won't you, Papa?'

Francis recalled a time where Daisy had been suffering from the same disease, as a baby. Against his advice, Siana had flown in the face of convention, using a controversial manner of body-cooling treatment which had pulled Daisy through. As a last resort, he would use it, too.

'I'll make her better. I promise.'

Francis knew he was about to have the fight of his life on his hands. It was a fight he was determined to win.

13

Thank God it wasn't consumption, was Francis's first thought. Nevertheless, Goldie was extremely ill. There was very little fluid in her lungs, which was a blessing. She had a dry cough, producing a minimum of mucus, but her muscles offered him hardly any resistance. Her skin was hot and dry, and when he gently pinched it between his finger and thumb it was slow to return to its natural state. Her stomach was beginning to bloat, too. She was suffering from dehydration and malnutrition.

Pneumonia was not always fatal, Daisy was living proof of that. But a body which had been deprived of basic nutrition had no strength to fight off infection, so became a breeding ground for all types of illnesses, which could easily be passed on to others. Until Goldie ingested some fluids, Francis wouldn't even know whether her other organs functioned as they should.

If the air was humidified and he got plenty of fluids into her, with an infusion of savoury, willow bark and honey to treat her fever and cough, as long as bacteria didn't take advantage of her weakened state she just might pull through.

Francis brought in Noah Baines to confirm his diagnosis.

Noah's prognosis was a little less encouraging than his own. 'As you're aware, Francis, a patient with pneumonia can deteriorate very quickly. Goldie will need observing night and day. She already has pustules on her body, which indicate a bacterial infection in the blood. If that spreads to her lungs it's unlikely she'll recover. I would advise that she be nursed in the infirmary, for I'm not sure that your personal involvement will be in her best interest.'

'You mean, you consider I'm not sufficiently recovered from my recent bereavement to cope. I assure you, I am, Noah.'

'Good. It's about time, Francis.'

Miss Edgar exchanged a glance with Pansy, who stated firmly, 'There's no question of placing Goldie in the infirmary when we can offer her the best of attention here. We'll all take turns looking after her, Papa. And a couple of the maids can help out during the day.'

'And me. I want to tell her about the theatre,' Daisy said.

'Not you, Daisy. You're not old enough.'

'Siana would have allowed me to help Goldie if she hadn't been sent away.'

There was an awkward silence, one during which Francis tucked Goldie's arm under the covers. He was astounded by the change in Daisy since he'd last seen her. It was as if he'd woken from a long sleep to discover everything had passed him by. How old was she now? Eleven years? Getting on for twelve? As far as he could see, her body remained undeveloped, but there were signs of a new maturity in her thinking.

'I'm aware only that your services wouldn't have been needed if Siana was still here, for she wouldn't have allowed Goldie to remain at her brother's house for such a prolonged length of time. Therefore, Goldie wouldn't have been in the workhouse in the first place However, past action and the consequence of it cannot be undone, it can only teach us to act differently. When Goldie has recovered some strength, then that is the time for her to hear the exciting adventures of Daisy Skinner in London. Then, and only then, will I allow you five minutes with her each day, in the company of your elders. But what I'm interested to learn is the story of how you found her. Perhaps you could write me a journal of your time in London, so I can read it for myself every evening after dinner.'

Mrs Edgar smiled slightly at that, for she'd discovered Daisy's secret journal and knew her employer would find it entertaining and illuminating reading. 'I'll provide you with a journal in which to record your adventures,' she said, hoping Daisy would omit certain passages pertaining to herself in the new one.

Reassured that she wasn't being sent away and, for once, the absolute centre of Francis's attention, Daisy beamed a happy smile at him. 'Perhaps I'll become a famous author and write a play like William Shakespeare's *Romeo and Juliet*.'

An ambitious project for a child who'd always found spelling a chore. Still, Francis nodded encouragingly at her. He'd always found Daisy's nonsense refreshing and

243

saw no harm in nurturing her various dreams for her future. 'Yes, perhaps you will.'

The crisis came suddenly in the early hours of the morning. Goldie's temperature rose alarmingly, causing convulsions. Miss Edgar roused Pansy, who in her turn roused her father.

Used to being woken from sleep, Francis came rapidly awake and emerged from his room a few moments later in his shirt and trousers, buttoning up his waistcoat.

The sounds of people rushing back and forth woke Daisy. Fear stabbed her to the core. Creeping from her bed she went to sit on the stairs, where the moon shone through the big window on the landing, making the colours glow. She was shivering all over, partly from fear for Goldie and partly from cold, though she never thought to fetch her robe and slippers.

She remembered Siana sitting in this very spot, sometimes, looking with sadness in her eyes at the mother and boy in the stained-glass window. Her sister had told her once that the boy reminded her of her lost son, Ashley Forbes. She said she liked to imagine the woman cupping his head was Megan Skinner, their dead mother.

Daisy couldn't remember Ashley Forbes very well. His death had coincided with Bryn coming into the house and the two boys always merged as one in her mind.

Where was Bryn now, and her sister? Did Siana feel unhappy living away from her family? Daisy knew she'd be left alone if Goldie died. Papa wouldn't want her then, for he was not her real papa. Somebody called Bill Skinner was.

Daisy couldn't remember either of her parents. Tears gathered in her eyes. It was hard being an orphan. She remembered Goldie was an orphan too, and Goldie didn't even have a brother now. At least she had Josh, and a sister as well. Pulling herself up, she crept up the stairs and through the open door of the sickroom.

What were they doing to Goldie? She was naked and they were slopping water on her. Goldie began to moan and jerk. There was a horrible sound of chattering teeth.

One of the maids had told Daisy about the noise her father had made when he was dying. 'It be called the death rattle,' she'd said. 'His eyes rolled up in their sockets and he foamed at the mouth. He looked something terrible, like a madman. His mouth was all stretched tight in an 'orrible smile and 'is teeth went clackity clack.'

Daisy gave a small, terrified sob.

Her attention drawn by the noise, Miss Edgar looked up, hurried over and guided her to the door. A hand in the small of her back gave a gentle little shove to propel her through it and towards her own room. 'Go back to bed, at once, Daisy.' The door closed, leaving her standing alone on the landing.

Panic filled her. She wanted her sister. Siana would make everything all right. She always did. Driven towards Siana's bedroom for comfort, she found the door locked.

Not that it mattered. The keys were all the same, for she and Goldie had tried them all one wet day, locking every door. She took a key from the nearest door and inserted it in the lock. The bedroom door creaked as it opened, and she almost expected to see Siana sitting in front of the dressing table. The moonlight poured through the window, showing an unmade bed with Siana's nightgown still lying where she'd left it.

'Siana,' she whispered. 'I'm scared.'

The room was cold, it smelled stale and dusty. As Daisy picked up her sister's nightgown a faint perfume of wildflowers and pine needles was released. Immediately, Daisy felt comforted, as if Siana was close to her.

Creeping under the covers she curled into a ball, hugging the nightgown against her cheek. 'Siana, Josh told me you have a very rare sense given to a few special people, and sometimes you know things or are able to help people without being told. So please help Papa to save Goldie's life.'

It was strange, but Daisy seemed to hear her sister's voice softly singing a lullaby. With tears streaming down her face, she began to sing it softly, too. Siana had told her it was a very special lullaby, one their own mother had sung to Daisy when she was a baby.

'Baby of mine, the sun has gone down and the shadows creep in like a mouse. But safe in my arms I'll keep you from harm till the morning light blesses our house . . .'

As Daisy imagined Siana's arms warm and comforting around her, peace gradually crept through her body, relieving the tension. 'Come home to us soon, Siana,' she whispered, just before she fell asleep. 'We need you.'

*

246

It was first light. Francis gazed sadly at the tear-stained face of Daisy, who was curled up in Siana's bed for comfort. He was racked with guilt, for his grief had caused him to lash out and, in his pride, he had punished the innocent.

He looked around him, at the dusty room, at the vase of wildflowers, now brown and brittle. The clock on the mantelpiece was quiet, the hands stopped at three minutes past four.

Did she still think of him, his beautiful, fiery peasant girl? He brought to mind the property in Van Diemen's Land. Siana would like the countryside there, for its wild and rugged beauty would probably appeal to the pagan side of her.

Marcus Ibsen, he thought, then frowned. His son-in-law had made it clear that he admired Siana more than was healthy. A streak of something akin to jealousy crept into his mind. Damm it! He was a grown man, not a callow youth. Why did he still feel this way over a woman who had deliberately deceived him?

Francis didn't want to think about Siana's deceit, because it brought Bryn to mind.

He was about to go and tell Miss Edgar he'd found Daisy when a streak of sunlight lit on a shard of glass scattered on the dressing table. The piece of paper lying next to it caught his attention. Siana's parting letter, the one he hadn't been able to bring himself to read. It was yellowed now. No doubt it contained an elegantly penned apology, for she was nothing if not eloquent, despite her lack of early education.

He stared at it, curiosity tugging at him. Finally,

deciding that whatever Siana had had to say to him then, couldn't possibly affect him now, he crossed almost impatiently to the dressing table and picked the paper up, his fingers trembling as he unfolded it.

Dearest Francis,

I have no excuse to offer you, but you must know I deceived you for the best of reasons. When you allow yourself the time to think about this, you, with your generous heart and your compassion for those less fortunate than yourself, will understand. I was driven by love, love for Maryse and for a helpless infant who was faced with a future of hardship, or no future at all.

I hope you can find the charity in your heart not to withdraw from Bryn the only possession of real value a parent can offer a child, the feeling of being loved.

My dear love, I cannot bring myself to regret my action. Bryn eased my heartache when I was grieving for our own dead infant. He is part of my heart, for Maryse lives within him. If I'm to be sent away, please be kind to this child, who is innocent of any wrong and should not be punished for the sin of his father. His mother was truly blameless.

Francis, I understand your anger. Know I will love you always.

Siana.

Damn this woman of his for trying to manipulate him! She wasn't even sorry for what she'd done. God, how miserable he'd been without her.

Marcus had said he'd offer Siana a home at Cheverton Manor. How dare he try to come between husband and wife? That would make a fine scandal in the district, his wife living with another man. Be damned if he'd have it. He didn't trust Marcus, and he was aware of the nature of his wife. Would she accept Marcus for the ease it would bring her? Would she seduce him with her eyes and body, as she'd often seduced Francis himself? He felt sick at the thought.

He remembered the softness of her, the way she teased him and laughed, her eyes sparkling. Then there was the pliant softness of her mouth when he kissed her. Sometimes, he remembered, she grew restless at being housebound and her eyes would turn to the hills. She would walk for miles and come back refreshed, her cheeks aglow and the mystery of the earth in the soft, mossy green of her eyes. Siana was his enchantress and he loved her. *Dammit! He did still love her, despite her deceit.*

But now he could do nothing more useful than to examine the depths of his own heart, and wait.

Daisy sat up in bed, rubbing the sleep from her eyes. Her hair was a tangled flaxen mess from where she'd tossed and turned. She gave a small cry when she saw him.

'I'm relieved to find you here,' Francis said.

From her heart came a plaintive plea. 'I want Siana to come home. I miss her.'

'I know, Daisy. So do I.'

A question grew in her eyes, along with dread. 'Goldie died, didn't she?'

He shook his head, grinning with his own sense of jubilation. 'She's out of danger now. You can see her later on.'

Scrambling from the bed Daisy ran across the room and hugged him tight. 'I knew you'd make her better, Papa. I told her so.'

'Thank you for having such faith in me,' he said gravely, for he was aware the girl needed a great deal of reassurance, despite her bravado. 'It's going to be several weeks before she'll be strong again, though. Come on, we must let Miss Edgar know you're all right. She's going frantic because she thought you'd run away.'

'I'm sorry, I wasn't trying to hide. I was worried about Goldie and I just wanted to be close to . . . someone.'

'And were you?'

She gave a little smile. 'I dreamed that my sister sang me a lullaby, like she used to when I was small.'

'Aye, you would remember that.' He ran a finger down her pert little nose, remembering hearing Siana sing it. 'Come on, I'll take you to Miss Edgar before she calls out the constables to search for you. You won't be punished.'

He handed Daisy over to her governess and made his way downstairs. It appeared to be a cold, bright day outside. The sun shone through the hall window, sending rainbows of light into the dimmest corners.

Opening the front door Francis stepped outside to take a deep breath of the crisp air. It was early, frost rimed the shadows on the lawn. Illuminated by the rising sun, the colours around him sparkled and shone, as if they'd been freshly painted onto the earth.

The world looked different to him today. The thin finger of a sunbeam touched against his face and pulled him into its golden light. He closed his eyes, allowing it to fill his body as his skin absorbed its warmth. He laughed for the first time in many months, feeling enriched by it, then turned and went back indoors. He would breakfast with his family today, then visit his patients.

It was with a lighter heart that he set out on his visits to the sick and afflicted. Abbie Ponsonby of Croxley Farm was pregnant again, despite his advice to the contrary. He smiled to himself, wishing there was some way to control her fertility. Abstinence obviously was not an option. All he could hope for was that Abbie's age would take control of her fertility after this one.

After that came Reverend Richard White, whose condition had been worrying Francis for the past few months. The reverend was showing increasing signs of advanced heart disease and he needed to rest. He must talk to his second cousin, who happened to be the reverend's superior, if he saw him at Christmas, and see if an assistant could be obtained for Richard.

But the church was part of the Cheverton Estate and perhaps Marcus Ibsen wouldn't be prepared to fund an assistant. Not that the man was in residence so he could not be asked in any case.

The size of the congregation had fallen since Siana's first husband, Edward Forbes, had died. The rule for compulsory church attendance by the estate workers had been done away with. Francis knew Richard was not well off. If the church decided to retire him, where would he go? He should, perhaps, broach the subject with Richard before he talked to anyone else.

The reverend was asleep in his chair in front of the fire when Francis reached the rectory.

Rosie, Siana's former maid until Francis had summarily dismissed her, stiffened, casting a reproachful glance his way when he walked into the kitchen. She was just putting the kettle on the hob. 'I'll fetch you in some tea when it's ready, Dr Matheson.'

'The reverend is asleep. I don't want to disturb him. How has he been over the past few weeks, Rosie? Has the tincture done him any good?'

'Aye, it helps when he gets puffed. If you asks me, he's not long for this world and he knows it. He misses her, who was here before me. But I don't know why he should be so taken with her. Some people are put on this earth to be destructive, and that Welsh shrew was one of them. I told him, "You had a lucky escape, for she had her clutches into you, all right."

'"Now, Rosie," says the reverend, "be charitable. Miss Lewis didn't know the trouble her words would cause."

'"Then she should've been charitable herself and sewn her mouth shut," I told him. For that interfering spinster forced herself on to others as family, when she wasn't invited. She broke the hearts of some good people around here, them whom I loved. Her wicked tongue deprived some innocent cheils of their parents, too.'

Her voice lost its fierceness and she dabbed a corner of her apron against her eyes. 'Though I daresay I shouldn't be saying it to you, Dr Matheson, you being the husband of my former employer. I miss my girls

252

something terrible. Though, mind you, I wouldn't desert the reverend in his time of need. A nice gentleman he be, though lonely.'

'Miss Goldie, Miss Skinner and Miss Matheson are now back home at Rivervale House,' Francis said awkwardly, for he hadn't considered how his actions would have affected others. 'Goldie has been very ill. If you wish, you may visit them in a week or two.'

Rosie stared rather damply at him through her dark lashes. She was a tall, plain-looking woman of late middle age. Francis had never noticed her much before. Vaguely, she reminded him of someone else. A smile parted her lips and her amber eyes began to shine. 'Thank you kindly, sir, I should certainly like to.'

'You're from these parts, aren't you, Rosie?'

'Born to a maid up at Cheverton Manor and farmed out to one of the village women. My mother ran off to London when I was five, and I never saw her again. I never knowed who my father was, either. The old squire, he who was father to Edward Forbes, fetched me back to Cheverton Manor when I be just twelve years old, and I was put to work to earn my keep. Very nice he was to me too, said he wished he had a daughter just like me. The poor old gent died not long afterwards.'

Noblesse oblige, thought Francis. The responsibility of a true gentlemen. But where did Bryn fit into such a moral convenience? Should he bring up the lad as a groom or a gardener? Was there even room in his house for the consequence of a violent assault on his daughter? If there was, how could the truth be kept from the boy? There were things Francis thought he must think about without being too hasty in reaching a conclusion.

He heard Richard give a rattling cough. So there was fluid in his lungs, as well. He must check the man's ankles to see if they were swollen.

Rosie began to butter some scones, which she served up with blackberry conserve and some bread and butter.

'I can always put the reverend in the infirmary towards the end, Rosie,' he said quietly.

'There be no need for that, sir. Most likely the reverend will go easy in his sleep one night. When he can't get up the stairs, I shall have his bed brought down to the parlour. He can shuffle to the church with my help on Sundays and has all the sermons the Welsh spinster wrote for him.

'Fire and brimstone, they be, and he lacking the energy now to deliver them as he should. That Wynn Lewis had the gift of the gab all right, and an evil eye to go with it. When she dies, no doubt the horned man will have her basting on a spit over his coals, and good riddance to her, if you asks me. I hope she burns to a crisp for what she set in motion.'

Francis tried not to laugh as he said ironically, 'You're a good woman, Rosie.'

Her smile told him she was pleased by the compliment. 'Folks is as folks does, I always say. Now, off you go, sir, and take a glass of sherry with the reverend. He needs the company.'

So Francis spent a good two hours being company, for there was really very little more he could do for the reverend, except make him comfortable and listen to him talk about the past.

'I made a mistake not marrying again after my wife died,' Richard said with a sigh. 'A man shouldn't journey through his life alone, but should have a good woman and children to fulfil him.' His eyes met those of Francis. 'I helped Edward Forbes deceive Siana into marrying him. It has long been on my conscience.'

'I'm not your confessor, Richard, and I know when you're leading me somewhere I don't want to go.' Francis growled, realizing he was condemning himself with his own words when he stated, 'Siana was happy in her short first marriage. Edward convinced both himself and her that she was loved. Thankfully, he didn't live long enough to disillusion the faith she had in him.'

'You've never been easy in the presence of faith, have you?'

'The dogma of the church annoys me. I've seen too many innocents die of disease brought about by lack of food, hygiene and shelter. There is too much hypocrisy in this good Christian country of ours.'

'Man is born of sin and you're angry because you're unable to acknowledge your own hypocrisy. Siana is part of you. She's the beat of your heart, the warmth in your arms, the fire in your loins. Siana loves you. Don't throw that away, Francis.'

Francis managed a smile. 'I didn't realize you were prone to such poetical turns of phrase, Richard. But please, kindly keep your parson's nose out of my personal business and concentrate on regaining your health.'

Richard chuckled. 'You don't fool me, Francis. And

since the Lord has me marked, I will disregard your advice by saying exactly as I please. I must admit, though, it's gratifying to discover you've regained some of your fight.'

'Such pride, and from someone who professes to be but a poor servant of the Lord,' Francis mocked. 'If God exists, I doubt whether you're that important to him, my friend.'

'I doubt it too, but I prefer to believe in life after death, then I'll know my time on earth counted. Rest assured, when I arrive at my destination I'll tell Maryse your grief for her was so profound, it excluded those who loved you most.' With that, Richard's eyes drifted shut and he began to gently snore.

Francis said softly, 'Dammit, Richard, I've never been able to win an argument with you. Don't do me any favours, for I'm doing a good job of pricking my own conscience at the moment.'

He didn't win that argument either. Richard died peacefully in his sleep a week later.

The new incumbent appointed by the bishop arrived in time to conduct Richard White's funeral. He was to be buried next to his wife.

Reverend Samuel Brannan was thin and upright. He had a kindly smile, a plump, pious-looking wife, two daughters and two sons.

The whole parish attended the funeral. After the funeral service the new reverend smiled benignly at the congregation. 'It seems my predecessor was well loved in his parish. So if any would like to speak on his behalf, please come forward.

Rudd Ponsonby shuffled self-consciously from his seat. 'I don't be much of a speechifying man, but I'd like to say my piece. The reverend was a right nice gentleman. Kind and helpful he was, to me and my family both. I hope God has a special place for him in his heaven.'

'Amen,' someone in the pews shouted out. 'The reverend give me some coal from his own cellar when I didn't have a ha'penny to my name.'

'And he gave me a dinner every night, when I was alone with the horses at Cheverton Manor,' a tall young man said, determined not to be outdone. 'Up till then I was eatin' oats and straw.'

'Didn't do thee much good, did it?' someone said. 'You'm be as tall and as thin as a willow stick.'

'I hears 'im neigh when the moon's full, Rob. And 'is eyes be all of a pucker.'

'It must have been all the horse manure he was standing in that done it. Some say 'tis good for making roses grow, but 'e don't look like a rose, do 'e, Tom?'

'Not 'zackly, lessen that bit of fuzz be a flower blooming on his upper lip.'

The tall young man sat down, flushing to the roots of his hair.

'Now 'e looks like a rose, don't 'e?' Rob said.

Francis smiled when the congregation began to laugh uproariously.

The new reverend rose hastily to his feet, saying authoritatively, 'Ladies and gentlemen, I would ask you to show respect for the dead. Pall bearers, perhaps it's time to take the coffin to the graveside.'

Mrs Brannan sniffed, shepherded her children in front of her and headed back towards the rectory, a determined look on her face.

So many lives gone, Francis thought a few minutes later, gazing around him at the several Skinner headstones, a family to whom Siana claimed kinship through Josh and Daisy. In the fenced-off area, there were Siana's first husband, Edward Forbes, and young Ashley, the son Siana had borne Edward. How it must have torn her heart out to have lost that son. And their daughter, Elen, buried on the Welsh hillside where she'd been born.

His own daughter Maryse was with her mother. A sob caught in his throat. For years he'd mourned his first wife, despising his own inability to save her life. It was Siana who'd brought him back to life. Her devotion to her sister and her brother, in spite of the despair of her destitution, had filled him with an admiration which had swiftly turned to love.

Siana had strength. She would still have that strength as she waited for word from him to come home. But would she come home to him now, after all this time? His woman had a mind of her own and acted on it. And there was Marcus to think of, a man of singular attractiveness, with whom Siana had formed a strong bond of friendship. How she'd laughed off his jealousy when he'd mention it. But would she still be laughing now?

The graveside prayers had been said, and a fine drizzle drifted down from a grey sky. People set off on wagons, horses and by foot, to get home before darkness fell. The road would be churned up by nightfall.

Someone pulled at Francis's sleeve. It was Richard White's lawyer.

'There will be no formal reading of Reverend White's will,' he said. 'He didn't have a great deal, but his late wife's dowry had been invested since their marriage and has grown into a useful sum. There are only two beneficiaries. One is Bryn Matheson. Richard suggests the legacy either be used for a decent upbringing and education, or be held in trust until the boy comes of age. The decision is yours to make. I'd be much obliged if you would step into my office the next time you're in Poole, Dr Matheson, so the sum can be handed over.'

'And the other legatee?' Though Francis didn't really need to ask.

'Your wife, Siana Matheson. The reverend has left her his entire library. He said he couldn't think of anyone better able to appreciate his books. You should arrange for their removal from the rectory as soon as possible.' Tipping his hat, the lawyer hurried off towards his rig, leaving Francis staring after him.

So, Richard had allowed him the last word on Bryn, after all, and in more ways than one. But Francis wasn't sure he was ready to pronounce it.

On the way home he stopped to pick up Rosie, who was struggling along the road hefting a heavy bag.

'That new reverend's wife couldn't wait to get rid of me,' she said. 'Packed my bag herself, she did, and left it in the porch. She said she and her daughters are quite capable of doing the housework and it was best I leave now. That be after making me scrub the house from attic to cellar last week and polish all them windows. She didn't even pay me my wage. Bleddy hippocratics, that's what they be.' Sitting on her bag she buried her head in her hands and wailed, 'What's to become of me?'

Jumping down from the rig, Francis helped her to her feet then picked up her bag and threw it into the buggy. 'I'll make sure you get your wage, Rosie. And you'll come home with me, where else would you go?'

14

It was the end of November before Goldie had the strength to leave her bed. Escorted by Daisy she walked across the room on thin, wobbly legs, grinning with the triumph of the challenge.

'Good,' Francis said, smiling himself, for Goldie's hair was a mass of bobbing, reddish gold curls where her hair was beginning to grow back. 'Don't overdo it. You must rest every afternoon until I say otherwise. And you need to gain some weight, so I expect you to eat all your meals.'

Rosie beamed a smile at the girl. 'Don't you fret, Dr Matheson. I'll make sure she eats every morsel.'

'Can Goldie move out of the sickroom now, Papa?'

'Haven't you got some lessons to do, Daisy?'

'You gave Miss Edgar a day off so she can go into Poole to do some shopping.'

'So I did. I don't see why Goldie can't be moved. I'm sure Rosie has seen to it that her bed is properly aired. But don't tire her out.'

'I won't.' Daisy sent a loving smile Goldie's way. 'I'll read you my journal, then you can see how we found you in London. I might write a play for when you're better. Papa gave me an idea for the title, The Amazing Adventures of Daisy Skinner in London. We can pretend to be famous actresses, then.'

With a title like that, Miss Daisy Skinner is bound to be cast as the heroine, Francis thought wryly, as he went down to the drawing room where Pansy was playing the piano. She stopped playing when he entered, gazed up at him and offered him a smile when he kissed the top of her head.

'Keep playing. That's a pretty piece.'

'It's a sonata by Franz Schubert. Aunt Prudence taught it to me.'

When she finished playing it he sat next to her on the piano stool and murmured, 'Do you remember this?' He started to play Maryse's favourite song, by the same composer.

Her head resting against his shoulder, Pansy began to softly sing, 'Who is Sylvia? What is she when all her swains commend her . . .'

They gazed at each other when they finished, appreciating this shared moment of closeness. Pansy kissed his cheek when he pulled her against him in a hug. 'Will we ever get used to Maryse leaving us so cruelly, Papa?'

'We'll have to. I'm glad to have you and the girls back, though. I've been remiss in my parenting, and for that I'm sorry. Everything came as such a shock and I thought of nothing but my own grief when, of course, you were grieving too.'

'Dearest Papa. You have been through such a lot. I forgive you . . . we all do.'

'And Siana,' he said heavily. 'Will she forgive me too, do you think?'

'She may, as long as you haven't broken her heart completely.' When Pansy stood and shook the creases from her skirt, Francis knew his daughter had left much unsaid. She was wearing a gown of pink watered taffeta topped by a fur-trimmed velvet jacket. Her hair was in ringlets, her eyes shone and roses bloomed in her cheeks. She was all woman now, as if Maryse's death had wiped away every trace of her childhood.

'You look beautiful today. Is something special happening?'

'Oh, Pa. You know very well that my . . . that you're to have a visitor today.'

'This swain of yours . . . he's waited a long time to declare himself to me.'

'He wanted to wait until Goldie had recovered, so you could pay proper attention to his suit. He's also a little . . . shy.'

Though Francis knew exactly who her intended was, he couldn't help but tease her. 'I don't see why you can't tell me who this mysterious man is. Are you ashamed of him?'

'Certainly not.' She shrugged. 'But he's uncertain of his status and wants to speak to you himself, so he can convince you of his worthiness.'

'Pansy, my dear, I trust your judgement in this. I want you to know how sorry I am that I ignored your feelings when I tried to press you into a match with Alder.'

'You're my father and sought only to do what you

thought was best for me. I can understand that.' The glance she gave him was full of appeal when they heard the sound of a horse and buggy outside. 'Please be kind to him, Papa,' she said, and turned to leave. As he heard her footsteps patter up the staircase there came a knock on the door.

Francis's eyes widened in shock when he opened it. 'Giles Dennings?' *Surely not!* 'But I thought . . .? You'd better come through to my study and take a glass of sherry with me, Giles.'

'Thank you, Dr Matheson. That's very kind of you.'

He couldn't allow it, Francis thought, pouring the golden liquor into glasses and handing one to Giles. He gazed at him over the glass. 'I'm prepared to give you a fair hearing, Giles, but I'll tell you straight away, I'm not in favour of a marriage between you.'

Placing the glass back on the table, Giles stiffened. 'Why is that, sir?'

'She's far too young for you.'

'But Sylvia is only a few years my junior.'

Francis stared at him. 'Sylvia?'

'Sylvia Edgar.'

'You mean you're here to ask me for the hand of *Miss Edgar* in marriage?'

'No, Doctor. I don't need your permission.'

Francis began to laugh. 'Forgive me, Giles. I've made a blunder. I thought you were here to request the hand of my daughter.'

'Miss Matheson?' Giles's eyebrows nearly disappeared into his hairline. 'Good Lord! I'm old enough to be her father. I'm here to collect Miss Edgar

264

and take her into town.' He picked up the sherry again, sipping it appreciatively. 'It's Sylvia's hand I'm after. If she accepts me I shall be the luckiest man alive and I'm afraid you'll have to find yourself another governess.'

'Accept my best wishes, then.' Francis glanced at the door when there was a tentative knock. 'Come in.'

Miss Edgar peered inside. She was handsomely turned out in dark blue. Her demure bonnet was trimmed with a posy of silk flowers and she carried a fur muff to match the trim on her jacket.

'How becoming the ladies of my household appear today,' Francis murmured, astonished to discover that his jaundiced view of everything had changed, so his surroundings and everyone in them appeared in a quite different light.

Surprise came into her eyes. 'Thank you, sir. Have you seen Mr Dennings?' She blushed when she saw her intended standing to one side. 'Oh! There you are, Giles.'

'Would you like a glass of sherry to ward off the cold, Miss Edgar?' Francis offered.

'No, thank you, sir. I rarely drink alcohol at this time of day.' Her glance darted towards Giles, her expression slightly schoolmarmish.

Smoothly, Giles informed her, 'Neither do I. However, on some occasions one cannot avoid being sociable.' He grinned as he swallowed the last of his drink. 'Thank you for your best wishes, Doctor. I must be off.'

Francis smiled and nodded to him.

'Best wishes . . .?' Miss Edgar was saying curiously as the door closed behind them.

Josh felt as if he was in a muck sweat. Running a finger under his cravat, he lifted each foot and polished the toes of his already immaculate boots on the back of each leg.

His double-breasted frock coat was of the latest style, with gathered sleeves and shaped back panel. Donkey brown in colour, it toned nicely with the fawn of his braided trousers.

His man, Mr Bentley, had advised him on the outfit. 'Very understated, sir, as befits a successful gentleman of business. We don't want to appear flamboyant now, do we?'

Who would have thought he'd come to this, proposing marriage? Siana, that's who. 'The women will be after you like a flock of seagulls,' she'd once told him.

Although that wasn't exactly the way things had been, there had been one or two women to show him the way of things, and several more who'd been attracted by his wealth. None of them could measure up to Pansy Matheson, who was gilt-edged in his book.

Mr Bentley had still been handing out instructions as Josh had left the house. 'Now don't you go fidgeting with yourself, sir, for a more turned-out gentleman you couldn't wish for. You're a real credit to me, even though I say so myself. Remain polite, but be a bit humble as you state your case, for the young lady is well-bred and her father will want only the best for her. A gentleman doesn't forget to remove his hat. Hand it with your coat and gloves to the servant in the hall.'

'What if there isn't one?'

'Then be positive and lay them on the hall stand. Have you got your gift for the young lady, sir?'

Josh patted his breast pocket and grinned. This was one surprise Pansy wouldn't be expecting.

'Giddy-up, Alder,' he'd said, and the horse had tossed its head, then given a spirited whinny and high-stepped towards the gate, taking Josh towards his future, he hoped. The beast had been springy with pent-up energy and he'd taken a firm grip on the reins, cautioning, 'Whoa, boy. Your former master has already given me a tumble I won't forget. As soon as we're out in the countryside I'll let you stretch your legs.'

He'd enjoyed the journey as much as the horse had. Now he stood outside of Francis Matheson's study, cleaning the dust from his boots on his trousers and feeling extremely nervous.

'Come in, won't you?' Francis called out impatiently, for the second time.

Josh sucked in a deep breath and opened the door. As he removed his hat and placed it on the chair, he groaned. He'd forgotten every one of Mr Bentley's instructions.

Francis rose quickly to his feet, concern on his face. 'Are you ill, Josh?'

'Who me? I've never been ill in my life, 'cepting when that damned fool nephew of yours tried to break my neck. Now, his horse is trying to do the same. I named it Alder, after him. It gives me great satisfaction when I have to lay the crop across his contrary arse.' That's right, Josh, make a good start by criticizing the man's nephew.

But Francis just smiled. 'The horse is a thoroughbred, he's bound to be mettlesome.'

'Whereas a non-thoroughbred is just troublesome, aye?'

Francis was not about to be drawn, and merely nodded. Josh cleared his throat and decided to get straight to the point. 'I have some business to discuss with you, Dr Matheson.'

'Would you like a glass of sherry first?'

'No, sir. I'm not partial to the stuff. I might need a brandy afterwards, though.'

'That bad, is it?'

'What is?'

'The business you intend to discuss with me, Josh.'

Josh gave an audible gulp and his words came out in one breathless rush. 'Ah that . . . it's about Miss Matheson, I intend to marry her if she'll have me.'

In the ensuing silence Francis picked up a paperknife and tested the blade against his thumb, saying softly, 'Do you . . . do you indeed?'

Josh kept his eyes on the knife, wondering if it was sharp. Francis was reputed to have a deft touch when it came to surgery. 'What I mean is, I'm here to ask for permission to marry your daughter, if you'll allow me. And if she'll have me, of course, so much the better.'

Francis looked up then, the expression in his eyes one of amusement. 'Do you love Pansy, Josh?'

'Love her? I'll say I do. Crikey, I get all of a pucker just thinking of her.'

'Why don't you sit down, Josh? I'm getting a crick in my neck looking up at you.'

Josh forgot about his hat until it buckled under his rear. Pulling it out from under him, he gazed ruefully at it, then shrugged. 'Dammit! Mr Bentley will have a piece of me when I get home. He's trying to turn me into a gentleman, though I keep telling him he's flogging a dead horse. I never could get the knack of wearing these things.'

'You certainly don't wear them on your backside. Now, about Pansy.'

Josh smiled broadly at him. 'You know how much I'm worth, Doc. Well, perhaps not, for I'm not really sure of that myself. I know Miss Matheson is far above me, but for all that, I think I'll be able to make her happy. She'll want for nothing.'

'Naturally, I don't want Pansy to live a life of poverty, but money isn't everything. I know how hard you've worked, Josh. I've admired you for that. But my greatest wish is for Pansy to be happy.'

With desperation in his eyes, Josh gazed at him. 'I'll do everything in my power to make her happy.'

'I know, Josh, so there will be no opposition to the match from me.'

The wind seemed to go out of Josh. Suddenly, he remembered the things he'd meant to say. He remembered his gift for Pansy and took the wad of papers from his pocket. 'Miss Matheson isn't the type to languish about the house playing the lady. I reckon she's got a brain on her that would put mine to shame, and it will need exercising.'

Puzzled, Francis nodded, interested in Josh's reasoning, nevertheless, since it concerned his daughter. If Pansy had been a man he would certainly have encouraged her to attend university and study science.

'With her having more than a touch of the Countess of Kylchester's influence trained into her, it got me to thinking she might decide to meddle in a man's business in years to come . . . no offence meant, of course.' Josh gulped and dropped the papers on to the desk. 'So I bought her this as a token of my deep regard. What do you think?'

Francis only just stopped himself from laughing as he unfolded the papers and scrutinized them. He looked up, his smile fading and shaking his head from side to side. 'You've bought Pansy a school?'

'Only a small one. The main part has two classrooms and has enough pupils enrolled to pay the bills. There's also a small outbuilding. It's full of junk, but if I clear it out and fix the roof it will serve as a classroom for some of the young uns from the workhouse. D'you think she'll like it?'

Francis reached out for the decanter. 'I think it's me who needs the brandy.' He began to laugh then, a loud roaring guffaw that would have woken the dead if the cemetery hadn't been a couple of miles away. 'A token, you call it. Most men would give their intended a brooch or a bunch of flowers. Only Josh Skinner could have thought of a gift like this.'

Anxiously, Josh said, 'But will Miss Matheson like it?'

'It isn't exactly a romantic gift, but, knowing Pansy, she—'

'– will love it,' Pansy said from the doorway, grinning when she gazed at her father. 'Well, Papa, will he do?'

'Most certainly. But you didn't need my permission, since you are both of age.'

'I told him that when I suggested to him that we run away together to Gretna Green. But he insisted on doing things his way. Men can be infuriatingly conventional, and I did so much want to put Aunt Prudence's noise out of joint,' she fumed. Pansy's words set Francis laughing all over again after they left, because Josh had compared Pansy to Prudence, and she'd sounded just like her. Then he sobered, wondering if his family would attend Pansy's wedding, since Pansy had jilted her cousin Alder in favour of Josh.

She'd also incurred the earl's displeasure by being extremely rude to him. Ryder had written to him at length to say Pansy's behaviour had appalled him. Pansy had offered no excuses except to avoid his eyes in a most embarrassed way and say, 'We quarrelled over a family matter, the subject of which I cannot relate to you. I lost my temper and became indiscreet.'

How indiscreet, Ryder had seen fit to inform him of.

Pansy had written a formal letter of apology to the earl, humbly begging his pardon, which was more than had been required of Alder when applied to the crime he'd committed against Josh Skinner.

Pansy was unrepentant, though. 'I've written this letter because the earl is your brother, and because you are my beloved father and you've asked it of me,' she'd said.

Still, Francis was pleased there had been no argument over it, because he had other things on his mind.

Francis having informed the authorities of the suspicious death of Sebastian Groves, as soon as Goldie was ready, the magistrate, Sir Oswald Slessor, came to the house with his clerk to obtain written statements from Goldie and Daisy.

Daisy gave a highly embroidered account of her part in the rescue. She seemed put out by the fact that she probably wouldn't be called upon to testify at the Old Bailey.

'We have Zeke to take the witness stand and a statement from Josh Skinner about what happened at the print shop. As long as Mr Skinner's account of what happened on that day at the shop coincides with yours, the statements will be accepted without you having to appear in court, since you've signed them in front of a magistrate.' Sir Oswald smiled broadly round at them. 'I imagine the girl and her mother will confess when pressure is brought to bear on them. If they don't, it's possible Miss Goldie might be called to take the stand, since she was an eye-witness. However, as Mr Skinner is an upstanding businessman with a considerable amount of property to his name, I'm sure his sworn word will suffice.'

'I'm scared in case Alice's Uncle Ned comes for me,' Goldie said.

'You don't have to worry about him, my dear. Her uncle is currently awaiting transportation for the term of his natural life.'

'Will Betty Groves hang?' Daisy asked the magistrate with a certain amount of relish.

'It depends entirely on the judge, my dear. I doubt if

the girl will, for she's young and would have been influenced by her mother. It's possible they'll be transported for life to New South Wales or Van Diemen's Land.'

Daisy gave Francis an accusing look. 'My sister is in Van Diemen's Land. She's been there a long time.' There was an awkward silence. A sob catching in her throat, Daisy rose to her feet and scurried from the room.

Francis didn't go to comfort her. In fact, he intended to give the girl a talking-to. It was just one example of Daisy's constant manipulative behaviour concerning Siana, and he wasn't about to bow to pressure. He would not insist on Siana's continued banishment if she wished to return, but he had no intention of inviting her to come back. Her deceit and its consequence was still an open wound inside him.

It was Bryn who was causing him problems, for the boy's absence was all the more noticeable by mention of his name being avoided. Francis sighed, knowing he'd prevaricated too long, and needed to make a firm decision.

So, later in the day, when Daisy stood in front of him looking angelically penitent, he was more lenient than he'd intended to be.

'I know you miss your sister, Daisy. So do I. However, you must not embarrass our guests by discussing our personal family matters with them. Siana will be home before too long.'

Undeterred by his stern voice, Daisy gave him a guileless smile. Her blue eyes searched in vain over the letters on his desk, then lit with curiosity on the crested card placed prominently on top of the pile. 'Papa, you never tell us anything. Have you received a letter from Siana, then?'

'No. This is an invitation to join my brother at Kylchester for the Christmas festivities.'

'And shall we go?'

The invitation was for himself and Pansy alone. Gruffly, he said, 'I haven't decided.'

'They've only invited you and Pansy, haven't they?'

She was astute. 'What makes you say that?'

'While you were away and we all thought you were drowned, your family never once invited Siana to stay. The earl and countess visited once, but uninvited, and only to inspect Bryn.'

Ah . . . someone had uttered his name, at last.

'The countess was unbearable. She kept nagging my sister to wear mourning for you, even though Siana didn't believe you were dead. And she tried to take Maryse and Pansy away. She wanted them to live with her, but they didn't want to go. In the end they *had* to. There was always an argument when it was time for them to come home.

'The countess said she was the one who raised your daughters and they shouldn't be living with someone from an inferior class. The earl said that since you had regarded Siana as a suitable stepmother for them, then so must they. The countess then went snorting and stomping all over the place and looking down her nose in fury.' The girl lowered her voice. 'Siana cried when Maryse and Pansy had to go away with the countess. She is a witch on a broomstick, really.'

'That's something a well-mannered girl should not say.'

Although he sympathized with Daisy's indignation at Prudence's interference, he tried to keep a stern expression on his face. He was interested in what Daisy was telling him, despite his reluctance to gossip with her. She had seen events through the eyes of a child, but what a perceptive eye she had. Her makeshift journal had born testament to that. 'Why didn't Siana believe I was dead?'

'She said it was hard to explain. She said you were joined by an invisible thread, and she could feel your heart beating inside hers.' Daisy gave a big sigh and placed her hand against her heart. 'So romantic, like *Romeo and Juliet.*'

Another nail in the coffin of his guilt. Then another, for Daisy's bright blue eyes suddenly impaled him. 'When is Bryn coming home to us?'

Uncomfortable under her scrutiny, he shifted things around the desk with his finger. 'I don't want to discuss Bryn.'

'I know what happened to Maryse.'

'Do you, Daisy?'

'People talk, and they think children don't under-stand. And sometimes children don't, but they remember things. As they grow older they piece those things together. I know I'm horribly precocious because the countess tells me so every time she sees me.' Daisy's hand slid across the desk and gently stilled his. 'We all loved our brother and you loved him too. Siana said love is too precious to be thrown away, so why did

Maryse punish us all by choosing to take her life, when we loved her so?'

Tears glinted in Francis's eyes as he gazed at this girl, so immature, but wise beyond her years. It had taken a great deal of courage for her to stand there in front of him and say what she did. Her question deserved an answer, one he didn't have.

'I don't know, Daisy. Perhaps Maryse had suffered too much and didn't consider the effect her death would have on others. People who carry out such acts are usually in an altered state of mind, so what seems rational to them, is irrational to others.'

He rose and came around the desk. 'I don't feel strong enough to talk fully about this yet, but I do appreciate your concern and have taken note of what you've said.'

Her arms came around him in a hug. 'I do love you so much. I wish you were my real papa. Don't make Siana choose between you and Bryn. She will do as you ask because she loves you, but part of her will shrivel and die without Bryn. We all miss him, you know.'

He held her for a few moments, a lump gathering in his throat, touched to the core by both her admission, and her attempt to counsel him. Siana, mine, he thought. Why was I such fool, to send you away at a time when we needed each other the most?

Marcus Ibsen said he would send her home. Francis knew that, if he could trust in the man's power of persuasion, she would be here by the spring. But would she still want to be his wife, or would she move into the heart and home of another?

*

Siana spent Christmas with the Stowe family.

They ate outdoors, where a pig was roasted on a spit over a pit of hot ashes. It spat and crackled allowing a delicious aroma to escape into the air as they took turns to rotate it. There was a dish stuffed with vegetables to accompany it, and a large pie filled with sliced apples to follow.

The elder Stowe boy had invited a family from the nearby town to join them, for he'd recently asked for their daughter's hand in marriage.

Siana couldn't get into the Christmas spirit here. The weather was too warm and she wondered what her children were doing. She constantly missed them all, and pictured them missing her, especially Bryn, whom she longed to have back in her arms. If she'd been alone, she would have broken down and cried for all the lost hours and the horizons of empty ocean between herself and those she loved.

Francine was on her best behaviour. She chuckled and smiled all afternoon until Siana took her into the bedroom to be fed, where she fell asleep against her breast.

'She's such a good baby,' Jean said, gazing down at the infant's dark, curling hair. 'I haven't asked you before because I didn't think it any of my business. You look so unhappy today. Is there anything I can do?'

'I'm just homesick. I was thinking of my brother and my children, wondering if they were keeping well and happy. My husband too.'

'Dr Matheson? He spoke so well of you when he

was living here, I can't imagine him deserting you completely.'

Tears trickled down her cheeks because Christmas had made her loss seem very great. She no longer felt strong, just angry and heartsick, because she'd never believed Francis would do anything so cruel and she was beginning to believe he was right, that she had been responsible for Maryse's death.

Convinced as Siana was that Francis would one day come for her, nothing would convince her that Bryn deserved to be deprived of the only family he knew and loved. No matter how much she loved her husband, she knew she'd be unable to return to him until that issue was resolved.

'I deceived Francis, Jean. I caused his daughter to take her own life. At the time, I thought my actions were a solution to a problem. But it just made it worse.'

Jean's arms came around her, holding her tight as the story poured from her. Finally, Siana fell silent. It had been such a relief to confide in someone, but what would the woman think of her now?

'I would have done exactly the same thing,' Jean said slowly. 'Grief affects people in different ways. Once your husband has thought about it he'll come to the same conclusion, I'm sure, for I formed the impression he was a man of compassion and good sense.'

Handing her a handkerchief to dry her eyes on, Jean gazed at her. 'I'm glad you've told me. It helps to share troubles. Dry your eyes now, for Bart will get his fiddle out soon, and the boys intend to dance you off your feet before they escort you home.'

Home? This wild, turbulent landscape with its wondrously strange animals and towering plants could *never* be her home. The native people who'd once lived here had been cruelly dispossessed, those who were not killed, hunted down and removed to a remote island to live. Sometimes, Siana could hear the melancholy voice of their sadness in the keening sigh of the wind. Mothers crying out for lost children, children for their homes and men for the loss of their pride.

Their spirits sometimes seemed to call her into the wilderness. The lure of it was almost irresistible, for she was vulnerable to it. If she answered their calls, instinct told her she'd be lost for ever. So she stayed within the boundary of cleared land around the house, and the well-trodden path to the stream and pool.

Dorset was her home. She closed her eyes, reaching into her mind for a fleeting image of daffodils in a lush green meadow. The air there was a pot-pourri of salt and pine resin, and the wind spun and tumbled the leaves on the beech trees. She reached further into her mind, grabbing images of undulating waves of golden wheat, gnarled and mossy roots pushing from the dark floor of the woods, and the mist rising from a quiet river, the surface dancing with mayflies. Then came a church-yard, quiet except for the wind sighing through the pines. There was a woman standing by a grave, holding a child.

'Who are you?' Siana murmured, already knowing it was her mother. When they turned towards her she saw the child in her mother's arms was green-eyed and dark-haired. He smiled at her, whispering, *Mamma*.

Then the image was gone, replaced by a seagull gliding on the wind.

Peace filled her as the image left her. Opening her eyes, she gazed down at Francine. The children were alike. Her firstborn, her dearly loved son Ashley, wasn't dead at all. He lived on in his sister.

Siana knew she'd been given a message. As usual, she didn't question her gift of the sight, for how could it be explained? She must make the right choice, else everything she'd worked towards since her mother's death would be for ever denied her.

She understood there would be two paths open to her and she would have to trust in her instincts to guide her.

'Sleep tight while your mother dances, little one,' she said. 'Soon things will change, for a messenger is on the way.'

15

While Siana spent a warm Christmas in Van Diemen's Land with her neighbours, in England, Francis had travelled to Kylchester Hall, in the county of Hampshire.

Having declined to spend Christmas there the year before, he had been undecided whether to accept the invitation to attend the family festivities at Kylchester this year. But he was aware that he had an important decision to make regarding Bryn, and he needed to consult with his brothers. So far, they hadn't pressured him in any way, but the question of the boy's future could not be delayed any longer.

He decided to take all the children with him, invited or not. Goldie was wrapped warmly for the journey. Her cheeks glowed with the excitement of spending Christmas at Kylchester Hall, for she was much in awe of the earl and the countess. Daisy had already begun to practice the airs and graces she thought she'd need for the occasion.

'The name Daisy is so plain,' she said to nobody in particular as they neared their destination. 'Perhaps I should choose a better name? Charlotte perhaps, or Adelaide.'

'For goodness sake, Daisy, your name is so very pretty. Just be yourself,' Pansy urged, rolling her eyes at her father, as the carriage neared the hall. 'You're perfectly all right as you are.'

Prudence nodded to herself when she set eyes on the two younger girls, as if she'd been expecting them. 'Ah, the children are back with you. I did wonder if you'd bring them, so I instructed the servants to air the bedding and light a fire in the room next to the one Pansy usually occupies. They are too grown-up for the nursery, but I've assigned a maid to look after their needs.'

At which pronouncement Daisy gazed at Goldie with an excited grin. Yet afterwards, overwhelmed by the grandeur of Kylchester Hall, Daisy was suddenly struck dumb. She clung to Pansy's side, though she managed a graceful curtsy when Prudence swept forward to greet them. It earned her an approving smile, and a kiss on the cheek from the countess, who slanted Pansy a sideways glance. 'I do so like a girl who has graceful manners.' She turned to peer closely at Goldie. 'You look pale, girl. Have you been ill?'

Dumbly, Goldie nodded.

'Goldie has suffered from pneumonia recently. She is improved, but is still recovering her strength,' Francis told her.

'Goodness, how unfortunate. I do hope she's strong enough to join in the jollity.'

'She is stronger than she looks. She must rest, of

course, but I wouldn't have brought her if she wasn't up to it. The change will do her good, too.'

'Allow me to dose her up with some blackberry tonic while she's here, then. It will soon bring the roses back into those cheeks. Come, give me a kiss then, my dear. We don't stand on ceremony here, especially at Christmas.' Which wasn't exactly the truth.

When Pansy moved off with the girls Prudence turned to him. 'My dear Francis, you look so much better than the last time we met. Your grief is lessening, I think. Such a shock to all of us. Rest assured, though shock made me speak hastily at the time, I have not mentioned Maryse's unfortunate episode to anyone.'

Maryse's unfortunate episode? How neatly the crime and the agony had been packaged, so it rolled off the tongue in a civilized manner without causing distress. Just as Siana had said, his daughter had been a victim. But then, even he, her father, who should have known better, hadn't seen it that way at the time. Prudence was such an insensitive woman, but he knew she meant well. He stooped to give her a kiss. 'My grief will never be less, Prudence. Neither will my guilt.'

'Guilt? You have nothing to feel guilty about. Now, we must forget sad events and have a jolly time together as a family. Your stepchildren are welcome, of course. A pretty pair. In fact, I rather like the cut of that Daisy.'

'Daisy is my sister-in-law.'

'Quite so, but because she regards you as her papa, one forgets. I'd assumed she'd been sent to her live with her brother.'

'Daisy brought Goldie home from London, and insists

on staying with her. No doubt you will be regaled with her role in the affair once she relaxes, for she admires you.'

'Like her sister, the girl has spirit. In fact, if the girl was quality she would be described as precocious, which is not a bad thing to be, since it gets one noticed by the right people. I was a precocious child myself.'

'Really, Prudence?' he said drily. 'One would not believe such a trait ever existed in you now.'

'Training and discipline, my dear. There's nothing like it. But Daisy's admiration of me has a dubious foundation. I confess that I'm ashamed of my reaction regarding the tragedy, since Maryse was subjected to an advance not of her making. You know, I would not have hurt the dear girl for the world and will be everlastingly remorseful of my conduct. If only Siana had asked for my advice over the matter I would have given it willingly. It would have been less of a shock for us all, then. The tragedy could have been averted, for the child would have been farmed out and none would have been the wiser.'

Francis wished she'd stop talking about it. 'Except Maryse, who was prevented by Siana from taking her own life over the matter at an earlier time.'

'Such a solution at the time would have been preferable to prolonging the difficulty. Now you have the child to deal with.' Francis only just restrained himself from placing his hands around her scrawny neck and choking the life from her. She must have sensed his anger, for she said lamely, 'Not that it was something I'd have wished to happen, of course.'

'Of course.'

Pity came into her eyes. 'You must allow your brothers to advise you while you're here, for the matter of the child cannot be delayed any further.' She took his arm and lowered her voice. 'But first, I wish to talk to you about Pansy and Alder. It is not too late, you know. Alder has held back on offering for the hand of Justina Parsons. Although I should tell you that he intends to accept her parents invitation to visit over Christmas. If he's turned down by her, although an affirmative answer is a foregone conclusion, of course, for the girl is quite gone on him, then Alder will take up a commission in the army. His patience over the affair is now quite at an end.'

So was Francis's. 'You should advise Alder to offer for Miss Parsons right away, then. Pansy is now promised to Joshua Skinner.'

'Joshua Skinner?' Prudence exclaimed with a dismayed gasp. 'That young man trounced Alder in a public park.'

'I understand Alder was both inebriated and aggressive at the time, and was arrested shortly afterwards,' Francis said. 'His conduct towards my daughter was ungentlemanly.'

'Be that as it may, Alder was defending his cousin's honour against a man who was trying to remove her from the bosom of her family.'

'Alder's plan was to abduct her. It was Josh who defended Pansy. He prevented her from being compromised and forced into a marriage she has never wanted. Moreover, he behaved perfectly properly by informing the earl of the unsavoury event and placing my daughter under the chaperonage of Miss Edgar, until he could bring her home. Which he did as quickly as possible. Joshua Skinner is a fine young man, of whom I thoroughly approve. They love each other, Prudence. I will not stand in the way of their happiness.'

'Does Pansy realize that many doors will close to her if she weds beneath her?'

'But surely not the doors of those people who are worth more than a damn to her, Prudence. You, for instance, wouldn't be unpleasant to a girl you've always professed to love. I've always considered you to be more generous in spirit than your bluff manner indicates. Ryder wrote and told me he'd informed you of what had taken place. You do understand that a marriage between Alder and Pansy is completely out of the question now, do you not?'

Colour seeped under her skin as she flustered, 'Yes, of course. Ryder has already counselled me on the matter.'

'Good. Then I hope you will heed him, for if Pansy is caused any embarrassment I will remove my family from your hearth forthwith, and will never return.' With his head slanted to one side he regarded her, hating to be obliged to put her so firmly in her place. 'I hope we can remain friends, for I have never regarded you as being deliberately vindictive.'

'Dearest Francis, you above all others know that I have always done my best for your girls, even though I may have been thoughtless at times.'

'And I've always appreciated it.' He kissed her on the cheek. 'Good, we understand each other, then. Now, where can I find Ryder?'

'In his study with Augustus. The pair were being disgracefully unruly, so I sent them packing from the drawing room.'

As he set off up the staircase Francis smiled at the thought of his two eldest brothers being sent from the drawing room in disgrace. No doubt, they'd have instigated their departure deliberately.

He heard the exchange of laughter before he found them. They were comfortably ensconced in leather armchairs at either side of a roaring fire, a couple of glasses and a half-empty bottle of brandy standing on the table between them. It was late afternoon, the lamps had not yet been lit, firelight licked at the panelling and shadows danced across the ceiling.

'Ah, Francis. Nice to see you this Yuletide, we missed your presence last year. Fetch yourself a glass and pull up a chair. Gus and I were just discussing how the conspiracy to turn you into a parson fell by the wayside, despite being christened with the name of a saint. Luckily, I have a son who leans towards the pious, and who will redeem the family honour in that profession.'

'Hmmm, he obviously doesn't take after his father, then. How are *you* finding married life?' he said to Gus, pouring a small amount of brandy into a glass and warming it between his hands.

His brother's smile had a contented edge to it. 'A man can get comfortable, but I must admit, marriage takes the excitement out of the chase. Still, I'm to become a father in May. Constance is hoping for a son.'

Something squeezed painfully at Francis's heart. 'My congratulations, Gus. Obviously there's life in the old sea dog yet. I hope you get your wish. How's the rheumatism, Ryder?'

'In this weather, painful.' The earl grinned. 'It helps enormously when the new maid massages my knees with warm peppermint oil. Unfortunately, Prudence hovers over her giving instructions. Lord, the countess is a martinet. Still, she was a good breeder of sons, for which I'm grateful, even though one of them is a fool. Is the delightful Siana with you?'

'My wife is still in Van Diemen's Land.'

Ryder leaned forward in surprise. 'After all this time? Surely you do not intend to leave her there in that isolated place, Francis? It would be such a waste.'

Staring into his glass he murmured, 'I have reason to believe she'll be returning to England before too long.' He changed the subject. 'Will Beckwith and Raoul be here for Christmas?'

'They intend to travel down from London together. Beckwith's wife and children arrived yesterday.'

The muscles in Francis's haunches bunched to lift him from the chair, for had a sudden urge to rush upstairs to the nursery to see if Bryn was there. With an effort, he managed to relax them again, said carelessly, 'Did they bring the boy with them?'

The earl's eyes sharpened. 'Of course not. While he's waiting to be apprenticed to the Royal Navy, he's been farmed out to a former servant, Lucy Tisk, who lives in

Christchurch. The Marine Society's naval school will have a place available for him in the new year. I did write to you about this.'

'So you did. It slipped my mind.' Which was an outright lie, for he'd deliberately put it from his mind as soon as he'd filed the documents away out of sight.

'It's a respectable society of which the late Lord Nelson was once a council member. I arranged the placing myself,' Gus informed him.

'But Bryn is only five years old.'

'The boy's nearing six. By the time he's fourteen he'll be educated, and will have been taught seamanship to a high level of proficiency on board a training ship before being signed on as a midshipman. It's an ideal solution for boys such as Bryn. As his guardian, all you need to do is sign the papers. Did you bring them with you?'

'Unfortunately, no. I meant to, of course.'

The earl sighed. 'Ah, yes, of course, I do not doubt that for a minute. Beckwith thought this might happen, so he intends to bring another set with him.'

Francis felt as if a noose was being tightened around his neck. Although he knew he'd already prevaricated too long over this matter, he prevaricated a bit more. 'When he died, Reverend White left money for Bryn's education, enough to take him through university later in life, or invest for his future.'

'Did he, by God! That was good of him. It will compensate you for the cost of his apprenticeship. He will grow up to be independent, but grateful to his benefactor, you'll see.'

Nearly two years ago Francis had been Bryn's father,

not his benefactor. He sipped at his brandy, feeling the darkness of his grief hovering at the edges of his mind. All the while, he wondered if Bryn would remember him if they met. He tried to squash the recollection of the love and pride he'd once held in the boy.

There came a knock at the door, then Raoul and Beckwith slipped inside, bringing with them the smell of horses and an aura of the winter cold outside the house. Long-legged Beckwith, the tallest and quietest of the five brothers, chaffed the cold from his hands. Raoul grinned from ear to ear at the sight of his brothers. The pair helped themselves to a brandy apiece and slipped to the fore to warm their backsides in front of the fire.

Once his father's study, now Ryder's, the room hadn't changed since Francis's childhood. There was a contented feel within it as the brothers chatted companionably together, as they always found time to do when they were together. Francis couldn't remember ever being unhappy during his upbringing, for his brothers were always there for him, as they were now.

The room was familiar to them all as a place of punishment. He could remember his late brother, William, hanging over the very chair Ryder was now seated in, having a birch laid across his rear, while he himself waited with great trepidation for his turn. Neither of them had cried out in front of the other, for that would have been to show weakness. He grinned as he remembered his backside being on fire, and guessed William's had been the same.

As if he read his thoughts, the earl chose that moment to lift his glass and murmur, 'To our brother, William.'

They drank to William's memory, then Ryder said, 'This Christmas, brother William's ghost has the fair Siana to keep him company.'

'Siana's still abroad?' Raoul drawled. 'You should bring the girl home before she takes a fancy to some other fellow. She's too young, and too exquisite a creature to be neglected.'

Francis couldn't ignore the stab of dismay he experienced. He was about to protest that his and Siana's was not a marriage arranged for convenience, but a true love match, when Ryder turned to Beckwith and said, 'Did you bring the papers from the Marine Society with you?'

Beckwith nodded, throwing the satchel he was carrying into Ryder's lap.

Francis demurred when the earl opened it. 'I'd like a little more time to think about this, Ryder.'

'Only two hundred boys a year are taken into the Marine Society naval school, so you cannot afford to lose the place reserved for him,' Gus pointed out. 'The papers must be signed while we are here, so you might as well do it now. Once the unpleasant business is over and done with we can enjoy the festive season and Ryder's hospitality without the question of the boy's future hanging over us.'

The desk lamp was lit, the papers were spread out in the circle of its glow on the table. The seal had a pair of comical sea dogs supporting a circular plate, within which a woman gazed down at a young lad. The design within the circle reminded Francis of the window on the stairs at Rivervale House. His train of thought brought

Siana into his mind, not that she was often far from it. If she'd been with him she'd have fought him tooth and nail over this issue, for where the children were concerned she allowed her emotion to cloud her good sense.

She'd told him she was expecting an infant before she left!

He shook his head. Surely it had been a ruse to soften him? If she could lie about an issue as important as Bryn, a smaller lie would mean nothing to her. He hardened his heart. 'Do we have pen and ink?'

Writing implements were brought. Ryder and Beckwith flanked him, Beckwith saying, 'We'll witness your signature, then Ryder will affix the Kylchester seal.'

Francis felt under pressure. He wasn't usually so indecisive about issues, but this one had been put aside while he'd grieved for his daughter. 'I would like to read the papers first.'

'There's really no need, Francis. I've examined every word. All is in order and you have already delayed the matter too long.' Beckwith handed him the pen. The nib glistened. The ink was the consistency of blood and the colour of the berries on the deadly nightshade. 'All you need to know at this point is that there's no room for negotiation and the contract is legally binding. Sign there.'

Bryn Matheson. Birthplace. Wales. Parents unknown. Benefactor: Francis Matheson.

All this to lift the stain from his dead daughter's character, when she'd been an innocent victim of the affair. Nothing could hurt Maryse now, but wasn't Bryn an innocent victim too?

Thinking about it was painful, much better to let his brothers do it for him. Francis placed the pen against the space left blank for his signature. Suddenly a line from the letter Siana had left him came into his mind, so vividly he could almost hear her voice whisper it accusingly against his ear.

I hope you can find the charity in your heart not to withdraw from Bryn, for the only possession of real value a parent can offer a child is the feeling of being loved.

But he wasn't Bryn's parent, he told himself with a certain amount of anguish. He was the boy's grandfather. *Damn Siana and her deceit! Damn her to hell!* How dare she bring this child into their happy home and pass him off as his? No wonder she'd called Bryn her cuckoo child.

As he angrily applied pressure against the pen a globule of ink rolled from the nib on to the page, like a shining, black teardrop.

Flinging the pen in the direction of the fireplace, Francis swore.

Marcus was having a comfortable journey.

His fellow passengers, having lost their earlier pretensions as seasickness robbed them of their dignity as well as their stuffing, had withdrawn to their cabins until they improved. They'd emerged one by one, whey-faced, to amuse themselves with cards. The majority were bad losers, becoming boorish and unpleasant when they lost to him.

There was one exception, a young woman travelling unaccompanied to join her brother in Hobart Town.

Her name was Julia Hardy, and her brother was a parson. She was no great beauty, being tall for a woman. Her straight brown hair was drawn severely back from her brow in a style that was unflattering. But neither was she plain. Her nose was neat and her brows well-shaped. When she smiled, her brown eyes sparkled and charming little dimples appeared in her cheeks. Her mouth formed a pleasant curve, too, with no lines of discontent.

Julia Hardy was capable, keeping herself busy helping women with children, who were afflicted with seasickness. The woman took it all in her stride, no task seemingly distasteful to her, from washing clothes to nursing the sick. She carried out her duties unobtrusively, her services taken for granted rather than commented on with gratitude. She didn't have the air of being a servant but rather, it seemed, she was used to being of service.

Julia Hardy interested him, so he cornered her when she was hanging some children's clothing on a makeshift line to dry, threading the cord through the sleeves so the garments couldn't fly away on the breeze. 'You're a paragon of virtue, Miss Hardy,' he told her. 'Would you care to spare some time amusing a perfectly able man who craves a little of your time and feminine attention? A woman of your station should not be bent over a tub of suds.'

Julia had a sense of humour, gently chiding him for his attempts at gallantry with a broadside. 'Charming as your approach is, Mr Ibsen, I *have* no spare time, for Mrs Morris and her children are in an unenviable state due to the motion of the ship. As for my station, I'm under no illusions as to that. I was raised up to keep house for my father, who was a penniless parson, and am travelling to join my stepbrother and his wife, who are of modest means and have three children in need a tutoring. I've been made aware of my lowly role in the family hierarchy, but have very little choice, since I've nowhere else to go. And since I'm plain and have no money of my own, I know I'm destined to be *craved* company for only as long as this journey lasts. You must find some way of amusing yourself, without me.'

The fact that she'd known his name gave him hope, though he was seeking nothing more than her companionship, for any romance on board ship wouldn't go unnoticed or remain uncommented upon, and that would badly mark her reputation. After that, though, he took the trouble to waylay her whenever he could.

Eventually, she relaxed in his company. He found that the more he grew to know her the more he liked her, for not only could Miss Julia Hardy indulge in an intelligent and lively conversation, there was nothing false about her. They began to play chess together in the salon every evening, in the company of the other passengers, totally absorbed in their game.

Towards the end of the journey, when he finally allowed her to win her money back, she grinned triumphantly, though he thought she may have seen through his ruse. 'There, Mr Ibsen. I have trounced you, at last. It's about time somebody did.'

'So you have, Miss Hardy. It's a warm night, would you care to take a turn around the deck? We might be able to see the lights of Hobart Town.'

The sails above them sang as the breeze slid from their surface. The rigging creaked, the dark sea hissed and slapped against the hull.

Marcus nodded to the first mate, who stood at the ship's wheel, a smile on his face as the ship respond to his overtures. 'A nice night, Mr Johnson.'

'It is that, sir. If the wind remains fair, we should be slipping into port tomorrow at dusk. Watch your step in the darkness. I'd be obliged if you'd give me a shout when you go below, so I don't set my mind to worrying about you.'

'We will. We're just taking a turn or two around the deck.' There was no moonlight to guide their steps. The stars were a spread of silver freckles across a black velvet sky, the breeze had a touch of humidity. 'Are you being met in Hobart Town, Miss Hardy?'

'I do hope so. Though my stepbrother told me in his last letter that Hobart Town is small, so I doubt that I'll get lost if he doesn't meet me.' She gazed up at him, said shyly. 'Mr Ibsen, I consider us to have become trusted acquaintances on this journey.'

'Friends would be a better word to use, I think.'

She drew in a deep breath. 'Then, as a friend, would you grant me a favour?'

'If it's within my power.'

'Oh, it is. Would you kiss me, please?'

The unexpected request surprised him. 'Kiss you?'

'Oh, I daresay you think I'm foolish spinster, and quite forward. But you see, I'm already twenty-six years old. I have never been kissed by a man, nor am I likely to be. It would be a memory for me to treasure.'

'Would you treasure it?' he said lightly, intrigued by such naiveté coming from a woman of her age, and reckoning she displayed a romantic heart.

She shrugged, saying in a mortified manner, 'Please disregard my request, then, for I believe I have embarrassed you.'

'On the contrary, I'm honoured by the request. If you would allow me . . .' He gently took her chin between thumb and finger, tipped up her chin and captured her mouth.

For a moment she stiffened, then she relaxed. Her mouth was soft and receptive and towards the end, as she grew used to the caress, satisfyingly responsive. Marcus parted from that kiss with some reluctance.

A faintly audible sigh reached his ears. 'Thank you. I will never forget it.'

'My pleasure, Miss Hardy.'

They resumed their walk in silence, as if nothing had happened. Julia said, after a little while, 'What about you, Mr Ibsen? Do you have someone meeting you? A wife, perhaps?'

He smiled at that. She had not thought to ask him that before the kiss, and he wondered if she now harboured romantic notions about him.

'I'm a widower with two young children at home in England. I intend to pay a surprise visit to a friend here.' He smiled at the thought of seeing Siana again.

'Tell me about your children. How old are they?'

'They are infants, still. The boy is called Alexander and the girl is named Jane Louise. They are twins.'

'Oh, how delightful. You must miss them enormously.'

'Yes.' He hoped she didn't ask about Maryse, and she didn't, though he could sense the question hovering about her. He didn't offer an answer to it, despite the familiarity of the kiss they'd exchanged. It was still too painful to discuss with strangers.

Marcus didn't see Julia again until it was time to disembark. He wondered if she'd been avoiding him. Spying her across the deck, he smiled and she blushed and averted her gaze.

He crossed to where she stood, took her hand in his and kissed it. 'It was nice meeting you, Miss Hardy. Perhaps we shall meet again before I leave.'

'I think I should like that.' When her eyes came up to his he could see laughter in them, and it was aimed at herself. 'Thank you for everything, Mr Ibsen, I did enjoy your company.'

He gazed at the small crowd on shore, at the unprepossessing Hobart Town, then at the majestic mountain behind the town, thrusting out of the earth into the sky. Marcus could feel the power of it, as if the sorrow of ancient spirits was imprisoned within its core and pulling him there. He shivered. 'Can you see your stepbrother?'

Her smile faded a little. 'It's a long time since I've seen him, but he's too much like my father to miss. He's standing to the left. That must be his wife and children with him. Goodbye, Mr Ibsen.'

'Miss Hardy.' He watched her step ashore with a faint sense of regret, a drab figure in grey following after a seaman with her bags.

Her stepbrother and his wife were sour-looking; in

fact, the whole family had hardly a smile between them to spare for Julia. They trooped off in single file, Julia struggling with a large bag and bringing up the rear. He felt sorry for her plight. She was a nice woman who should be married with a family of her own to look after.

When she turned to gaze back at him he blew her a kiss and she smiled. Such a small, happy memory for her to treasure in years to come, and it had cost him nothing.

He found himself a boarding house for the night, his room little more than a few rough boards nailed to a couple of posts to form a partition. There was a palliasse for a bed. Although he'd slept in worse conditions, his horse had a better stall at Cheverton Manor! There was precious little sleep for him, for the fellow in the next stall snored loudly.

The next morning, Marcus rose early and changed into his robe, which was comfortable to travel in and often got him mistaken for the theologian he'd once studied to be. People trusted clerics, and his robe had opened many doors on his travels, as well as helping him merge into the landscape on occasion.

For all his discomfort, there was a hearty breakfast of ham and eggs to consume. He purchased a loaf, some hard-boiled eggs, and cheese and fruit from the landlord for the journey. The man had given him clear directions to where the trail began, and had offered him the services of a guide. Marcus had rejected the offer. He had always possessed a good sense of direction and, whenever possible, he liked to travel alone.

He gazed up at the dark, brooding mountain

dominating the landscape. It would be there long after his fellow men had gone, a silent witness to their folly.

Throwing his bag across his shoulders, for he always travelled light, Marcus set out at a steady pace.

16

Christmas and New Year had proved to be yet another milestone for Siana to pass, for time progressed slowly. She delighted in the development of her daughter, who was eight months old now.

Bart Stowe's eldest son, Thomas, was managing Francis's estate, which ran a few cattle, sheep and poultry for local use. The logging brought in most of the income, for it was run on convict labour.

For the sake of propriety, Thomas Stowe lived in a cottage over by the sawmill, which was a mile or so away. Siana had never been there, neither did she want to see it.

'Best you don't,' Bart Stowe had advised. 'Although they're guarded, the convicts are a rough lot and are no respecters of women. It would be best if they remained unaware you were in the district.'

She had no visitors except for the neighbouring Stowes, for there was nothing but wilderness beyond the adjoining properties.

Aware of her isolation, Siana was vigilant. She kept the rifles clean and ready to be loaded, checked the house was secure each night and made sure the out-buildings were kept locked. Jean Stowe had given her a pair of geese to look after, which had produced a clutch of goslings. Fierce towards strangers, they made noisy but effective watchdogs, harassing with their honks and thrashing wings any animals who happened to wander by.

'I must keep faith that Francis will come for me soon,' Siana told Jean, for they'd become closer since she'd confided her troubles to the woman at Christmas.

'I'm sure he will. Your husband seemed a good man. He didn't speak of his sufferings to me, but I know he was birched aboard the ship he arrived on.'

'Did he say why?'

'Elizabeth Hawkins told me he took the punishment for a young convict girl who was assigned as a servant to him. The girl drowned when the ship overturned. I believe she reminded him of one of his daughters. Elizabeth said he accepted punishment in the girl's place. She was locked in the prisoners' quarters when the ship went down. Dr Matheson thought he might have been able to save her life if she'd still been on deck.'

'Ah . . . I see,' Siana said, and she did. Francis found it hard to believe that events which had passed by in life had to be let go of. There were bound to be regrets, of course, but they must be set aside in order to serve the present. Her husband tended to spend too much time deliberating over what might have been.

But Jean was still speaking of Francis, giving Siana an insight into what he must have been through.

'The second time he was flogged it was a case of

mistaken identity, and undeserved. They used the cat on him. He was ashamed because he couldn't stop himself from crying out with the pain and shock of it. They almost broke his will. I understood he wished for death so he could escape the pain.' She shuddered. 'Apparently, they lived like animals in the prison, fighting over scraps of food.'

Odd that Francis had confided these things to Elizabeth when he hadn't been able to tell his own wife. He must have thought Elizabeth would have understood because of her own convict status. Tears filled Siana's eyes. If Francis had been here she would have taken him in her arms and held him close. Not liking himself very much, he'd come home to heal, only to experience more sorrow, shame and degradation.

Now it was February. She placed Francine against her breast and experience the surge of her mother's milk into the child's mouth, she sighed as she remembered how. Francis had lashed out at her, said he would never father her child. Would he deny this daughter of theirs when he saw her?

Francine, pausing to take a breath, opened her eyes and turned her head to gaze up at her mother. Her eyes glinted greenly. For a revealing instant they seemed to contain all the pagan mystery and wisdom of her Welsh great-grandmother. It was a moment of recognition between them.

Then Francine's sweet lips curved into a smile, like the sun coming out from behind a cloud. Siana's breath caught in her throat. That smile of hers was all Francis.

Bryn suddenly thrust into her thoughts. What had

happened to him? Francis wouldn't have farmed him out for long, surely? He was too compassionate a man. Was Bryn happy, and would he have forgotten her after all this time? And what of Daisy and Goldie, were they well?

Something was going to happen soon, Siana knew it. There was an air of expectancy rising in her, a restlessness. It wasn't that uneasy dread which had always foretold sorrow. This was something optimistic and promising, almost light. Siana could feel the faint cowl of the melancholy she wore begin to lift.

February was the hottest month of the year. The day lived up to its promise, heavy with humidity. No wind came to relieve it. Sweat soaked the cloth between Siana's shoulder blades and trickled between her breasts. Taking Francine into the forest, they bathed in the cool cascade of water coming over the fall, revelling in the relief it gave them.

Towards evening, Siana sat on the verandah watching the shadows lengthen over her lonely domain. A spider which lived in the darkest corner of the verandah came out to weave its web, attaching it by a strong thread to one of the posts. The mother goose harshly called her family together. They waddled in a bunch back to the safety of the barn, honking noisily at each other.

All was then peaceful. The dusk drifted around her in an amaranth haze. Birds settled into their nests and an owl hooted nearby. Soon, the sky would darken and the stars would blaze like silver campfires upon a wide desert of navy blue.

Behind her, the lamp she'd lit sent a faint glow through the window.

Siana didn't know how long she sat there, listening to the siren song of the earth calling her as it grew darker.

Siana . . .

She smiled. She must be hearing things.

Siana Matheson.

The geese set up a clamour and there came the alarmed beat and flap of several pairs of wings as the army of birds came charging from the barn as one.

She stood up, her eyes straining down the slope. There was a dense moving shadow in the gloaming, and it was heading rapidly towards her. Going into the house she took down a rifle, returning to the door to call out, 'Don't come any closer, I have a rifle turned on you. State your name and business.'

The shadow stopped moving. Then, from amongst the honking of the geese she heard a familiar chuckle. 'Call off your watchdogs, Siana, they're trying to peck me to death.'

She closed her eyes for a second, blood rushing to her face as she said in wonder, 'Marcus? How wonderful that you've come. I've been so lonely.'

'And if I'd had a gun you'd be dead, for against the light you make a perfect target. Could you point the rifle elsewhere? You're making me nervous.'

She laid it on the chair. 'It's not loaded.'

Stepping into the light spilling from the door, he held out his arms to her. 'Come here.'

'Shoo!' Moving forward, Siana scattered the scolding birds and was swept into his arms. The moon rose from behind the trees to bathe them in white ethereal light as they hugged each other tight. The geese waddled back to the barn like a group of old women, their feathers fluffed and ruffled, gossiping indignantly amongst themselves.

Until Marcus had shown up, Siana hadn't realized exactly how lonely she'd become.

'What are you doing here?' she said to him when they went indoors. 'Are you hungry? I have eggs and some chicken and I baked some fresh bread this morning.'

He dropped into a chair, yawning hugely behind his hand. 'One thing at a time, Siana. That was a hell of a trail up here on foot. I'm tired and dirty. I need a wash and some sleep. Tomorrow, I'll eat.'

Lighting the candle in the bedroom, she fetched the metal tub from the lean-to, sending a lizard sprinting up the wall in fright. Marcus took it from her, carrying it through to the bedroom and pouring cold water into the bottom. He spoke inconsequently of his journey and the people he'd met aboard ship while the water in the kettle heated, as if to keep himself awake. She added the hot water to the cold, giving it a stir with her hand, then passed over her precious tablet of soap, and a bath sheet to dry himself on.

'Please don't leave the soap in the water. It's all I have and we'll have to share it for the time being. In summer, I usually wash in the stream, for there's a small pool and waterfall. I'll show you where it is tomorrow. There's a clean shirt and some cord trousers in the cupboard. They're old, but I washed and repaired them. Jed Hawkins left them behind, so they'll be a bit loose.'

He frowned. 'I understood from Francis that Jed Hawkins was managing the place.'

'Jed bought a property in New South Wales. He and his family have left?'

'Susannah is with them?'

She nodded. 'It didn't take her long to settle down with her mother.'

'Then you're here all alone.'

She smiled as she thought of her precious daughter, sleeping peacefully in the next room. She'd surprise Marcus with her in the morning. 'Not quite. You're here.'

His frown became a slight smile, his coal-dark eyes glittered. 'So I am, and I'd forgotten how exquisitely beautiful a woman you are.'

And Siana had forgotten how dangerously attractive Marcus was. Her hand went nervously to her untidy braid and she grimaced. Her hair needed washing. She didn't bother much with her appearance these days, usually wearing a skirt and bodice with an apron over it, and leaving her feet bare when it was warm. Marcus's remark had made her conscious of herself as a woman. She gave a wry smile when he chuckled, saying crossly, 'There are blankets in the storage box. Goodnight, Marcus.'

After she went to bed she heard him moving about for a while, then all went quiet. The moonlight shone peacefully through the window, a white backdrop for the spider, spread dark against the glow. Strange, how having another person in the house made her feel so safe, especially a man – and Marcus was all man.

A very attractive man, she thought, just as she was drifting off to sleep. Suddenly, she was brought wide awake again, aware of her body, which had been without a man for too long and was now aroused from its dormant state. Throwing back the sheet she lay there in the moonlight, spreadeagled like the spider, the perspiration glistening on her skin like honey, and the musk of her all too apparent. She was ashamed of this sudden need in her, aware of the thin wall between herself and Marcus.

Safe, was she, when she couldn't even trust herself? Tomorrow, she would clean out one of the cottages and banish Marcus from the house.

Unaware of her mother's turmoil, Francine slept peacefully next to her, occupying the cot Jed had woven from branches for his sons. It reminded Siana of the hurdles they fashioned the Dorset sheep pens from.

It was a long time before she was able to curl on to her side to sleep.

Francine brought her awake just as dawn spilled over the window sill. Siana made her infant comfortable, then put her to the breast before dressing.

Marcus's door was still closed. It was early, so she imagined he was still asleep. She fed Francine some milk sops, then placed her on the floor, where she got to her hands and knees and rocked back and forth, gurgling happily to herself. She was a good-natured child, even though she was cutting her teeth.

Stoking up the fire, Siana cut some rashers from a flitch of bacon she'd smoked over the fire and placed some eggs next to them, covering it with a muslin cloth to keep the flies off.

The water bucket was empty. Marcus had placed the soap in a saucer on the dresser. The day promised to be warm and, after the sleepless night she'd had, Siana needed a good wash anyway. Placing Francine astride her hip in a sling fashioned from her mother's old shawl, she picked up the bucket and headed for the stream, about a quarter of a mile away.

Tied to a tree by a string around her waist, Francine played happily on the bank while Siana waded into the cool, waist-deep water. She enjoyed the feeling of goosebumps racing over her body as she soaped her hair and body, then rinsed it. Without bothering to dry herself she slipped back into her clothes, rubbed her hair as dry as possible with her skirt, then filled the bucket from the stream of sparkling water cascading down over the rocks upstream.

The pair headed back to the house.

When Marcus saw Siana coming, an exquisite woman with a damp tangle of wild, dark hair, bare feet and a baby balanced on her hip, his breath caught in his throat. The earth mother in her was so striking, the impact hit him at full force.

He moved forward, taking her face between her hands. Her eyes reflected the green glow of Dorset pines. 'You look wonderful.'

'Marcus, don't say such things. Let me go else I'll spill the water.'

He kissed her soft mouth while her hands were full, taking his fill of her warm lips. She didn't resist, but neither did she encourage. The infant chuckled as its hand explored the buttons on his shirt. He was smiling when he let her go. 'A daughter?'

She nodded, then gazed at him, her face troubled. 'We mustn't let that happen again. You make me feel too much the woman.'

'I know, but you are *too much* the woman.' Laughing, he slanted her a sideways look. 'Did you sleep well last night?'

'No . . . yes. I slept very well. I felt . . . *safe* with you around.'

'I doubt it.' He took the bucket from her, gazed at Francine and chucked her under the chin. The child smiled widely at him, her sharp front teeth gleaming whitely in her gums. 'She looks like you. Does Francis know about her?'

'I told him. He didn't believe me.'

'Ah . . . he takes things hard, your husband.'

'Did he know you were coming to see me?'

Marcus raised an eyebrow. 'I told him.'

'How did he react?'

'That's an odd thing to ask.'

Though not so odd when she gave an apologetic shrug and said without guile, 'He thinks you admire me.'

'He knows I admire you. I made that very plain to him. He should be worried.'

Her laughter filled him with exquisite pleasure. 'No, he shouldn't be. I still love him, Marcus.'

'I know, and he doesn't deserve you. You're a free spirit, not someone to be confined to his rules and regulations.'

'Not like you, who makes your own rules to suit the occasion. How are your children?'

'Siana, my dear, your defence strategy is all too obvious, but you are wise to have one. You'll be asking me if I miss Maryse next.'

'Do you?'

He considered for a moment, deep sadness in his eyes. Siana was the only woman he could discuss his late wife with. She listened to him with more than her ears and more than her heart. She listened with her soul. 'Maryse is dead. Since she left me I've discovered I'm still very much alive.'

'Were we to blame for her death, Marcus?'

'The decision to die was hers. I have puzzled over it often. Was that decision born of courage or cowardice? To me it was selfish decision, for she sacrificed the happiness of two families to ease her own pain.'

'I loved Maryse, yet I let her down. When she took her own life she wasn't in a fit state to think rationally.'

'I'll tell you something you're unaware of, Siana. Although Maryse professed to love me, she couldn't bring herself to be a wife to me, no matter how gently I treated her. I know this was not her fault. I could never understand, though, why she could not love our children.'

Siana gasped. 'That cannot be true.'

'It is true. Although she tried to hide it, Maryse avoided them when she could. She would not put them to the breast as you do. Everything she did was for her own comfort. I'm not blaming her, for the assault on her was not her fault. But I believe Maryse was not strong enough to be a woman of real substance. You, myself and Francis have been carrying her guilt around with us. We are blaming ourselves and each other, and we're tearing ourselves and our families apart in the process. It's like throwing a stone in a pond. The ripples keep spreading wider and wider.'

Siana remembered her time in Wales, where Bryn had been born to Maryse. Siana's great-grandmother Lewis had visited the house of *Bryn Dwr* at the time.

'Last night I dreamed of ripples widening on a pool,' she'd said in her high, fluting voice. But then she would say no more. Siana knew now that her great-grandmother had foreseen the tragedy, and the trouble surrounding it. Her fingers strayed to the silver Celtic cross at her throat. It had belonged to her great-grandmother, with whom she shared a name.

The anger she felt made her tremble. But instinct told her the old ways couldn't be fathomed, and sometimes, the sight was a gift she'd rather not have. Savagely, she kicked open the door. 'I don't want to shoulder the burden of Maryse's pain any more. Would you please fill the kettle, then amuse Francine whilst I cook us some breakfast?'

He pulled her into his arms to cradle her head against his shoulder, running his hands through her hair to relieve the tension in her. 'You're angry with her too. But as nothing will bring her back, you must go home and fight to reclaim that which she stole from you.'

'I don't know if I can face Francis. However justified he feels it was, he has not only deprived me of everyone I loved most, but he has punished them too. Although I still love him, if I'm forced to stay here much longer, I'm frightened I'll learn to hate him.' She pushed him away. 'What did he do with Bryn? I cannot believe a man who displays so much compassion towards the poor could love a child as his son one moment, then discard him the next.'

'I don't know what has happened to Bryn. You must take Francis to account for that, yourself. There's a packet leaving next week. I've booked a passage on it for you.'

'What if he won't have me back?'

'There's a home for you at Cheverton Manor. Go there first, where you'll be within easy distance of Rivervale House. Take my advice, make Francis work to have you back.'

She stared at him for a moment, then gave a tiny, unbelieving laugh. 'Damn you, Marcus, would you have me shame Francis?'

'I won't be in residence at the manor for several months. It depends how quickly I dispose of *my business*.'

Her eyes met his, absorbed some of the turmoil in his soul. She nearly recoiled from the darkness of it, but touched his cheek, a light caress with her fingertip. 'Dearest Marcus, you're hurting so much, still. Will it be over soon?'

A time to kill, and a time to heal, he thought, and he closed his eyes for a moment, his smile mirthless. He hoped it would be over soon, for he could find no satisfaction in revenge, nor embrace the balm of mercy in his soul.

He nodded. Taking Francine from her arms, he

smiled down at the child, avoiding Siana's sympathy. She brought all his sadness to the surface and he wanted to cry like a baby. The child he held in his arms had eyes as wise as the earth itself. She made a soft, cooing sound, like a little dove. 'Francine is going to be a heart-breaker, just like her mamma. If I'd set eyes on you first, Francis wouldn't have stood a chance. We would have suited each other in many ways, you and I.'

'I know,' she said, unconsciously flirting her long eyelashes at him. Turning, she strolled off towards the kitchen, leaving him with a glint in his eye and an inconvenient hardness in his groin. Suddenly, she flung over her shoulder at him, 'You should take another wife, Marcus. One who will share your bed and mother your children. It might stop you lusting after me.'

'I doubt it.' He followed after her, grinning at her bluntness. 'I will never stop lusting after you and I can never love anyone as much as I loved Maryse.'

'That won't matter as long as she needs you. If you are good to a woman, she will respond. If you find someone you like and trust, love might grow between you and it might turn out to be a better way of loving in the end. Last night you spoke with some warmth of a woman aboard ship.'

'Miss Julia Hardy?' He gave a faint smile. 'You don't miss much, do you? I found the lady to be most admirable, in a sensible sort of way.'

'There is nothing wrong with sensible. The most sensible thing I ever did was marry Edward Forbes, my first husband, since I was destitute and needed a home. I grew to love him because he was good to me, though he was much older and not an easy man to live with. I love Francis differently, and in a much deeper way.'

Marcus had never admired Siana more than at that moment. She was desperately erecting her defences, and not only could he could see right through them, he would delight in tearing them down. They would be alone here for several more nights yet. He was well aware of how to woo a woman as hot-blooded as this one. He would enjoyed the chase and the kill, though. So would she, he'd make sure of that.

The morning was bright in the country Julia Hardy found herself in. It was very beautiful here, she had to admit. Her brother's small house was set on a slope, allowing a fine view over the sea.

Her bedroom was a disgrace, part of a storeroom on the back verandah which had been curtained off. The room had no window, and there was nowhere to hang her clothes except for a couple of hooks attached to the wall. Rusting corrugated tin was nailed to rough wooden beams to form the roof. By day, the space heated up like an oven. By night, it was stuffy and airless. Julia dreaded the arrival of winter, when it would probably be exactly the opposite. There was a gap under the door of at least two inches, which would invite the draughts in. Rainwater stains ran down the walls and there was evidence of rodents.

From the drawing-room window she morosely watched the packet she'd arrived on, as it disappeared over the horizon. It was heading back to England and she wished she was on board. She'd gone to the wharf, taking the children with her so she could watch it set sail.

Marcus Ibsen had been there – with him, a woman who'd been carrying a small child. He'd drawn the woman into the shelter of a cart and, taking her face between her hands, he'd kissed her before they'd turned to go on board. There had been a closeness between them that Julia had envied, for the woman had laughed and caressed his face afterwards. The smile Marcus gave her took Julia's breath away and an ember of envy lodged in her, for the woman was beautiful and her own indifferent looks had never attracted the attention of a man.

Then Mr Ibsen has come ashore by himself, striding off without a backward glance.

Watching the ship sail was like parting with an old friend. As the sails unfurled she had a dreadful sense of being cut off from all she'd known in the past, and the friends she had made. Julia had never been happier than aboard that ship, and she wondered bleakly what her future held now.

She didn't have time to wonder for long.

'Gazing out of the window doesn't get the work done, Miss Hardy,' Millicent, her sister-in-law told her. 'After you've finished polishing the floors you can help the convict labour with the laundry.'

Julia turned to gaze at Millicent, whose sour face topped such a tightly corseted gown she could not help but remain uncomfortably upright. She said, 'I understood I was brought here to tutor your children, Mrs Hardy.' The woman had made it clear that familiarity was not to be encouraged by the use of first names.

'Idle hands get into mischief. I am the mistress of this house. You will do as I require of you. I'll draw up a list of your duties, which you will follow to the letter. Catherine told me you chastised Master Timothy yesterday.'

'He kicked me and raised a bruise on my leg.'

'You are forbidden to chastise my children in any way. If they misbehave you must refer them to myself or to Reverend Hardy, who will discipline them.'

'I must insist I be allowed to discipline them myself, and in my own way. Also, I have tested their ability. Their education as regards to letters and numbers is very poor. They will need to work hard to reach a good standard.'

'Have you, have you, indeed, Miss Hardy? And on whose authority did you undertake such a task?'

'My own, as their tutor. I needed to discover the standard they'd already reached before I set work for them. That is my position, after all. The children must be taught to respect me if they're to learn.'

'Respect you? Miss Hardy, you are acting way above your station. You are here to be of service to us, not the other way round.' The woman's eyes glinted. 'I advised my husband that bringing a poor relation into the household would cause trouble. Try not to prove me right.'

Julia knew she'd have to learn not to argue with this woman if her life was to be tolerable, so she swallowed her anger when her sister-in-law said coldly, 'Let me remind you, once again. You're here because your stepbrother considers it his Christian duty to be charitable towards you. You should be made aware, perhaps, that I do not share his sentiment. As you're little more than a servant, you're in no position to insist on anything. If you do not like the arrangement you may leave, but not until you've worked off the money laid out for your passage.'

Julia bit her tongue. Even when she'd done that, she'd still have nowhere else to go. In the week she'd been part of this household, she'd come to dislike her stepbrother and his family intensely. Reverend Hardy was sanctimonious, as their father had been. He liked the sound of his own voice and expounded at length about the virtues, or lack of them, in his friends, neighbours and acquaintances.

Charity? *Hah*, she thought, her anger transferred to a vigorous slathering of beeswax over the floorboards, an action which was the cause of much chagrin to her arm muscles. This family didn't have a charitable bone in their collective bodies.

Two days later Julia emerged from the evening service to see a familiar figure waiting by the gate. When Marcus smiled at her, she remembered the kiss they'd exchanged and the blood rushed to her face. 'Mr Ibsen,' she stammered. 'What are you doing here?'

'Looking for you.'

'Miss Hardy. We are waiting,' Millicent said ominously.

Marcus placed a hand on her arm to detain her. 'Miss Hardy, may I have a moment of your time? There is a matter of some urgency I wish to discuss with you.'

She nervously gazed at her stepbrother and his family, who had turned to watch the encounter with avid curiosity and much disapproval.

'Who is this man?' her stepbrother said to her.

'He is Mr Ibsen, who was a passenger aboard the ship I arrived on.'

'What is your business with Miss Hardy, sir.'

She saw a nerve in Marcus's jaw twitch. 'My business is private, and is with Miss Hardy, alone.'

'Is it, indeed? Miss Hardy is a relative who is under my care. Any business with her is my business too, so anything you wish to say to her will be uttered in my presence.'

Amused dark eyes gazed down at her. 'Is that your wish too, Miss Hardy?'

It wasn't, but she really had no choice. Her eyes appealed to him for understanding when she nodded.

He gave her an altogether wicked grin, sank down on one knee and took her hand in his. 'Very well, then. Would you do me the honour of becoming my wife, Miss Hardy?'

'Your wife?'

There was a gasp from behind her.

'As I've already told you, I have two children who are in need of a mother. I also have a fairly comfortable home in Dorset.'

Julia felt her eyes saucer with shock, yet at the same time she wanted to laugh with the unexpected delight at receiving the proposal. She didn't have to think about it. 'Yes, Mr Ibsen. I'll become your wife. Please get up, you're making a complete fool of yourself.'

'I sincerely hope not, Miss Hardy. Shall we shake hands on it and consider the agreement binding, then? I'm shortly to go to New South Wales on business. As soon as that business is completed, I will return to claim you.' As he rose and took her hand in his, he slipped a piece of paper into her sleeve and gazed into her eyes.

'Just a moment, sir,' the reverend said. 'I went to considerable expense to bring my stepsister here from England. The girl has not yet worked her passage.'

'And neither will she.' Marcus Ibsen took a purse from his pocket, removed several coins and handed them to the reverend. 'That should cover my fiancée's expenses. Good evening to you, Reverend. The ship sails at midnight and I have things to do before I board.'

Julia watched him stride away, a smile on her face. Her life was about to change, and she couldn't help but think it was for the better.

'You did not mention any man when you came to us, so what are we to make of your morals now, Miss Hardy?' Millicent sneered.

'No doubt you will make of them as you wish, as you do of every other unfortunate person you cast your eye upon.'

'Mr Ibsen is an adventurer. I'm surprised you allowed him to take you in. Do you really trust him to return for you?'

'I'd trust him with my life,' she said, and smiled, for she was about to do exactly that.

'You will not leave me without help,' Millicent said triumphantly. 'While you're under our roof you'll still be expected to carry out your duties, else you'll find yourself on the street.'

Julia shrugged. She'd be more than happy to leave this household, and at this instant. Unfortunately, she had nowhere else to go. But, later that evening, Julia chuckled as she read the note Marcus had slid into her sleeve.

Dear Miss Hardy,
You struck me as being an adventurous type of woman with a mind of her own. If you'd care to elope with me to New South Wales, we can be married there. It will save me the inconvenience of coming back. I will wait for you in the shadows beyond the gate until eleven o'clock. Trust me.
Marcus Ibsen

He'd said the ship sailed at midnight.

Julia offered the reverend and his wife the courtesy of a brief note of farewell, leaving it on her pillow. Then, packing her bag, she crept from her poorly equipped accommodation and, with a great sense of freedom and excitement, joined her future husband.

17

Francis thought his grandchildren to be handsome. Alexander was growing to resemble Marcus more each day. Jane Louise was a dark-eyed, dark-haired beauty, with waving hair and a mischievous smile. Neither of them resembled their late mother to any great extent, though he searched their features for signs of Maryse every time he visited them.

He came every week to Cheverton Manor, sometimes bringing Daisy and Goldie, so the twins would have other children for company. Today, he was alone.

He enjoyed his visits, and was satisfied the children were well treated and cared for. They were walking now, and talking after a fashion. They recognized him as their grandfather, indeed, addressing him as 'ganfer' in their almost unintelligible infant prattle.

Jane Louise held her arms up for a hug as he was about to leave. As she snuggled against him, her plump little arms holding him tight, love for her raced through him. How lucky he was to have them to care for. How could Maryse have deliberately left these two beautiful children motherless? It was something he wouldn't have expected of his daughter.

Halfway home, it occurred to him he'd done exactly the same with Bryn. The boy had regarded him as his father. As a father, he had loved Bryn without reservation. What had happened to that love to make him withdraw it from Bryn, a lad he'd also deprived of a mother?

He could feel that love inside him still, crouching like a wounded animal gone to earth. He coaxed it out to examine it. How bewildered Bryn must have been in the weeks following the move. Had he waited and watched for his parents to come for him until he'd finally run out of hope? Francis's heart ached for the boy now. Indeed, who was he to censure Maryse for the state of her mind, when his own attitude towards Bryn had been less than charitable?

For his own peace of mind Francis knew he had to reclaim Bryn before his brothers took matters into their own hands for Ryder was quite capable of using his position to sign on his behalf. His family was incomplete without the boy, the house felt empty without him. The need for him to bring Bryn home became suddenly urgent.

When he returned home to Rivervale House he found Pansy in the schoolroom with Miss Edgar, supervising a poetry recitation. Daisy was at her melodramatic best, her hands clasped over her heart and her eyes turned to the ceiling. Goldie wore a false moustache. He grinned at the sight and, pushing the door a crack wider, beckoned to Pansy.

'What is it, Pa?' she said, closing the door behind her in case the girls saw him and were distracted.

'I'm going to Christchurch in the rig. I'll probably stay at Kylchester Hall overnight.'

A smile spread across her face. 'Are you going to fetch Bryn?'

He nodded. 'I admit, I have been torn apart by this affair, but I've reached a conclusion that Bryn will be better off living with us than left to the mercy of strangers.'

'Dearest Papa. I knew you would come to this realization sooner or later. I'll inform the staff and will make sure Bryn's bed is aired. I'm sure you'll never regret this decision.'

'Pansy, my dear, I certainly hope not, but the truth of his parentage cannot be kept concealed from Bryn indefinitely, for too many others know. He must be prepared for his future honestly and accordingly.'

'He'll be proud to have you as a grandfather, and I'll adore you for evermore for bringing him home. I've missed him so much.' Her declaration was reinforced by the warmth of her hug. 'Wrap yourself up warmly, Papa. I'll prepare you a food hamper, for you'll miss dinner.'

Francis left within the hour, shivering a little, for the wind had become blustery and brought driving showers with it. Now he'd made his decision he couldn't wait to see Bryn again. But would the boy remember him after all this time?

It was three hours before he crossed into the neighbouring county of Hampshire, then travelled on to the east of Bournemouth Cove. Another thirty minutes passed before he reached Christchurch. The reflection of the square Norman tower of the priory, a later addition to the various contributions to its earlier style, was wavering on the wind-rippled water of the Avon river.

The evening shadows were lengthening when Francis found the cottage of Lucy Tisk. His knock at the door brought the sound of shuffling feet. The door opened a chink to reveal the withered face of an old woman. She gazed short-sightedly at him, her head jerking back and forth with palsy. 'What do 'e want?'

'My name is Francis Matheson. I'm here to collect the boy.'

'The boy, is it? And about time, too, for my grandson, Ben Tisk, had to take the birch to him this morning. He wouldn't do his chores, and me so crippled with rheumatics I can hardly walk.'

Her grandson appeared then, a man of solid appearance in his early twenties, who filled the door frame of the back room. The scars on Francis's back, placed there by a flogging when he'd been mistaken for a convict in Van Diemen's Land, began to burn at the thought of Bryn being birched. 'Where is he?' he said roughly.

The woman might have been old, but she wasn't stupid. 'First, there's the matter of bringing the payment of his board up to date. I was only supposed to have him till the end of the year.' A grubby palm was extended. 'Thirty shillin', I be owed.'

The man moved forward to stand behind his grandmother, arms folded.

The sum dropped into her palm was shoved into the pocket under her apron, and the woman pointed to a ladder leading to a loft. 'He's up there.'

Noticing the bolt securing the trapdoor, Francis frowned. 'You've locked him in?'

'The ungrateful little tyke keeps trying to escape,' the man said. 'He's as sullen as a river rat. If you asks me, the discipline of that there school he's being sent to will do him good.'

Francis was curt. 'I didn't ask you. Would you fetch my grandson down, please.'

'Fetch him down, Ben,' said Lucy Tisk, as she shuffled off. 'Make sure he don't take the smock that boy be wearin', less'n it be paid for, first. There was nothin' to say I had to provide him with clothes and that smock cost me two shillin' at the market.'

Francis placed two shillings in Ben Tisk's hand, then watched him open the trapdoor and poke his head and shoulders up through the hole. 'Come 'ere, you,' he growled. 'There be someone here to fetch yer.'

There was a shuffling noise from the ceiling above, then the sound of a foot thudding against flesh. Giving a howl, Ben Tisk ducked out of the trapdoor with blood dripping from his nose. 'I'll kill that little bastard when I gets hold of him.' Ben shot swiftly up through the trapdoor again, his whole body propelled by muscular arms. There came the sound of a struggle, followed by a high-pitched squeal. Suddenly, the near-naked body of a boy came hurtling through the trapdoor.

Francis was in time to catch Bryn, but the force sent him staggering backwards and they rolled together onto the floor. Immediately, the boy began to kick and punch him.

'Enough, Bryn,' he said. Pinning the child's arms to his sides, he rose to his feet and carried him outside. He didn't want to risk a confrontation with the burly Ben Tisk. As the door slammed behind them, Bryn was beyond reason in his passion, swearing and screaming at the top of his voice. Francis kept him captive until he reached the phaeton, where the boy suddenly ran out of energy.

This was not the lively, healthy child he'd left with Beckwith to farm out. This was a boy who'd suffered. Francis understood now why Siana hadn't been able to leave him at the farm in Wales. She would have known what his fate was likely to be. Now her worst fears with regard to Bryn had been realized.

'Look at me, Bryn,' Francis said to him. A pair of grey eyes came up to his and stayed there. There was no recognition in them, just pain and defiance. 'I'm not going to hurt you. Do you understand?'

Bryn nodded, but his body was tense with fright. He was filthy, his hair was shoulder length and matted, his smell feral. Marks on his wrists and ankles indicated where a rope had chaffed and burnt his skin, welts from a recent birching striped his legs, arms and back. A piece of rag, the remnants of a filthy smock, was all the clothing he wore. Dear God, what had this boy gone through?

'I'm going to wrap a blanket round you. Then I'm going to give you some medicine to help you to feel better.' The truth was, Francis couldn't risk driving away if there was a chance of Bryn throwing himself from the rig.

He released the boy's arms, said, 'Do you remember who I am?' Bryn stared at him, mistrustful and sullen. Francis had no time for self-recrimination. That would come later, even though he was finding this reunion, coming on top of the condition Goldie had been found in, an extremely bitter pill to swallow. He reached for the hamper and opened it. 'I'm your grandfather, come to take you home. Are you hungry?'

The boy snatched the bread, cheese and ham he offered, stuffing it into his mouth and choking on it as it went down. A few minutes after he finished bolting it, he pressed his hands to his stomach and groaned with pain. The food was immediately brought up again. Leaning over the side of the rig, Bryn's thin body jerked and heaved with the involuntary effort.

Wiping the boy's mouth he said gently, 'I should have known better. When we get to Kylchester Hall, we must try you on some broth, instead.'

Again that disconcerting stare, but there was a spark of recognition in the depths of his eyes now. Bryn swallowed the laudanum Francis gave him and allowed himself to be wrapped in the blanket. Afterwards, he edged over to the corner, as far away from Francis as he could get.

It didn't take long for Bryn to begin to relax, for the dose had been a large one and the rocking movement of the rig was soothing. His lids closed gradually and reluctantly, jerking open as soon as they closed, as if he was frightened to fall asleep, then gradually closing again. Finally, they stayed shut. As he brought the rig to a halt Francis knew Bryn would sleep until morning. Laying the child on the seat beside him, he secured him with a rope around his waist, so he couldn't slide off. Clicking his tongue at the horse, Francis gently set the rig in motion again and they headed for Kylchester Hall.

It was almost dark when he arrived there. Ryder and Prudence were about to go into dinner, but came to greet him instead.

'I'd be grateful for a bed for the night,' he said to Ryder.

Ryder sent a servant scuttling, then gazed down at the boy in his arms. 'What are you going to do with him?'

Anger at himself made Francis short. 'He'll never leave my home again until he's of an age when he can make that decision for himself.'

Placing a hand over her mouth, Prudence gasped. 'Surely that child is not Bryn.'

'Yes, it is.'

'But . . . what a state he is in, that disgusting smell! I had no idea . . . oh, Francis . . .' She began to weep, clearly rattled by the sight of the poor child. 'I'm so sorry. Lucy Tisk was my own recommendation. She used to be a maid of all work until she became too old and her grandson took her in. But she was always so reliable. I don't understand how this can have happened. You must let me tend to the poor child.'

Francis was weary, for he'd been up much of the previous night trying to patch up a woman who'd been beaten half to death by her drunken husband. She'd survived with two ribs broken, her face bruised and swollen. She'd also lost the baby she'd been carrying. He'd have liked to place her in the infirmary, but she had five children to care for.

He'd had words with her husband. 'The next time this happens I'll report you to the constable.'

All swagger, his belly full of scrumpy, her husband had grunted, 'A man has the right to treat his wife as he sees fit.'

'Not to this extent. You've killed the infant she was carrying.'

'Got enough of the little beggars running around as it is. A man can't get a moment's peace.' And indeed, there had been a row of scared, dirty little faces such as Bryn's gazing out from behind a curtain.

He sighed with the depth of his sorrow. As a husband he had also treated his wife and children despicably. Worse, for he'd denied the children in his charge the love and guidance of a mother.

'Bryn probably has body lice. I've dosed him with laudanum, but he should sleep until morning. Bathing him is not a job for a lady such as yourself.'

Prudence placed a hand on his arm. 'I'm a mother of five sons, Francis. I know you think I'm an interfering idiot –' an assessment not far removed from the truth, Francis thought – 'Ryder would be the first to agree with you. I do have some common sense, however, and I'm not entirely devoid of feeling. Hand the child to me. I will summon a servant. We will make sure he's clean, and apply soothing salve to his sores before settling him for the night.'

'Place him on the chaise in my chamber then, Prudence, for I'd not want him to wake in the night and be frightened. He will lash out and be hard to handle if he feels the need to defend himself.'

'He needs mothering again.' To Francis's surprise, Prudence took the child from him and gently kissed his forehead. 'Poor lad,' she said softly. 'This has been a tragedy with far-reaching consequences. What can we do to help you forget what you've been through?'

Ryder took him into the drawing room, handing him a brandy while they waited for Prudence to return. 'Are you sure you know what you're doing, Francis?'

'For the first time in several months, yes, I do. I'm bringing my family back together again, for I've been too harsh and I'm miserable without them. Don't think I'm ungrateful for the help you and my other brothers offered, Ryder. However, Siana loved the boy and so did I. I see no reason why he should not remain with us.'

'And when he finds out the truth of his past . . . what then?'

'He'll hear that truth from me, his grandfather. When the time comes, I can only hope the affection with which we raise him will give him a sense of worth. He has, after all, got Matheson blood in him, which, Pansy aside, is more than the rest of my family have.'

'My advice to you is—'

'With all respect, Ryder, I believe I'm old enough to manage my life without any more advice. Being married to Siana has taught me that whatever their lot in life, all people have feelings. Over the past two years I've sent away the woman I love, and have been the cause of two children experiencing unimaginable horror and degradation. In the process, I've lost all respect for myself.'

'You're being too hard on yourself, Francis. This whole affair was caused by that damned Welsh woman making mischief.'

'It was caused by a crime being committed against my daughter. Nothing more, nothing less. Had I been more observant at the time it happened, instead of setting my mind on the property William had left me in Van Diemen's Land, I would have noticed Maryse's distress at the time and looked for further signs.

'Siana did what she thought was right. She's not the type of woman who would turn away from a child who was in need of her, which is one of the very qualities I admired in her when I decided to wed. Now, I might have lost her.'

'Send for her. She's your wife and must do as you bid.'

'You don't understand, Ryder. I want Siana to be happy. There has already been too much sadness in her life.'

'I applaud you for that,' Prudence said, coming into the room with a smile on her face. 'I knew from the first time I saw you together that Siana was perfect for you. I told her so.' He received a kiss on the cheek. 'Now, you mustn't worry about the boy. He's peacefully asleep with a maid to watch over him for the time being. I have found some clean clothing for him, which although rather large, will suffice for now.

'I'll order some broth to be made for the boy.' She slid her arm through his. 'Now, let us have dinner, for my sons will be as hungry as a pack of wolves. Perhaps we'll discuss Pansy's wedding to that Skinner fellow, between us.'

'I think not,' Ryder said with a grin. 'Francis has decided he can manage the affairs of his family himself.'

'Has she someone else to advise her, then?'

Francis laughed. Prudence would never change. 'The wedding is to take place in the local church. Pansy said it's to be a small wedding with only close family and Josh's business friends in attendance.'

'My dear Francis, I wonder if my niece is aware of how very large the Matheson family is.'

'To be honest, Pansy expects them to display their displeasure of the event by refusing the invitation.'

'Even if they do not all attend, they'll need to be invited. And although that drawing room of yours is a handsome size, I'm not sure it will accommodate us all should everyone decided to follow my good example, and accept.'

Francis exchanged a relieved grin with Ryder, who winked. He would not like Pansy to be snubbed on her wedding day. 'I understand the reception is to be held at Pansy's future home. Josh has added a large conservatory to the drawing room which leads out onto a terrace.'

'Ah yes. As I recall, that house at Poole has a fine view.' She gave him a dark and exaggerated sigh. 'I also recall that I had an argument about you with Siana there. She objected to wearing mourning for you. For

333

some strange reason she was quite convinced you'd return from the dead.'

'And she was right.'

'On that occasion she *guessed* correctly . . . but it's quite annoying to be constantly contradicted when I'm not used to it. All your family do it. I really don't know where they get it from. Certainly not from you, Francis, for you're always such congenial company. Still, we must leave irritations in the past for the sake of future generations.'

Francis wished she'd do just that. Too much of Prudence was certainly an irritation, like wearing a hair shirt. He didn't envy his brother for having a wife with no quietness in her.

He also didn't envy his brother for the servants, trappings and responsibilities of estate that came with being the Earl of Kylchester. Suddenly, he was glad he was the younger brother, Dr Francis Matheson, physician, and sometimes a surgeon, which was the lesser of the doctoring professions, but a deserving one when a life and death consideration was needed. He was a man who earned his respect, who lived at Rivervale House and could allow his daughter to wed a self-made man, without too much fuss.

'Joshua Skinner,' Prudence suddenly said. 'As I recall, he's an enterprising young man who has done well for himself.'

'His company has vast property holdings and has expanded into London. In years to come, he'll probably end up as one of the wealthiest men in England,' Francis predicted.

Prudence gave him a beaming smile. 'That's something in his favour, then. Pansy has always had a good head on her shoulders. I'll write a list of family in order of preference, and you will give it to Pansy on my behalf, for she will never remember them all. What happened to that dreadfully deformed creature who used to work for Skinner?'

'Sam Saynuthin? He lives in Poole, and earns a good living from his drawing skills.'

'Ah yes. He did a drawing of me once. Very unflattering, for he made my nose look like a raven's beak. You will tell Pansy I'm available for advice at any time. I have always wanted a daughter so I can arrange a wedding for her. Perhaps I can do something with those younger girls instead. Daisy is promising, if pert, and Marigold has such a sweet, shy nature.'

'Perhaps,' Francis said with a smile, and his mouth began to water as a tureen of steaming soup was carried in by a footman. He had not eaten since breakfast.

Francis didn't leave Kylchester Hall until the following noon. Prudence had sent one of the maids into the nearest town with a list and Bryn was now suited out with a wardrobe of clothing. It was a gift to relieve Prudence of her guilt over the affair.

His hair neatly trimmed, bathed, and garbed in a sailor suit, Bryn now looked more like his old self than the stinking animal Francis had collected from the cottage. His eyes lacked lustre, though, and the tenseness lingering about him couldn't be dispelled.

Personally attended to by Prudence, who was

obviously doing her best to make amends, Bryn con-
sumed a bowl of chicken broth without major mishap,
even though he tried to grab the bowl and drink from it.

'We will use a spoon, boy, otherwise you'll be sick,'
Prudence told him in a manner which made it plain she
was going to be obeyed. Afterwards, Bryn went to sit on
the floor in the corner of the room, his face turned to the
panelling, as if hiding his face would make him
unnoticeable. He cringed away from Francis when he
was picked up.

'You mustn't be frightened of me, Bryn. I won't hurt
you.' But Francis's soothing words had little effect.

The unnerving silence continued all the way to
Rivervale House. When they reached Poole, Bryn made
a tiny mewing sound as if his memory was being
triggered by his surroundings. Indeed, the nearer they
went to Rivervale House, the more alert he became.
When Francis slowed the rig to allow several deer to
cross the road, Bryn gazed intently at them.

'Do you remember this place?' Francis asked him.

The boy ignored him and turned his head away.
When they passed through the gates he displayed signs
of restlessness. They pulled to a stop in front of the
house. Just as the front door was opened by the maid
and Francis freed Bryn from the restraints keeping him
safely in his seat, the boy became quite agitated.

Francis was about to climb down when Bryn flung
himself from his seat to the ground. Picking himself up
he tore up the steps and into the house. By the time
Francis followed him in it was to see Bryn dashing up the
stairs at a fast pace. He shot straight past the astonished-

looking trio of young ladies who were coming down to greet them.

'Mamma,' he heard Bryn shout out, then a door slammed back against the wall. There was silence for a moment, then a loud scream of frustration. *'I want my mamma!'* and the boy burst into a frenzy of heart-rending sobs.

Pansy exchanged a glance with him. 'He needs a woman's touch, I think, Papa. I'll attend to him.'

'Me too,' Daisy and Goldie said together, unable to hide the accusation in their eyes.

As if he didn't already feel like an ogre. Going into his study, Francis placed his head in his hands, trying to stem his own tears. He wished there was an easy way to right the wrong he'd brought about.

'Come home, Siana,' he whispered. 'We need you.'

A few weeks later, the ship Siana was sailing on sighted the Cape Verde islands off the African coast.

'We'll turn east towards Spain then sail up the coast and across the channel into Bristol. If the weather remains fair, we should sight the coast of England within two weeks.' The captain showed her where they were on the charts. A kindly man, he had patiently responded to her interest during the journey, answering any questions she might have. She'd been keeping a journal of her time in Van Diemen's Land, and now, of the journey home. The ship would be putting into Bristol first he'd told her, then going across to Ireland to provision and pick up immigrants for a trip across the North Atlantic Ocean to the American continent.

'You must have seen many interesting places,' she said.

He smiled. 'Aye, you could say that. I've been at sea since I was a boy, first sailing with my father when I was nine years old. I know of no other life.'

'Then you have no wife and family?'

He said soberly, 'I married when I was young and we had a baby daughter. I intended to give up the sea and settle down ashore, but I left it too late. One day I came home from sea to find them gone. Cholera had taken them both. It didn't seem fair to take another wife.'

'I'm so sorry.'

'And what about you, Mrs Matheson. Will you be met in England?'

'My family doesn't know I'm on my way home. I thought I'd find a livery stable and hire a carriage and driver to take me to Dorset.'

'Bristol is a rough port. I'll make sure you're escorted to the ship's agent, who will forward you safely on your journey. He can arrange decent accommodation for you and the babe, if needed.'

'Thank you, Captain. You're very kind.'

The weather took a turn for the worse as they neared England. The wind was blustery and cold, the water white-crested and choppy. The ship wallowed and bucked this way and that, so most of the passengers became ill and were confined to their cabins.

The movement affected Siana and Francine not at all. Siana's daughter had found her legs over the past few weeks, and had to be constantly watched lest she lose her grip on the furniture and fall.

Wrapped in a warm cloak and, with Francine protected by her body from the wind, Siana watched the coast came closer and closer. The sight of the small green island that was home brought a lump to her throat and tears to sting her eyes, for her travels had made her realize how truly small and precious it was to her.

The ship tied up the following morning. Siana had said her farewells to the ship's crew and the other passengers. The ship's agent kindly hired a carriage and horses whose driver was willing to take her to Dorset, and within two hours she was on her way home. Not to Rivervale House, though. She didn't know if she'd be welcomed there.

It was warmer on shore than it had been on the water. There was a drift of soft rain, almost like mist.

The rich aroma of Dorset was a balm to her senses. As she passed fields where sheep and cattle grazed, she had a sense of never being away. Life on the land never changed. Root vegetables were being sown. She watched the men and women bending to the earth, their skin nut-brown and toughened to the elements.

The corn fields were an undulating ocean of verdant wheat and barley. She felt the hills call, and experienced the urge to walk there again. But not now. She was travel weary. Her legs were still unaccustomed to dry land, so it came up to meet her feet unexpectedly, sending her side-stepping. She would need to find her land legs again before she could walk a distance.

The Cheverton housekeeper, Maisie Roberts, met her at the front door, her face wreathed in smiles. 'Mrs

Matheson? How nice to see you at Cheverton House again.'

'I'm to be a guest, Maisie. I have letters in my bag to that effect from Mr Ibsen.'

'Before he left, Mr Ibsen gave instructions that you were welcome to stay here at any time.' Her eyes widened at the sight of Francine. 'There's a bonny cheil. And so like you. Dr Matheson never mentioned her on his visits here to see his grandchildren.'

'Dr Matheson is, as yet, unaware of her existence. Does my husband come here often?'

'As regular as the sun rises, every Sunday morning. He stays for an hour or two, playing with Alexander and Jane Louise. He says it gives him an excuse not to go to church.'

Siana smiled at that, but she needed time to collect herself before she confronted her husband. 'For the moment I don't want Dr Matheson to know I'm back, Maisie.'

'I understand, Mrs Matheson. I'll instruct the staff not to say anything. Now come in out of the rain, for though 'tis fine, it will soon soak you through. Still, a little rain be good for forcing the crops on this time of year, they say, and we've had precious little this year. Very dry, it be. In some parts the farmers be turning the crop in. Cheverton Estate was lucky, as we got just enough to grow a decent crop.'

Tears pricked Siana's eyes at the sound of Maisie's rich dialect. 'It's lovely to be home. I've missed the place so much.'

Maisie patted her shoulder. 'There, there, my bonny.

I'll bring you some refreshment and get you settled in before I send someone to tell Phinas Grundy you be here.'

'Thank you, Maisie.'

'Likely, the two young uns will enjoy having a playmate for a while. I'll fetch one of the nursery maids down to make the little one's acquaintance.'

After Maisie had gone, and Francine had charmed the nursery maid with her smile and been willingly borne off to the nursery, Siana sank into the chair and gazed around her. Her marriage to her first husband had been celebrated in this room. She'd been eighteen years old. Her marriage to Francis had been celebrated here too. Yet Cheverton Manor had never felt like a home to her. It still didn't.

Not more than two miles away was her home. Would she be welcomed at Rivervale House by the man who still held her heart, she wondered.

18

Sydney Town had pleasantly surprised Elizabeth Hawkins. A bustling place, it had many fine sandstone buildings and a sense of order about it. To the west a range of mountains rose into the sky. They were as beautiful as they were formidable.

For four hundred pounds, Jed had purchased some three hundred acres of partially cleared land on the Hawkesbury River at the mandatory price of one pound per acre, from a widow woman who was returning to England. He'd considered the extra money well spent, for it included a homestead, albeit one of modest proportions, plus livestock consisting of approximately one hundred sheep, six sows and a hog to service them. Jed was a hard worker. Already, he'd added two extra rooms to the house.

Seven convicts had been assigned to work on the farm. Most were set to clearing the land. One of them had once worked the fields of Cheverton Estate when Jed had held the stewardship. A shepherd, serving a nine-year term for slaughtering one of his master's sheep to feed his family, he was the only one trustworthy enough to work near the homestead. Jed paid him a small wage to keep him loyal, the sum to be set aside until he gained his ticket-of-leave.

The rest of the convicts were housed in small shelters made from any material that came to hand. They were situated a good three miles away from the house, and guarded by a trooper. Jed took them a weekly ration of flour, sugar, tea, molasses, and a carcass of mutton. There was native wildlife to be trapped, too. The odd, hopping creature called a kangaroo made a hearty meal, tasting a little like venison.

Generally, the convicts were an unkempt lot, for their beards grew wild and matted and their clothes became ragged. There was rarely any trouble, for they were worked to the point of exhaustion each day. Neither did Jed have any compassion for them. To varying degrees of brutality, they were all criminals and he didn't trust them further than he could throw them.

Jed Hawkins had a plan. Thorough and deliberate in his ways, he knew the future of the property rested in the hands of their two young sons, and his task in life was to build the property up for them before his life was over.

'This is a fine country. I have everything I need to make me contented,' Elizabeth's man of few words said to her one day.

'Being your own master, for one thing.'

'Aye, there's that, though it was a long time coming.' He smiled at her then. 'There's something to be said for having a loving wife and some young uns, though, and no guessing which I'd choose between the two if I was asked.'

Elizabeth's life now was a far cry from her former situation in England. Although she'd been unjustly convicted of a crime, because of it she was truly happy for the first time in her life. Susannah had settled down, too, now she'd been made aware of how much she was loved. Susannah's two younger brothers adored her, and the girl revelled in their admiration. Elizabeth schooled her along with the boys, as well as teaching her the household skills she would need in the future. She was proving to be an apt pupil.

Dainty and feminine in her ways, Susannah's pretty manners endeared her to everyone she met, thanks to Siana. Elizabeth expected her daughter to marry well when the time came, for marriageable females were in short supply. Most of the properties in the district were flourishing and had sons who would need partners.

From the window, Elizabeth watched her daughter, who was sitting astride one of the horses learning to ride. Jed had the horse on a long rope so it could only go in circles. At the moment a horse trained to a lady's side saddle was an unnecessary expense, since the beasts had to work as well as provide transport. Jed was careful with their money, but when they were more established a proper mount would be obtained for herself and Susannah, and Elizabeth would undertake to teach her daughter the accepted manner of riding. But at least Susannah was becoming used to handling a horse, and that would hold her in good stead for the future.

Aware of the eyes of her brothers upon her, Susannah appeared to possess more confidence than she actually had. When she slowed to a stop, Jed went up to her and said something. When she nodded, he freed the rope from the bridle. Hand going to her mouth, Elizabeth held her breath. For a moment Susannah looked unsure, then she was off, walking the horse across the paddock then going into a trot. Wheeling the horse around she went into a canter and brought it back to where Josh stood, a proud grin on her face. The boys began to whoop and holler when Jed lifted her down.

The day was cold. Something moving in the eucalyptus trees bordering the paddock caught her attention. A puff of dust. It might have been a kangaroo, though Jed's dog had heard something unusual, for it began to bark.

'Quiet,' Jed growled, shading his eyes with his hands. Although visitors were more frequent than they'd been in Van Diemen's Land they were still rare, so those living on isolated properties had to be cautious.

The children came running indoors and lined up by the window. Elizabeth took the rifle down. Loading it, as Jed had taught her, she went to join her man.

Making no attempt at stealth, a man and woman were walking towards the house. The strangers stopped a little way off, the man shielding the woman with his body, in much the same way as Jed shielded Elizabeth. 'My name is Marcus Ibsen. I'm looking for Jed and Elizabeth Hawkins, and it seems as though I've found them.'

There was a click as Jed disabled the rifle. 'Mrs Matheson has told us of you. Welcome to my property, though if you want me to go back and manage

Cheverton Estate for you, the answer is no. I'm my own master, now.'

'I already have a good agent managing the place.'

The two men shook hands, appraising each other all the while. A mutual relaxation between them seemed to take place. Marcus smiled at her. 'Mrs Hawkins, it's nice to meet you, at last. Susannah and I have been acquainted for some time. She's very much resembles you.'

Indeed, Susannah had come forward to gaze up at him, her brothers in tow. With a shy smile on her face as they reacquainted themselves, she then introduced her two brothers.

Elizabeth sensed an odd mixture of menace and dependability about Marcus Ibsen. Siana had told her that Marcus Ibsen was a man who knew his own depths and acted accordingly, much like Jed. His dark eyes were both astute and assessing. 'I have a message for you. Mrs Matheson sends you her love and hopes you and your family have a prosperous future.'

'Was Siana well when you last saw her?'

'I've never known her to suffer from any malady. Mrs Matheson has returned to England with her daughter.

'Her daughter! Siana was expecting a child?' Elizabeth turned to Jed, remorse in her eyes. 'Oh Jed, if I'd known I'd have never left her there alone. I'd have insisted she came with us.'

'Which is probably why she didn't tell us in the first place. That little lady has always been capable of running her own life, and the lives of everyone else around her, if she can.'

Elizabeth's eyes narrowed when she saw the gleam of a grin in Marcus Ibsen's face. It was the smile of a man who thought he had the measure of Siana. But then the grin became self-deprecating, and she saw those coal-black eyes of his were intent on her. His head slanted to one side, he regarded her steadily, as though he'd read her thoughts. He was intriguing, and slightly uncomfortable to be with. Siana would like that aspect of him, for she'd find it a challenge.

'What name did Siana give to her daughter?'

'Francine Megan. The infant is the very double of her mother.' He drew the woman with him forward. 'This is my wife, Julia. We have recently been wed in Sydney and will be returning to England as soon as my business here is finished. I wondered if you would be kind enough to offer her your hospitality for a day or two. We've been travelling by foot and she's tired of living rough, I think.'

Elizabeth held out both hands to Julia, drawing her forward to kiss her cheek. 'We would be glad to. You do look fatigued. Come indoors, my dear. I'll make you some refreshment and boil some water so you can bathe.'

Marcus watched Julia being led away. He was well pleased with his wife of two months. She'd turned out to be congenial company, possessing a wry sense of humour in the most trying of circumstances. She had also applied herself with some enthusiasm to her marital duties, which had surprised him greatly, considering her background.

The first night of their marriage had been spent in the

open. Being almost strangers, they had become suddenly awkward with each other when it was time to retire. Marcus had just been pondering on how best to approach the subject of intimacy, or indeed, whether he should approach it at all after the debacle of his union with Maryse, when she'd said, 'Marcus, now we are wed, sooner or later I must become you wife in truth. I would prefer it to be now, so it's put behind us. I have some knowledge of what is entailed, but no experience. I would be grateful if you would instruct me in my duties.'

So, instruct her, he had. She'd confessed her enjoyment of the experience through the soft pleasurable noises and the involuntary response of her body as she submitted to him. He knew he'd found a willing bed partner in her. That, he intended to exploit to the fullest, for she had a shapely, long-legged body and her skin was as soft as satin.

She'd laughed softly afterwards, and said, 'I hope your home in Dorset has a soft bed, for there are several stones digging into me and I'll be peppered with bruises in the morning.'

'*Our* home in Dorset,' he'd said, and although she became curious about Cheverton Manor he wouldn't tell her any more, for there was a childish urge in him to surprise and please her with the sight of it. Though now Jed had made her aware that it was an estate, no doubt Julia would quiz Elizabeth about it when they were alone, for women were curious creatures.

'What business can you have on my property, when there is nothing beyond?' Jed asked.

Marcus didn't bother to lie, for he sensed that the man has already guessed why he was here. He'd learned enough about Jed Hawkins from Siana to know it was best to be straight with him. 'I have a score to settle. I'm looking for a convict called Henry Ruddle. You've heard of him?'

'Aye, you know I have. He used to work on the Cheverton Estate as an itinerant labourer.' The man didn't betray his thoughts by as much as the flicker of an eyelid.

'I've learned he's part of a convict clearing gang a few miles inland.'

'Could be.'

'There's no could be about it. I'm going there to kill him.'

Jed nodded. 'I understand you have cause. There is a trooper guarding that clearing gang. How do you intend to get past him?'

'I'll observe the routine of the camp first.'

Jed jerked a head towards the house. 'Aside from your good woman, who should I inform if you don't come back?'

Marcus shrugged. 'I have every intention of coming back. Maryse blessed me with two children to rear. That, I intend to do.'

'An incentive to be careful, then.'

'A good incentive.' The two men exchanged a significant glance, then Jed nodded. 'Will you be staying for supper, Marcus?'

'Thank you, Mr Hawkins, but be warned, I have appetite enough to eat a horse.'

'Mutton will have to suffice. Call me Jed,' he said, holding out his hand in an uncharacteristic gesture of friendship, for he was rarely drawn so easily to a man.

Marcus departed as soon as it was dark, heading for the line of trees that bordered the property. Two hours later, when everyone but himself and Elizabeth was fast asleep, Jed fetched his warm jacket and picked up his rifle.

'You're going after him?'

'Marcus Ibsen won't even know I'm there.'

Elizabeth fastened the buttons on his jacket one by one and, holding on to his collar, gazed up at him, worry shining deeply in her eyes. 'I don't want you to get involved.'

'The man has a strong urge in him to avenge Maryse. I can't blame him for that. After Siana told me what had happened to Maryse, I'd toyed with the same idea myself, till I reckoned it was none of my business. I won't step in unless I have too.'

'Be careful then, Jed Hawkins. You're a stubborn mule, but I love you.'

Jed grinned at that, kissed her lightly on the mouth and said, 'Unhand me then, woman.' When she did, he slipped out through the door and closed it gently behind him.

It was the evening of the second day before Marcus found the work gang. He'd slept a little, huddled in his brown robe under the branches of a fallen tree, with the hood pulled over his head, ready to wake in an instant.

He'd kept to the river bank until he'd come to a place where a track was cleared into the bush and the mud was churned by many feet. He'd been drawn to the clearing camp by the smell of woodsmoke.

On the way to the camp he'd had the feeling he was being followed. His caution and observations came to nought, though. Nothing he could see moved in the shadowy bush land other than the creatures which ought to be there. In the end he'd relaxed. Were there natives out to cause him harm, most certainly they'd have sent a spear thudding into his back by now. They'd had ample opportunity.

After several weeks going from place to place Marcus was used to the noises of the bush. He'd learned to be cautious of snakes, though he'd heard that, at this time of year, the cold weather caused them to be sluggish. They were cold-blooded creatures which concealed themselves in hollow logs or under rocks in the winter.

As he lay in the dawn shadows watching the camp come awake, the trees above him rustled in the wind, or gave faint cracks as loose branches fell. The local eucalyptus trees were not as sturdy as English trees. The foliage was supported by spindly grey trunks and branches soaring skywards. The oil they contained made them highly flammable.

The thorny undergrowth he'd pushed through had scratched his face and hands. Three days of beard decorated his chin. But he was not as disreputable-looking as the convicts with their long matted beards, he noticed, as the camp woke to the sound of groans, rattling coughs and breaking wind. Men shuffled into the undergrowth to relieve themselves, returning to form a ragged line for role-call.

'Smith . . . Meredith . . . Taggert . . . Ruddle . . .'

Marcus's eyes honed in on the wretch he'd come to kill. Henry Ruddle was still powerfully built, despite his deprivations, for hard labour had kept him muscular. The very fact that such a man would have forced himself on his gentle Maryse brought the blood roiling in fury to his face. Hard pressed not to rise from the spot and throw himself upon the man, Marcus wished he'd brought a weapon with him, for he could have shot him from concealment.

But his wasn't the coward's way. He wanted the man to know the crime he was dying for. He gazed at his slender fingers with doubt in his eyes. Ruddle had a thick, muscular neck, and he'd have to take him by surprise.

The convicts were given a portion of gruel to eat, and chained together. They shuffled off with the overseer in charge of them. Luck was running his way, for Ruddle was left behind with the guard.

The trooper sat on a log, his gun slung over his arm, barking orders at the convict. 'Tidy up the camp, then put the billy on.'

Ruddle went down to the river with a leather bucket for water, then came back and washed the utensils. The remaining water was set aside.

Marcus saw his chance when the bucket suddenly tipped over, spilling the water into the ground. He grinned when he saw a grey snake retreat into the undergrowth, disturbed by the heavy load placed on it.

Moving swiftly towards the river, Marcus stepped out as Ruddle bent to fill the bucket for a second time.

'Henry Ruddle?'

The man's head jerked up. 'What of it?'

'My name is Marcus Ibsen. I'm the owner of Cheverton Estate, in Dorset.'

'Come to offer me a job 'ave you? As you can see, I'm otherwise engaged.'

'Actually, I've come to kill you. Remember a girl you raped on the night of the harvest supper, over six years ago?'

The convict's body tensed and his eyes narrowed as they darted about Marcus's body, looking for signs of a weapon. 'A tasty little pie, as I recall. Nice and tight. I nearly skinned my thrasher getting it inside her.'

'She killed herself because of you, you lump of shit.'

Ruddle grinned as he goaded, 'The slut didn't have to do that. She wriggled and sobbed, made it even more exciting. A pity she killed herself, I wouldn't mind doing her all over again.'

Even knowing he'd probably left it too late, Marcus launched himself at the man.

Sinewy arms wrapped around him in a bear hug. Ruddle might be chained at the ankles but his arms were free, and he was intent on breaking Marcus's neck.

A knee to his groin loosened the hold and the pair went down. The mud prevented Marcus from getting a good grip as they rolled around grunting and punching at each other.

Nearly felled by a blow to the head, Marcus fell on to this back, dazed.

Staggering to his feet, Ruddle picked up a rock and lifted it over his head. But he seemed to jerk as if he'd been stung. He slipped, and the rock fell from his grasp.

Marcus rolled to one side before the rock landed, scissoring the convict's ankles with his legs to bring him down on to his stomach. Kneeling on Ruddle's back and capturing the man's head with his arm, Marcus applied force with his knee and jerked his neck backwards. The sound of the crack went unheard amongst the sound of axes in the undergrowth.

He checked that the man was dead and, breathing heavily, rose to his feet, aware that luck had been on his side. 'You can rest easy now, Maryse,' he whispered. 'And so can I.'

He saw it then, another thin snake sliding off into the bushes, but this one was brown and braided. 'Not this time, I think, my friend,' he breathed.

'Ruddle,' the trooper shouted out, 'get yourself back here.'

Grinning, Marcus melted into the bushes and headed back towards the Hawkins farm at a fast lope. It wasn't until two hours had passed that he stopped to rest on a fallen log.

Before too long he heard his tracker, who was making no effort to hurry or conceal himself, now. He stepped into Jed's path, grinning when the rifle swung up, though knowing he wouldn't have stood a chance if the trigger had been pulled. 'I thought it was you.'

Jed grinned from ear to ear. 'You're good, Marcus.'

Marcus pushed the barrel of the rifle aside with his hand. 'You're just as good. That trick with the stick was

354

a new one on me. As for the whip tip stinging Ruddle's leg . . . I thought a snake had struck him the second time, until I realized I'd never seen a snake made of braided leather before. You're too familiar with the camp not to have been watching it.'

'Of course I'm familiar with it. The convicts are assigned to me, and I've my wife and children to consider if those convicts get loose.'

'And Ruddle? You must have known him, since you managed Cheverton for most of your life.'

'Aye, I recognized him, and Mrs Matheson told me what happened to young Maryse.' He shook his head. 'A sad business, for a nicer lass you couldn't wish to meet. I had the same idea as you, but couldn't figure out how to kill the scum and get away with it. My instincts were weighted on the side of my own good woman, for I'm no good to her, dead.'

'They'll think he slipped and fell on the rock.'

'There's no reason for them to think otherwise, is there? They'll dig a hole and bury him deep and it will be as if he never existed. Is this business over now?'

Soberly, Marcus nodded.

'Then put it behind you. Go back home. Cheverton is a fine estate and needs a master in residence. Be nice to that sweet woman you've wed. I know a good un when I see one. Elizabeth thinks she might be with child.'

'Already? We've only been wed for a few weeks.'

Jed chuckled at his astonishment. 'When a man takes his ease with a woman he should give some thought to the consequence. Go home. Be a good father and set a decent example for your young uns to follow.' He grinned widely. 'Though that father be covered in muck and dressed in a skirt. We'll have to wash your sins away in the river before we take you home.'

'I was never much of a preaching man and my sins are part of me. Let them be, so they can warm me when the devil takes me.' Laughing, for he was exhilarated now his gruesome task was over, Marcus dragged the ragged and muddied robe over his head and threw it away. He wouldn't be needing it again.

He would be glad to get home to Cheverton. His little Alexander and Jane Louise needed a mother as well as a father. Who better than Julia to set them an example? 'A good un,' Jed had called her, and Marcus knew he was right. He smiled at the thought that there might be another child on the way. Cheverton Manor was a big house.

Suddenly, he couldn't wait to take her home. He hoped Siana would like Julia, for her opinion was of the greatest importance to him. He began to chuckle at the thought.

'What's tickled you?' Jed said, the beginnings of a smile on his face.

'I was thinking of Siana Matheson and wondering what she'll make of Julia.'

'Grabbed you by the balls, has she?' Jed said, matter of factly, which made Marcus laugh out loud. He only wished she had.

Siana had returned to Dorset, Francis knew it.

There had been nothing tangible. No note from her, no gossip. He felt her in the dappled shadows under the trees, in the steady beat of his heart, in the very air he breathed. He heard her in the church bells that rang her name to float upon the summer breezes. The grasses seemed to whisper her name. *Siana . . . Siana.* Sometimes he could smell the faint elusive perfume of her, wild-flowers, wood musk and bergamot.

Odd, he mused, grinning, for it ill behove a sensible man of science, such as himself, to be receptive to such nonsense.

''Tis the midsummer moon. You be fair mazed by it,' Siana's maid, Rosie, had told him, grinning when he'd asked her if she could smell his wife's perfume too. But her eyes had slid away from his.

There were subtle changes in the house. The servants stopped whispering together when he came into a room. They put an extra sparkle into their polishing and they sang about the house and laughed. There was an air of secrecy about the children. Pansy had been evasive when he'd asked her if she'd heard any gossip.

'If Siana has returned, no doubt she'll let you know in due course, Papa,' was all she said, then she bustled off to perform some seemingly urgent task.

Francis found an excuse to visit Josh in Poole. Josh's man, Mr Bentley, ushered him into the hall. 'I'll enquire if the master is receiving visitors, sir.' He shuffled off towards the drawing room with Francis's card on a silver salver. 'Dr Matheson wishes to see you, sir,' Francis heard him say.

'Thank you, Mr Bentley. Dr Matheson doesn't need to stand on ceremony. He's welcome any time.'

'Yes, sir. I'll tell him to come in then, sir, shall I?'

'Sorry about Mr Bentley,' Josh said cheerfully to him a couple of seconds later. 'He takes his duties very seriously and acts as though I were Prince Albert, himself.' Josh lowered his voice. 'I'm glad you're here, though. I'd like you to take a look at the old feller. He keeps gettin' short of breath and is tottery on his feet.'

'I don't need to look at him.' Francis knew exactly what ailed Bentley. He had dropsy and was finding it hard to breathe. All were indications of advanced heart disease. 'He's old, Josh. He shouldn't be working.'

'I know that. But he's a proud old fart who won't accept charity, and he insists on making himself useful. Can you give him something to make him feel better?'

'A little brandy for medicinal purposes, perhaps.'

'You don't need to worry about that. He helps himself to nips of my best during the day, and falls asleep in the chair in the kitchen in the afternoon. The maids have been told not to disturb him.'

Francis nodded. Josh had a kind heart. First it was Sam Saynuthin, who had been deformed in infancy due to a lack of nutrition, and who was also profoundly deaf. Josh had befriended the lad, given him a life and brought out the best in him. Now it was Mr Bentley, the former butler to the Bainbridge family, who'd been cast out on the death of his master. Josh had taken the old man in when he'd been tramping the streets looking for work.

'It will be kinder to let him go on doing what he's doing. Be prepared, though. I doubt if he'll last over the winter.'

'Poor old thing. I hope he goes off peacefully in his

sleep when he's not looking. But not before the wedding, for he's looking forward to it.' Josh suddenly smiled. 'What can I do for you then, Doc?'

'Have you heard from Siana?'

'Ah . . . I see. A letter, you mean. No, I can't say I've received news from her lately. Come through and take a look at the new conservatory. Pansy's given me a plan of where all the plants have got to go. I'm not much of a gardener, myself. Are you?'

Francis placed his hand on Josh's arm, and said with some asperity, 'Stop the small talk, Josh. Tell me, is Siana here, staying with you?'

Astute blue eyes gazed into his. 'Take my word for it, she is not here; or take a look around if you'd prefer.'

'Your word will suffice.'

'Can I be frank with you, Francis.'

'You usually are, so go ahead.'

'Be that as it may. You didn't treat my sister right and fair, parting her from everyone she loved. Not after everything she went through on your behalf.'

So, he was being forced to eat crow again, and by Josh. 'Do you think I'm unaware of that? I've thought of nothing else these past few months.'

The scrutiny Francis underwent from Josh was disconcerting, then the younger man suddenly said, 'I imagine you must be sorry, at that, under the circumstances. Truthfully, I've not seen Siana, but I did hear a whisper. Have you been to see your grandchildren lately?'

'Not for three weeks. There's been an outbreak of chicken pox in the village and I didn't want to expose them to infection.' His eyes narrowed. Surely the worst he'd imagined hadn't happened. Had Siana returned in the company of Marcus Ibsen to shame him by living openly with the man in Cheverton Manor?

Drawing in deep breath, he headed for the door. 'Perhaps I should call in on the way back.'

'Perhaps you should.'

Mr Bentley couldn't shuffle fast enough to open the door to let Francis out. 'The doctor's not staying for refreshment then, sir?' he said, as the door swung shut behind him.

'No. He remembered somebody he urgently needed to see.' Josh gave the old man a smile. 'I don't need you this afternoon, Mr Bentley, so you can go off and have a nap if you want. Miss Matheson will be here with Miss Edgar in attendance. The catering company is coming to discuss the food for the wedding and to inspect the kitchen and reception areas.'

'I see, sir. Bentley's manner became slightly frosty. 'And what will my duties be during the nuptials?'

'Duties?' Josh scratched his his head. 'Can't rightly say you'll have any, since you'll be my guest. 'Cepting, of course, I'd appreciate you helping me dress, if you would.'

'Me, a guest, sir?'

'Damn me, if I didn't see Miss Matheson writing your name on an invitation just the other day.'

'That's very kind of her. Thank you, sir. I'll be happy to assist you in any way I can.'

'You're welcome, Mr Bentley. Having you here gives me a bit of class, you know. We'll be mingling with the

360

blue bloods, so I can't let Miss Matheson down.'

'Indeed, you cannot. Miss Matheson is a lovely young woman, if you'll pardon the liberty. And you have more class than any other man I know.'

'I think I'm the luckiest man alive.'

'And so am I, sir. It's a privilege to serve you, sir.'

As Mr Bentley shuffled off, Josh squashed the warm feeling rising up inside him. He was a hard-headed member of the businessmen's institute now. People looked up to him. It wouldn't do to show emotion in front of the servants – it wouldn't do at all.

19

For once, the spaniels had not come out to greet Francis. They were in the kitchen, most likely, for this was not his usual visiting day. Though if Marcus had returned, they were possibly with him. Had he returned?

'Is Mr Ibsen expected home from his travels soon?' he asked the maid who took his hat.

Her eyes slid away from his as she said evasively, 'I can't rightly say, sir.'

Of course, her evasion could have been his imagination. He was not his usual perceptive self at the moment.

'I'll run up and tell the nursery maids you are here, for they won't be expecting thee, it not being your regular day.'

The relief he experienced as she quickly skittered up the stairs made him feel light-headed and he was thankful he hadn't made fool of himself by asking if his wife was in residence. He'd soon find out, for signs of occupancy couldn't be concealed.

There were no gloves on the hall table, no lace-edged handkerchiefs left about. No hints of feminine pursuits, such as embroidery frames or sewing boxes, were in evidence. The furniture in the main living rooms he walked through were shrouded in dust sheets.

He could not, though, search the chambers in another man's house. Such behaviour would be erratic in the extreme and would draw notice. Yet, any one of those closed doors could hide his wife from sight, for some of the guest chambers had private sitting rooms attached.

He went up the stairs quietly, his ears alert for a sigh, a feminine laugh, the rustle of taffeta skirts or just the flutter of her heartbeat, for he was sure he'd recognize it if he heard it.

He stood on the top landing outside the nursery door, the blood pumping against his ear drums, his elation plummeting when he thought miserably: She is probably still in Van Diemen's Land.

Inside, the children were giggling and the nursery maids were laughing about something.

'Hush now, my bonny,' one of them said. 'I'll take you through to the other room so you can rest. If you're good and go to sleep, I'll sing you a pretty song when you wake.'

His mind sifted through the familiar sounds and discovered an odd note, a giggle which didn't quite fit. Was it a different voice? His mouth dry, he pushed the door open.

'Ganfer!' With squeals and giggles Jane Louise and Alexander swarmed over him, lifting their arms to be cuddled.

One nursery maid was folding clothing. The younger one smiled as she stepped through from the room the children slept in, which was curtained off. She looked ill at ease when she said brightly, 'Good day, Dr Matheson. You're just in time to have some tea with us. Cook has made us some oatmeal biscuits today, and there is some gooseberry conserve to spread on them. Though I daresay you'd prefer tea to milk. Cook will bring some up directly, now she knows you're here.'

'Thank you.' Preoccupied as he was with his grand-children, it was some time before he noticed the smallness of the garments being folded. He gazed at them for a moment, then said, 'Surely they don't fit these two now?'

'No, sir. It's quite amazing how fast children grow, isn't it?' The clothes were quickly bundled back into the basket and set aside.

A soft noise took his glance to the curtain separating the room, and under it he saw a small pair of chubby bare feet. As he watched, a face peered at him from the side. The child was standing there, holding on to the door jamb. When he smiled at her, she let go, staggered like a drunken sailor towards him, then folded heavily on to her rear. Jane and Alexander clapped their hands and the three of them dissolved into paroxysms of giggles as she struggled to stand and rolled over on her back with her legs in the air.

One of the nursery maids hurried forward to pick the child up, gazing awkwardly at him. 'Francine should be resting.'

Francine! Something familiar about the child drew his eye. 'Is that your child?'

'No, sir.'

He placed the other two down on the floor and his

heart leaped as his memory was triggered. Siana had told him she was expecting a child and he hadn't believed her. 'Bring her here to me. I want to take a look at her.'

The child didn't protest at being picked up by a strange man. She scrutinized him intently through eyes as dark as pines. Her hair was dark, curling in a riotous cap over her head. Little fingers came to explore his face. She did it in a deliberate manner, cupping her palms over his nose then pressing them flat against his lips, as if to mould them. She made a face when she stroked against the grain of his whiskers and, after gently exploring his eyes she placed her hands over her own eyes.

'Boo!' she shouted, flinging her hands away from her.

He laughed and so did she, a hearty giggle which made her whole body jiggle like that of a plump little puppy. It was love at first sight for him, for she was the very image of Siana.

'Where's her mother?' he growled at one of the nursery maids.

'Out walking, sir.'

'Has she been gone long?'

'Since early, an hour, perhaps.'

Siana could walk for hours, so he could afford to spend some time with the children. He played with them until they tired, and were taken off to rest, though his mind was elsewhere.

'Have my wife's and daughter's things packed and taken to Rivervale House. We'll be back for our daughter,' he instructed as he left.

The two maids exchanged a grin. 'Didn't take 'e long

to run her to earth, did it?' one of them said. 'Lord, but his eyes lit up when he saw the little un.'

As Francis strode towards the hills, his mind was filled with a vision of Siana standing on the cliff top, her hair tumbling about her, her skirt blowing in the wind and her feet bare to the grass beneath her feet.

And thus it was when she came into sight. Her bronze taffeta skirt had a hint of cream petticoat beneath, and was teamed with bodice the colour of toasted almonds. Transfixed, he gazed upon her stillness and was drawn into the relationship his woman had with the elements surrounding her. He had no doubt that the pagan part of her had pulled him to her side.

'You complete me,' she'd said to him once, and he knew with absolute certainty that it was the other way round. Siana completed him. So he stood there to watch and wait, feeling his love reach out to surround and protect her.

He waited – waited for her to feel his presence and to allow her heart to accept him again.

That morning it had been much the same kind of sky as on the day Maryse died, only less violent. 'Red sky in the morning, sailor's warning,' Siana had murmured.

As the morning progressed the red sky had become a stipple of apricot clouds banding across to the horizon, then a race of ragged rain clouds had appeared to soak her through.

The day was warmer than that fateful day nearly two years before, the breeze was as kind as a caress. The difference between that awful winter and the summer of Siana's return was marked by hope, not by the loss of it.

Maryse's sky would have been just as glorious as today's early red sky, with its same warning. Her eyes would have absorbed it as a last beautiful memory as she'd fallen to her death into the shadowy rocks concealed in the surging tides below. It would have filled her heart and mind and remained with her as she'd stepped forward into the light.

She would not have thought of the children she'd born for Marcus, nor the horrible shaming of her at the christening. Maryse would not have felt fear. She would have felt nothing but the most fleeting, exquisite pain.

Time had become meaningless to Siana. The wind blew her hair about her face and shoulders in damp strands. She didn't mind. Up here on the cliff with the turbulent summer sea stretching into the sky, she knew her place within the landscape. Her heart was too open to the elements for her body to feel uncomfortable.

She could feel Francis and her children, so close and yet so far. She had contacted nobody since her return, yet those who mattered to her would suspect she was home.

From the poppy-covered grass on the hill above Rivervale House, where she'd once laid with her love, she had watched Goldie and Daisy at play, ignoring the need to reach out and hold them close. The earth had warmed beneath her body when she'd caught a glimpse of Francis leaving the house. There had been no sign of Bryn, and she'd been heartsick over his absence, for she'd hoped Francis had softened towards him.

Francis would know she was here now. She could feel the uncertainty of him, the need he had in him to retain his pride. He was close to her, this love of hers, and she must guard her instincts, for the need to punish him was strong in her, too.

But the conflict between them must be resolved. Her mind reached out to his, connecting with the love he held for her. Feeling his heart beating, her own picked up its rhythm. The measure of his tread trembled in the grass beneath her bare feet and the voice of her great-grandmother Lewis came to her like a sigh on the wind.

He is come to you, cariad. *Your one true love.*

'Don't come any closer, Francis,' she said, keeping him at arm's length, as he approached her from behind.

His voice was filled with the male gruffness of him. 'I thought I'd find you here. You'll catch cold standing in the rain.'

'It makes me feel alive in a way you'd never understand.' She turned, her heart churning at the sight of him, for his grief over Maryse's death and the aftermath was written indelibly on the gauntness of his face. His hair had silvered more too, but fire burnt in the grey of his eyes. Tears filled her eyes as she closed the gap between them and gently touched his cheek. Her resolve to punish him weakened. 'You've suffered greatly.'

'I shouldn't have sent you away.'

She drew in a breath, drawing strength from the bracing saltiness coming off the ocean. There was a need in her to tell him, to redeem herself in his eyes.

'We nearly lost Maryse once before. Here, in this very

spot. It was when she first knew of the burden she must bear. There was a storm, and lightning struck the earth. Without my intervention Maryse would have died then, and her infant would not have been born. Marcus came upon us and it was as if he had been sent as part of the storm. That's how we met, and the events that followed afterwards seemed fated. I must bear responsibility for Bryn, for I made myself the guardian of his life back then, when I saved the life of his mother.'

Francis said nothing.

'I must have him back, Francis! Even if you can't accept him as a son you can be his grandfather and love and guide him. Already, I've lost two children. My heart is aching for them, but it's aching more for Bryn, because he's alive and needful of me. The circumstance of his birth was not his fault and I won't let you punish him for it. You've experienced first-hand what that does to the innocent.'

He made a gesture of defeat with his hands.

'You once loved Bryn, but what price do you place on love when you can send those you love away?' She forgot to be strong and pleaded with him. 'You cannot love people one moment and hate them the next. I tried it with you, tried to hate you so your coldness didn't hurt so much. I discovered that love is stronger than my will, and to love you is a burden as well as a blessing. There can be nobody else held so close to my heart. Even as you spurned me, I still loved you. But for pity's sake, Francis, return Bryn to my keeping, for the child was nurtured at my breast, and without him I feel bereft.'

There was a noise deep in his throat. A sob. 'Don't condemn me for that, Siana, not when I feel so wretched.'

'I know I don't deserve your love. Would you have me beg on my knees for the life of the boy? I will, if you ask it of me.'

'I love you. I want you to come home.'

Her heart gave a leap, but her smile was uncertain, for she couldn't abandon Bryn. The child was within her heart and she could feel his uncertainty and his need to be loved. 'I cannot return without Bryn. He's part of me now.'

Francis took a step towards her, his eyes searching her face. He said, 'I knew you would not, for I wounded you too much when I took him from you. But in doing so, I hurt myself more.' A faint wintry smile touched his lips. 'You brought me a gift in Francine.'

When her chin lifted a fraction he knew she would fight for her children without giving him any quarter. 'Remember what you said to me when I told you I was with child? That you would never father any child of mine. Francine is *my* daughter.'

The air between them quivered with tension, for his past remark had wounded her badly. Yet she had the feeling she'd gone too far, for his face tightened as he gazed at her. 'It was something said in the heat of the moment and immediately regretted.'

'You forgot to tell me you regretted saying it. A letter would have sufficed. You could have sent one with Marcus Ibsen.'

'There is much to regret. My lack of communication

is one of them.' He gave her a tight smile. 'Isn't it time we stopped playing games?'

She stared silently at him. This wasn't going exactly as she'd planned. 'You're a surgeon as well as a physician, Francis. Tell me, how many times can a person be stabbed in the heart without bleeding the death?'

'You're being overly dramatic. We're talking about the paternity of a child.'

'Francine is part of my heart. All the children are.'

He made a soft, exasperated noise in his throat. 'Let me put my question thus. If I'm not Francine's father, who is? The fact that you've chosen to conceal from me that you've returned to England and are living in another man's house, could give rise to speculation.'

Blood rushed to her face. 'Hah! I thought your eyesight was adequate enough to see past the end of your nose.' Picking up her skirts she pushed past him and began to run.

He grabbed her wrist when he caught her up, swinging her round to face him. 'I love you,' he said, his voice breaking with the emotion he usually found so hard to express. 'I know Francine is my child. I know you're my wife and I'm aware I've treated you badly.'

'Francis, can I just say—'

He placed a finger across her mouth. 'Hush, it is me who is begging now, in the best way I know how. There will be no more recriminations and no more apologies, for it will only prolong the hell of living without you. You and Francine will come home with me now. Much has happened in your absence that you need to be made aware of, and we will talk of it later. The children need you, and we need each other.'

In an instant she was in his arms, her head against his chest, reluctant to mention Bryn again, for although she'd pleaded the boy's case with all that was in her, Siana knew she would learn to live without Bryn rather than lose Francis, despite her resolve to the contrary.

She couldn't resist one last try. 'I shouldn't have given you the impression I would choose Bryn over you, even though my heart is breaking into a thousand pieces at the thought of losing him. I will bend to your will, but only if I have to.'

He chuckled at that. 'Your heart is stronger than you could possibly imagine, and Bryn is waiting for you at home.' Tipping up her chin he gently kissed her, chasing all thoughts of Bryn out of her head. They stood for what seemed an eternity just holding each other tight, then, hands joined, slowly walked back to Cheverton Manor together.

As they drove up to Rivervale House, Siana felt she had truly come home.

Suddenly, there were Daisy and Goldie, sitting on the step together, grown older now, though Goldie had a frail look to her. Their smiles crumpled into tears at the sight of her. 'Mamma!'

She left her daughter with Francis, almost leaping from the rig in her haste to cuddle them close. Soon they were all damp-eyed.

'Look how you've grown, Daisy. Goldie, have you

been ill, my love? Oh, I've missed you all so much. I'm so glad I'm home.'

She sensed rather than saw someone in the shadows of the hall beyond. Standing, she gazed into the darkness, her body tensing when her eyes adjusted to the dim interior. She saw a forlorn little figure gazing at her through the banisters of the stairs. This was not the outgoing child she had last seen. Sadness emanated from him, and loneliness too.

'Oh God! . . . Francis, look how much he's grown, but what has happened to him?' She went went to where he sat, and drew his stiff little body against hers. 'Do you remember me, my dearest Bryn?'

'Mamma,' he whispered.

He needed a very special kind of loving from her now. 'My sweet boy, I love you so much and I've missed you so.'

When Bryn began to tremble and weep she pulled him onto his lap and hugged him tight, rocking him back and forth. 'You need a very special kind of loving, my little cuckoo, and that you will have.'

His smile came at the mention of her pet name for him, uncertain, like the sun lurking behind the tragic cloud of his face. His eyes were a mixture of excitement and shyness.

'I've missed you so much, my Bryn. So much,' and she grazed kisses over his face and head.

'You stayed away a long time and I had to go away, then Grandpa came for me,' he said, sounding all forlorn.

Grandpa, now, was it? She gave Francis a speculative

glance and, noting the smile on his face, thought perhaps it was the best compromise, after all. Lying did not sit easily on him.

'My darling boy, I'll never leave you again,' she promised. Francine had climbed the stairs with Goldie and Daisy in close attendance. 'See, I have brought you a baby sister to look after. Her name is Francine.'

Francine produced her most winning smile for Bryn. Seeming not to mind in the slightest that her mother's sole attention had been removed from her and she was cuddling a stranger in her lap, her daughter climbed up and hugged him too.

Her children crowded in on her then, smiling and touching her, loving Bryn and bringing another smile to his face. Floating in their love, although she stretched her arms as far as they would reach, Siana couldn't encompass them all until Francis joined them, taking her hands in his so they were all reunited.

'Thank you for bringing me home,' she whispered, choking on her own emotion.

Then later, it was the turn of Pansy who came in with Josh, the pair of them shining with happiness so the whole world could see they were in love, rendering the wonderful news they had for her superfluous.

After dinner she and Francis talked. Francis held nothing back, telling her of Goldie's misadventure, and not sparing himself in the process. 'I should have gone to London and checked that all was well instead of trusting to those letters. I should have known it was not Goldie's way of saying things.'

'What of Betty Groves and her daughter? Were they punished for their crime?'

'I heard from Beckwith just two days ago on the matter. The pair are awaiting transportation. He's in the process of settling Sebastian Groves's estate. An offer has been made for the business, including the machinery. I thought I might ask Josh to find a suitable property to buy on Goldie's behalf, one which can be rented out until she comes of age.'

'And Bryn? Have you decided what his future will be?'

'He knows me as his grandfather now. I'll tell him the truth of his birth when he's old enough to understand, for he must be trained in a profession to provide for himself in the future. Reverend White left Bryn a legacy, which will carry him through university. And my brothers will help in any way they can.'

'That's good of them.'

'They bear some responsibility for what happened to Bryn in your absence, for I followed their advice. But, no more recriminations, Siana. We must live for the future, not in the past. Go and say goodnight to your children. I'll be up later to do the same.'

But when he went upstairs he found the children's rooms empty. He found the children asleep on Siana's bed. Daisy and Goldie were propped on pillows at the foot, looking like a pair of angels with their golden hair spread all around them. Francine was lying between them. His daughter's thumb was jammed firmly in her mouth, her plump fingers curved over her nose. The three of them were tucked under a blue and white quilt.

He recognized it as the one the Welsh woman had left behind for Siana, and wondered fleetingly what had happened to her.

Bryn was snuggled up against Siana. All were asleep. Siana had been reading to them, for *Robinson Crusoe* was lying open on the bed.

As if they hadn't had enough trauma, he thought, gazing wryly at the face of his sleeping wife. Stooping to gently kiss them all, he went through the dividing door to his own chamber.

Siana woke just before the candle guttered out. Being careful not to disturb the sleeping children she rose to light another candle from the stub.

A few moments later she was through the connecting door and gazing down at her husband. He looked more relaxed in repose. All she had ever felt for him was now a river of love in her veins. She kissed him until she felt the softening response of his mouth against hers, and knew he was awake.

'Allow me to tell you about Marcus Ibsen, for I know you are wondering,' she whispered, when she saw the glitter of his eyes in the candlelight.

'Must you?' he said painfully.

'Marcus is not like other men I know. We are at ease with each other and he understand me as no other man does, not even you, my Francis.'

'I have been torturing myself with the thought of him being alone with you in that house, so isolated from everyone.'

'Ah . . .' she said softly. 'Then torture yourself no

more. I have always loved you, and only you. Marcus slept in one of the cottages.'

Siana grinned to herself then, for Marcus had been so sure of himself. She had to admit his attention had been flattering when she'd been vulnerable, and she'd been sorely tempted. But becoming lovers would have been wrong for both of them and would have complicated matters. He'd looked like a small, lost dog when she'd banished him from the house. But he'd laughed at himself from then on and had accepted his defeat gracefully, except for taking advantage of her with a long, lingering parting kiss when her hands had been full. Oh, Marcus, she thought, thank goodness you didn't kiss me like that back at the house.

'Why did he go to Van Diemen's Land at all?'

'His sole purpose was to send me back to you. Before he placed me on the ship he told me to come home and take back that which is mine.'

'You left him in Van Diemen's Land?'

'I understood there was a woman he'd travelled out with living there. Julia Hardy, she was called. Marcus expressed his admiration for her on many occasions and I believe he was considering proposing marriage to her. So don't be surprised if he returns with a bride.'

'What was his business in New South Wales, then?'

'I considered it best not to pry too closely into what his business might be, for I suspect it involved those who dealt so badly with Maryse.'

When he gave a distressed sigh, she reminded him, 'There were others who loved her too, Francis, and they were hurting just as much. Marcus doesn't possess a nature that would allow her attackers to remain unavenged.'

'Yet he married her, even knowing what he did about her.'

'And would have taken her child under his roof too, had it been necessary. He loved her. Maryse was perfect in his eyes. She always will be, and he'll always remember her young and in need of his protection. That's not a bad memory to grow old with.'

He reached up to touch her face, his voice soft. 'Aye, it's not. You're perfect.'

'There's no such thing as perfection. We all have blemishes.' Pulling the covers from his body she slid in beside him and murmured, 'Didn't I promise you a son?'

'You did, but my daughter was a unexpected gift and I'm content with her. For now, I'd just like to hold you, for I've missed the closeness we had.'

And hold her he did, but not for long. He'd forgotten the potency of her caresses, the teasing wanton movements of her body, the silky touch of her skin under his fingertips and mouth, and the seductive perfume of her. He lost himself as her caresses brought the man in him surging against her, so she took him into the fragrant moist depths where all was sensation until she cried out with the joy of him and captured him inside her with her thighs.

Then came the frenzy of his last frantic thrusts as she arched to meet him, and the swift, hot flood of him into her honeyed lair.

When he collapsed, hot and perspiring against her,

she was loving as her fingers strayed to the welts on his back. 'Tell me about these, my Francis.'

And since she'd unmanned him with her loving, he told her about the floggings he'd received. 'It was as if I was inhuman, a man without without pride in himself.'

She cried a little, then stopped his words with her mouth over his. It was just a few moments before he was ready to love her all over again.

It was in the early hours of the morning when she fell asleep. He brushed the dark tangled hair back from her face and gazed at her. She looked as smug and as satisfied as a cat, and he had not felt so relaxed for a long time.

He kissed her mouth, already swollen from his kisses, and when she muttered his name in her sleep he smiled to himself, for he was filled with the contentment of just loving her, and he had been made whole. He would not lose her again.

20

The countryside was a blaze of colour as the procession of carriages headed towards the church. Inside, the occupants, dressed in their finest, looked forward to celebrating the nuptials of Pansy Matheson and Josh Skinner.

Behind them came the bridal carriage, decorated with streaming ribbons and jingling silver bells. Pansy and her father bowled through the countryside. The horse's coat glowed like burnished copper.

Pansy was dressed all in white, her billowing skirts draped softly over stiff petticoats. There were touches of lace, flowers in her hair and dreams in her eyes. Pansy had no qualms about marrying Josh. He understood the need in her to live a useful, productive life. Who else would have thought to give her a school as a wedding present?

Not once had she regretted her decision to discard Alder, who was now an officer in the army. She was pleased he wouldn't be at the wedding, even more pleased that Justina Parsons had turned his proposal down in favour of an impoverished viscount. Alder had treated Justina with much disdain.

Francis turned to smile at Pansy. His daughter had never looked lovelier. She'd stepped out of Maryse's shadow to reveal herself as a capable young lady of rare good sense. Not only had she pandered to Prudence by asking her advice about the wedding, she had also invited her aunt to become patron of the new charity wing of her school when it opened at the beginning of the following year.

'Your patronage will set the seal of quality on the school. The charity scholars who do well at their lessons will perhaps be offered worthwhile employment because of it.'

The countess had thought for a moment of two, then murmured, 'Perhaps I could sponsor a scholarship. It could be called the Countess of Kylchester bursary, and would provide the money to pay for an apprenticeship for the recipient.'

Which was exactly what Pansy had been hoping for, Francis thought.

Siana had gone before them in an open carriage driven by the Cheverton groom. Daisy and Goldie were seated in a quiet, ladylike pose, lest they crush their frothy white gowns or scuff their kid shoes. They were to wear the same gowns for the marriage of Miss Edgar to Mr Dennings the following month.

Bryn was quiet, clinging to her hand and self-conscious in his velvet trousers, silk shirt and brocade jacket, for he was to stand beside Josh during the ceremony, holding the wedding rings on a cushion. The boy had regained some confidence over the past few weeks. With plenty of attention and loving she knew he was young enough to forget his ordeal in the years to come. Francine had been left with the nursery maid.

The church was a crush of people. Siana left the girls in the porch with Miss Edgar, then made her way to the front pew, handing Bryn over to Josh. As she went to sit in the Cheverton Manor pew, her glance fell on Marcus, seated with his new wife at his side.

A smile crossed Siana's face. 'Marcus, how lovely to see you. Why haven't you called on us?'

'It's only been two weeks, after all. I thought we'd wait until after the wedding, when you wouldn't be so busy.' He rose to his feet. 'May I present my wife, Julia, to you. This is Mrs Matheson, Julia, who once owned Cheverton Estate.'

'Ah, yes, Elizabeth Hawkins spoke of you to me, though I believe I saw my husband assisting you aboard a ship in Van Diemen's Land.'

When Marcus gave Julia a surprised look and she grinned at him, Siana knew she'd like this woman.

'Yes, Marcus did see me safely aboard the ship. I'd been staying at my husband's property there for a while. I do wish you'd come forward, then. Since my son-in-law mentioned you so many times in conversation, I've been most curious to meet you. May I offer you my congratulations on your marriage, and much happiness in the future.'

A faint flush touched Julia's face and her eyes shone, making her appear beautiful. 'Thank you, Mrs Matheson. You're most kind.'

'Call me, Siana, please.' Siana smiled to herself, noticing the slight bulge under the woman's skirt. 'How are you finding your new home, Mrs Ibsen?'

'Since you've requested first names, I'd be pleased if you'd use mine.' Julia gazed at Marcus with a slightly incredulous edge to her smile. 'Actually, the house is much larger than I was led to expect. '

'It will not take you long to get used to it. I'm so pleased you were here in time to attend Pansy and Josh's wedding. Marcus, thank you so much for the use of the carriage and groom. Francis and I are most grateful.'

'It's my pleasure.'

'How do you find your new stepchildren, Julia?'

Her eyes lit up. 'They are so delightful and I quite adore them. I'm so pleased they're young enough to accept me as their mamma.'

Marcus's smile had a satisfied look to it.

'You must bring Julia over when you are settled again so we can get to know each other properly,' she told him. May I sit next to you, so I can keep an eye on the children? Francis will need to sit here too, for there are too many guests for the church to comfortably hold. I never knew my brother had so many friends.' She blew a kiss to Josh who was waiting for his bride to arrive and who looked radiantly happy.

Marcus and Julia obligingly moved along the pew. When Marcus provocatively tickled the palm of his new wife's hand as she seated herself, Siana gave a faint grin and ignored it.

The reverend came in, smiled at everyone, then glanced to the back of the church. There was a sudden rustle, as if heads had been rotated towards the door by a strong breeze.

However, it was not the bride arriving, but a grand parade of the Matheson family, headed by the stately Earl of Kylchester and his countess. They were a splendid sight, the women clad in pastel silks, flowers and feathers, the men top-hatted, their heads resembling a forest of tall grey chimneys.

Ushered into the pews reserved for them, they appeared unaware of the craning necks. All of them greeted Siana as though she'd never been away. Prudence gave her a kiss on the cheek and the benefit of a few wise words before she seated herself. 'One must forgive and forget, Siana.'

Who should be forgiven and who should forget was unclear, though. But for Pansy's sake, Siana was thankful the Mathesons had accepted their invitation. She had no time to ponder on it before Pansy appeared on the arm of her father. Preceded by her attendants, the bridal party made their way down the aisle. Francis slid into the seat beside Siana when the pair began to exchange their vows, taking her hand in his.

Beside her, Marcus drew in a trembling breath. She could feel his anguish and knew he was remembering the vows he'd exchanged with Maryse in this very church. Just as certain, she knew Julia would lessen that pain for him in years to come, for this woman with her warm nature, her kindness and intelligence, had been born for that very reason.

Pansy and Josh had also remembered Maryse in their happiness. When the ceremony was over, Josh led Pansy to her sister's grave, where she placed her posy of wedding flowers. It was a touching and precious moment, one that brought the Matheson family closer.

Looking around her, Siana saw the graves of so many people once close to her. Her mother, whose life had been cut tragically short in childbirth after a traumatic fire. Her first husband, Edward Forbes, and Ashley, the beloved son she'd borne him.

Then there was Reverend Richard White, once her mentor and friend, who had nurtured the thirst for knowledge inside an impoverished peasant girl, and helped her along the path to the woman she'd become today. Siana had come a long way since then, but he had left her his library of books, which, once again, had opened a treasure trove for her.

Her glance fell on the grave of the tragic Maryse, her sweet stepdaughter. What had they become, these people she'd loved? They were nothing but a bitter-sweet memory. A handful of ashes. The bounty of autumn covered their remains in a thick blanket of glorious copper leaves.

Life pulsed through her body as she gazed towards the hills and felt their pull. But today was not a day to heed the pagan call of them. Today, they had guests and were celebrating the union of life. It wasn't part of Siana's nature to remain sad for ever. With her heart overflowing with love for her family, she had no choice but to leave the dead to their rest. Amongst them was no place for herself and Francis, not yet, for their season of living had hardly begun.

The marriage celebrations proved to be lively, ending

just before darkness fell. The guests departed, leaving the newly married couple to their own celebration.

Rivervale House welcomed them back. The children were settled in their beds and kissed goodnight.

'It's good to be home,' Francis said, sliding his arm around her waist and gazing down at the sleeping Francine, tucked into her cot.

'You're my home, Francis. You always have been.' Gazing up at him, Siana never thought she'd feel such contentment again as when she told him, 'I'm carrying your son.'

That beautiful smile she'd always loved so much appeared on his face. 'Aye, Siana mine.'

'You knew?'

'From the very moment of his conception.' He chuckled and, entwining her fingers with his, bore her knuckles to his mouth to be kissed. Together, they strolled downstairs to their chamber, and closed the door firmly behind them.